12/4/23

Isabelle Broom was born in Cambridge nine days before the 1980s began and studied Media Arts in London before a 12-year stint at *Heat* magazine. Always happiest when she is off on an adventure, Isabelle now travels all over the world seeking out settings for her escapist novels, as well as making the annual pilgrimage to her second home – the Greek island of Zakynthos. Currently based in Suffolk, where she shares a cottage with her two dogs and approximately 467 spiders, Isabelle fits her writing around a busy freelance career and tries her best not to be crushed to oblivion under her ever-growing pile of to-be-read books.

ISABELLE BROOM

Hello, Again

HODDER

First published in Great Britain in 2020 by Hodder & Stoughton
An Hachette UK company

1

Copyright © Isabelle Broom 2020

A CIP catalogue record for this title is available from the British Library

Paperback ISBN 978 1 529 32507 2
eBook ISBN 978 1 529 32504 1
Audio ISBN 978 1 529 32506 5

Typeset in Plantin Light by Hewer Text UK Ltd, Edinburgh
Printed and bound in Great Britain by Clays Ltd, Elcograf S.p.A.

Hodder & Stoughton policy is to use papers that are natural, renewable
and recyclable products and made from wood grown in sustainable
forests. The logging and manufacturing processes are expected to
conform to the environmental regulations of the country of origin.

Hodder & Stoughton Ltd
Carmelite House
50 Victoria Embankment
London EC4Y 0DZ

www.hodder.co.uk

For Tamsin, whose wish for a hot German
is where this whole thing began . . .

I

Pepper Taylor visited her mother at the same time every Tuesday.

It was part of her routine, something she had done for a long time, without question.

Today, however, everything felt different. Because this particular Tuesday should have been her sister's thirtieth birthday.

Bethan had been dead for almost twenty-three years now, and while the anniversary of her accident was always a difficult day, in some ways Pepper found birthdays the hardest of all.

She was not the only one.

'Hello, Mum.'

Her mother always opened the door with the chain still fastened, and now she squinted at Pepper through the gap, apparently surprised to see her.

'Oh,' she said wearily. 'Is it that time already?'

'I brought cheese straws.' Pepper held up a Tupperware box. 'Baked them this morning.'

There was a pause as the door was closed and the chain removed. Pepper heard the soft patting sound of her mother's slippers against the plastic hallway runner and wondered, not for the first time, why she didn't just get rid of it. Once upon a time, it had served as a barrier between the muddy soles of her children's shoes and the carpet, but now all it did was serve as a reminder that one of those children was gone, while the other was old enough to wipe their feet on the mat outside. Pepper had asked the question a few years previously, only to have her words waved vaguely away.

'You know I prefer things spick and span,' her mother had said airily, running an eye over the paint-stained shirt and leggings that Pepper had been wearing at the time.

While Pepper was by no means fastidious when it came to her home or her appearance, she was very particular about her work, and so she had let the matter slide. She had learnt over the years that it was easier to accept her mother's foibles than attempt to change them, and now, to keep her happy, Pepper abandoned her tatty pumps by the door and ventured barefoot towards the kitchen.

She knew her mother must know what day it was, and how significant a year, but neither of them raised the subject of Bethan. Pepper watched on in silence as her mother made tea, humming faintly as she opened first the fridge, then the cutlery drawer. Her hair, once ash blonde like Pepper's, was fine and silvery now, and she kept it cut short and neat around her face. Everything about her mother was unobtrusive; she dressed in mostly creams, whites and the palest blues, her nails clean, her make-up immaculate yet understated. Pepper, who favoured bold prints and colourful patterns, and never left the house without a slick of bright-red lipstick, often felt almost garish by comparison.

'Shall we sit in the conservatory?' her mother asked, and Pepper nodded. The small, glass-walled room was a relatively new addition to the house, and as such it always felt less oppressive somehow. There were no memories lingering in there, no traps liable to snap.

Pepper waited for her mother to sit first, then settled herself into the squashy wicker-framed chair opposite and brought her knees up under her chin. The weather had been unable to make up its mind all day, and the sky beyond the windows was the same sullen grey as a pigeon's wing. It felt to Pepper as if spring was taking an awfully long time to arrive, and she said as much to her mother, who muttered something back about her daffodils having bloomed later than expected.

'How's work?' they asked in unison, and Pepper braved a tentative smile.

'You go first,' she said.

'Oh, you know,' her mother said with a sigh. 'Busy. Mr Patel retired last week, so we organised a small send-off. Just some party food and fruit punch, nothing too extravagant.'

'Party food, eh?' Pepper sipped her tea. 'I thought dentists frowned upon anything sugary.'

The corners of her mother's mouth did not so much as flicker.

'Business is good,' Pepper went on, when her mother said nothing further. 'I'm getting regular bookings in London now, plus a slew of children's parties. Oh, and did I tell you I'd branched out into candle-making?'

The clock in the kitchen chimed the hour.

'Well,' Pepper continued, 'people kept asking about it, so I thought I'd best supply their demand. I'm hosting the first session at my studio in a fortnight, if you fancied joining in?'

Nothing. Her mother was staring hard at a point on the wooden floor, not listening.

'Or instead, we could dye our hair purple, put tutus on over our normal clothes and dance along Aldeburgh high street reciting *Wee Willie Winkie*? What do you think?'

'I see.' Her mother did not look up. 'Lovely. Well done you.'

Pepper fought hard not to sigh. She knew her mother didn't mean to ignore her; it was more a symptom of her perpetual misery. She could not work up enough energy to engage, and it had been years now since she had pretended to try. To distract herself, Pepper dived into the cheese straws, cupping her spare hand under her chin so as not to drop flaky pastry crumbs.

'Have you spoken to Dad lately?' she asked between mouthfuls. This, at last, caught her mother's attention and she looked up sharply.

'Martin? No. Why? Should I have?'

Pepper had spoken to her father that morning. He had remembered the day, of course, had called to check that she was OK, to chat about Bethan for a time, share some stories.

'I just thought that he—' Pepper stopped abruptly when she saw the heat beginning to rise in her mother's cheeks.

'Never mind. Forget I mentioned him. Are you done with that tea? I can make us another cup, if you like. Or a pot? Why don't we have a pot?'

Anything to escape the suffocating tension that had descended.

Pepper hurried back into the house, her heart battering against her chest, only letting go of the breath she had been holding in when the kettle began to boil, soothing her with its familiar sound. She was thirty-six years old, but still scared of her mother, too timid to pull at the threads of the past or stray into a conversation that she knew would cause upset. She had thought that today of all days the two of them might have found a way to talk about her sister, but it was clear now that the topic of Bethan was not only off the table but swept neatly under the rug beneath it.

When she returned to the conservatory a few minutes later, she found her mother distractedly picking dead leaves off a potted fern, the remains of one of Pepper's homemade cheese straws on a plate beside her.

'Are you busy on Saturday?' Pepper asked, putting down the teapot.

Her mother glanced up, arched a questioning brow.

'There's a big fête happening over at The Maltings – that care home on the outskirts of town, where I go and volunteer sometimes.'

'I thought you volunteered at the RSPCA shop?' her mother countered.

'I do,' Pepper said. 'But that's only every other Monday. And The Maltings is far more fun – I do art and crafting sessions with some of the residents, help out with lunch, that sort of thing. Some of them are only young, and it's—'

'I'm afraid I can't do Saturday.' Her mother went back to pruning. 'Perhaps another time.'

'Please come.' Pepper curled her bare toes. 'I'm hosting a bric-a-brac stall and you know how terrible I am at maths. I'll end up giving people the wrong change.'

For a moment, she thought her bait had actually worked. Her mother had stood, a look of agency on her face, and promptly wandered off in the direction of the hallway. Pepper heard the creak of the banister, then another of the floorboards upstairs. It was always so quiet in this house, so different from Pepper's home, where the radio was barely off and the television chatted late into the night. She was overcome suddenly by an urge to scream and had to stuff her fist into her mouth to stop herself, removing it just as her mother came back into the room.

'Here,' she said, handing Pepper a large cardboard box. 'This was all in the attic. I only just got around to having the ladder fixed. You know it's been broken since your father— Well, it's probably no good to anyone, but perhaps you could take a look through, sell anything you don't want at the fête?'

'Thanks.' Pepper shook the box gently and heard a clunk. When she went to prise open the lid, however, her mother raised a hand.

'No. Open it later,' she said quickly, gesturing around. 'The dust will go everywhere, and I only just polished in here.'

'OK.' Pepper frowned. 'But what's in there? Surely you can tell me that?'

She studied her mother's expression, watched as her pale eyes flickered with discomfort.

'Some clothes,' she said snippily, sitting down and turning her attention back to her plant. 'Toys, books – that sort of thing.'

'Oh.' Intrigue inflated like a bubble inside Pepper's chest. 'My old stuff?'

'Some,' her mother replied, through what sounded suspiciously like clenched teeth.

Pepper moved the box from side to side, thinking.

'Mum?' she began, her voice small. 'Is this? Are they? Beth—'

'Please, Philippa.' Her mother shot her a warning look.

'Just take the box and go.'

2

Taking the beach route was neither the quickest nor easiest way for Pepper to get home, but she turned off the high street regardless, blinking as the blustery wind picked up strands of her hair and flattened them across her cheeks. Agitated gulls were picking their way over the pebbles, as restless as the sea that was swirling and frothing below them, and in the far distance, she could just make out the shape of a man walking his dog.

Pepper put down the cardboard box and contemplated the murky water. It was not quite brown, not quite blue, not quite grey – as if all the painters of the world had used it to rinse off their brushes. She had always seen the world in this way, always strived to find the familiar in the new, or the magic in the mundane. There had been occasions in Pepper's past where she saw her artistic nature as a curse, but not even that had stopped her from pursuing a career where she was able to indulge in all things creative. Although it was not the dream she had set out to achieve, Pepper was still proud of her little teaching business, Arts For All, and for the most part, she found it both satisfying and rewarding.

She enjoyed meeting people, inviting them into the studio at the end of her garden to learn a new skill, make a new friend or two, then go home with something beautiful they had created, something they could display or give away as a gift. Solitude was the enemy of creativity, and Pepper did anything she could to avoid it, to shield herself from loneliness.

Aldeburgh was one of Suffolk's more beautiful towns, but it was also one that people left behind. Pepper had watched each of her school friends move away in turn, be it for a job or a relationship, and as time had ticked by, the bonds between them had started to fray. For Pepper, the whispers of the past had always been more insistent than the beckoning hand of the future, and so she stayed where she was, bound by a mixture of duty and fear.

The next gust of wind felt as if it had passed right through her, and she shivered, cursing the lacklustre April weather as she retrieved the box from the ground. Pepper didn't stop again until she reached the wooden bench in the sheltered courtyard not far from the fishmongers' huts. It was too early in the season for any of the vendors to bother opening, but there was still enough ripeness in the air to wrinkle her nose. The fresh catch of the day carried a scent that settled into cracks, submerged underneath layers of damp wood and burrowed into plaster and stone – yet she found it oddly comforting. It was the smell of home, of growing up, of long summer days chasing Bethan across the stones, of chips wrapped in newspaper that stained your fingers, of a time when their family was still together, still intact, not broken by tragedy, the pieces scattered and muddled, the picture of happiness destroyed.

It felt right to be here today, even if the memories were making Pepper feel increasingly melancholy. In a bid to distract her mind, she decided to have a look through the box now, rather than waiting until she was home, and slid a hand under the cardboard flap to open it. Inside, she found a plastic Care Bear with a single tuft of pink hair, a metal Slinky twisted into a thousand knots, and a crude drawing of four people with arms dangling out from where their ears should be, oversized feet and huge, wide-apart eyes. There was an ancient bottle of bubbles, its lid stuck fast, a light-up yo-yo that needed new batteries, a deformed-looking teddy that had been washed one time too many, a battered piggybank, a whistle on a string and a My Little Pony purse. It was all rubbish, yet precious – each item a memory of a made-up game, a shared giggle, an imagination permitted to flourish without constraint. Some of the things had been Pepper's, but many had been Bethan's – the sketch, the bubbles, the bear.

As she took out each object in turn, Pepper was reminded of how much her younger sibling had begged to play with her toys, had wanted to be grown up enough to have her own Barbie doll, or her own set of smart pastels instead of crayons, and wished she had given in.

Right at the bottom, tucked underneath a Get Along Gang Montgomery Moose doll and a toy barn that mooed when you opened the doors, Pepper discovered her and Bethan's *Book of the World* and exclaimed in delight.

This had been their favourite, the one they had pored over together in their tent of many sofa cushions. Pepper felt her eyes fill with tears as she began flicking through, remembering how her sister had asked her to read it to her again and again, to tell her the story of Tutankhamun and the Egyptian Pyramids, of Mount Everest and the South Pole. They had folded down the corners of all the pages bearing countries they wanted to visit, then turned to the world map at the back and charted their course with a finger, soaring across from England to France to Spain to Greece to Africa to China to New Zealand. She couldn't believe she had forgotten about this book, about their plans, about that intrepid need the two of them had shared for adventure.

All this time, all these years later, and Pepper had not gone on a single trip.

Shame coloured her cheeks, the compulsion to cry suddenly so strong that she felt compelled to stand up again and move, get herself back to her cottage before her emotions had the chance to overtake her. When she emerged from the courtyard, however, Pepper saw someone she recognised on the beach. The older woman was set up in front of an easel that was wobbling precariously on spindly legs, her body mostly concealed beneath an acid-green coat that would make even a colour-blind person baulk.

As Pepper dithered on the spot, deciding whether to say hello or tiptoe past, her friend stood up and began to pack away her things, only to stagger to the side and fall over.

'Josephine – are you OK?' Pepper was by her side in an instant.

Ditching the box, she crouched down and wrapped an arm around the woman's shoulders, feeling the sharp edge of a jutting collarbone through the coat.

'Oops,' proclaimed Josephine in amusement. 'What a prize pillock I am.'

Although she had followed this up with a bark of laughter, Pepper noticed that she was trembling.

'Don't try to stand,' she soothed. 'Give yourself a moment.'

Josephine had dropped her bag as she fell, so Pepper scooped up the scattered belongings. As well as pastels, a stick of charcoal and an old rag that smelt deliciously of turps, there was also a miniature set of paints, complete with tiny brushes.

'Oh, don't worry about the picture,' the woman said, as her sketch book was blown open by another gust of wind. 'Utter tosh – only good for the fire.'

'I think it's beautiful,' Pepper told her honestly, running a practised eye over the faint lines and daubs of grey and blue. 'Very atmospheric.'

'Poppycock!' came the retort. 'Now, if you wouldn't mind helping me up.'

Pepper stood first, then slowly levered Josephine back to her feet, noting the lines of exhaustion on her friend's face.

'Do you think you should see a doctor?' she asked.

'Good Lord, no!'

'Sorry.' Pepper was contrite. 'I just thought—'

'No, I don't want a fuss, darling. Doctors these days have enough whingers to deal with.'

'Hmm.' Pepper eyed her with disapproval. 'Will you at least let me walk you home?'

'I will do you one better than that,' replied Josephine, her blue eyes full of mischief as Pepper folded the easel and lay it across the top of the box.

'Ready? Righto – follow me.'

3

Josephine Hurley had swept into Pepper's life for the first time the previous summer, when the two of them had ended up on adjacent seats of a rail replacement bus. Unlike most of the other passengers, who were chuntering grumpily about 'the state of the trains these days', Josephine had clapped her hands together and proclaimed it 'an adventure'.

After telling Pepper her name, adding mischievously 'I longed to shorten it to Fifi when I was in my teens, but my father said people would assume I was a go-go dancer', she explained that she had only recently moved to Suffolk from London, having sold her home following the death of her husband.

'It was far too large for one old biddy,' she had remarked dismissively. 'I would finish cleaning one damn room, then discover cobwebs had gathered in the next.'

By the time they had reached their stop, Pepper had deduced that not only was this whirling dervish of a woman demonstrably sharp of wit, she was also one of those refreshing souls who say exactly what is on their mind as soon as it occurs to them.

'If it was up to me, I would have carried on working until I dropped dead,' she had told Pepper of her successful public relations company. 'But I was overruled by the offspring. Do you have any children?' Then, when Pepper shook her head. 'Very wise – they spend the first half of their lives ignoring most of everything you tell them to do, then the latter half complaining that you never gave them the right guidance.'

As well as being in firm agreement about the merits of Pepper's home county, they found that many of their likes and dislikes were similar, too, and Josephine had clasped her hands together in delight when she found out what her new friend did for a living. She was an ardent fan of both arts and crafts, she told Pepper. 'But certainly not a practitioner – I have less creative prowess than frogspawn.'

Clearly, however, that was not the whole truth, and Pepper said as much as they settled in at a cosy corner table in the Turbot pub on the high street.

'You told me when we met that a stickman would be a stretch,' she said. 'But from what I just saw down on the beach, you have some real talent.'

'Hogwash,' Josephine replied, reaching for her gin and tonic. 'If you must know, the easel was just a decoy – an excuse to sit and stare out at the water for a while. It's therapeutic, don't you agree?' Josephine stared at her thoughtfully. 'The voice of the sea speaks to the soul, and all that.'

'Does it?' Pepper asked, seeing a flicker of amusement flash across the older woman's face.

'Lord only knows.' Josephine's stack of bracelets jangled as she put down her drink. 'I cannot, for the life of me, recall where I read that quote – perhaps inside a fortune cookie or printed on a tea towel?'

'Keep calm and speak to the sea?' Pepper suggested, and was rewarded with a chortle.

'Something like that. Although, I find that the beach is a good place to sit when you have some thinking to do – and,' she added, with a satisfied sort of flourish, 'it just so happens that I was thinking about you.'

'Me?' Pepper paused with her lemonade halfway towards her mouth. 'Why me?'

'Because,' Josephine was tapping her fingers on the table top now, as if mulling over what exactly to say. 'No, that won't do,' she went on, more to herself than to Pepper. 'I suppose I need to start at the very beginning.'

Pepper waited, feeling utterly mystified.

'Have you been abroad much, darling?' Josephine asked, her gaze direct.

Pepper thought about the book in the box beside her, of folded-down pages and dreams of exploration and adventure.

'No,' she admitted. 'Never.'

'You've never wanted to travel? See the world? Go and "find yourself" or what have you?'

This was a question that required a more complicated answer, and Pepper hesitated.

'I did want to,' she said at last. 'But the opportunity never came up when I was younger, and since then, I can't remember a time I wasn't busy – especially since I started the business.'

'I understand.' Josephine smiled to reassure her. 'Holidays are an indulgence.'

Pepper went to agree, but Josephine cut across her.

'But they are also a necessity.'

'I wouldn't go that far,' Pepper said lightly, watching the bubbles in her lemonade. 'It's really not that big a deal. I live by the beach, after all – it's not like I'm missing out on the whole seaside thing.'

What she didn't add was that she had never had the guts to go alone. Most people went away with their partners, but Pepper had never held onto one of those long enough either – her most serious relationship to date had lasted less than four months.

Josephine didn't say anything for a while, she merely shook her head slowly from side to side, before stopping to stare hard at Pepper, as if trying to work her out.

'There is something I want to tell you,' she said finally.

Pepper felt a cold stone of dread drop down from her throat into her stomach.

'There's no need to look so aghast.' Josephine reached across and patted Pepper's wrist.

'I suspect you might even enjoy this story.'

'Really?' Pepper said warily. 'Does that mean it has a happy ending?'

Josephine thought for a moment.

'That,' she said, breaking off to sip her gin, 'very much depends on you.'

'Me? Why me?'

'In order for you to understand completely,' she said, 'you need to know everything. But for that to happen, I will need to take you back to when I was a young woman – right back to 1966.'

'OK.' Pepper was perplexed, but she was also eager to listen. Josephine's stories were invariably as enthralling as they were entertaining.

'As you know, many people in this country claim that 'sixty-six was a great year,' Josephine began, giving Pepper a sidelong glance. 'England won the World Cup for the first – and seemingly only – time in July, colour television arrived with much hurrah, and everyone was in agreement that the Beatles were just about the most wonderful thing to ever happen to music. I think John Lennon himself claimed that the band was more popular than Jesus – which tells you something about the man's ego – but regardless, it was certainly a year of celebration and liberation.'

Pepper could sense a 'but'.

'The mood was very much "can do", which I suppose is why I felt brave enough to head off abroad by myself. I had always wanted to explore, and defying my poor mother and father felt like such a rebellious thing to do.'

Pepper, who could relate to this, nodded in agreement.

'I chose Portugal simply because I had read about it in a newspaper that same week,' Josephine continued. 'A bridge had been erected that connected Lisbon to Almada, and there were photos, so I knew it was beautiful. I wanted to get a suntan and see all the azulejos – those are painted tiles, of course. I thought I was so grown-up and cultured, but I was only seventeen. I barely knew my ankle from my earlobe at that age.'

The door of the pub opened, and Pepper glanced up, waving back at the two women arrivals, both of whom were regular customers at her mosaic classes. Josephine fell silent, waiting while the three of them exchanged pleasantries, and there was an awkward moment when it looked as if the ladies might attempt to join them.

'We're just—' began Pepper, pulling her best 'please don't sit with us' face. Luckily, the two women cottoned on fast and, with smiling apologies, moved towards the other side of the bar instead.

'So,' Josephine went on, so quietly that Pepper had to lean forwards in order to hear her. 'That is exactly what I did. I packed a bag, booked my ticket, and off I went.'

'Just like that?' Pepper was impressed. 'You must have been so scared?'

'Oh, not a bit of it – quite the opposite, darling.' Josephine shook her head. 'Being alone felt natural to me. I had never really been given the opportunity to look after myself and put my own needs first until that point, and the freedom it offered felt like a revelation. No, no – I was far too excited to be afraid.'

Pepper gazed at her friend with awe. 'What was it like?' she asked eagerly. 'Was it every bit as beautiful as you'd hoped it would be? Did you find the things you were looking for?'

Josephine smiled, her whole demeanour softening as her memory transported her back to another time. She drank some more of her gin and tonic and seemed to relish the feel of it slipping down her throat. Pepper waited, perched as she was on the literal edge of her seat, for what came next.

'My dear girl,' Josephine said, fixing Pepper with an expression that was both wistful and mischievous. 'What I found was not some*thing* at all – it was someone.'

4

'Do you believe in love at first sight?'

'Oh, yes,' Pepper said gleefully. 'Not that it's ever happened to me – unless you count Robbie Williams?'

'Is he a former partner of yours?' Josephine asked, and Pepper laughed.

'If only. No, he was a member of a very popular boyband in the nineties – my friends and I used to squabble over which one of us would marry him one day.'

The pub was beginning to fill up with early diners now, and Pepper kept being distracted by people passing by their table to say hello, ask what new sessions she had coming up and tell her how much their husband, friend or colleague had loved the gift Pepper had helped them create. Josephine did not seem to mind, and smiled warmly at everyone, introducing herself merrily as 'the resident troublemaker', gaining herself much laughter in return.

'We were talking about love,' Pepper reminded her, as she returned from the bar with a second round. Despite Josephine's plea that she join her on the gin, Pepper was sticking resolutely to soft drinks. She had not forgotten how close she'd come to breaking down on the beach earlier and knew that alcohol would likely push her over the edge.

Josephine extracted the wedge of lime from her glass and squeezed it delicately.

'As far as my husband Ian was concerned,' she told Pepper, 'he was the one who turned my insides to mush. And it's true – I was drawn to him the instant we met. It was on Aldeburgh beach, you know – have I ever told you that?'

Pepper shook her head.

'My family and his had taken us there for a holiday over the same long weekend. He taught me how to skim stones and, because he knew the area so well, he also knew where to find all the best shells.'

She smiled faintly at the memory.

'But he wasn't your first love?' Pepper said.

Josephine looked down towards her lap. The hand that was clutching the gin and tonic quivered slightly.

'His name was Jorge,' she said. 'And without sounding too trite, he was simply the most beautiful man I had ever seen.'

'Was he Portuguese?' asked Pepper.

'Yes. But he could speak English perfectly; he had spent some time over here when he was a boy, so although he spoke with a rather heavy accent, I could understand him. We understood each other, you see, that was the thing. We had this connection, right from the first moment we met until the day I left him behind in Spain.'

'You travelled around together?' Pepper sat back in surprise. 'For how long?'

'Oh, only for a few weeks,' Josephine said, her voice faint. 'Jorge was an aspiring artist, you see – he had always wanted to see the magnificent architecture in Barcelona, so we went there together from Lisbon and it was all so perfect. The two of us were so in love that we felt invincible.'

Pepper was enraptured.

'Why did you leave so soon?' she asked. 'Surely, you could have stayed longer?'

'I had promised my family that I would be back,' Josephine said. 'I had barely any money and it wasn't as easy to find work abroad as it is now. I thought I would go home and get a job, save some funds and make the return trip when I had the means. Jorge and I were in love, and of course, that felt like everything. We agreed that a few months apart would not break us, that we would stay in contact and see each other as soon as possible. The day I left, I truly believed that I would see him again.'

'And did you?' Pepper wanted to know, even though she could sense the answer.

Josephine's mouth was pulled down at the corners, but she looked resolute rather than sad.

'I never heard from him,' she explained. 'I wrote to him, of course, sending the letters to his apartment in Lisbon, but I have no idea if any of them reached him. Perhaps he did get them and sent replies that never found their way to me? I don't know for sure, but at the time, it hurt me so much, being ignored like that. I was proud, you see, even then.'

She gave Pepper the ghost of a smile.

'When I didn't hear anything back from Jorge after three months had passed, I stopped trying. I did my best to put him out of my mind. And not long after that, I met Ian.'

Pepper pressed her fingers against her cheek.

'And you fell for him in the same way as you had for Jorge?' she asked.

Josephine's expression was unreadable.

'It was different with Ian. More straightforward, I suppose one might say. Ian and I wrote to one another at first, and then, the third time he came to visit me in London, he proposed. That was that. I was happy, and until our first child, Georgina, came along, I was settled, too. The relationship and wedding were adventure enough to satisfy that urge I had always had to push the boundaries.'

The sun had broken through the clouds beyond the pub windows, and dappled light flooded across the table. Pepper blinked, rubbing her eyes at the sudden brightness.

'And you really never heard from Jorge again after that?' she asked, feeling rather sad.

Josephine sighed. 'Sometimes I wish that I had, but most of the time, I simply accept it for what it was. We had our moment – and it was a wonderful one – but fate clearly had bigger things for each of us to do, things that carried more weight than our feelings did. I have been lucky, Philippa dear, to have loved and been loved by two very special men. And the love I feel for Jorge now is the same as it was all those years ago – it has never been tarnished. It has kept me smiling for all these years, kept me ticking in here,' she said, bringing a hand up to her chest.

'Have you ever felt that way about someone before, my darling?'

Pepper shook her head.

'Well.' Josephine sat up straighter. 'There's still plenty of time.'

Pepper made a non-committal snuffling sound and dropped her chin towards the floor.

'We're not talking about me,' she chided. 'And I have a feeling we're not at the end of this story yet.'

Josephine chuckled. 'Correct!' she exclaimed. 'There is a little more I need to tell you. As a matter of fact, I have been thinking a lot about Jorge recently, and about the journey we went on together. I thought I was content to simply leave it all behind me in the past – but then today, I thought, why don't I go back?'

'To Lisbon?' Pepper asked.

'Yes, to Lisbon!' Josephine clasped her hands together. 'And Barcelona – to all the places that meant something to me and Jorge. I want to retrace the steps of our love story, recapture my youth, have another adventure, perhaps even find him.'

'Then you should absolutely go,' Pepper enthused.

'My dear girl,' Josephine said, stretching a hand across and resting it on top of Pepper's. 'Thank you for not judging me too harshly. Many people would, you know.'

'Not me,' Pepper said simply. 'You can't help who you fall in love with, can you? It is a force much stronger than any of us. Just ask Shakespeare! Or Richard Curtis! Or Ed Sheeran!'

'Is he something to do with sheep?' she asked, to which Pepper burst out laughing.

Josephine chuckled.

'You are fun,' she said. 'And what's more – I trust you, Philippa, I really do. Which brings us to why I was thinking about you earlier. I want you to come with me.'

'You *what*?' Pepper stopped laughing abruptly.

'It's high time you had a holiday. I will pay for everything, of course. You would be acting as my companion, but I promise I won't cramp your style.'

'I can't,' Pepper garbled. 'I have work. My schedule is full.'

And what would my mother say?

She could see that Josephine was not going to give up easily.

'I'm very flattered you would think of me,' she interjected, as the older woman opened her mouth to speak. 'But surely there's someone else you'd rather go with? Someone who actually has some experience of travelling for a start.'

Josephine finished what was left in her glass.

'I appreciate that I have rather flung this on you,' she allowed. 'Of course, you must go away and mull it over. All I ask is that you do really consider it – do you think you can do that?'

Pepper chewed the inside of her cheek.

'For me?' Josephine pleaded.

It was all so much to take in, the story, the offer, the fact that it had landed on her lap on this day of all the days – Pepper felt as if her brain had been spiralised.

'OK,' she said at last, returning Josephine's wide smile with a more uncertain one of her own. 'I promise I'll think about it.'

5

The Maltings didn't look like a care home from the outside. With its immaculate white stone walls, tall arched windows and vast entrance flanked by a pair of neatly clipped Japanese maples, it looked more like something that would pop up in a BBC period drama. Pepper always half expected young ladies in bonnets and corsets to come skipping down the steps as she approached.

She had been volunteering here for almost a year now, ever since the duty manager – a woman named Jilly Howarth – had turned up at one of Pepper's life drawing classes and the two of them had got chatting. Because she was able to choose the hours and days she ran her sessions, Pepper was the ideal candidate for voluntary work, and she enjoyed it immensely. Not only did it feel good to be helpful, it was also a great way to meet lots of new people, and she had become quite friendly with several of The Maltings' staff.

Jilly, a kind but crumpled-around-the-edges woman in her mid-fifties, greeted Pepper warmly as she arrived at the front desk.

'Hello, Philippa love. Nice to see you. Gosh, is that all for our fête?'

Pepper was wheeling a large suitcase behind her and carrying two boxes. Most of the bric-a-brac items she had collected came from the cupboard under Josephine's stairs, which the older woman had insisted Pepper rifle through and take whatever she wanted. There were also a host of knick-knacks from her own home, but nothing from the box her mother had given her had made the cut. Pepper could not face parting with anything that had once been played with by her sister.

'Yep,' she said now. 'All for you. I'm so glad you gave me bric-a-brac rather than cakes – I'm afraid cheese straws are about my limit when it comes to baking.'

'Not to worry,' Jilly said, retrieving her glasses from where she'd pushed them up into her salt-and-pepper nest of hair. 'We put our resident culinary expert on the case. If you hurry through, he'll let you know where you can set up. Fête kicks off at two.'

Pepper ventured further into the house before turning right and making her way down a wide corridor. There were doors spaced at regular intervals along one side, while the other consisted of floor-to-ceiling windows that looked out over a wide, paved courtyard. She knew from earlier visits that there was a well-stocked pond in the middle, as well as raised flower-beds, a sprawling herb garden and, come the summer, so many tomato plants that you could smell them the moment you stepped outside.

There were no residents in the main sitting room as she passed, and nobody in the kitchens when she peered through the propped-open door, but she found the wide lawn at the back of the house littered with colourful tents, picnic blankets and an array of mismatched garden furniture. Pink and purple balloons were tied to the surrounding trees and many of the residents' wheelchairs, and Pepper recognised lots of faces as she made her way across the grass, smiling back at anyone who called out a greeting. There were a large number of elderly folk living at The Maltings, but Pepper spent most of her time volunteering with the younger contingent, all of whom were here because they needed round-the-clock specialist care.

'Oi, Taylor – over here!'

She turned to see a tall, slim, black man beckoning her over, and grinned. As well as apparently being a culinary expert, Samuel was one of the home's most popular carers – and a wind-up merchant of the highest order. A born-and-bred Londoner who proudly referred to himself as a 'Bantersaurus

Rex', he was a hero among his young charges and often sat in on Pepper's sessions. Samuel seemed to have an uncanny ability to make every single person he came into contact with feel special, and despite the taxing nature of his job, always made time for people. The two of them had settled quickly into an easy friendship, and Pepper invariably came away from her encounters with him feeling as if the world was a better place, even if he did have a fondness for taking the mickey.

'That's quite a haul you have there,' he said by way of a greeting, running an approving eye over Pepper's boxes. Plucking a rather deformed-looking stuffed cat from the top of the nearest one, he laughed.

'This is . . . interesting.'

Pepper tutted good-naturedly.

'I'll have you know,' she said, 'that is an original Arts For All creation, hot off the sewing lesson press – highly sought-after and a true one-of-a-kind.'

'In that case,' Samuel rummaged in the pocket of his shorts and pulled out a ten-pound note, 'consider me your first customer.'

'It's actually twenty quid,' she told him, then laughed at his expression of pure horror.

'Not really! You should see your face.'

'Do you want the stall between my two?' he asked. 'I mean, obviously you'll get way more footfall if you're hanging out near the Chief.'

'I assume by Chief, you mean yourself?' Pepper shook her head in mock exasperation. 'Let me guess – you gave yourself that name?'

'A man's gotta believe in himself,' he said, as she followed him across the grass.

'What are you selling other than the cakes?' Pepper asked, peering at the plain blue sheet Samuel had tossed over the front of his second stall.

'Glad you asked that,' he said cheerfully. 'I thought, seeing as it's such a sunny day, that I would . . .' He paused to bend over and pick up a bucket of water, lifting a big dripping sponge up and holding it out for Pepper to see.

'Wash cars?' she guessed, and Samuel slapped his free hand across his face.

'Now that would have made sense,' he said. 'Where were you when I needed you, eh? In the planning stages? But I've made my flyers now and handed them out. Here,' he added, digging one out of his back pocket and giving it to Pepper.

'Soak a Bloke?' she read out loud. 'You're going to let people lob wet sponges at you?'

'For a fee!' he protested. 'I reckon a quid a go is reasonable.'

'In that case,' Pepper said, getting her purse out of her bag and extracting her own ten-pound note. 'You can count *me* as your first ten customers.'

Five hours later, dripping wet but swelling with pride at having raised over four hundred pounds, Samuel helped Pepper pack up the few items she had not managed to sell.

'I can't believe nobody wanted this,' he exclaimed, picking up a truly grotesque ornament of a naked man sitting cross-legged on a toadstool.

'Or this,' Pepper replied, pointing to an *Ultimate Pan Pipes* CD.

'I dated a girl once who could play the pan pipes,' he said. 'Her name was Aurora and she was obsessed with *Wuthering Heights*.'

'My last boyfriend played the guitar,' Pepper told him with a grimace. 'Very badly. I'm not sure if he was obsessed with anything – certainly not me, in any case.'

'Mother-plucker.' Samuel beamed his mega-watt smile as she rolled her eyes.

'I see what you did there.'

'Not just a hat stand.' He tapped the top of his head.

'Is that what it says on your dating app bio?' she joked.

Samuel made no secret of the fact that he was looking for a girlfriend and seemed to have a new dating-disaster anecdote every other week.

'I might have more luck if it did,' he said, pretending to sound sad. 'Although, saying that, I did meet up with someone just last night.'

'Oh?' Pepper loved a good first-date story. 'Any sparks?'

Samuel considered. 'We'll see,' he allowed. 'Gotta let these things develop naturally, right?'

'You don't believe in love at first sight, then?' Pepper replied, thinking of Josephine.

Samuel laughed. 'Lust maybe – love is the big one, innit? You can't go throwing out the L-word to someone you barely know – therein madness lies.'

'What about Romeo and Juliet?' she protested. 'Or Anna and Vronsky?'

'Who-sky?'

'He's from *Anna Karenina*.'

'So, fictional characters only, right?'

'It happens in real life, too,' she insisted, only just stopping herself from blurting out Josephine's story. 'Trust me,' she went on, crouching down to zip up her case. 'It can happen.'

'Have you got a net?' Samuel asked.

Pepper stared up at him in confusion.

'You know, to catch all the tiny birds that are flitting around your head,' he said, giving into a laugh. Pepper arranged a look of fury on her face as she stood.

'You're mocking me,' she stated.

'Maybe a little . . .'

'Where's your sense of romance, man?'

Samuel put his head on one side, his eyes bright with amusement.

'If you ask me,' he said, 'love is a trap, out to get us. It wants us to fall but falling is dangerous.'

'Falling in love isn't like jumping into a well,' Pepper retorted, as Samuel started to fold up the sheet that had been spread over the stall.

'I think I would prefer that,' he said. 'At least in that scenario, there would be a rope and bucket to help me climb out.'

'Sorry.' Pepper felt as if she'd overstepped a mark somewhere, but she wasn't sure how.

Samuel turned to face her, the sheet bundled up in his arms.

'Don't be daft,' he said. 'Pay no attention to me, I'm just bitter and twisted because nobody has swiped right for me all day.'

'You'll meet the perfect person one day,' she said, wanting to reassure him even though she knew as soon as she'd said it how clichéd it sounded. 'And when you do, you'll know.'

Samuel looked as if he was trying not to laugh. She could see the merriment dancing in his eyes and shifted uncomfortably. He thought she was a fool, but Pepper knew she was right.

Love was out there somewhere, waiting to make everything better.

All she had to do was find it.

6

If you asked a roomful of people to choose their favourite day of the week, Pepper would be willing to bet that most of them would opt for Sunday. As tranquil as Saturday was tumultuous, the latter half of the weekend undoubtedly felt to many the more enjoyable, like a second sip of wine, or series two of a sitcom once you knew and loved all the characters.

Pepper understood the reasoning, but she was not in agreement. She would have preferred to work, but barely anyone booked into the Sunday sessions she arranged, while the charity shop she volunteered at was closed and The Maltings was busy with visiting family members. It had been a strange week, what with Bethan's birthday and Josephine's offer, but by keeping herself busy throughout most of it, Pepper had managed to delay actually thinking too deeply about either. Now it was Sunday, and time had caught up with her.

In a half-hearted attempt at some self-care time, Pepper decided to start her day with a bubble bath, into which she promptly dropped the latest Katie Marsh novel. After letting out the water and making her way downstairs to make a soothing camomile tea, she discovered that her temperamental kettle must have blown a fuse in the night, because half the contents of her freezer were now soggy. Turning on the oven to cook the three packets of vegetarian sausages before they went off, she knocked a stack of plates off the draining board and swore as two of them broke across her bare feet. Now, fighting back tears of pain and frustration, Pepper hobbled outside to deposit the shards straight into her pot of odd bits and bobs she used for art projects, and found that next-door's cat had left her a little present on the mat.

'Shitting hell!' she swore, which pretty much summed up the situation.

All of a sudden, the house felt as if it were closing in on her, the ceilings too low and the furniture too small. She couldn't settle and limped on her bruised feet from room to room, fussing and fidgeting until she became irritated with herself. Picking up her mobile, she scrolled to Josephine's number, only to change her mind before pressing the button to call. Her friend would definitely know what to say to snap her out of this strange mood. She would beckon Pepper into her cluttered front room and feed her ginger cake and eye-wateringly strong beakers of gin and tonic, make her laugh by shouting at the racing on Channel 4 or fill her in on the latest slice of town gossip. Josephine's house was a treasure trove of trinkets, paintings and sculptures, and Pepper loved to poke through them all, asking questions about how they came to be there. Josephine could remember the details of every gallery she and her late husband had visited on their forays through the French countryside, every flea market where she'd uncovered a treasure, and every back room of an antique shop she had talked her way into. She remembered things in a sensory way, recalling not just events and words exchanged, but smells and sounds, too – it made her stories all the more vivid.

The problem was, Pepper still did not have an answer to Josephine's question, and until she did, she was steadfastly avoiding her.

After solemnly chewing her way through two slices of toast coated in three inches of crunchy peanut butter, Pepper headed to her studio at the end of the garden, thinking that she may as well get on with the grouting from last week's mosaic class. It took forty-eight hours for the glue to properly dry, so none of her customers could do the finishing touches to their pieces during the day-long session. Instead, Pepper offered them a small bag of grout to take away, along with an instruction sheet, or promised that she would do the work herself and drop the mosaics off once they had dried.

Turning her plug-in radio up as loud as she could get away with, so the chatter would keep her company, Pepper rolled up her sleeves, donned her mask and latex gloves and got stuck in. The work was simple yet satisfying, the dark grout transforming the mosaics from pretty pictures to something with far more clout. She spread the grainy goo over the top of each piece in turn, using her fingers to ease it into all the gaps between the cut tiles, then leant in closely to search and destroy any remaining air bubbles that could ruin the overall effect.

The dust from the dry grout hung in the air, coating Pepper's disposable face mask with grime and making her sneeze behind the protective cardboard barrier. It was a bad idea to breathe any in, but that didn't stop Pepper loving the smell. It was earthy and rough and reminded her of sitting in her parents' front garden as a child, Bethan beside her and the two of them elbow deep in mud. Pepper would dig until she uncovered something exciting – a broken piece of pottery or soft-edged lump of glass – holding it up triumphantly for her sister to admire, before dropping it into her plastic bucket. They'd had one each, Bethan and herself, a blue one for her and a yellow one for her sister.

Pepper shook her head, dislodging the memory before it gained too much clarity, and began removing the excess grout with a wet sponge. It never failed to lift her mood when she saw the picture below beginning to emerge, and for a while, the repetitive action was enough to soothe her. She tried to recall the last time she had made anything for herself and couldn't. As a child, Pepper had drawn, painted, moulded and sculpted obsessively – art was all she ever wanted to do and the only subject she really cared about at school. It was what she turned to for solace after her sister died, and how she expressed her dismay when her father left not long afterwards. Painting was what she loved most of all, and she experimented with all sorts of materials and canvases, spurred on by her own need to create, but also by the reactions of those around her, all of whom seemed to think she had serious potential. When asked by her careers advisor what she wanted to do, Pepper had replied simply that she was going to be a world-renowned artist – not that she 'wanted' to be, but she 'was going' to be – and she had believed it, too.

Brimming with confidence having breezed through her A-level exams, Pepper began her degree foundation course without so much as a tremble of trepidation and dashed out her first assignment – a collage that told a story from her life – with easy self-assurance. When she presented it to her teacher, however, the woman's face fell.

'I can see what you tried to do,' she had remarked, her tone straying close to pity. 'But where is the emotion? Where are you in this work?'

Impossibly stung but determined to prove her worth, Pepper started the project again from scratch, only to get much the same feedback again. When it came to creating a self-portrait, her marks slipped even lower, with the same teacher telling her that although she was technically gifted, she was so far failing to create anything that would make people stop and feel something. It was that connection, she explained reverently, that separated a good artist from a great artist, and sent Pepper home with a list of examples to look up.

This she did, but try as she might, Pepper could never get her grades back to where she wanted them, and by the end of that academic year, she was so disheartened that she gave up. On the rare occasions that she created art now, she always found it lacking, and each failure pushed her self-confidence down further. As far as Pepper was concerned, teaching the very basics was all she was good for, and so that was the level at which she stayed.

The grouting was finished now, so she set each block aside to dry, and sat for a while looking out towards the garden, at the colourful banks of flowers, the terracotta pots decorated in mosaic patterns, the neat little pond surrounded by painted stones, and the bird table she had constructed from driftwood washed up on Aldeburgh beach.

The urge to paint was needling her. It had been so long, yet perhaps, this time, she would achieve something special. If she

didn't give in, the compulsion would drive her to distraction –
prevent her from sleeping.

Mind made up, Pepper got to her feet and moved quickly, her
body making the decision before her head had time to interfere.
Switching off the radio, she searched through the music on her
phone until she found the Prodigy and, turning it up to its highest volume, plugged in her headphones, pressed play, and
selected a blank tile from the stack beside the door. Snatching
up her paints, she daubed on first green, then pinks, purples and
creams. The frothy outline of the lilac flowers appeared within
moments, and Pepper barely waited for the paint to settle before
she changed brushes to add details to petal and leaf. Her heart
raced as the music thundered to a crescendo in her ears, and all
the while her hand moved seamlessly across the tile, daubing,
tweaking, perfecting. It was so easy, so joyful, so uncomplicated
– Pepper could feel her shoulders knotting with effort, yet she
continued to work, so set on finishing what she had started that
she failed to notice the light begin to fade beyond the windows.

Once she was satisfied, Pepper took a deep breath and
switched off her music, closing her eyes briefly as vibrations of
silence rushed into the void. Lifting the tile carefully so as not to
disturb the paint, she carried it across from the table to the more
solid work bench and set it down almost lovingly amongst the
sawdust and curls of stripped wood. The delicate floral pattern
was so lifelike that she could almost smell its sweet aroma.

Hearing a noise in the garden, she swung round to find
Josephine making her slow way along the path, her hand raised
in greeting. Pepper opened the door.

'Hello, darling – there you are!' Josephine beamed. 'I knocked
and knocked, then tried the door and found it open – I hope you
don't mind?'

'Of course not,' Pepper said, wondering why her friend
hadn't tried to call.

'I'm afraid I forgot my mobile,' Josephine explained, as if she
read Pepper's mind. 'I would forget my arms and legs these
days, if they weren't attached – oh!' she exclaimed, gazing down

at the tile on the workbench. 'How wonderful – did you just paint this?'

Pepper reddened.

'It really is quite remarkable,' Josephine appraised, bending over for a closer look.

Pepper leant over reluctantly until their noses were level, then her blood seemed to come to a halt in her veins. The breeze coming in through the open door had blown some of the stray chippings across the tile, smudging the wet paint in several places, and dust had adhered itself to the petals.

As Josephine continued to offer praise, Pepper gathered up a small key from a hook on the wall and made her way to the cabinet in the far corner, unlocking a drawer and extracting the tool she needed. Before she had time to change her mind, she returned to the workbench and, in a single decisive motion, brought down her hammer and smashed the tile into tiny pieces.

Josephine recoiled.

'Good God! What on earth did you do that for?'

Pepper shrugged, her eyes on the broken shards.

'It was ruined,' she said simply. 'Worthless.'

'Darling, it absolutely was not,' Josephine assured her. 'I thought it was beautiful.'

'It wasn't good enough,' Pepper insisted firmly. 'It was just a silly tile,' she added, when Josephine looked as if she was going to protest further. 'Forget about it.'

Scooping up the pieces, she tossed them into the bin.

'Tea?' she suggested brightly, reaching for the light switch, but Josephine shook her head. If Pepper didn't know any better, she would have said her friend looked sheepish.

'What's up?' she asked suspiciously.

'With me? Oh, nothing, darling. I was just wondering if you'd given any thought to what we discussed at the pub?'

Pepper cast her mind once again to the book she had found, and to what Bethan would say if she were here. What would her sister make of the fact that she had never been abroad, simply because she was too scared, too anchored in Aldeburgh? She had thought that there were a hundred reasons not to go, but now she saw there was only really one – herself.

'I have,' she said, starting to smile. 'And I think . . . Oh, sod it. I'm in. Let's do it!'

Josephine clapped her hands together in delight. Pepper suspected that she would have jumped up and down on the spot if she were able.

'I am so glad to hear you say that,' she said, still looking slightly shamefaced. 'Because I am afraid there is a small chance I may have already booked the two of us a flight that leaves next week.'

7

The rain that greeted Pepper and Josephine as they emerged from central Lisbon's Santa Apolónia train station began so rapidly, and fell with such insistency, that for the first few minutes, all they could do was stand and stare – watching in open-mouthed awe as the droplets pummelled the surrounding trees and drenched the canvas umbrellas propped open outside a café on the opposite side of the street.

There was that smell, too – the warm, metallic tang that sun-bleached paving stones give off when they have been doused in water. Steam seemed to rise from the ground beneath Pepper's feet, as if the earth itself was sighing in contentment. She took it all in, her senses reeling and her mind whirling at the ludicrousness of her situation – of her being abroad for the first time, on a mission to retrace the steps of a love affair from the distant past. But while it might be bizarre, it was happening – she was here now, and she was determined to make the absolute most of every single moment.

She and Josephine waited until the downpour had slowed to a trickle before making their way to one of the waiting taxis, Pepper's wheelie case making a pleasant clackety-clacking sound as she pulled it across the cobbled street. They told the driver where they were staying, then relaxed back against the cracked leather seats as he started the engine.

Pepper had fired up her ancient computer a few days ago and spent an enjoyable evening scrolling through images of the city, but it was a very different experience actually being here. Houses of all colours, from primrose yellow to faded pink and cool mint green, sat shoulder-to-shoulder along curved narrow streets, each one leaning against the next like packed-in concertgoers at a sold-out gig. Pepper tilted her gaze upwards as they drove and saw toothy grins where there were balconies, and dark eyes where painted shutters had been pulled together behind tall, elegant windows.

They passed gift shops, wine bars, laundromats and tiny art galleries, all with their doors propped open in genial invitation. Chalkboard signs outside restaurants boasted of fresh fish caught that day, craft beers, and port sold by the glass. As well as the kaleidoscopic window displays, there was graffiti scrawled artfully across walls, and azulejos of all patterns and colours plastered up the facades of the buildings.

The rain had stripped the petals from a vibrant bougainvillea overhanging the entrance to their hotel, leaving them strewn like confetti amongst the cobbles. Bending over to pick one up, Pepper caught the sweet, unmistakable scent of just-baked bread drifting out from a patisserie and felt her stomach rumble with longing.

'It's every bit as beautiful as I remember,' murmured Josephine, whose entire demeanour seemed to be softening by the second.

'I love it,' Pepper agreed, smiling across at her friend. 'I can't believe I'm actually here.'

Josephine clutched her arm, giving it a quick squeeze.

'Darling, this is just the very beginning of our adventure.'

Half an hour later, having unpacked, showered and swapped her comfortable flight ensemble of leggings and oversized shirt for a lime-green playsuit covered in toucans, Pepper ventured back downstairs and found Josephine propped up at the hotel bar.

'Nice hat,' she appraised, taking in the UFO-sized adornment that her friend had balanced across her lap. She had changed, too, into a long flowing dress covered with flowers.

'Feel free to shelter underneath it if it rains again,' Josephine said, gesturing for Pepper to sit on the stool beside her. 'Do you want anything to drink?'

'No, thanks.' Pepper frowned at the glass of what looked suspiciously like gin and tonic in her friend's hand. 'Bit early for me.'

'It's sparkling water, darling,' Josephine lifted her drink so that Pepper could smell it. 'I'm not half as much of an old lush as you think I am.'

'I think you're very lush,' Pepper told her loyally.

She was remarkably serene, considering she was back in the place that meant so much to her, where so many memories were lurking around corners waiting to be rediscovered. Pepper was about to ask her how she was feeling, when Josephine disarmed her with one of her mischievous grins.

'The fizz has done the trick,' she announced. 'I feel fit as a Cossack dancer, about ready to skip through the streets.' Then, when Pepper gave her an incredulous look, 'Come along, then – toodle-pip!'

Outside, a late-afternoon sun had broken through and ushered away any remaining rainclouds. The higher they climbed through the twisty, shaded streets of the Alfama district, the better the view across the city became. Lisbon's famed terra-cotta rooftops glowed like embers against a periwinkle sky, the Rio Tejo sparkled sapphire blue below them, and tramlines slithered like silvery eels across the roads and up around corners.

Josephine seemed content to simply wander for the time being and reacquaint herself with the area, so she and Pepper followed what seemed to be the natural direction through the backstreets, eventually finding themselves at the edge of a wide, tiled viewing platform. There were tables and chairs arranged haphazardly around a small kiosk, but every single spot was occupied by a mixture of tourists and locals. Pepper could tell the latter from their deep tans and casual manner, while the pale-limbed British were all stiffness and sunburnt faces.

Around yet another corner, in the shadow of a vast white-stone church, they came across a quaint yet rather shabby court-yard. The flowerbeds were unkempt, and cracks crisscrossed the surrounding walls, but little could detract from the beauty of a large blue-and-white mural. Pepper ran her eye over every individual tile, absorbing each brush stroke with mounting pleasure. The city was steadily working its ambient magic on her – she already sensed that there was less noise inside her head, fewer drumbeats inside her heart.

There was a second courtyard below the one they were in now, and Pepper could see that it had a long shallow pool at its centre, as well as a tiled seating area overhung with yet more gaudy fronds of bougainvillea. As she followed Josephine down the steps, Pepper noticed a man walking up from the other direction. Tall and broad-shouldered, with a flop of golden hair hanging over his eyes, he was incongruous among all the small, dark Portuguese.

As they drew level with one another, Pepper sneaked a closer look, only to blush as she realised he was staring right back. As their eyes met, the man smiled at her with such warmth and familiarity, that for a moment, she was taken aback, wondering if she somehow knew him.

'Hallo.'

Pepper felt her cheeks heat up all in a rush.

'Er, hello.'

Grinning as she dropped her gaze, Pepper fixed her eyes firmly ahead and tried to resist the need to turn around. The urge to have another look at this handsome specimen was a strong one. Whoever this man was, he was easily one of the most attractive Pepper had ever seen. He might even be *the* most attractive.

She suppressed a ridiculous giggle and forced herself to keep walking, but the encounter had made her feel so skittish that she almost collided with Josephine at the bottom of the steps.

'What's the big hurry?' she asked, looking over Pepper's shoulder with intrigue.

'Nobody. I mean nothing.' Pepper cringed.

Josephine removed her sunglasses and squinted up the steps.

'Hello. Yes, you there,' she called. Then, to Pepper's horror, began to beckon with her hand.

What on earth was she playing at?

To the blond man's credit, he did look rather embarrassed to have been summoned, and the smile he offered Pepper looked a lot like one of defeat.

'Hi.' Pepper shifted from one sandalled foot to the other.

'Hello, again.' He didn't offer either of them a hand to shake, but when Josephine extended one of her own, he took it.

'Sorry,' he said then, sounding amused. 'How are you today?'

He had an accent, Pepper realised – Dutch perhaps, or maybe German.

'We are extremely well, thank you,' said Josephine, who was eyeing him in the same way Paddington Bear might a jar of marmalade. Pepper opened her mouth and shut it again. She couldn't seem to stop smiling, but the ability to speak had apparently abandoned her completely

The man beamed at her.

'I thought that—That we . . .' He looked helplessly at Pepper.

'Liked the look of each other?' suggested Josephine.

The man nodded, rubbing his hand across his jaw as he did so.

'Perhaps, yes.'

'How wonderful,' she exclaimed.

Pepper was torn between wanting to laugh and wishing the ground would open up and swallow her whole. She had gone past standard humiliation and into a realm of mortification previously unknown. Was it possible to simply stop living because you were so embarrassed? Pepper felt sure she would soon find out.

Josephine was now busy introducing them.

'And this is my very good friend, Philippa.'

'Pepper.' So, she could speak after all.

'Finn.'

Another smile. He was grinning wider than the Tiger Who Came to Tea – after he'd emptied all the kitchen cupboards.

Pepper searched in vain for some more words – for any words. She was aware of Josephine looking back and forth between the two of them as if she was watching a tennis match, her unbridled delight at the situation threatening to bubble over like microwaved porridge.

'We should . . .' Pepper began, feeling herself redden. 'I, er, we have to be somewhere.'

'Ah.' The man took a step backwards. 'Perhaps I can take your number?'

Pepper's face must have registered her surprise, because he immediately started to apologise.

'Sorry,' he said, folding and then unfolding his arms. 'You must think I am a madman. I promise, I don't do this. I have not done this before.' He motioned towards the steps.

Pepper wondered if this was a TV show, if any minute now, the old ladies she had seen selling cherry liqueur in open doorways would throw off their black shawls and reveal themselves to be the hosts of a hidden-camera series, designed to humiliate lonely, love-starved women.

'That's OK,' she managed. 'And I don't think you're mad – not yet anyway.'

Looking more hopeful now than before, Finn took his phone out of his pocket.

'Why don't I take your number instead?' she blurted, yanking out her own phone and holding it out triumphantly.

'OK,' he agreed, his smile slipping a fraction. 'How many days will you stay?'

'Oh, not long,' she garbled, talking across Josephine. 'Just a few.'

Finn took her phone from her and tapped in his number.

'You will send me a message?'

'Yes, sure. I mean, why not?'

The sun had slipped down between a gap in the buildings and was shining right into her eyes. Pepper blinked, wishing she had Josephine's hat to hide under.

'OK,' said Finn, sounding more cheerful. 'Maybe we can go for a coffee – or a beer?'

'Yes. Maybe.'

'Right.'

He looked as if he wanted to give in to laughter, as if this entire situation was pure comedy. 'I will go now,' he said. 'Nice to meet you both.'

'Oh, the pleasure was all ours,' called out Josephine, waving with unbridled enthusiasm as he strode away.

Finn made it only a few steps before he stopped and looked down at Pepper once again, his gaze sending a bolt of delicious electricity right through her insides. She had been in Lisbon for less than two hours, and already it felt as if her life had changed.

Was history about to repeat itself? Was she going to fall in love just as Josephine and Jorge had done all those years ago?

In that moment, Pepper had never wanted to believe in something more.

8

After the relative serenity of Aldeburgh, Pepper was surprised by how invigorating she found the bustle and noise of Lisbon.

Scores of people meandered lazily through the braided backstreets, many of them slipping off the edges of the slim pavements like lemmings, spilling onto the wide roads only to stumble back a few seconds later as a passing tram jangled past. Music filtered out from the open doors of restaurants and bars, the sound competing with the buskers who seemed to have set themselves up at every second corner.

They reached the outskirts of Alfama with relative ease, stopping every now and then at Pepper's insistence to allow Josephine to rest. The streets became wider as they crossed into the neighbouring district of Bairro Alto, with its kooky boutiques and steep labyrinthine pathways. The wasp-like buzz of moped engines filled the air, as tanned youths in shorts and flip-flops zoomed past them at speed, one carefree knee cocked out to the side in a gesture of insouciance.

There was evidence of the city's artistic heart at every turn, from the patterned tiles – or azulejos, as Josephine reminded her – on the buildings to the posters stapled onto boards and lampposts, advertising everything from outdoor concerts to exhibitions. Pepper was enchanted by all of it – even the graffiti – and stopped numerous times to take photos. There were barely any tags or political statements, such as those she was used to seeing scrawled across surfaces in England, but rather Banksy-style cat-and-mouse stencils, colourful rows of aliens and what looked to be a teddy bear riding a sardine. Much of the more impressive street art had been created from mosaic tiles, and Pepper gazed in appreciation at a peacock, an elephant and the image of a vase filled with bright blue hydrangeas.

The temperature that morning was comfortable, a mid-dial warm rather than sticky, and the faint breeze that danced along Pepper's arms felt like a caress. Despite taking out her phone every ten or so minutes – far more than she ever did at home – Pepper had yet to contact Finn. What had felt so exciting yesterday now just seemed silly. While Finn had undeniably got her attention, he was by no means the first man to catch Pepper's eye as she passed him. He was, however, the first who had ever come back.

Men *never* came back.

Josephine had been very keen to bring up the subject of Finn as they had breakfast.

'For what it's worth,' she had said, smearing butter across slices of dark, nutty rye bread, 'I don't think men like that come along very often.'

'Men like what?' Pepper asked, feigning ignorance.

'A gentleman,' Josephine stated, fixing her with one of the no-nonsense stares Pepper had come to know so well over the past year. 'One that is handsome, polite, clean, and has all his own teeth.'

Pepper had been forced to fight the rising tide of a grin. 'OK,' she allowed. 'I'll let you have the handsome – but how can you really know if he's polite all the time? He might curse his mother behind closed doors, for all we know. And he might have looked clean, on the outside, but what if he's been wearing the same pair of pants for a fortnight?'

'Not possible.' Josephine lifted her water glass. 'A man with fingernails that well-tended definitely looks after himself – mark my words.'

'Why on earth were you examining his nails?'

Josephine had given her a wry smile. 'I was checking for a wedding ring, darling.'

'Even if he is single,' Pepper allowed, taking a sip of coffee. 'And we have no way of really knowing. But even if that is the case, I still don't think I should message him. I'm here to keep you company and help you find Jorge. I'm hardly going to bugger off and leave you by yourself just so I can meet a strange man I'll probably never see again. Who, by the way, could be an axe murderer who doesn't wash his pants.'

She had torn a slice of bread into pieces as she talked, and Josephine eyed the crumbs with amusement.

'If you don't mind me saying,' she remarked, 'you seem rather . . . frustrated. In fact, might I be so bold as to suggest that a date with an attractive man might be exactly what you need.'

'Stop!' Pepper had given in to helpless laughter. 'Please! I'm begging you.'

Josephine had relented then, but not before telling Pepper that she must 'pay attention to what fate is telling you'.

Pepper, however, had already made up her mind that she was not going to message Finn. So many times, she had met a man and felt the same fizzing excitement, only to have her hopes dashed after the first few hours, when it became apparent that the two of them had little in common, or that she liked him far more than he liked her. Twice she had accidentally ended up on dates with married men whom she'd met on dating apps, and once she had gone for a coffee with a local farmer who seemed perfect, only for the two of them to be accosted mid-latte by his ex-girlfriend, who told him through sobs that she had made a big mistake and wanted him back. Pepper had left them kissing at the table, bewildered and frustrated at having made yet another bad choice. Against all that, the allure of love – real love – was a strong one. Pepper still wanted to find it and remained convinced that she would, but she needed more of a sign than merely bumping into someone.

'If the universe really wants me to see Finn again,' she told Josephine, 'then I'm sure it will find a way of bringing him back to me. For now, though, this trip is all about you – deal?'

'Spoilsport,' Josephine had declared, but she tapped her coffee cup against Pepper's, nonetheless.

'Was Lisbon this busy when you were last here?' Pepper asked Josephine now, as the two of them waited for a packed tram to clatter past.

'Oh gosh, no. People were still using donkeys to transport themselves and their goods back then, and there were far less cars on the roads, far fewer people milling about. But the essence is the same,' she added. 'All these colours, and all the decoration, those have remained. I did worry that some godawful town planner might have come along and stripped away all the azulejos, but thankfully that doesn't appear to be the case. It would be utterly devastating if it was ever allowed to happen. Have you ever been over to Cambridge and seen what a disaster they have made of the city centre?'

Pepper had not.

'Bloody criminals.' Josephine sniffed in disgust. 'I'd like to put whoever signed it off over my lap for a good spanking.'

'Ooer, missus,' Pepper murmured, and saw the glint return to her friend's eye.

'So,' she said, taking Josephine's elbow as they hurried across the road. 'Do you think Jorge could still be here? Do you think you would recognise him if you did see him?'

'Of course.'

Pepper could hear the conviction in Josephine's voice, and felt something give inside her chest. It reminded her of the film *Titanic*, when you know that Jack has been claimed by the sea, but you still hope that, somehow, he will come back at the end, see Rose as an old lady and recognise her immediately.

'It wouldn't be his features I would know, so much as the feeling I would get when I saw him,' Josephine said. 'The body remembers even that which the mind cannot, and the heart is the most powerful, most vital, part of us.'

Despite the heat of the day, Pepper got goosebumps.

'I hope we find him,' she said. 'It feels like that's what should happen.'

'Well then,' Josephine took a breath in and dabbed at her eyes. 'Shall I take you somewhere that he took me?'

'I thought you'd never ask.'

Leaving the busy Bairro Alto and Baixa districts behind, they continued downhill until they reached Ribeira das Naus – a wide riverside promenade dotted with benches, kiosks, and tall, arching trees. As Josephine found them a place to sit down, Pepper fetched them both a coffee in the reusable cups she had brought along in her bag.

'Thank you, darling.' Josephine grasped hers with both hands. 'Did they add cream?'

'Warm cream.'

'Golly, how decadent.'

They sat for a while in companionable silence, watching as a shrill contingent of little birds squabbled over a discarded paper bag. The weather had turned hazy, a white sky brightened by the promise of sun and putty-coloured clouds sitting in a fat swell above the water.

'Jorge and I used to come down here all the time,' Josephine said, turning until she was staring up towards a vast, distant statue of Christ the Redeemer.

'Cristo Rei, the Portuguese call him,' she said, as Pepper followed her gaze. 'When I first came here, he was a relatively new fixture. He lends a certain something to the landscape, don't you think?'

Pepper put her head on one side.

'I think I'd prefer him if he was more colourful.'

Josephine gave Pepper's pink denim shorts, zebra-print vest and battered tartan Converse the once-over.

'In a city like Lisbon, it is those that are absent of colour who stand out the most,' she said. 'If Christ was dressed in a Technicolor Dreamcoat, how would he hope to compete with all the azulejos?'

'You said before that Jorge was an artist,' Pepper prompted, and Josephine's expression softened.

'Yes – at least, he wanted to be. He was also fanatical about cooking, would you believe? I guess you have to be an artist to create beautiful plates of food, just as you would a painting. All

I know is that colour and vitality seemed to stream out of him – that is what it felt like to me. But then I was young and infatuated, not to mention a little bit bananas,' she added, tapping the side of her head.

'Is there anywhere else you want to go today?' Pepper asked. 'Any other places that you and Jorge went together?'

'Do you know, I think I may have overdone it on the gins last night.'

As she said it, Pepper noticed a tremble in her hands. Josephine was gripping the reusable cup so tightly that her knuckles were white.

'Shall we go back to the hotel?' she asked. 'So you can take a nap?'

Josephine visibly relaxed. 'That might be for the best. You can keep yourself occupied for a few hours, can't you, darling?'

9

Pepper knew immediately where she wanted to go.

As much as she had enjoyed ambling around the central hub of the city, it was the older district of Alfama, with its crumbling cathedrals, cracked tiles and cosy art galleries, that had won her heart.

She settled on Castelo de São Jorge as the landmark to aim for, thinking that she would meander through the streets and reach the city's sprawling fortress in time to watch the sunset. The Castelo had the added allure of being situated in the area where Josephine and Jorge had met for the first time. Josephine had told Pepper the story in the taxi ride back along the water-front, and while she wasn't able to recall the name of the road, or which buildings were nearby, she did remember that she had been sitting on a bench in the middle of a small square, staring up into the branches of an orange tree.

'All I could think,' she told Pepper, 'was how much I wanted to taste one. I had never seen oranges growing on a tree before then, but I didn't know if it was bad form to pick one. So, when this gorgeous young chap appeared and sat down beside me to roll his cigarette, I asked him outright, just like that. Instead of answering me, Jorge jumped up onto the bench and plucked one for me to try.'

'That is so romantic.' Pepper sighed.

'He peeled it for me, too,' Josephine went on. 'I watched his thumb go through the rind, saw the juice run down over his fingers, and somehow, I knew, right from that moment. I understood that there was something special about him – about me when I was with him.'

Pepper was now determined to locate this square with its tree of unforbidden fruit. It would mean so much to Josephine to see it again – and it was where her love story had begun.

She already felt as if she blended in quite well here in Lisbon. Nobody gave her more than a cursory glance as she pounded along the pavements, her calves burning as much due to the gradient of the hills as the sun, which had made good on its earlier promise and was now sitting high in a cloud-strewn sky.

Pausing to catch her breath and admire a batch of gold, green and purple azulejos, Pepper noticed a stream of people disappearing down a nearby alleyway. They looked purposeful enough to pique her curiosity, so she followed, and found to her delight that the pathway led to a huge sprawling flea market. Back home in Suffolk, she often got up with the dawn to get first dibs at car boot sales, which were invariably a treasure trove for any artist. Pepper could use pretty much anything as a basis to create something new: second-hand books, old clothes, mismatched pottery and crockery that could be broken and used for mosaics, discarded children's toys, CDs, costume jewellery and more. She was a firm believer in the 'one man's trash' mantra, and turning other people's unwanted items into new and beautiful treasures made her feel more content, somehow.

Despite this, however, Pepper stalled. She was supposed to be searching for a square with an orange tree. But then again, what harm could a quick half-hour browse do? She might find something truly remarkable amongst all these knick-knacks – something she could give Josephine as a gift or keep as a memento of the time she had spent here.

Most of the stalls consisted simply of sheets laid across the ground, the seller's goods spread out across them like sugar sprinkles atop a cake. Pepper crouched down to inspect a collection of trinkets, picking up each item to examine it in more detail. There was a pocket-sized china swan with a chipped beak, some blue metal jewellery pliers, a neat leather sack fastened with a velvet ribbon, a whole range of copper taps and pieces of piping and at least seven ornaments of the Virgin Mary, all in various states of disrepair.

'All one euro,' a woman with Brillo-pad hair who was manning a tin of coins informed her. 'Very good price.'

'*Obrigada*,' Pepper said shyly, putting her hands on her knees and hoisting herself up. At a rough guess, she estimated that there must be close to a hundred more sheets on the ground, and perhaps fifty or so proper wooden stalls, each one piled high with items for sale. Determined to stick within her self-imposed thirty-minute window, Pepper decided not to bother looking at the paintings, large antiques and furniture – if she fell in love with something, she wouldn't be able to get it home anyway – and focused instead on a stretch that seemed to be mostly jewellery, glassware and other small oddities. After ten minutes of picking through boxes, untangling nests of necklaces and turning teacups over to check the bottom for date and place stamps, she had amounted quite a haul for under ten euros.

Stopping at the end of one row to replenish herself with some water, Pepper's eye was drawn to a narrow table covered with a cheerful red cloth. The girl standing behind it could not be more than fourteen and was pleating the front of her dress with nervous fingers. As she edged closer, Pepper noticed the paint stains on the girl's hands, and smiled in recognition of a kindred spirit.

'*Olá*,' she said, and the girl glanced up timidly, quickly returning Pepper's greeting in English.

'Did you make these?' Pepper asked, gesturing down at the colourful array of ceramic key holders, vases, plant pots, pet food bowls, soap dishes and a range of model dogs. Everything had been painted beautifully, and with the kind of unselfconscious finesse that Pepper wished she was able to teach her clients.

'Yes.' The girl glanced down at her hands, her face flushed.

Pepper extracted a key holder with two cats painted on it.

'How much?'

The girl smiled.

'Five euros.'

'In that case . . .' Pepper opened her purse. 'I'll get this and one of your dogs, too, please.'

She had just stowed her new treasures – each one cocooned carefully in bubble wrap – in her rucksack, when the air turned abruptly cold with the threat of rain. There was a unified kerfuffle as customers and stall owners took evasive action to avoid a soaking, and Pepper almost tumbled over onto the cobbles as an elderly couple barrelled into her sideways.

Just as it had when she and Josephine arrived the previous day, the deluge fell like a waterfall – heavy and powerful and with a total disregard for anyone who might be yet to find cover.

By the time Pepper had dodged, slipped and slid her way along a narrow street and found a tree under which to shelter, she was drenched, her hair plastered against her cheeks and her pink bra clearly visible through the thin material of her top. One of her laces had come undone and was trailing along the ground, so she propped up her foot on the arm of an adjacent bench and bent to tie them. Her back was turned to the road, so she was only vaguely aware of someone running towards her, seeing only a flash of blond and a wide grin before she had time to register who it was.

Finn skidded to a stop beside her. He was wet through, just like her, his navy shorts sodden and his white T-shirt even more translucent than her zebra-print vest. Clocking Pepper as he pushed his dripping fringe out of his eyes, Finn started to laugh.

'It is you,' he said, beaming at her. 'Hello, again.'

'Hi.'

Pepper's heart was trying to smash its way out through the front of her chest.

'You're soaked.'

Finn appraised her. 'You are the same,' he said, and after twisting the bottom of his T-shirt with both hands in order to wring it out, he added, 'Shit, man – this rain is crazy.'

'I like it!' Pepper had to raise her voice to be heard over the deluge, laughing at the look he gave her. 'Summer rain. I always have. I think it's the smell.'

'The smell?' Finn wrinkled his nose.

They would need to build an ark from the branches of this tree soon, she thought, glancing up and noticing the oranges for the first time. Water was hurtling down the tram tracks and washing away scattered petals. From somewhere high above them, Pepper heard the sound of window shutters being slammed and shivered.

'You are cold,' Finn stated. 'I don't have anything to give you.' He lifted both his arms, and for a thrilling moment, Pepper thought he was going to offer her a hug.

'I'm fine,' she told him, inwardly cursing the polite British reflex that always made her default to immediate reassurance. 'I mean, obviously I'd be happier if I didn't look like one of those sea birds that's been caught up in an oil spill, but, you know . . .'

Finn frowned at this, but only with the top half of his face – the lower portion was still smiling at her, and Pepper found that she had no choice but to grin back. It was as if someone had tied a helium balloon to each corner of her mouth.

Finn took his phone out from the back pocket of his shorts, wiped the screen dry with the flat of his hand, then lifted it up to show her.

'No message.'

'I was just about to send one,' she spluttered, registering heat in her cheeks and wondering if she had gone full plum, or merely radish. 'I was busy,' she added, turning so he could see her bulging rucksack. 'Shopping.'

'At the market?' he guessed, and she nodded, swallowing as she took in the muscular shape of him beneath the wet material of his T-shirt. Thank God for the rain – the longer it fell, the longer she and Finn would be trapped here together.

'Will you show me?' he asked, nodding at her bag. 'I want to see what I missed.'

Pepper extracted her spoils one by one, explaining that no, she wasn't a weird collector of old mismatched cutlery and broken jewellery, but that she was planning to put everything to good use. Finn smiled politely as she handed him one item after another, only becoming more animated when she unwrapped the ceramic key holder.

'Nice,' he said, holding it up so he could examine it in more detail. 'I like this very much.'

Pepper told him about the girl and Finn listened, his fingers testing the join of the hooks and the quality of the edging. Josephine was right – he really did have impeccable nails.

'Can I buy it from you?' he asked, and Pepper was so surprised that she laughed.

'Um, OK, I suppose so – but wouldn't it make more sense to buy a different one? That way the girl would get the money, rather than me.'

'That is true,' he said. 'Or, you could just give it to me.'

'You want me to give you *my* new key holder? The key holder that *I* found, from in amongst all those stalls – my pearl in a pile of old oyster shells. You want me to just hand it over?'

Finn folded his arms, his T-shirt becoming even tighter as the damp material was pulled downwards.

'It will make up for not sending me a message – and for pretending that you were going to.'

'I was!' she insisted.

Finn was shaking his head and tutting now, his mouth still open in a smile. His features were so alive – there was so much expression in his face, and playfulness in his eyes.

'I have changed my mind – you can keep it,' he said, his head cocked at a slight angle. 'In exchange for a drink.'

'You're incorrigible.' Pepper zipped up her bag.

Finn shone his headlight-beam smile.

'I know where we can go, there is a good place not very far from here.'

Pepper peered out at the continuing downpour.

'You mean right now?'

'Yes, now.'

'We'll get drenched – even more drenched!'

'OK, so we get wet. So what?'

He was even worse than Josephine when it came to accepting no for an answer.

'Come on.' Finn held out his hand. 'I know a shortcut.'

There was a beat or two where Pepper considered refusing, telling him thanks, but no thanks – that she had to be somewhere and it couldn't wait. But then another feeling stole through her, one that she had been doing her best to bury ever since she first saw him.

Hope.

IO

When it came to relationships, Pepper had always struggled.

It wasn't that the boys – and later men – she dated were all bad people, more that the elusive connection she so longed to find never seemed to materialise. Once those heady first few weeks were over, her feelings started to slowly but surely drain away. And it wasn't always the partners she chose that let her down, so much as herself. The little niggles that she tried so hard to suppress always squirmed through and demanded to be heard. Sure, they would say, this man is nice and everything, but are there fireworks going off in your heart? Do you long for him every moment of every day? Do you feel like the heroine in a romantic film?

The answer was always no.

She had laid out a challenge to the universe yesterday after bumping into Finn, telling both Josephine and herself that this time, she was not prepared to give chase. This time she wanted a concrete assurance that fate was pulling the strings, and that the stars were finally ready to align in her favour.

The universe, it seemed, had been listening.

She and Finn sought refuge from the rain in a tiny café, where they ordered a large pot of fresh mint tea to share and sat facing each other on low stools. Finn's bare knee kept brushing against Pepper's whenever he shifted position, and every time, she felt currents of tantalising warmth trickle through her body. Their conversation was mostly polite at first, but because they could not stop smiling at each other, every other reply was punctuated by tinkling laughter. Finn was open yet interested – and unlike many of the men Pepper had met, he really listened when she spoke.

'Tell me about your family,' he said now, lifting a hand to push his still-drying fringe off his forehead. Pepper admired his symmetrical features – a wide expressive mouth, large but pleasingly shaped nose and deep-set smiling eyes – and wondered where to begin.

'There isn't all that much to tell,' she said. 'There's just me and my parents. Dad left when I was a teenager and has had a series of younger women in his life ever since, and my mum . . .' She paused, debating how much to tell him.

'She has remarried?' Finn asked.

'No.' Pepper cast her mind back over the few men her mother had dated since her divorce. All of them had been nice enough, none had lasted beyond a few months. 'Not yet, anyway.'

'So, you are an only child like me?'

'Yes.' Pepper coughed to mask the croak in her voice. 'But I didn't used to be. I had a younger sister. She died a long time ago.'

'Ah.' Finn looked momentarily downcast. 'Sorry.'

'What about you?' she replied, keen to divert attention away from the subject of Bethan.

'I am an Army brat,' he told her. 'My father was a captain in the Royal Engineers – he is English – while my mama is German. I was born in Hamburg, but I spent some time in England as a boy. We moved around the place quite often.'

'That must have been hard?' she guessed, but Finn seemed nonplussed.

'Not especially. I think, when you are a child, you are more adaptable to change. I travel a lot still – I like to discover new places, see new things.'

'Is that why you're here in Lisbon?' Pepper fished a mint leaf out of her cup and laid it carefully on the saucer. 'Just a holiday?'

'Partly.' Finn gave her a half-smile. 'But also, to do some work.'

'What do you do?'

'What do you think that I do?'

Pepper sat back on her stool, her hands raised.

'I have no idea!' she exclaimed. 'I barely know you after all.'

'You know me enough to make a guess,' Finn said. 'I will give you three questions, then you must make your guess.'

'Same deal for you?' she checked, and he nodded.

'*Ja* – why not?'

Pepper thought for a moment, allowing herself the luxury of looking him up and down, examining his hands, his clothes, and his expression for clues. Then she remembered how much he had liked the ceramic key holder she'd bought from the flea market.

'Would you describe your job as creative?' she asked, waiting while he mulled this over.

'*Ja* – at least a little bit. But I am no artist. I appreciate art, and when I was younger, I tried to become good at it. But some people are not born with the right talent.'

'Talent can be taught.'

Finn looked across at her, his beam now back to full capacity.

'I know a lot of artists who would disagree with you,' he said.

'Are you a gallery owner?'

'*Nein.*'

'Gah! As if I just wasted a whole question with that guess.'

'One question remaining,' he prompted.

Pepper wracked her brain, searching in vain for something to ask. Finn was far too clean and well-groomed to work with animals or machinery. He didn't give off a teacherly vibe, or a particularly outdoorsy one either. Despite his upbringing, there wasn't so much as a whiff of the military about him, and she doubted very much that he did anything as beige as real-estate agenting or insurance brokering.

'My turn,' he said then, taking his time to scrutinise Pepper as she had him.

'You are a designer,' he decided. 'Perhaps you make prints and patterns for clothes, or logos for big businesses.'

He wasn't exactly wrong, but he hadn't guessed quite right either. Pepper drank some tea.

'Sort of,' she told him. 'But also, no – and no.'

Finn squinted in mock exasperation.

'My final question is this,' she said. 'Do you love your job?'

Finn smiled easily.

'*Ja!* Of course. I would not do it if I hated it.'

'Many people do,' she pointed out.

'Then I feel sorry for them. Life is too precious a thing to waste being sad, or bored.'

Pepper could not help but think about all the weeks and months she had spent feeling nothing but the former, driven half-mad with grief.

'I think you work in advertising,' she said. 'That would make sense – it's a bit creative, could easily involve travel, would account for the lovely neat nails.'

'These nails?' Finn examined his fingertips and laughed. 'I just have a good set of clippers.'

'Artists notice these kinds of things,' she protested, then slapped a hand over her mouth as she realised she'd given the game away. Finn bellowed with even more laughter, then reached across and put a hand on her shoulder.

'Don't worry,' he said. 'I had a pretty good idea that you were an artist the first second I saw you.'

'But I'm not!' Pepper was very aware of the heat rushing into her cheeks. 'I teach art, but I'm nothing special, really – nothing.'

Finn still had his hand on her shoulder, but as Pepper continued to blabber, he removed it, letting it hover in the air beside her face for a moment.

'You are not nothing,' he said, returning his hand to the handle of his cup.

'I think you are really, you know . . . something.'

II

They finished the mint tea just as the sun came back out, the bright shafts that poured in through the front windows of the café enticing them back out onto the curved cobbled street.

Lisbon was drenched, but rather than appearing dreary, it seemed to sparkle even more than before. The rain had washed away the dust coating the azulejos, and Pepper sighed with contentment as she took in yellows intertwining with blues, curls of red and fronds of green, purple and pale pink. The uniformity of the patterns pleased her; she liked the way every line matched up, and the way the tiles had been laid, so neatly, each beside the next.

'Shall we walk?' Finn asked.

'Up to the Castelo?'

'Good idea.' He turned towards her. 'How long do you have?'

Pepper pulled her phone out to check the time and saw she had missed a call from her mother, but nothing, as yet, from Josephine, who she presumed was still resting back at the hotel. It would be so easy to spend the rest of the day with Finn – *or the rest of my life, for that matter*, Pepper could not help but add internally – but she mustn't forget her real reason for being here.

'I have an hour or so,' she told him.

He didn't reach for her hand again, as he had when they ran together from under the orange tree, and Pepper tried not to feel too disappointed when he slipped his own into the pockets of his shorts.

'I am afraid you were wrong, by the way,' he said as they set off. 'I do not work for an advertising firm. I part-own a restaurant and wine bar back home in Hamburg. My friend Clara, she is the chef, and Otto, he runs the bar. I do all the other stuff.'

'Other stuff?' she echoed, emitting a small yelp of surprise as a drip fell from some sodden washing hanging high above them and landed right on her nose.

'Marketing, events, social media, finance,' Finn said, before adding, as Pepper wiped at her face, 'Better than a bird poo.'

'People always say that it's supposed to be lucky,' she said. 'But how can it be? It is literally being shat on by a bird – and it happens all the time to me back in Suffolk. I live by the beach,' she explained, telling him a bit about Aldeburgh as they clambered up a steep flight of rough-cut steps. The houses on each side slotted in against the stonework like pieces of a Tetris game, some painted in the softest peach, others a blend of raspberries and cream. The higher they climbed, the broader the streets became, and the more of the city's dark-orange rooftops came into view. Everywhere Pepper looked, she noticed another detail – a half-moon window winking like the closed lid of an eye, pots overflowing with plump trailing leaves, stained wooden shutters, sprigs of wildflowers and polished brass doorknobs, as well as tall, weary-looking palm trees and decorative wrought-iron balconies.

There was so much to see that Pepper could easily have found herself overwhelmed, but rather than fret about taking photos or committing every last inch to memory, she simply let the whole tableau settle over her, concentrating on how pleasant it felt to be amongst all this beauty, and relative stillness. She and Finn had somehow managed to find a route that drew them away from other travellers and locals alike, and it was nice to have their own small corner of the city.

'So, you said you travel as part of your job,' Pepper said, pausing to catch her breath as they finally reached the top of the steps. 'I'm curious – how does that work exactly?'

'Ah.' Finn fiddled with his fringe. 'The travel is linked to my other job – my secret occupation.'

'Don't tell me – you're a spy!'

Finn pointed a finger at his chin.

'With this awful poker face? No chance!'

'Nothing awful about your face,' Pepper blurted. 'I mean, speaking as an amateur artist, you have great bone structure.'

Finn beamed.

'*Danke.*'

'Is your secret job to do with art?'

'*Ja!* Good guess.'

Pepper felt her smile widening as he talked her through his business plan – a website to rival Etsy, showcasing all the best purveyors of art in the world, but with a new twist. This work, he explained solemnly, would all be handpicked by him. A bespoke collection that he himself had seen, touched and – perhaps in some cases – even helped create. He wanted to source pieces that moved him and give a platform to artists who may not have the means to reach as big an audience as their work deserved.

'There are so many talented people all over the world,' he said. 'I want to find as many of them as I can.'

'I think that's amazing,' Pepper told him, only just stopping herself from adding, '*And I think you're amazing, too.*'

'I wish my papa agreed with you – he believes that the art world is full of "sissies and work-shirkers".'

'It is not!' Pepper was affronted. They had reached the final stretch of road leading up towards the Castelo now, and were surrounded on all sides by groups of tourists. Where before there had been quiet and calm, now there was noise and chatter, but the melee did not seem to bother Finn. His attention was solely on her, and Pepper wished her hair hadn't dried quite so crinkly. When she had escaped to the bathroom in the café, she had actually sworn at her reflection in the mirror above the sink. Mascara had been smeared under each of her eyes, her ponytail was a frizzy disaster, and her waterlogged Converse squelched with every step.

'When my website makes me a millionaire,' Finn went on, 'he will be forced to apologise to me. But for now, it must remain a secret. If Mama and Papa ask me why I am travelling so much, I tell them it is to source wine. The restaurant and bar are doing very well, so they are happy. When Papa sees a queue of people waiting to eat or drink, it helps him to feel as if his son is a big deal.'

'And if it was an art gallery?' Pepper asked, and Finn lifted his shoulders in a gesture of defeat.

'Then, I think, less proud.'

Pepper thought of her own parents, of her father's donation to help her start up Arts For All and her mother's muted yet genuine pride when she heard it was doing well, and her heart went out to him.

'I know it is his problem,' Finn went on, 'but knowing that does not help me care less about his opinion. I don't know why I still let it bother me so much.'

He sighed, then looked at her questioningly.

'Why is it, do you think, that we must forever try to please our parents?'

Pepper came to a stop outside a gift shop packed to the rafters with colourful ceramic plates, bowls, dishes and ashtrays, blinking as she looked up at him.

'I guess, because at the point where you pass from childhood into adulthood, you feel responsible for them? Or maybe it's simply an ego thing – the better you do, the more they praise you. And nobody's praise means more than a parent's – at least for most people.'

Finn looked at her with new respect.

'I think you are right,' he said. 'And if I was holding a drink right now, I would toast to that – to our big egos.'

She laughed. 'OK . . . Anything else?'

Finn considered.

'*Ja.* To Lisbon, and to art, and to rain!' He glanced up at the sky as he said it, and his hair fell away from his eyes.

'And to Josephine, too?' suggested Pepper. 'I would not be here at all if it wasn't for her.'

'Is she your grandmother?'

'God, no! Although, she's much nicer than either of mine were.'

Finn looked sympathetic, but before he had a chance to reply, Pepper barrelled on.

'Josephine is just a friend. She came to Lisbon in the sixties and wanted to see it again, and kindly invited me along as her companion.'

She stopped short of explaining about Jorge. That was Josephine's story to tell.

'She seems like fun,' Finn said. 'The same as you.'

'Oh, I don't know about that,' Pepper muttered, ready to brush the compliment away. Finn quickly silenced her by folding his arms across his chest.

'Are you having fun with me?' he asked.

Pepper smiled.

'Yes.'

'Well, then – you see. It would not be fun if you were not fun.'

'Are you always so . . .' Pepper searched for the word.

'Direct?'

She nodded.

'*Ja*, I guess so. It is the German in me. We always say what we mean. Mama is the same.'

'Us Brits are all mumbling apologies, self-deprecation and pretence,' she joked, and Finn chuckled.

'Not my papa. Maybe he is an alien?'

'I fear he and my mother might have that in common,' Pepper added, feeling slightly guilty, and Finn laughed even harder.

'I think,' he said then, taking a step towards her, 'that we have a great many things in common. It is good that we met – and then met again.'

Pepper wanted to agree, but all she managed was a gargling sort of cough. Finn was standing so close to her now that she could see the sprinkle of stubble across his jaw, and the dark smudges under his eyes. Where had he come from, this miraculous man, this person with whom she felt so alive, yet so at peace? She kept waiting for the uncertainty to tap her on the shoulder, for the practical side of her subconscious to point out all the reasons why this thing between her and Finn, whatever it was, could not last – but nothing came. Not so much as a murmur. The more time she spent with him, the more she got the feeling that something inside her was mending.

Something she hadn't even realised was broken.

12

'Do you prefer sunrise or sunset?' Finn asked, as he and Pepper stood side by side, each staring out across the city. The Castelo grounds were rough and dusty underfoot, and the gardens surrounding them were dotted with gnarly trees.

Pepper had heard the bells ringing in Lisbon's many churches and knew her time with Finn was almost up, yet she could not seem to drag herself away – not from him, or from the view spread out below them. A sun as dark and slick as honey had trailed down behind the rooftops, leaving behind a sky shot through with fiery reds and smouldering yellows. The dying embers of a day that Pepper knew she would never forget, no matter what happened.

'Sometimes I go down to the beach at home to watch the sunrise,' she told Finn. 'Usually, I hate being all by myself, but it's different at dawn. It feels like I'm the only person in the world privileged enough to see it, as if Mother Nature is show-ing me her hand under the table. And the more beautiful the dawn,' she added, turning from the view to look at him, 'the more beautiful I feel the day must become.'

Finn nodded.

'I know what you mean,' he said. 'But I have always preferred the sunset – it is so much more dramatic. And if you are a night owl, like me,' he went on, 'a sunset signals the start of the fun.'

'Are you trying to tell me that you're a party boy?' she asked, but Finn chuckled.

'Maybe once upon a time,' he said. 'But not any more. Now, I am too old.'

'How old is too old? No, don't make me guess!' she added, seeing him about to retort. 'That never ends well. I went on a date last year and the guy guessed that I was forty-four.'

'No!' Finn laughed out loud.

'Yes,' she promised. 'The very next day, I started using face cream.'

'I like faces with lines,' he said then, and Pepper screwed up her own on purpose.

'I do not mean yours!' he protested, jabbing her arm gently with a finger. 'I mean, in general. Lines equal life lived, stories to tell, wisdom to be shared.'

'That's why I don't have any, then,' she quipped, although it was not strictly true.

Finn shifted until he was facing her and began to examine her through his fringe.

'For example,' he began, raising a hand. 'Can I?' he asked, pausing a few inches from her cheek.

'Yes.'

Pepper's voice sounded hollow.

'This line,' he said, lightly running his finger along the top of her cheekbone, 'tells me that you smile a lot, that you are a happy person. While this one,' he continued, stroking her forehead, 'shows me that you use your eyes to work, that you are often concentrating.'

If he carried on touching her like this, Pepper thought, it wouldn't just be the sun that was sliding down towards the ground.

'But these,' Finn said, his fingers coming to a stop on the fleshy part between her eyebrows, 'prove to me that you worry sometimes, that you care about people, feel concern.'

'What, my frown lines?' Pepper asked, trying to make a joke out of the situation. 'They're so deep you could hide soldiers in them.'

Finn smiled, but she could tell he was only humouring her.

'Look at mine,' he said, squinting hard so that two trenches appeared in the same place as hers. 'Too much sun,' he muttered. 'And probably too much wine. My friend Otto drinks far too much. He is only thirty-six, but he has the skin of a fifty-year-old.'

'Thirty-six is a good age,' she replied, and Finn smiled properly this time.

Removing his hand from her face, he said, 'Thirty-eight is not so bad either.'

'When I was still a teenager, thirty felt impossibly old,' she told him, digging through the dusty earth with her foot. 'I thought that my whole life would be sorted by then, but I am so far away from where I imagined I would be, aren't you?'

Finn considered this.

'No,' he said simply. 'I am exactly where I want to be, doing what I want. And I am happy.'

'Do you mean in general?' Pepper asked, then could not help but add, 'Or right now?'

'Right now,' he repeated, drawing out each word until he could tell she was hanging on them, 'I am very happy indeed.'

'Really?' Pepper whispered, holding her breath as Finn moved closer.

'*Ja,*' he said.

She allowed her eyes to travel downwards until she was staring at his lips. It felt like such a first kiss moment, up here overlooking the city, the fading light of the day colouring the sky. She was so sure it was going to happen that she closed her eyes, only to open them a second later as she heard Finn clear his throat. He had stepped away and was resting his elbows on the Castelo's outer wall, his gaze drawn by the thousand twinkling lights that signalled a city's transition from day to night.

'I should go.' Pepper sounded as dismal as she felt. 'I've been way longer than an hour.'

'OK.'

Finn seemed neither happy to see her go, nor sad that she was leaving. Pepper hesitated for a moment, stepping from one still-soggy Converse to the next.

'I guess this is goodbye, then?' she said. But as she turned to leave, her cheeks burning, Finn reached across and looped his arm through hers.

'Don't run away,' he said, sounding puzzled. 'I will walk with you.'

Pepper let herself be led along, wondering how she could have read the situation so wrong. Linking arms was not something you did with a person you fancied; it was something she did with Josephine. And why had he done all that face stroking if he wasn't planning on kissing her afterwards? She was caught between embarrassment at having made it so obvious she liked him and disappointment that he clearly did not feel the same way. Here she was again, reading signals worse than a blind train driver, believing that butterflies in the belly meant love, when what they were really doing was beating out a percussion to accompany the words: he's just not that into you.

Finn said very little as they wandered back down through the Alfama streets, but he seemed content, and every time she braved a look in his direction, she found him smiling down at her. He must be relieved to be on the verge of escape, she surmised grumpily, then shrieked as Finn pulled her suddenly and forcefully backwards. She had been so lost in thought that she hadn't even noticed the tram hurtling around the corner.

'That was close,' Finn said. 'Too close. You might have ended up flat, like a crepe.'

It was such a ludicrous image that Pepper could not help but laugh.

'I'd rather be a pancake,' she said. 'You know, being British and everything.'

'Both are sweet,' Finn agreed. 'Like you.'

Was he mocking her now, or did he mean it?

Pepper unlooped her arm from around his.

'My hotel is just at the bottom of those steps,' she said, pointing across the road. 'You don't have to walk me all the way down there – I'll be fine.'

'OK,' he said, with the same reluctant acceptance as before. 'OK.'

Pepper paused, took a step back, then forwards again towards him.

'OK,' he said again, this time with a grin.

'OK,' she repeated.

Finn extended a hand, his fingers brushing the tips of hers as she began to finally walk away. She got to the top of the steps before she turned once more to look at him, then laughed as he started waving exuberantly with both hands.

'Send me your number and I will message you!' he shouted, his voice carrying over the sounds of traffic and travellers, of music and voices.

Very quickly, before the nagging voice of self-doubt could pipe up again to talk her out of it, Pepper brought her hand to her mouth and blew him a kiss.

13

The number twenty-eight tram set off with a rattle and a jangle.

'Jorge and I used to ride this route every day,' Josephine said, grasping Pepper's hand in her own. 'Back in those days, the tourists hadn't cottoned on yet, so it was mainly the local folk that used it. Very lazy of us, given how young and spritely we both were at the time, but we never could resist.'

'I can see why,' Pepper replied, waving back at a group of schoolchildren through the tram's open window. 'I feel as if we've travelled back in time.'

'Now you see why we had to get a taxi to Praça Martim Moniz this morning,' Josephine added. 'The only way to get a window seat on the left side is to get on board right at the beginning of the journey. Jorge taught me that. Quite often, however, the two of us would simply leap up and hold onto the bars at the back, rather like we were surfing the thing.'

'You daredevils!' Pepper said in delight. 'I can one hundred per cent picture you doing that – probably even now.'

'You are far too generous to me, darling.' Josephine chuckled. 'If I jumped up onto anything these days, it would likely be the last agile thing I ever did.'

There was a loud screech as the tram brakes were applied, and a chorus of 'oohs' and 'ahhs' from everyone riding inside as they began to descend an almost-vertical road. Pepper fell into the same contented silence as Josephine, enjoying the feel of the sun-warmed air as it streamed in through the open windows. The city was bathed in a sleepy, butter-coloured light this morning, the sun yet to reach full mast. As they trundled and clanked into the Alfama district, the views became increasingly mesmeric, and Pepper gazed out as a kaleido-scope of pastel houses, smooth cobbles, dazzling azulejos and abundant plant life flashed past.

'Do you see?' Josephine whispered. 'Do you see why I fell in love here?'

Pepper could only nod, her mind straying predictably to Finn. Thinking about him made her feel as if she were standing right on the edge of a precipice, but rather than being struck by the fear of falling off, she felt free, as if she could fly, just as she had in her dream last night. Right out into the open, dipping and soaring and leaving the rest of the world far behind.

Glancing from the view to her friend in the seat beside her, Pepper was surprised to find tears trailing down the older woman's cheeks.

'Oh no, what's the matter?'

'Don't mind me; just being a silly, sentimental old bat.'

'You are neither silly nor an old bat,' Pepper scolded gently. 'And there's nothing wrong with feeling sentimental.'

'Being back in this city, and travelling once more through all these memories, it makes me feel young again – in here.' Josephine tapped a hand against her chest. 'But all that does is remind me in the same breath of how decrepit I am – and how much of my life has vanished in what feels like the merest whisper.'

'But you've had such a full life,' Pepper argued. 'Four chil-dren, a long marriage to a man you loved, career success.'

'You're quite right, my dear girl.' Josephine extracted a proper handkerchief from her handbag and dabbed at her cheeks. 'I had everything I wanted – and now I have this. And I have you. What a joy you are.'

Pepper was about to reply with a rebuttal, but then she remembered Finn's light-hearted telling-off from the previ-ous day and stopped herself. She hated it when people attempted to push aside the compliments she gave them, so why did she persist in doing the same thing to others? She must try to stop.

'Thank you,' she managed, pressing her shoulder against Josephine's. 'And thank you for bringing me here, for broadening my very limited horizons.'

'Nonsense!' Josephine tutted. 'Darling, you have an artist's soul, just like dear Jorge. When you see the world in the way that you do, there are no walls or bars at the windows. I would wager that you could be in the smallest, darkest place in the world, and still find beauty in the shadows.'

Pepper's voice cracked as she started to reply, and she was forced to clear her throat.

'Perhaps once,' she said. 'But not for a very long time now. The truth is, since Bethan died, I sometimes feel as if my whole life exists inside a small, dark room.'

'Grief can feel like that,' Josephine said softly. 'The key is not to allow it to box you in. Think of the person you lost, and what they would want for you.'

Pepper thought of Bethan's zest for adventure, of her little sister's hopes and dreams, dashed before she had a chance to realise any of them.

'What about what they would want for themselves?' she said. 'That counts, too.'

'Of course it does, darling. But one of those things would surely be a desire to see those you love happy. Not long before I lost Ian, he made me promise that I would not retreat into the space he left behind, but that I would keep living for the both of us – keep striving to do all the things he would have done if he had the chance. I think about that every day.'

'That makes sense.' Pepper was nodding, but her insides twisted with sadness. All at once, the colours beyond the window seemed to lose their vibrancy, and the serenity that had settled over her was replaced by a churning wave of sorrow.

Pepper had always struggled with feelings of guilt surrounding Bethan's death. She didn't blame herself for what happened – it was an accident – but she did feel a strange kind of shame at having been the one who survived. And she suspected that she was not the only one.

As if on cue, Pepper heard a buzzing sound coming from her bag, and for a fleeting second, her heart leapt in hope that it was Finn, calling to bring the sunshine back into her day.

But it wasn't. It was her mother.

14

'Philippa.'

Her mother had not called her Pepper since Bethan died.

'Your father is getting married,' she announced wearily. 'To his secretary.'

'Hang on a sec, Mum.' Pepper clamped her phone against her ear with her shoulder as she helped Josephine down the steps of the tram. They were in the Chiado area of the city now, not far from the next location on Josephine's list. She shouldn't really have answered, given the fact that she was supposed to be giving her full attention to her friend, but when she saw her mother's name on the screen, Pepper had remembered the missed call from the previous day and been walloped by a thump of guilt.

She could hear her mother sighing with obvious displeasure at the other end of the line and could appreciate why. This would be her father Martin's second attempt at another marriage since he had left her mum. Since he left both of them.

'Sorry,' she mouthed to Josephine, who waved away her apology and motioned towards a nearby bookshop. Pepper watched her go in through the open door, then let out a breath she had not realised she'd been holding. Looking around for a place to sit down, she settled on a low wall that had been decorated in yet more patterned tiles. She would be willing to bet that if you reached out a hand anywhere in the city, the first thing you would touch would be art in some form or another.

'So, I guess that means there's going to be another wedding?' she asked, staring down at her sandalled feet. Pepper had painted her nails that morning, choosing a rich ruby red to match the scarf tied up in her blonde hair. For the first time in ages, she had thought carefully about every element of her outfit, even treating herself to a white sundress from a shop not far from the hotel. It was the first item of clothing she had bought new in years.

'He wants us there again, of course,' her mother said. 'Something about a show of unity, merging his old family with his new one.'

'Are we allowed a plus-one?' Pepper asked, even though she was not sure who she would invite if this was the case.

'I have no idea.' Her mother's voice lurched a notch closer to shrill. 'They're doing it over in Guernsey, would you believe? Like we're all made of money and can afford flights and hotels.'

Pepper closed her eyes and took a slow breath in. Her mother always became more agitated when she was talking about Martin, and although she had assured Pepper many times that she harboured no hard feelings towards him, it was painfully apparent that the opposite was in fact true.

'I went ahead and booked us a room,' her mother went on. 'I thought I should, before the hotel filled up. She's very young, his new—' Her mother could not bring herself to say the words 'wife-to-be'. Instead she mumbled something unintelligible, before adding, 'She's bound to have a lot of friends coming. Your father's probably only inviting us to swell his numbers, make him look more popular.'

Ouch, thought Pepper, but she made no comment.

'I hope he doesn't expect a gift,' her mother rattled on. 'They will probably have a list at John Lewis. Well, they're not getting so much as a card from me.'

'I can pay for our flights,' Pepper replied, thinking as she did so how strange it was that she would be taking another trip in the near future. The Channel Islands were not exactly exotic, but it still meant a plane journey.

'When is it?' she added, interrupting her mother's protestations about travel costs.

'Towards the end of the summer, I think,' she said. 'I can't remember the exact date, or perhaps Martin didn't think to mention it. That would be just like him. He always has been forgetful.' Her tone had softened now, as if her ex-husband's absentmindedness was something she remembered fondly. It was a sentiment that rankled.

'Your dad has gone because he is too sad to stay,' her mother had told Pepper, who was fourteen when her father moved out. 'We make him too sad.'

Pepper had tried to make sense of those words at the time, had chased them around in her mind almost constantly, but they had never become any clearer. Because how could it feel right, after losing one daughter, to leave the one you had left? How would that make the sadness go away? Surely, she had reasoned, choosing to go would only make him sadder still? Years later, disinhibited by alcohol, Pepper had asked her father to tell her his reasons why.

'I just couldn't stay,' he had said. 'I couldn't do it any more.'

Couldn't be a husband. Couldn't be a father. *Couldn't.*

It still stung.

'That sounds like Dad,' she agreed, because it was always easier to humour her mother. 'Just check the hotel booking and text me the dates, so I can block those days out from work.'

'The hotel booking?' For a moment, her mother sounded completely lost, then she remembered. 'Oh. Yes, of course. I see. Yes. It's this wedding – it's thrown me. My mind is tied up in knots.'

'Don't worry about it, Mum.'

Pepper stared unseeingly at the blur of mopeds and stumbling tourists, unaware of the sun on her bare limbs, and the strutting dance of the pigeons as they picked at paving stones beneath her feet.

'It will be fine,' she soothed. 'We'll dress up nicely, hold our heads up high and act like we're happy for them, even if we're not. We'll smile, eat their food, drink their champagne, then we'll come home again.'

'It's not your father's fault,' her mother said then, her inner pendulum swinging from affection to loyalty. 'He deserves to be happy.'

'So do you,' Pepper reminded her, but she could already sense a rebuttal.

'You say that,' her mum said with a sigh, 'but it's an empty platitude, Philippa.'

Pepper understood it, of course; knew that the absence of Bethan meant an absence of happiness for her mother. As she sat there, her phone pressing her ear against the side of her head, Pepper found herself assailed by the same guilt she always experienced whenever she saw or spoke to her mother. Guilt that her own pain did not run deep enough, that she dared to hope for elation in the wake of tragedy.

'I'm sorry, Mum,' she whispered, standing up to pace in a circle. 'I shouldn't have said anything. I just worry about you, that's all.'

'I know you do.' Her mother sounded almost sleepy. 'I know you do.'

Her nose stinging now with unshed tears, Pepper said a hurried goodbye, then jabbed at her phone to end the call.

This was it – this was what it would always be like with her mother. The pattern of their relationship would keep repeating, just like the designs on all this city's azulejos. The same picture, over and over. The same outcome, forever inevitable.

15

'Fabulous, isn't it?'

Josephine had to fold up the rim of her UFO hat in order to admire the curved stone arches of the Convento do Carmo – a grand yet ruinous cathedral nestled in the heart of the city.

'Very,' agreed Pepper, who was still feeling bruised after her phone call.

'I can remember being here with Jorge as if it were yesterday. It hasn't changed a dot. Do you know, part of the original structure collapsed during an earthquake in 1755, but instead of attempting to rebuild her, the Portuguese simply chose to nurture what remained. I think she's rather beautiful, in an eerie way. Jorge brought me here because he wanted to paint me, but I never had the patience to sit for him. Now, of course, I wish I had.'

Pepper found it strange to walk through a nave that was open to the elements, the cracked stone pillars bleached pale gold by a sun they were never meant to see. She avoided churches at home because she always felt as if silent condemnation was emanating from every pew and flickering candle. It did not feel the same here, though, with the sky so blue above them and the breeze so warm. There were no echoes of death here, no corners shrouded in darkness, or whispering voices.

'Do you want to go inside?' Pepper asked. As well as being a church, the Convento do Carmo site also had an adjoining archaeology museum.

Josephine pulled a face. 'Not especially. I always find looking at old artefacts a bit depressing. They remind me of how fusty I am.'

'Oh my God, woman!' exploded Pepper. 'You are ridiculous.'

'Ravenous is what I am,' she replied, offering Pepper the crook of her elbow. 'And as luck would have it, the next place I want to see has the added benefit of pastel de nata by the barrowload.'

'Pastel de who?'

Josephine tittered. 'Nata. Utterly divine and exceedingly delicious custard tarts. You must have seen them – they're in the front window of every other bakery we walk past.'

'Oh, those!'

'So, what do you say?' she enthused. 'Shall we go to Belém and see how many we can eat before we're sick?'

Pepper estimated that walking the five kilometres along the river to Belém would take them at least an hour, and was therefore out of the question for Josephine, whose fall on the beach she had not forgotten. Instead of flagging down a taxi, however, she suggested they took the bus, only to find it packed to the doors with passengers. A young mum near the front offered a seat to Josephine, while Pepper stood towards the back, wedged in between two elderly women in long, black dresses and a group of rowdy teenage boys.

Hoping to find a message from Finn when she took out her phone, Pepper was disheartened to be greeted by a blank screen. *I like him*, she thought. Being within his orbit yesterday had felt to Pepper as if she was inside a happy bubble. Life had been better for those few hours; Finn had rubbed away the dullness that had settled over her former shine.

Chewing at a curl of skin on her thumb, she used the other to tap out a rapid message to him, pressing 'send' before she had a chance to reconsider. The bus trundled from one stop to the next, groaning under the weight of its human cargo, and all the while Pepper clung to the pole, trying her best not to bash into people whilst also keeping track of how far they had come.

Her phone pinged.

'Hallo,' Finn had written, followed by an emoji of a waving hand. There was a pause, then another message came through.

Pepper had asked him what he was up to, and now she let out a squeak of pleasure. The universe wasn't just listening, it was *doing*.

Finn was sitting on the bus stop bench when she and Josephine arrived, and smiled when they came into view. Getting to his feet, he strode smoothly across to greet them.

'You look nice,' he said, looking Pepper up and down. 'Like a raspberry ripple ice cream.'

Josephine nodded in enthusiastic agreement, eyeing Finn like a cat might a goldfish bowl.

'And you look lovely, too,' Finn added, running an appraising eye over Josephine's green trousers and pale yellow blouse. 'The colours of a summer meadow.'

'I remember rolling around in those, once upon a time,' she chuckled, and a mortified Pepper covered her face with her hands.

'I would not suggest that you do the same here,' Finn replied. 'Not in front of so many people.'

Josephine thought this was hilarious and waggled a mock-offended finger at him as she complimented his crisp white shirt with its polo player embroidered on the breast pocket.

'How wonderful that you two young things keep bumping into each other,' Josephine said now. 'I warned Pepper that this city has a history of bringing people together.'

'Perhaps the stars want us to know one other,' he agreed, beaming at both of them without a trace of humour or irony. Pepper could not imagine any of the men down at the Turbot having the gumption to talk like this.

'I seem to recall Pastéis de Belém being this way,' Josephine said, as another bus pulled up and a second crowd of occupants spilled out onto the pavement. The Rio Tejo lay, vast and glittering, to their right, while across the road there was a rectangular sprawl of lawn bordered by orange trees. Ignoring the path, Josephine beckoned them with a hand and made her way over the grass instead, stepping over outstretched legs and picnic baskets as she went.

It was impossible to miss the Mosteiro dos Jerónimos – an enormous dreamscape of carved stone on the far side of the park – but Josephine was clearly a woman on a mission for a custard tart, and aside from a brief appreciative glance in the building's direction, she made no comment, instead continuing determinedly towards what looked to be the main street. Pepper could see souvenir shops, bars, and a line of electric scooters for hire, but it was the queue outside Pastéis de Belém that really drew her eye. All around the entrance in the shade of the bakery's blue awning, tourists stood in excitable huddles, many posing for selfies with pastries raised up towards their mouths.

'It smells like cinnamon,' she said, her nose in the air. 'And sugar.'

Finn glanced down. His sunglasses were hiding his eyes, but the upward trajectory of his lips was a clear indicator of his mood.

'Then we have come to the right place.'

In any other circumstance, for any other food source, Pepper could not imagine ever waiting in line for close to thirty minutes in order to sample it. But this situation was different for two reasons. One: she got to wait in said queue with Finn, and two: when it came to the actual eating part, it turned out that pastel de nata genuinely were more than worth it.

'Oh my God!' she exclaimed between mouthfuls, as the gooey, warm, custard filling oozed over her taste buds and the thin layers of pastry cracked delectably. The flavour – a perfect balance between sweetness, richness and spice – was like nothing Pepper had ever experienced before.

'Wow,' she said, using a finger to scoop up the extra filling that had leaked out into the cardboard tube. 'These are – wow!'

Finn, who had ordered eight pastries to her four and still had his mouth full, articulated his wholehearted agreement with a brisk nodding of his blond head.

'Even better than beer,' he declared, when he was done chewing.

'Utterly sublime,' Josephine agreed, wiping delicately at the corner of her mouth with her handkerchief. 'Jorge and I would buy a bagful for the equivalent of pennies and eat them down by the riverbank,' she went on. 'Do you know, once upon a time, they would have sold them over in the monastery there, as a ruse to attract more people inside.'

'I can understand the logic behind that plan,' Pepper enthused, going in for a third helping.

'It says here on the bag that the recipe is still the same,' Josephine said. 'The secret ingredients have been passed on from one generation to the next.'

'I like that idea.' Finn folded his empty carton in half. 'I think it is important that we learn from our parents, and our grand-parents, just as we will one day teach our children.'

Josephine was looking at Pepper.

'Can we add friends to that list, too?' she asked him. 'Even I know that a person is never too old to learn a new lesson – or to teach one, for that matter.'

Pepper wanted to reply, to explain to her friend that she had already taught her so much about the importance of grabbing moments as they passed, and how vital it is to cherish the time you have. She knew that if Josephine could find a way to heal Pepper of the hurt that she still carried, she would. But simply knowing it didn't make it so.

When it came to forging a future free from guilt, Pepper still had a lot of work to do.

16

It was early evening by the time they left Belém and braved the bus for the second time that day. Pleasantly pink from a day spent in the sun and with a nicely full stomach courtesy of Pastéis de Belém, Pepper stared out of the window at the passing scenery. Real life, with its antagonistic parents, bills to pay and work to be done, felt very far away.

Finn was in the adjacent seat, his leg tantalisingly close to her own, while Josephine sat facing them. Every time Pepper glanced in her direction, the older woman offered her an expression laced with mischievousness, a single, suggestive eyebrow raised up like a feather duster.

'I wonder,' she said airily, examining one of the many bracelets that decorated her wrist. 'Do you two urchins think you could amuse yourselves for the evening? I rather fancy a nap, then I thought I might go for a stroll. By myself,' she added, seeing that Pepper was about to interject.

'But—' Pepper began.

'Honestly, darling. I really would rather be alone for a bit, if it's all the same with you? There are so many memories coming back to me, and I fear some are being chased away by all our chatter.'

'I can stay quiet,' Pepper protested, but Josephine shook her head.

'Yes, but that is hardly fair on you. What would please me most of all is if the two of you were to toddle off and do something fun together. Perhaps go to a Fado club?' She nodded to Finn. 'Or explore those exciting-looking bars you keep telling me I'm not allowed to venture into?'

'Finn probably has his own plans,' Pepper pointed out, but Josephine was not going to be deterred that easily.

'I very much doubt that he's had an offer better than this one.'

She had posed it as a question, and Finn did not let her down.

'That is true,' he agreed, pressing the bell to alert the driver that they were nearing their stop, then helping Josephine to her feet when the bus began to slow.

'But what about dinner?' Pepper went on as they clambered off. 'You can't survive on just custard tart.'

'I am perfectly capable of dining at the hotel.' Josephine tempered. 'Alternatively, I can eat out somewhere later. Jorge's family used to run a restaurant, you know, and I should like to see if they are still there. I promise I won't go far – I will stay within the boundaries of Alfama.'

'But what if something happens?' Pepper argued, lowering her voice a fraction. 'These cobbles are treacherous enough in daylight hours.'

'My dear.' Josephine put a hand on her arm. 'This trip is all about us having fun, so if you please, stop being a worry goblin and let me have mine.'

It was only after she promised to text every hour and avoid unnecessary steps that Pepper let her go, and after they had waved her off, she and Finn stood facing each other on the pavement, their shared smiles doing the work of all the words they were unable to find.

Pepper spoke first.

'Beer?'

Finn removed his hands from the pockets of his shorts.

'*Ja!*'

This time it was Pepper's turn to take the lead, Finn falling in step beside her as she guided them up winding stone steps and along alleyways that appeared from between the tall houses as if from nowhere. There was a place in Alfama that she wanted to show him – a bar she and Josephine had passed on their first day – and she found her way back to it without too much trouble, trusting her own memory rather than relying on her phone.

'This place looks great,' said Finn, ducking to avoid hitting his head on the doorframe as they went inside.

The bar was laid out like someone's living room – albeit one in a house belonging to an eccentric kleptomaniac with a penchant for hoarding, thought Pepper – and every available surface was piled high with an astonishing array of ornaments, pictures, candles, framed photos, records and postcards. Someone had fashioned a disco light out of a gramophone, and the furniture was a jumble of mismatched pieces in varying states of disrepair. Pepper pointed to a mirror-fronted cabinet in the corner that someone had decorated in stick-on goggly eyes, a battalion of costume dolls on one of the wooden shelves above. There were shisha pipes stacked against the walls, a rickety table groaning under the weight of board games, and a large grandfather clock with graffiti-green chimes.

After ordering two cans of beer from a red-haired woman who was manning the kitchen-cum-bar area, they sat down on a chintzy sofa that promptly coughed out a fog of dust.

'*Obrigada*,' said Finn, thanking the same woman as she plonked a small basket of nuts down on the table in front of them.

'So,' said Pepper, pouring her beer from the can into a glass.

'So,' said Finn, following suit.

Before she had time to conjure up something interesting or witty to say, he had plucked a dog-eared menu off a nearby shelf and began reading the cocktail list aloud.

'Sloe comfortable screw?' he suggested.

Pepper choked as her beer went down the wrong way.

'*Nein?* OK . . . Perhaps, then, a Climax?'

'Stop!' Pepper laughingly poked his leg. 'You're lowering the tone.'

'Between the Sheets sounds good, *ja*?' he teased. 'White rum, cognac, triple sec and a splash of lemon juice.'

'Very nice,' she said obediently. 'But to be honest, I'm more a simple beer or wine girl.'

'Yes,' he said, putting down the menu. 'That is why we get along so well, I think. You like the simple things in life, and I am simple.'

'Simple suggests you're not interesting,' she pointed out. 'And I would argue that you are.'

'*Ja?*' He was fishing now.

'You co-own a bar and a restaurant and you're launching your own website. You apparently speak at least three languages – including Portuguese – and spend the majority of your time travelling around the world. Oh, and there's also the fact you accost strange women in the street.'

As she talked, Pepper ticked each attribute off on her fingers, watching in amusement as Finn's smile grew wider and wider.

'Given all the evidence,' she went on. 'I would say that you're extremely complex. Not simple at all – the very opposite of simple.'

'I don't talk to every woman I see,' he assured her, taking a swig of his beer. 'Only those that are wearing pelicans.'

'Toucans, actually,' she corrected. 'But I'm glad they made an impression.'

'The birds did catch my eye,' he admitted. 'But it is the rest that keeps me here still.'

Pepper shifted position on the tatty sofa. As much as she wanted to be seen by him – really seen – she was unused to being scrutinised so openly. Finn was staring at her now as he might a work of art. He was not afraid to make his feelings known, and Pepper wondered if her own features were giving away even half as much. Being this close to Finn had heightened her senses, and every nerve ending seemed to be pulsing at once.

'Tell me more about your work,' he said now, scooping up a handful of nuts. 'Do you teach only adults, or is it children, too?'

'I'll teach anyone who wants teaching,' she said simply. 'Anyone who wants to learn. Adults are more difficult, because they invariably come with a bag of bad habits and a very firm idea of what they want the finished creation to look like, even if it might be beyond their reach in terms of skill.'

Finn had finished his beer, and in a bid to keep up, Pepper

downed what was left in her glass and went up to get another round. She couldn't resist turning back to look at him as she waited, the pull between them like that of a tow rope, connected to the centre of her chest.

'Teaching children is better?' he asked when she returned, picking up the conversation where they had left it.

'I guess so.' Pepper thought for a moment. 'Children are great, because you really feel as if you're helping them to see the world differently. You ask them what colour the sky is, and they say "blue", so you take them to the window, tell them to look a bit harder, and then suddenly they can see greys and pinks and smears of white. Only once I get them to that point do I feel satisfied, because only then do I know for sure that I have given their lives so much extra colour.'

Finn stretched an arm around the back of the sofa, his hand coming to rest on the cushion behind Pepper's shoulder.

'I think we can all be guilty of that,' he said. 'Sometimes we can stare so hard at something, yet still never see it. That is why I love art – it gives you permission to stop and look.'

'You need permission to do that?'

'Perhaps permission is the wrong English word,' he allowed. 'What I mean is that it reminds us. We all learn that a painting, for example, deepens the more you examine it, and gives away more of itself.'

'I would agree with that.'

'What I try to do,' he went on, 'is apply the same rule to everything I come across in my life – not just art or nature, but people. I try to look beyond what someone is showing me on the surface and see what is hidden underneath.'

Taking a deep breath and raising both her eyebrows in appreciation of how deep their conversation had become, she said lightly, 'Remind me never to show you any of my darker work in that case. It'll scare you right off.'

Finn removed his arm from the back of the sofa, and even though he hadn't been touching her, Pepper still felt suddenly colder.

'I would like to see it,' he said, going in for more of the nuts. 'Can you show me some pieces? Do you have any photos on your phone?'

Pepper shook her head. 'I told you yesterday. I don't do much of my own stuff. I'm too busy teaching.'

'I don't believe that you do nothing.' Finn gave her a sidelong look. 'You must have one picture you can show me.'

'I honestly don't,' she insisted. And it was true – she never photographed her work, never kept it long enough to do so. The examples of art on her website were those done by her pupils, and anything she created as part of a session, she invariably gave away, painted over, or broke down into pieces to use another time. None of it warranted showing off – it was never good enough.

'OK,' he said, swilling beer around in his glass. 'But how can I hope to find out more about you if you refuse to show me?'

Pepper uncrossed her legs, the skirt of her white dress falling between her thighs. The red-haired woman was humming as she mixed drinks for a couple that had just arrived, a tune that felt familiar despite being indistinguishable. There was chatter and laughter coming from other tables, and the dancing lights of the gramophone disco ball were playing a fruitless game of chase on the far wall.

'You could just ask me,' she said, her knee now against his.

'*Ja*, I could.' Finn turned a fraction, so he was facing her.

Once again, she felt sure that he was going to kiss her, but rather than lean over towards her, Finn shifted his weight to the other side of his sofa cushion instead. Feeling foolish, Pepper grabbed her glass only to knock it over sideways, flooding the basket of nuts and half the table with beer.

'Bugger!' she swore, lurching over sideways to save her dress from the overspill.

Finn was already on his feet fetching a cloth from the bar and laughed at the stricken look on Pepper's face as he knelt down to mop up the mess.

'I'm so sorry.' She cringed. 'I'm a liability – you should escape while you still can.'

'Escape?' he said, mock solemn. 'No, sorry – it is far too late for that.'

'Really?'

Just like that, Pepper felt awash with happiness again.

Still on his knees, Finn shuffled forwards until his nose was level with hers.

'Really,' he said. And then, before she knew what was happening, he had leant over and finally, blissfully, pressed his lips against hers.

17

It was with an almost dreamlike serenity that Pepper wafted around the Royal Palace at Sintra the following morning. With its brightly coloured walls, toilet-roll turrets and endless swathes of exquisite tiles, the palace could easily have been plucked right out of the pages of a fairy tale, and it felt fitting to Pepper to be somewhere so otherworldly.

She still could not quite believe the events of the previous evening, of Finn kissing her with such tenderness that even the merest recollection made her lungs and stomach contract. She had known him for such a short time, but already he felt like an intrinsic piece of her life – one that had slotted in with such ease.

Josephine had known at once, of course. She had taken one look at the expression on Pepper's face and rubbed her hands together with glee.

'I'm very happy for you,' she said. 'It's high time you met a chap who put a proper leap in your lollop.'

Finn had stayed in the cluttered bar with Pepper until the dark beyond the windows was absolute, then afterwards, the two of them had wandered through the streets hand-in-hand, sharing stories, kisses and trading wishes as they picked out the stars far above. She knew it was corny, but it hadn't felt at all contrived. She liked him and he liked her – it was as simple as that.

Hopelessly caught up in the romance of the moment, Pepper only thought to check the time when it was long past midnight and found four messages from Josephine on her phone as promised – one for every hour she had been away. Finn saw her back to the entrance of the hotel, but he made no move to accompany her inside, instead giving her a final, lingering kiss and promising that he would be in touch the following day. Pepper had stood and watched him as he walked away, clutching her arms around herself and feeling the thud of her heart as it tried in vain to keep up with her whirling thoughts.

She had accepted the fact that sleep would most probably remain elusive, only to be surprised when she fell into an effortless slumber almost as soon as her head was down. It wasn't until Josephine knocked loudly on her door just after six a.m. that she awoke. Her friend had enjoyed her solo amble through the old streets of Alfama the previous evening, she told Pepper – had discovered the restaurant once owned by Jorge's family and gone inside to enquire after him.

'I don't know what I expected to find after all these years,' she said to Pepper, as the pair of them boarded the train that would take them from Sintra back to Lisbon. 'My former lover sitting there behind the counter, simply waiting for me to turn up and find him.'

'If he managed to make it as an artist, then there would be information about him online,' Pepper said, taking out her phone. 'What's his surname?'

'Montalvo,' Josephine said, rolling out the 'L' across her tongue.

Pepper opened her Internet browser and typed it in. Several results came up for Facebook and Twitter accounts, but when she clicked through and showed the corresponding profile pictures to Josephine, the older woman shook her head each time. There was also a film actor called Jorge Montalvo, who was – as Josephine succinctly put it – 'a handsome beast', but not only had he been born around thirty years after the Jorge they were seeking, he was also Spanish. It was a dead end, but the search had only made Pepper more determined.

'We can find him,' she said. 'I know we can. There will be a way.'

'Let me think about it some more,' Josephine replied. 'See if I can't rustle us up some better clues.'

They were two stops away from the city when Pepper's phone chimed with a message.

'Finn wants to know if we're both free this afternoon,' she said, unable to keep the smile from spreading across her face. 'He says he has a surprise planned.'

'Gosh!' Josephine exclaimed. 'For both of us? That is kind. How could I possibly refuse?'

It had been another overcast morning, but now the sky was an optimistic blue. Lisbon was beginning to feel familiar to Pepper now, and thanks to her endless wandering, she had become far more confident at finding her way around. It was impossible to get lost in small, linear Aldeburgh, but here it felt at times as if they had wandered into a labyrinth. The fact that Pepper had mastered the higgledy-piggledy lanes with relative ease made her love the city all the more, and she had switched rapidly from being anxious to leave Suffolk to reluctant to return. She couldn't believe she had waited so long to travel – and been so scared. It felt utterly ridiculous now.

Finn did a little bow as they approached the Alfama café he had chosen as a meeting place, and Josephine curtseyed back without missing a beat.

'Hello,' he said then to Pepper, bending to brush his lips against her cheek and making all the hairs stand up on the back of her neck. Instinctively, she touched him – put a hand on his arm and closed her fingers around it, the shape of him still so unknown, yet wonderfully familiar. Her breath caught for a moment in her throat, and when she smiled, she found that he was smiling too.

'We can walk there,' Finn told them. 'It is not very far.'

They set off in the direction of Baixa, passing yet more houses painted in shades of peach, jade, primrose, sage and marshmallow pink. Every time a new spread of azulejos came into view, Pepper scanned each one with eager eyes, committing the pictures and patterns to memory. Being surrounded by so much art was making her itch for her own materials, for her studio workbench or even a simple pencil and piece of paper on which she might sketch. She was so accustomed to pushing the urge back down when it reared its head, that at first it made her feel strange and exposed, but the further they ventured, and the tighter Finn held her hand, the more she began to relax and give in to what she was feeling.

Finn took them in multiple circles once they reached the town centre, frowning as Pepper pointed out that they'd walked past the same sardine shop four times. Not once did he drop so much of a hint as to where he was taking them, though, and when he did finally give in and consult his phone for directions, he held it up out of reach so she wouldn't be able to snoop.

'Naughty,' he reproved. 'You will ruin my surprise.'

Pepper had envisaged the treat to be lunch at one of the city's rooftop eateries, or perhaps a visit to a gallery or museum. Lisbon was famed for its cork, so perhaps they were on the way to source some of that? Or taste some Port? Josephine would enjoy that.

'I think we are here,' he said at last, coming to such an abrupt stop that Josephine almost walked right into him.

'We are?' Pepper took in the cracked wooden door with its sparse rinds of white paint.

Finn, who had been consulting his phone, looked up and nodded.

'She said that it might be difficult to find.'

There was a large iron knocker on the door, as well as a buzzer set to the side, and Finn tried both. Pepper, who was a few steps behind him, took the opportunity to admire the breadth of his shoulders and the spun-gold sheen of his hair.

The woman who answered the door reminded Pepper starkly of herself. Her skirt was long and flowing, the blouse above it dotted with flowers, and her hair, which was dark and shiny like treacle, was piled up and held in place with a slim paintbrush of the kind a child might use. She was wearing an ink-stained apron and enough metal bangles to topple a boat.

After they had all greeted each other with a chorus of *olá*s and *como está*s, the woman beckoned them in and along a dark hallway that opened out into a neat paved garden. Pepper saw long wooden tables piled with paints, blank tiles, pots of beads, glue and scissors. There were jam jars full of pencils, pens and brushes, stacks of coloured paper and cardboard pinned down with large shells and, on a chair that had been pushed into a far corner, a large rubbish sack full of what looked to be feathers.

Finn had somehow discovered the Lisbon equivalent of an Arts For All session.

The woman swept an arm around, breaking into clumsy English as she explained that they were welcome to use any materials they wanted, and that she would be around if they required any help. She didn't appear to be as hands-on as Pepper herself generally would be, but the set-up was almost identical. And the three of them weren't the first customers of the day, either – a gang of surly-faced teenage girls were gloomily sketching a bowl of fruit at one table, while a man with wild ginger hair was busy sculpting what looked to be a family of trolls out of clay at another.

'Are you happy to stay?' Finn asked, sounding less self-assured now that they were here. 'She told me that she never gets time to create any art for herself,' he added to Josephine. 'So, I thought . . .'

He looked at Pepper.

'We can go, if you want to?' he said. 'I don't want you to feel under any pressure.'

'Oh no,' she hurried out. 'This is lovely, so thoughtful, so sweet of you to be so clever – and so kind.'

She was babbling now as her mother sometimes did, desperate to reassure him. Finn had really listened to her; he had acted on what she told him. Pepper was so used to fulfilling her own needs – her independent streak born from years of being left to her own devices – that she had forgotten how nice it felt to be treated to something that she had not planned herself.

'What shall we make?' she asked, accepting an apron from the dark-haired host while Josephine fastened the ties on her own.

'You told me last night that you like mosaics?' Finn said. Then, when Pepper nodded, 'OK then, that is what we should do.'

Josephine had opted to sculpt with the clay and set herself up on the bench alongside Pepper while Finn sat opposite. They each had a rectangular block of wood on the table in front of them and plastic tubs full of tiny coloured tiles arranged within reach. Finn insisted on erecting a propped-up cardboard barrier between them, so they would not be able to see what the other was creating. This suited Pepper, who knew almost immediately what she was going to make. Selecting a pencil from one of the jars, she quickly sketched an outline of her design straight onto the wood, then began picking out white, grey, pale blue and yellow tiles to cut. Finn thought for a while, then beamed as an idea came to him. Using one hand as a shield, he rifled through the nearest tub for his own materials with the other, raising a comedy eyebrow as Pepper pretended to sneak a look.

At home, she only ever worked with deafeningly loud music or the radio blasting in her ears, but here gentle jazz drifted across from a distant window. Birds twittered away out of sight, the teenage girls mumbled things to each other occasionally, and every so often, there was the sticky slap sound of watery hands against clay from either Josephine or the troll man. Other than that, it was quiet, and for once Pepper found the lack of noise soothing rather than distracting. Or maybe, it was Finn that soothed her? There was something so capable, so reassuring, and so calming about him, yet he had also made her howl with laughter as they talked last night. She felt switched on – alive in ways she had not felt for many years.

'Making a mosaic is much harder than it looks,' he said, after half an hour had passed. Pepper, whose well-practised hands were cutting, placing and gluing with easy speed, tutted in good humour as Finn sent a shard of red tile shooting across the table.

'Here,' she said, 'cup your hand under the cutters before you snip, then all the pieces will fall into your open palm, see?'

Finn stood up so he could watch over the barrier, and Pepper only just hid her creation in time.

'You make it look simple,' he said. 'I see now why you are a good teacher.'

'Hardly!' she argued, only to be told off by Josephine.

'Pay no heed to her,' she warned him. 'I'm afraid this talented and wonderful young lady has a tendency to put herself down. She is immeasurably good at what she does, but she will never hear it, never admit it.'

Finn's eyebrows knitted together as he frowned.

'Why not?' he asked. 'If you are good at something, it makes sense to be proud – it is important.'

'I get by,' she said, then, before he had a chance to challenge her, 'where did your interest in art come from, anyway?'

'Mama used to take me to galleries when I was a child,' he explained. 'Much of the time, we lived close to the Army barracks, because of my father. And they were not always the best places. Mama was my best friend when I didn't have any of my own, and we would play drawing games together, or make models, that kind of thing.'

'What about your father?' Pepper asked.

'Ah, with Papa, it was always football,' he said with a sigh. 'Or cricket. Sometimes boxing. Always sport or fighting. My mother stopped putting my drawings on the wall, because he would take them down. He thought it was pointless to encourage me in something I was very bad at – which I was – but it felt unfair to me then. When he was sent abroad, or went away on Army exercise, those were the best times, because my pictures stayed up for weeks, even though they were terrible.'

'You poor little mite,' remarked Josephine.

'That is sad,' agreed Pepper, putting down the tweezers she had been using to nudge the smaller pieces of her mosaic into place.

Finn shrugged. 'I was never that good at any of it,' he said, trying for a laugh that came out as a sort of grunt. 'Not the art or the sport, so neither Mama nor Papa won that battle in the end. I chose to study business and accounting at university, which was very *stumpf* – dull – but now I can look after the money side of my business. I don't think I would be able to launch a website if I could not crunch the numbers.'

'Maths brings me out in hives,' Pepper confessed. 'Sums may as well be written in Egyptian hieroglyphics for all the sense they make to me.'

Pepper was relieved that the conversation had moved natur ally away from discussions about childhood. She didn't feel like telling them that there had never been any of her drawings displayed at home – not after Bethan's accident.

'Is this beginning to look anything like a bowl yet?' Josephine asked, raising hands that were covered in clay in a gesture of mild exasperation.

'Erm . . .' Pepper clenched her teeth together. 'Is that what it's supposed to be?'

'I thought that you were making a boat,' Finn observed, his knee finding Pepper's under the table. In every other relation-ship Pepper had ever been in, she had assumed the role of the giver, while the men had been the takers – but intuition was tell-ing her that Finn was different. How could she fly home to Suffolk tomorrow and leave him? It did not seem fathomable.

With her mosaic finished and set aside to dry, Pepper fetched some paper and charcoal and started to draw him, barely look-ing down as her hand moved easily back and forth. She sketched in the neat curve of his ears, the wispier hairs on his temples and the dent of concentration that had appeared between his eyebrows. His mouth was slightly open, his lips smooth, the blond stubble around them a scattering of sand, and his eyes were like brushed velvet in their softness, so rich with integrity.

For the first time since meeting him, she wished that instead of being here in Portugal, they were back in Suffolk, sitting together in her studio. There she would have the right paints to mix, her own easel and a teapot keeping warm under a cosy. They could lock the door, shut out the world, and bask in the pleasure of having found one another.

Pepper added smudges under Finn's eyes – a private tell of the late night they had shared – and the shaded hollow of his throat, pinching the stick of charcoal so she had an edge to add in the buttons of his shirt, and the lashes that were casting faint shadows on his cheeks. She was so absorbed in her task, that at first she didn't notice that Finn had finished his mosaic and was now watching her intently.

'All done?' she asked brightly, blowing the dust off the portrait and propping it gently against her chest.

Finn flashed her his megawatt smile. '*Ja!*'

'Going to give us a gander?' enquired Josephine, who hadn't looked up. She was still immersed in her bowl-cum-boat and was using a wooden stick to scratch on a pattern.

'I think it must be ladies first,' he said. 'I had a plan for mine, but it is—' He clenched his teeth together. 'Not exactly what I imagined.'

'I'm sure it's brilliant,' Pepper enthused. 'Mine is just silly.'

'What is this?' he said then, reaching across the table and trying to pluck the sheet of paper out of her hands.

'Nothing,' she said, gripping it tighter. 'Just a few scribbles.'

'If it is nothing,' he said, the corners of his mouth lifting amicably, 'then surely you can show me.'

'It's not finished,' she told him. 'It's rubbish. Please don't. I'll be so embarrassed.'

'It is most certainly not rubbish,' approved Josephine, putting down her stick.

Pepper loosened her grip slightly, looking from Finn to Josephine and back again.

'Oh, all right,' she said, giving in, then put her head in her hands as Finn swiped the paper out of them triumphantly.

'It's awful, I know,' she muttered. 'Chuck it in the bin – use it for scrap. Burn it!'

'Hush.' Finn's eyes were wide. 'This is *sehr, sehr gut.*'

He turned it around so Josephine could see, and the older woman whistled.

'What did I say? Barrels of talent.'

Finn stared first at Pepper, then again at the portrait. 'You drew this? Just now as we were talking?'

'Well, in the last ten minutes or so,' she admitted sheepishly. 'But it's not finished – it needs work.'

'Can I keep it?' Finn asked.

'It's not done,' she said again. The attention was causing her to squirm. 'It's not fit to be seen.'

'I really want it,' he pressed, clutching it just as close to his chest as Pepper had done.

'Honestly,' she pleaded. 'It's crap – it's better off in the bin.'

'I would take it, if I were you,' Josephine said to Finn. 'It will likely be worth a lot of money one day.'

Finn was still staring at Pepper, his expression hard to read. She was aware that she was coming across like a moron, but it was true what she was telling them – the portrait wasn't good enough. Not as far as she was concerned.

'Show me what else you have made,' Finn said, rolling up the portrait as if that settled the matter. Lifting away the cardboard barrier he had put up between them, he peered down at Pepper's pelican mosaic and immediately began to laugh.

'And yours?' she prompted, standing up.

Finn surprised her then by looking almost bashful, and when she saw what he had made, she almost wept.

It was a large, red pepper.

18

The muted Aldeburgh palette had always served to soothe Pepper in the past, the greys, blues and whites an antidote to her often fractured mind, but now that she was home, she found them too subdued. She missed Lisbon's terracotta rooftops and bright explosions of flowers; she wanted to be stirred, not stilled, to laugh, to feel the sunshine warming her limbs and too many custard pastries filling her belly. She craved the flames that the Portuguese city had ignited within her, and the fiery spirit that had driven her towards Finn. Home had always been where she belonged, but now it felt as if she had left a piece of herself somewhere else.

But Pepper did not have any time to dwell – she had promised that as soon as she was back from her trip, she would head over to The Maltings for a few hours to do a painting class with some of the more able residents. After arriving late due to the battery of her ancient Volvo being flat, she encountered pupils who were restless from the off, and by the time her allotted two hours were up and the session had come to a fractious and noisy end, Pepper felt too shredded by exhaustion to face the drive home straight away.

After piling all her paints, brushes and canvases into the boot, she decided to take a stroll around the grounds of the house. It was a pleasant enough day, all cotton-wool clouds and tepid sunshine, and once she had crossed the lawn and was following the narrow pathways between the rose bushes, Pepper began to feel better. She could see The Maltings' grand but lichen-covered water fountain in the distance, and was struck by a sudden urge to run over and toss a penny in for luck.

Drawing nearer, however, she saw that someone else had beaten her to it.

'Nice day for a stroll,' she said, as Samuel stood up from the circular wall to greet her.

'Mrs Howarth told me the roses were out,' he said, gesturing back the way Pepper had just come. 'I thought I'd take a look, but there are so many chuffing bees.'

He was dressed for work today, in a soft grey tracksuit and battered pair of Nikes, while Pepper was wearing a black jumpsuit covered in sunflowers that she'd found in a charity shop. Thanks to her few days in Lisbon, she was sporting a tan for the first time in years.

'You been away?' Samuel asked, and Pepper nodded.

'Portugal.'

'Mate, that sounds lush. You look as if you've been smooched by sunshine.'

And other things . . .

'Thanks,' she said, stretching out her bare arms and admiring the soft caramel hue. 'It went past so quickly. I felt like I'd just got to know the place before we had to leave.'

'Holiday blues?' he asked, and she smiled.

'Something like that.'

They continued to chat for a few minutes about all the usual things – work, weather, what TV series they had binged on recently – and Pepper found herself wanting to tell him about Finn. Why, she didn't know – it wasn't like the two of them were all that close. Perhaps she simply had a severe case of mention-itis. In an attempt to steer the subject her way, she asked Samuel if he'd had any more dates lately.

'Yeah,' he said. 'A second one with the girl I told you about before.'

'And?' Pepper flicked a coin up into the air.

Heads Finn will call tonight, tails he won't . . .

'Queen side up!' Samuel declared. 'Nice one.'

Pepper tossed her two-pence piece into the water, watching as it sank down to join the others. All those wishes. When she and Bethan were little, they used to tell each other everything; whisper secrets to one another after lights out, share stories and giggle with their fists stuffed into their mouths in case their parents heard them. Bethan had always been a fragile child, even before the accident, and Pepper could remember how much she loathed letting her sibling out of her sight. She felt as if she always had to be two steps behind her baby sister.

Until the day she wasn't.

'You didn't answer my question,' she said, forcing herself back out of her momentary gloom. 'Is there going to be a date three?'

'Nah.' Samuel aimed a kick at a stone, sending a cloud of dust up into the air. 'I'm a busy bloke, so if I'm not, you know, feeling it, I don't think there's much point wasting my free time.'

'I thought you believed in letting love grow?' she teased. 'None of that thunderbolt crap for you, right?'

'All right.' Samuel folded his arms. 'Don't get me wrong – I am a big believer in lust at first sight. But if you don't have that, you're probably never gonna have the other. That's the way I see it.'

'I guess in an ideal world, you'd be after both,' she said, giving him a sidelong look.

'Hang on a mo,' he exclaimed. 'Are you trying to tell me that you met someone? Ah, no – you have, haven't you? You went and had yourself a holiday romance.'

Pepper laughed in surprise.

'Is it that obvious?'

Samuel bent down so he could examine her face.

'Afraid so – your eyeballs have turned into hearts.'

'Funny.'

'Come on then – spill.'

So Pepper spilled. She told him about Finn walking past her on the steps, how he'd turned around and asked for her number, how she'd been unsure of whether or not to contact him, only for fate to intervene yet again, and put him beneath the very same tree that she had chosen to shelter under. Samuel kept his arms folded as she explained about Belém, then raised an eyebrow when she told him what Finn had said about the stars wanting them to meet.

'How do you know he doesn't say that to all the girls?' he joked. Then, seeing he had upset her, hurriedly added, 'I'm only pulling your chain.'

'I know it sounds soppy and mad,' she admitted. 'But it didn't feel that way when I was there – it just felt, I dunno, like he had always been there, waiting in the wings. I just had to meet him.'

Samuel smiled then, but he was no longer mocking her.

'If that's the case,' he said, 'then you're lucky. I had someone like that once, a long time ago. But she left. I lost her.'

'Her loss,' Pepper countered, but Samuel was shaking his head.

'Believe it or not, I was going to be a doctor,' he told her. 'I went to medical school, did all that. I was good, too – I was known as "Steady Hands Selassie". Everyone thought I would become a surgeon one day, including me.'

'Good name,' she said. 'What changed your mind?'

Samuel chuckled. 'Thanks for assuming it was my choice,' he said. 'And not down to the fact that I messed up or something.'

'You don't seem the type to fail.' Pepper regarded him for a moment. He was a doer, she could tell. A man who got things done – the opposite of a ditherer. It was a trait he shared with Finn.

'If you're not willing to fail, you're not ready to succeed,' he said gravely.

'Deep,' she drawled. 'Did you just make that up?'

'Nah.' Samuel grinned. 'I saw it printed on the wall of a gym once.'

The clouds had started to huddle together since they'd been talking, their white plumes reminding Pepper of a gaggle of geese, and she shivered.

'Do you mind if we walk – I left my cardigan in the car?'

They took the long route back towards the big house, past the wildflower meadow and The Maltings' resident pair of donkeys, both of whom stuck their furry faces over the fence. Samuel delved in his tracksuit pocket and unearthed a packet of Polos, scratching each animal behind its large floppy ears as they crunched away.

'Truth now,' he said. 'I bloody loved being a doctor. I loved the pace, I loved how demanding it was, that no two shifts were ever the same. I didn't even mind the lack of sleep. I think I thrived on it, you know. Junior doctors get into a sort of competition with each other and themselves – who can last the longest, score the best cases and cope most admirably with an emergency. I saw a lot and learnt so much. When I look back now, it feels like it wasn't even me doing those things, you know? Three years sped past in a mad sort of blur, and I was at the stage where I had to make a decision about my speciality, and my future. And it was then that it struck me.'

Pepper was about to ask what the 'it' was when he continued talking.

'I realised that all the best work I'd done was not the medical stuff – putting lines in, stitching bashed-up faces and setting broken bones. It was the other stuff, the hand holding and the listening. The people stuff. Often, you see, a kind word can heal far better than a pill or a bandage. Oi, don't make that face. I know what you're thinking – that all this makes me sound like some sort of new-age hippy type.'

'On the contrary.' Pepper shook her head. 'I was thinking that I agree with you.'

'My doctor mates wanted to get patients through the system as quickly as possible,' he went on. 'Whereas I wanted to spend time with them, follow up with them. I'm not sure when it happened, but at some point over the past ten years or so, we have all stopped talking to each other, and I reckon we've stopped listening, too. There's too much interference,' he added, making circular motions around his head that were brisk enough to alarm the donkeys. 'Too much noise.'

'I know what you mean,' Pepper agreed. 'It never seems to stop, does it?'

'It does if you switch some of it off,' he said simply. 'But I reckon when it comes to most people, there's a real fear of becoming disconnected, of missing out, you know?'

'What did you do when you realised all this?' she asked. 'Did you just quit?'

'I did.' He shrugged. 'Just like that. And it was the best decision I ever made. It lost me some friends; and my girlfriend left me—'

'No!' Pepper was appalled. 'Just because you resigned?'

Samuel shrugged. 'She had a plan, and the salary I would eventually have made as a surgeon was a large part of it.' He cut Pepper off before she got the opportunity to say something disparaging. 'She's honestly not a bad girl, just the wrong girl for me. Last I heard, she was happily married to a consultant and they'd had a few kids, so I'm sure she's got no regrets.'

'And you think she was The One?' Pepper asked earnestly.

Samuel laughed. 'The One?' he repeated, making inverted comma marks in the air as they continued walking towards the house.

'I'm telling you, Pepper – there is no such thing.'

19

It felt strange to be applying make-up so late in the evening, but Pepper wanted to look her best for her date. The FaceTime date she had arranged with Finn.

She had tried on at least three different outfits since receiving his message, eventually settling on a plain black vest top and checked pyjama shorts. Over this she threw her chunkiest, floppiest jumper – a gift from a client she had taught to knit the previous year – before pulling a brush through her freshly washed hair.

She felt nervous, but they were the good kind of trembles. The ones that transformed your belly into a bubbling cauldron and made it impossible to sit still. Pepper found that she couldn't concentrate on anything – not her novel, not the radio, not a BBC crime drama series starring one of her favourite actors – so she eventually gave up on all three and went on a cleaning spree instead. If this was how she was going to feel before every call with Finn, her house would resemble a show home within days.

She wished she had a friend that she could speak to – someone her own age, who would give her advice about where to position herself for her call, and how she could angle her face to make it look less like a big looming ham. Why were phone cameras so unflattering? How did all those influencers manage to look so perfect on their Instagram stories? It was a mystery to Pepper, and one she knew Josephine would have no answer for.

She scrolled through her contact list, but every name she paused at was a client, or a school friend who had long since moved away. She had seen gangs of mums having coffee together along the high street, some of whom she recognised vaguely from college, but Pepper had never plucked up the courage to go over and reintroduce herself. Most women her age had several big groups of friends, from work, university or their NCT groups – but Pepper only had her mother, Josephine and, she supposed, although it was a stretch, Samuel. And she was not about to text him and ask for some tips of how to look desirable on a FaceTime date. He would laugh her into the middle of next month.

Pepper had assigned Finn his own special ringtone, but she still jumped about a foot in the air when she heard it. Giving her hair a final fiddle and rubbing a finger along her teeth in case any of her red lipstick had somehow ended up on them, she arranged a smile on her face and answered.

'Hallo!'

Finn's slightly blurry face came into view, his smile so wide that it didn't fit the screen.

'Hey, hey you.' Pepper felt heat in her cheeks. He looked so handsome, so clean, so exactly as she had pictured him over and over, ever since she and Josephine climbed into a taxi and drove away from him. Finn was still in Lisbon, he told her, turning his phone around and giving her a sweeping glance at his hotel room, but he was flying home in the morning.

'Did you find any more artists for your site?' Pepper asked, glancing down at her own image in the bottom corner of her screen. It was really hard not to, and every time she did, the urge to grimace overwhelmed her. She looked like Phil Mitchell from *EastEnders*, only more like a thumb.

'*Ja*,' Finn told her happily. 'One who does ceramic fish, and another who is making these,' he went on, rustling in a bag before holding up a white plant pot with holes cut out for eyes and a mouth.

'He is . . . cute,' Pepper said. 'That smile is very enigmatic, isn't it? He's the Mona Lisa of pots.'

'That is what I said!' Finn exclaimed, even more animated now. 'We are like this,' he added, tapping the side of his head and then pointing towards her.

'Great minds,' she agreed.

'I like your hair like this,' he said then. 'And the black – it suits you.'

'Thanks.' Pepper dipped her chin. 'I hardly ever wear it.'

'Well, you should.' He paused for a moment, his mouth twisting to one side, and then he said, '*du siehst umwerfend aus.*'

Pepper tried to repeat his words, but he laughingly cut across her.

'In English, it means you look staggering – or stunning.'

'I'm sure I don't.' Pepper cringed. 'I can see myself, you know.'

'Will you show me your house?' Finn asked, and Pepper breathed with relief, glad to be off the subject of how good she might or might not look. Getting up from where she had arranged herself on the sofa, she took him on a mini tour which started in the front room and ended upstairs in her bedroom. When she turned the phone back around, she saw that Finn was now under the covers of his hotel bed and had also removed his shirt.

'Oh,' she said, unable to stop her eyeballs from bulging in appreciation. Finn was in very good shape and seemed wholly at ease to be half-naked on her phone.

'My flight is early tomorrow,' he said, by way of an explanation. 'It is bedtime for me.'

'Do you want me to go?' Pepper hastened, sitting down on the edge of her bed, but Finn shook his head.

'No – please stay. Perhaps . . .' He stopped and eyed her for a moment or two. Pepper felt as if she had newsprint all over her face, and that he was trying his best to decipher it.

'Perhaps what?' she asked.

'Perhaps we can both get into bed, and then it will be like we are together, under the covers.'

Pepper almost dropped her phone.

'Er, OK,' she said, standing up once again and folding back her duvet. A few seconds later, she was snuggled up against her pillow, her arm stretched out far enough to allow Finn to see her.

She had taken off her cardigan, but left her vest on, although from the way he was now looking at her, she felt as if Finn could see straight through it.

'This is nice,' he said, as Pepper tried not to fuss with her hair. Being under the duvet certainly offered a more flattering light, but she was concerned about her face looking scrunched up, or her nose too big.

'Are you OK?' Finn asked, as Pepper chewed uncomfortably on her bottom lip.

'Fine,' she said. 'This is my first FaceTime call – I'm still getting used to it.'

'Ah,' he replied, nodding as if he understood. 'I am honoured, then. I am your first?'

'First FaceTime,' she clarified.

'And first German?'

'Yes,' she agreed. 'That, too.'

'And first man you have met abroad?'

'Lisbon was the first time I've ever been abroad,' she confessed, and Finn's eyes widened.

'And did you catch the bug?' he asked. 'The travel bug?'

Pepper thought for a moment. She had loved every minute of her time in Lisbon, had not stopped thinking about it and was counting down the days until she and Josephine headed off to Barcelona for the second part of their quest.

'Maybe a bit,' she told him. 'But I'm not sure where I would go next, if it was up to me.'

Finn moved his face closer to his phone, until his lips felt as if they were only inches away. Pepper could feel herself unfurling as desire began to nudge its way through her body; her limbs felt loose and her lips heavy. What she wanted more than anything was for Finn to be here, so she could kiss him, so she could press herself against him.

'I miss you,' she murmured, making herself look right into his eyes. They were almost black under here, beneath the covers, deep pools of the darkest water.

'*Das ist gut,*' he said, his voice low. 'Because I miss you, too.'

They had not discussed when they would next see each other before Pepper left Lisbon, but the suggestion that they would was absolute. She had assumed he would offer to visit, but so far Finn hadn't mentioned it. Perhaps he was waiting for her? Pepper was struck then by a flash of courage, her need to see Finn – to properly see him again – smashing down the boundaries that she would usually cower behind, too polite or too fearful to peer over them.

'I know,' she said, reaching out and touching her phone, her finger on his lips. 'I know where I would go first, if it was up to me.'

Finn said nothing, he simply smiled at her expectantly.

'Hamburg,' she told him. 'I would come and see you. Is that mad? That is mad, isn't it?'

'*Ja*,' he agreed, nodding as she laughed. 'I think mad, yes. But mad *ist gut*!'

'You're funny,' she told him. 'But I can't just fly over to Hamburg.'

'Can't you?'

'Can I?'

'Pepper,' Finn said, and she could see from his expression that he was no longer joking.

'You are a grown woman. You can do whatever you want.'

20

When Pepper knocked on her mother's front door the following morning, it was with all the confidence of someone who was taking charge of their life, making decisions, being bold, and booking a flight over to Hamburg to see the man they were pretty sure they were falling for as hard and as fast as a bulldozer.

'Hi, Mum,' she said cheerfully. 'No, I won't take my shoes off, because we're going out. Come on.'

'What are you talking about?' her mother replied, rather irritably. 'Go where?'

'Ipswich. I thought we could go shopping, get something to wear at Dad's wedding, maybe have lunch?'

Her mother gaped at her.

'Come on, Mum,' she chivvied. 'It's not as if I've asked you to come and climb to Everest Base Camp with me – it's just the shopping centre.'

'Shopping?' her mum echoed. 'Now?'

'Yes! Why not? You don't have anything else planned for this afternoon, do you?'

The plastic hallway runner creaked as her mother shifted from one slipper to the other.

'No,' she said. 'But I don't think that—'

'That settles it, then.' Pepper started to back away before her mother could come up with an excuse. 'I've left the engine running in the car, so you get your things together while I turn around.'

Giving her mother a beaming smile of encouragement, she skipped back towards the Volvo, proud of herself for being so assertive. For over twenty-three years she had been mostly tiptoeing around her mother, terrified of saying anything that would upset her, but today she felt galvanised – by Finn, but also by herself. Nothing would ever change unless she did something to change it, and that meant she must find the strength to alter her routine and behaviour.

Pepper watched as her mum closed the front door behind her, double locking it and checking three times to make sure it could not be opened. Despite the May sunshine doing a grand job of pushing aside the clouds, she had put a smart camel-coloured trench coat on over her navy slacks and pale grey jumper and was hunched over as if she was cold. Pepper leant forwards and switched on the fan heater.

'I'm not sure we'll find anything worth wearing in Ipswich,' she grumbled, as Pepper manoeuvred the big car out of the cul-de-sac.

'Shall we go to London, then? I can drive us straight to the station and—'

'No. For heaven's sake, Philippa. London? What a thing to say.'

It took all of Pepper's self-control not to laugh out loud, and no matter how much her mother acted as if she had been kidnapped throughout the remainder of the drive, Pepper refused to allow her buoyant mood to be affected. She hoped that eventually, her mother would give in, would laugh at one of Pepper's jokes or ask her how her trip to Lisbon had been. She did neither, however, preferring to stare gloomily out of the window as Pepper prattled on about whatever subject came to mind next.

Her mother's mood did not improve when she saw the queue trailing out of the multi-storey car park, nor when Pepper used her sat nav to hunt for an alternative, only for it to direct them a mile out of the town centre.

'We can walk it?' Pepper said lightly. 'It's a nice day.'

Her mother sighed.

'I just want to get this over with,' she muttered, and Pepper felt her resolve beginning to crack.

In the end, she drove them back to the original car park, and after ten or so minutes of waiting, a space became free and they were in. Her mother said nothing as they ventured towards the central shopping centre and shook her head at the suggestion that they stop for coffee and cake first.

Pepper's resolve cracked further.

'How about this?' she asked, twenty minutes later, holding up what she thought was a chic and feminine floral number.

Her mother pulled the sort of face one would if they had stepped in a cow pat.

'Flowers,' she said disparagingly.

'And?' Pepper said beseechingly. 'Flowers are nice.'

A tut.

'OK, then – how about this?'

She had selected the fluorescent pink jumpsuit with the diamanté straps on purpose to provoke her mother into laughter, but not even this seemed to work. Her mother merely sighed again, as she had been all morning, and folded her arms across her chest.

'If you're not going to take this seriously, Philippa, then why did we come?'

'I was only joking,' Pepper complained. 'You remember what jokes are, don't you? Those things you tell to make people loosen up a bit.'

'Perhaps I just don't find your particular brand of humour funny,' her mother threw back, sounding prim. Turning away, she ran a hand down the silk front of a plain, cream blouse.

'This is more like it,' she said, and Pepper came to stand beside her.

'It's nice,' she agreed cautiously. 'But cream? At a wedding?'

Her mother scowled so ferociously that Pepper held both her hands up and took a step backwards.

'Hey,' she said. 'Don't shoot – I'm only trying to help.'

'This whole thing is ridiculous anyway,' her mother went on, pushing the blouse away.

'What, us going shopping?' Pepper asked.

'No! Well, yes – but I meant the wedding. The whole charade of us being there and pretending everything is hunky bloody dory.'

Pepper stared at her mother. She never swore usually – not even a 'bugger'.

'Don't go, then,' she said, and her mother wheeled around to face her.

'Don't be ridiculous, Philippa.'

'Why is that so ridiculous? If you don't want to go, if you think it will upset you, then stay at home. Lie, if you have to – pretend you're ill. I'll back you up. There's absolutely no point going if it's going to make you miserable.'

Her mother retorted with a flat, irritated noise.

Pepper made herself think of Finn, of seeing him again soon, of his hand in hers as they strolled through the starlit Lisbon streets.

'I'm going to Hamburg next weekend,' she said, to which her mother's mouth actually fell open.

'That's right,' she went on. 'I met a man when I was in Portugal – a German man – and, well, I want to see him again, so I'm going.'

'Portugal?' her mother said, as though she had no idea what Pepper was talking about.

'Yes, Mum – I was there a few days ago. You called me, remember?'

'What about this?' her mother said, striding away and leaving Pepper mid-sentence. She had spotted another blouse, this time in pale blue.

'*I think it's boring,*' Pepper wanted to scream. '*Boring like you, constantly ignoring me, constantly making me feel like I don't count, that I don't matter.*'

Instead she said, 'Blue was Bethan's favourite colour, wasn't it?'

There was a horrible, long silence.

'I remember,' Pepper went on, 'because she was always so jealous of my bucket-and-spade set. I never had a favourite colour, because I liked all of them, but Bethan was obsessed with blue. She asked me once how old she'd have to be before she could dye her hair blue. I called her Smurf after that. I wonder, if she was here now, which dress she would choose. This one?' she said, pulling a lace-panelled slip off a nearby rack. 'Or maybe this?' she added, shoving a denim pinafore under her mother's nose.

'Maybe I'll buy something blue,' she said, not caring now how much her mother's face had fallen, and how much fear she could see in her eyes. 'Then it will be like she's there at the wedding with you, instead of me. That's what you would prefer, isn't it, Mum? That I had died, and Bethan was still here?'

'Stop,' her mum whispered, her hands raised. 'Please stop.'

'Why?' Pepper had broken through her resolve now, the pieces scattered on the floor around her. 'It's the truth. I've always known it, always felt it.'

'Philippa,' her mother's hands were now over her ears and she was shaking her head, her eyelids squeezed together. She was doing what she always did and shutting out the world – shutting out the people she was supposed to love the most. Her misery was palpable, and just as quickly as it had overcome her, Pepper felt her anger ebb away.

'Mum.' Pepper stepped forwards, but her mother shook her head violently.

'I'm sorry,' she said. 'I don't know what came over me. I didn't mean it.'

But it was a lie. She had meant it – she had meant every word.

It took her mother a full minute to lower her hands and open her eyes once again. When she did, Pepper was so ashamed of the pain she saw reflected in them that she backed away, hurrying through the shop until she was standing outside on the pavement, her heart racing as the enormity of what she had just done settled over her.

She had thought herself so smart that morning, had imagined the two of them bonding over dresses and hats, sharing coffee and cake as Pepper told her mother all about Finn. But she had been a fool, she saw that now.

When her mother finally emerged almost fifteen minutes later, she thrust a carrier bag at Pepper before she had a chance to say anything.

'For you,' she said.

Taken completely by surprise, Pepper mumbled a thank you and opened the bag to find a small, square box.

'What is it?'

'Open it,' her mother said, tucking her neat bob behind her ears.

Pepper couldn't work out how they had gone from a horrible argument to this. She almost didn't want to open the box, scared that whatever was inside would bring her awful, needless antagonism to the surface again.

'You really shouldn't have,' she said, but the next words died on her lips as she eased off the lid. Inside was a gold brooch in the shape of an art palette, coloured cut glass set around its edges in blue, green, yellow, orange, red and pink, and two thin brushes laid across its centre.

'Oh my God.' Pepper felt a tide of tears rising. 'It's beautiful.'

'I thought so,' her mother said, shouldering her bag and looking purposefully along the street.

'Now, shall we have that coffee?'

Pepper could only nod. After years of unimaginative birthday and Christmas presents, her mother had brought her a gift that she loved, that was *her*.

It wasn't a 'sorry', a 'thank you', or a promise that things would change.

But it was something.

21

'Pepper!'

Finn made his way across the arrivals lounge of Hamburg Airport and took her in his arms, planting a proper kiss on her before she had time to get a single word out. All Pepper's nerves about the journey, flying alone, and – most of all – seeing him again, evaporated as she melted against him, kissing him back with a fervour that would have made any Richard Curtis fan proud.

'Hello, again,' he murmured when they finally broke away from one another, grinning at the friendly round of applause they were receiving from bemused onlookers.

'Hey.' Pepper beamed back.

'I missed you,' they said in unison, laughing and clinging to each other as Finn led the way towards the train depot.

'It is very early,' he said, yawning through his smile. 'So, I am taking you out for breakfast.'

Pepper gazed up at him, at the ripe-apple hue of his cheeks, his heavy flop of spun-gold hair and his dark-blue eyes. She was barely aware of the scenery flashing past beyond the windows, registering only the odd cluster of parkland and the mink-grey clouds that were scattered liberally across a pale sky.

'No rain today, hopefully,' Finn said, hooking his arm around her shoulders and pulling her gently against his chest. 'I cannot wait to show you my city; it is important to me that you like it.'

He explained that he lived in an area called St Pauli, not far from Freunde, the bar and restaurant he co-owned with his two best friends, Clara and Otto, adding that much of Hamburg's nightlife was concentrated in and around the Reeperbahn – the so-called longest party street in Europe. Pepper's face must have registered her concern, because Finn immediately started laughing.

'I am not planning to take you out to any strip bars,' he assured her. 'We can leave all of that to the stag and hen parties.'

Having never been to Germany before, Pepper was not sure what to expect, but in the end she found herself charmed by Finn's hometown from pretty much the moment they emerged from the underground station. While the buildings they passed were far taller, grander and more imposing than those at home, the attractive little details that she loved so much were the same. Late-spring blooms the colour of jellybeans were packed into window boxes, bold swathes of street art gave new life to exposed brick walls, and everywhere Pepper looked, she saw groups of friends hanging out together. A few were walking their dogs, some rode past on bicycles, while others sat in artful heaps on benches and kerbs with hand-rolled cigarettes and visible tattoos.

Finn seemed to know everyone, and exchanged cheery greetings and waves as they walked, Pepper's trusty wheelie case clattering merrily over the paving stones behind them.

'Are you secretly the Mayor of Hamburg?' she asked.

'Far more famous than that,' he joked. 'Freunde is very popular around here – you will see later.'

Pepper was greeted by people in Aldeburgh all the time, but that was because it was a small town and she favoured an eccentric outfit, not because she was highly rated. On the contrary – she had always felt distinctly average. Finn, by contrast, did not seem to be self-deprecating at all, as far as she could tell, and it was interesting to get a glimpse of the world through his eyes.

'We are here,' Finn announced, as they arrived at the door of a cosy, one-room café with a few fold-up tables propped outside.

'In or out?'

'In,' she decided, gazing through the large open window and taking in a clutter of mismatched wooden furniture, threadbare cushions, framed photographs and bedraggled-looking flowers in vases.

'*Guten Morgen*,' Finn said to the two women behind the counter, then launched into a further stream of German. Pepper, unable to follow a word of what was being said, lingered awkwardly in the open doorway.

'Sit anywhere that you like,' one of the women urged in English. Then, turning back to Finn, '*Essen Sie?*'

'*Ja, bitte*,' Finn replied, accepting two menus and heading to a table beside the window.

'I come here on most days,' he told Pepper, as she stowed her case under her chair. 'Sometimes for my breakfast, other times to do some work with a cup of coffee, that sort of thing.'

'It's nice,' she said, looking around admiringly. 'Oh, wow – what an amazing cat.'

There was a large ginger tom stretched out on one of the café's many cushions.

'*Ja*,' Finn agreed. 'That is König – it means king.'

The cat twitched its ears and flicked its stripy tail.

'It suits him,' she said. 'I think every cat I have ever met has thought of itself as a royal – perhaps we should all be a bit more cat?'

'You are purr-fect already,' he joked, and Pepper groaned in good humour.

'You are cheesy,' she informed him. 'But luckily for you, I am crackers.'

The coffee arrived, thick and creamy and dusted with cinnamon, and after a cursory glance at the breakfast menu, which was fortuitously printed in both German and English, Pepper opted for the intriguing 'egg in a glass'. Finn made no comment, but when their breakfast arrived ten minutes later, hers consisting of two poached eggs in a glass served with nothing but a sprinkling of salt and chopped chives, he found it hilarious.

'This is your first German lesson,' he said. 'We always mean what we say – and we are very literal.'

'And my second?' she asked, jabbing her spoon through the fragile white of her egg and watching the rich, golden yolk ooze out into the glass.

Finn pressed his knee against hers under the table.

'When we have finished here,' he said, 'I will take you home and show you.'

22

In all the many fantasies about Finn that Pepper had indulged in, the single common denominator was an urgent, all-consuming passion – one that she had been sure would take hold the moment the two of them were alone together. But there was something about being in Finn's home that made her come over all shy, and once he had given her a quick tour of his split-level apartment and fetched them both a glass of water, she was not sure what to do next.

She had been brave enough to get herself here, travel to a foreign country for the second time in her life to visit a man she had only met a handful of times, but now she was frozen. In the moment where confidence was most ardently required, it had completely abandoned her. She had no moves, no shimmy, no 'come hither' sexy finger-hooks.

Stealing a glance a Finn, she found that he was looking at her intently, and had to suppress a nervous laugh. He was so playful most of the time, light-hearted, if a little stiff on occasion, but he was never serious, as he was now. Pepper reminded herself that he was a man, and a mature, capable and strong-willed one at that. Of course he would not find sex funny; he was too grown-up for that.

She caught her breath as he came towards her, his movements so swift and decisive that for a moment she almost stepped backwards. Finn did not smile until he was standing right in front of her, and then he slid a finger under her chin, lifting it slowly as he lowered his face, kissing first her lips, then her cheeks, her neck, the soft hollow of her throat. Pepper knew it was corny beyond comprehension to rattle on about a 'connection', but she couldn't find a word that better suited herself and Finn. It was as if he knew her in an intrinsic way, and she him, and it wasn't long before all her worries were forgotten, tossed aside along with their clothes and inhibitions. Pepper let herself go, let herself be taken, and it was bliss to feel so free, so unburdened by anything other than Finn, in this room, in their moment.

Afterwards, he wrapped them both up in his bedsheets and took Pepper from room to room, giving her a more thorough tour of all the paintings, photos and sculptures he had on display. When she saw the portrait she had drawn of him in Lisbon framed and hung up in pride of place in the lounge, Pepper almost buckled with shyness, and Finn was forced to kiss her again to silence her protestations.

Sunshine had broken through the clouds by the time they ventured back outside, and the air felt warm and clean. Finn offered her his hand to hold as they walked along the wide, tree-lined street, and she grasped it with pleasure, happy to be in this bubble with him. She had never been with a man she was so proud to be seen with before, and Pepper found herself relishing the stares that the two of them got as they strolled back past the same groups of people they had passed just a few hours earlier. In Hamburg, nobody knew who she was, or what had happened to her family, to Bethan – and it was a liberating feeling. Pepper was unshackled from the past and felt able to luxuriate, for once, in the present.

The further they ventured, the more she found herself falling for the old city, for its cleanliness and friendliness, its bespoke themed cafés and pretty resting spots.

'It is a shame you missed the cherry blossom,' Finn said, as they passed a churchyard coated in pink petals. 'We celebrate a spring festival in Alsterpark every year, with performances and fireworks – this time Freunde had a pop-up kiosk, and we did very well.'

'And here I was thinking that Germany was all beer and bratwurst.'

'Do not worry,' he countered. 'We have a lot of those as well.'

The atmosphere in Hamburg was different from that of Lisbon – which Pepper had adored for its artistic and romantic soul – but it was no less easy to love. She was enthralled by the metal palm tree structures casting irregular shadows in Park Fiction, and found her eye drawn again and again to the glittering sweep of the Elbe River that lay beyond it. The Portuguese city's winding alleyways had been fun, yet challenging, to navigate, while everything here was laid out in a straightforward way that made exploring on foot a breeze. When they eventually began to tire, Finn took her to StrandPauli, a beach-style bar on the river, where the two of them drank rotund bottles of Astra beer and crunched their bare toes through the sand underfoot.

'Happy?' he asked, and Pepper grinned.

'Very.'

'I am afraid that Hamburg is not as beautiful as Lisbon,' he said, almost apologetically, but Pepper shook her head.

'I was just thinking the opposite,' she said. 'Because it is – just in different ways. Besides, variety is such an important thing. Imagine if every place looked exactly the same, and every person – that would be beyond dull. Then again,' she added. 'If every person looked like you, it would be no bad thing. I think I could get used to that.'

'Oof!' Finn exclaimed. 'But then, how would you know me?'

Pepper poked him with her big toe.

'I would know.'

'*Danke*,' he said then. 'For this weekend – for coming all this way.'

'Oh, well, thanks for letting me. I think it's the first time I've ever invited myself anywhere. It's mad. A few weeks ago, I had never even been on a plane, and now look at me. I don't recognise myself.'

She took a swig of beer to mask her blushes.

'I like this new Pepper,' he said. 'I have thought about you a lot. About the way we met, and then met again for a second time, and a third. This kind of thing does not happen often.'

'True,' she agreed, watching a bead of condensation trickle down the outside of her bottle. She wanted to say that it felt like fate, that she had asked the universe to show her an unequivocal sign that Finn was The One, and it had – but something stopped her.

'I have thought about you a lot, too,' she said instead. 'You are very distracting.'

'Good!' he declared, his standard grin back in place. 'It is funny, because I was not trying to meet anyone. I had decided that I must focus on the website this summer, but then – poof! – there you were. And I could not let you walk away.'

'Although you did – at least at first,' she reminded him. 'We have the rain to thank really.' Pepper drank some more beer and settled herself against the canvas back of the deckchair.

'If it wasn't for all that Lisbon rain, I wouldn't know what egg in a glass is.'

Finn raised his bottle in a toast.

'That,' he said, 'would definitely have been a tragedy.'

Pepper clanked her bottle against his and stretched out her legs. A DJ had set himself up in a booth above the bar, and people were beginning to get up and dance. It was a world away from Aldeburgh, with its cosy tea shops and proper British pubs. What would Finn make of it, she wondered? That was if he ever visited. Pepper liked the idea of spending more time with him, of course she did, but the thought of him in her home-town was oddly troubling. She supposed it was because there were things she had yet to tell him about her life, about those shadowy moments from her past that she was still struggling to come to terms with, even now, so long after Bethan had died. And then there was her art, which she knew Finn admired. How could she explain to a man as confident as he that she simply wasn't good enough – that nothing she did had felt good enough for a very long time?

'Another?' Finn was holding up his empty bottle of Astra, and Pepper realised she must have drifted off for a moment, swept out as she so often was by the rip current of her emotions.

'My turn,' she told him, getting to her feet as gracefully as anyone can be expected to when they're sitting in a deckchair. She had just wriggled her feet back into her shoes when Finn grasped her hand, drawing her down until her nose was level with his and cupping her face in his hands. When he kissed her, Pepper's knees began to tremble, and she had no choice but to collapse into his lap, her eyes closing as his hands moved into her hair. She kissed him back until her breath became ragged, not caring who saw them or what anyone might be thinking.

Pepper had thought she was destined to stand on the shoreline of her own life forever, trapped by the tides of fear and of loss. Now, however, there was a boat on the horizon.

And inside that boat was Finn.

23

Their two beers soon became four, then six, then eight, the last tipping Pepper over into that wobbly stage of drunkenness where everything feels soft-edged and a bit silly. Finn, who was demonstrably less tiddly than she was, kept patting her hand and asking her if she was OK.

'Fine!' she told him, sticking out her tongue, then laughing when he pretended to look shocked.

'Sorry,' she said happily. 'I'm not very ladylike, am I?'

Finn gave her a look that made Pepper feel as if all her clothes had fallen off.

'You are very much a lady,' he assured her. 'A perfect lady.'

His use of the word 'perfect' made her feel slightly uneasy all of a sudden, and she glanced away, concentrating on the dregs in her bottle rather than him.

'You do not like compliments,' he stated.

'No. I mean, I do. I just . . . I guess I struggle to believe them, that's all.'

Finn reached for his beer.

'Why?' he asked, and he sounded genuinely interested. Not fed up with her, or judgemental, simply intrigued.

'Because I'm not perfect,' she said.

'Ah.' Finn narrowed his eyes. Pepper could not tell whether he was confused or amused. Then he said, 'So, tell me – what do you think is wrong with you?'

Was he seriously asking her to list all her faults?

'Er . . .' she began, feeling stupid. 'Well, first of all, I dress like a mad clown most of the time.'

'I love the way you dress,' he said. 'Next.'

'My chin is massive – from the side it looks like a foot.'

Finn bellowed with laughter.

'*Lächerlich!*' he chorused. 'Ridiculous.'

'I am also a really bad dancer,' she added. 'And an even worse singer.'

Finn grinned.

'So?' he said. 'I am the same.'

'But you're good at everything!' she said challengingly.

'*Nein,*' he said gently. 'Nobody can be good at everything.'

'I bet you're a better singer than me,' she continued. 'We should have a sing-off!'

Finn laughed hard at that, but Pepper had begun bouncing up and down on her deckchair.

'Let's do it!' she urged him. 'There must be a karaoke bar somewhere around here?'

'Karaoke?' Finn echoed. He looked unable to believe what he was hearing.

'Yeah! Come on – it'll be fun. Help you loosen up a bit.'

The flicker of something passed across Finn's eyes, but he didn't argue. Instead, he reached for his bottle of beer and downed what was left.

'Come on,' he said, grabbing her hand and pulling them both up. 'I think there is a place on the Reeperbahn.'

It was not yet six p.m., but already Europe's longest party street was pounding with tourists. Pepper knew they weren't locals, because Finn made that particular fact very clear, explaining that everyone he knew gave the area a wide berth – and she could see why. Stag parties of twenty or more trailed past them in matching slogan T-shirts, scantily clad girls handed out drink vouchers, and everywhere Pepper looked there was a flashing neon sign, or a staggering drunk.

'I feel embarrassed to be British,' she muttered dully, but Finn merely shrugged.

'You make up for it,' he told her.

The karaoke bar didn't look like much from the outside. The front window was covered in a dusty plum curtain, and a rather battered sign saying 'Liederhaus' flickered above the door. Finn led the way inside and down a dark set of steps, and Pepper followed, wrinkling her nose at the smell of stale beer. The walls, floor and ceiling were all painted in various shades of red, and bass hummed out from underneath a corridor of closed doors.

Once they had paid for a two-hour session at the reception desk, a bored-looking girl with spiky red hair – to match the décor, Pepper wondered – showed them into a booth. As well as a large flat-screen TV, there was a low table, two microphones and a brown leather settee, onto which Pepper tossed her bag and denim jacket while the girl talked Finn through how to use the touchscreen controls.

'She will be back soon with more beer,' Finn said, as the girl closed the door behind her. 'I hope that is OK?'

Pepper, who was now drunk enough not to worry about how drunk she was becoming, nodded enthusiastically, snatched up one of the microphones, and pirouetted on the spot.

It had been years since she had done anything like this. In fact, when Pepper tried to cast her mind back, she was not sure if she'd done karaoke once since her late teens. Her father's first girlfriend after he moved out had been a big fan, and on the weekends Pepper spent with them, she was invariably dragged along to whichever local pub happened to be running a karaoke night and encouraged to have a go. Not wanting to upset her dad, who was still wobbly then and prone to bursting into tears at the mere mention of her sister, Pepper had obliged, even though she could see people in the audience wincing.

'You can choose.' Finn stood back from the screen, which was now displaying a list of songs by various artists. 'These are the most popular choices,' he explained, breaking off as the girl returned with drinks.

Pepper studied the options, chuckling to herself as she selected 'Private Dancer' by Tina Turner, 'It's Raining Men' by the Weather Girls and 'I Will Survive' by Gloria Gaynor. The thought of Finn singing any of these was enough to make her laugh, but when she turned to hand him a microphone, she saw that he was now looking more apprehensive than anything else. She knew full well that Finn had a playful side – he teased her often enough – but she couldn't deny the fact that he sometimes seemed rather strait-laced, too. They had broken down physical barriers in his apartment earlier that day, but now what she wanted more than anything was for him to kick back and relax a bit more, maybe even laugh at himself.

The opening bars to Tina Turner's sultry hit filled the tiny booth, and Pepper grasped her microphone with both hands, throwing back her hair and staggering forwards and backwards on her tiptoes.

Finn's eyes widened behind his fringe.

'Come on!' she urged, when she had warbled out the first two verses in her best Tina-drawl alone. Finn was making short work of his tall glass of beer, his eyes darting from the words on the screen over to Pepper. When the second chorus chimed in, he finally opened his mouth and began to sing. Very, very badly.

'Hooray!' Pepper cheered, laughing as Finn began to copy her strutting moves. For a man who moved so fluidly and seemed so comfortable in his own skin, Finn had absolutely no coordination when it came to dancing. But it was this ineptitude that made Pepper's heart burst with affection for him.

He was taking himself way out of his comfort zone – for her.

He was making an absolute tit of himself – for her.

In a strange way, being here in this booth with him, singing songs at the top of their lungs while they lurched about like three-legged tortoises, felt even more intimate to Pepper than their earlier lovemaking had. Finn had not been at all vulnerable in that scenario, but here he was unsure of himself, and it made her trust him more, and like him more, to see it.

By the end of the third song, he had got into his stride, and did not bat so much as an eyelash when Pepper selected 'Islands in the Stream' for them to sing as a duet. Never had the lyrics meant so much, or felt so apt, and never had the looks they were exchanging felt so loaded with feeling.

Perhaps love at first sight was a myth after all, wondered Pepper.

Maybe it was love at first song.

24

Night had fallen by the time Pepper and Finn left the karaoke bar and swayed together back through the streets of St Pauli. They were on the way to Freunde, the bar and restaurant Finn co-owned together with his two best friends, Clara and Otto.

'I think maybe I shouldn't drink much more,' she decided, punctuating her words with a comically timed hiccup.

'You can try,' Finn told her, as they arrived at their destination. 'But most of the time, the only question we ask here at Freunde is red or white?'

With a comforting squeeze of Pepper's hand, he bounced them both up the two steps into the wine bar, giving her only a few seconds to take in the vast queue that ran along outside the restaurant next door.

Like all the most exclusive venues, the bar was quite small inside, with two wooden tables and a bench seat built in around a large open window. The walls were white brick, the floor polished oak, and a family of plants were trailing leaves over the edges of a macramé hammock that had been strung up between two brass hooks. A shelf the length of the room groaned under the weight of bottles, and an artful web of fairy lights dangled from the ceiling.

Pepper was busy admiring a collection of potted succulents lined up along the bar when a small, lithe man bounded out from behind it and enveloped Finn in an enthusiastic hug.

'Hallo, hallo,' he exclaimed, letting go of his friend and throwing two skinny arms around Pepper.

'This is Otto,' Finn said.

Releasing a bewildered Pepper, Otto looked at each of them in turn.

'Where have you been hiding, heh, you fuckers? In bed all day, I bet?'

Finn threw up his hands and began berating his friend in German, and soon they were both laughing uproariously and slapping each other on the back.

'This guy,' Otto said, one of his spider-monkey arms draped around Finn's neck. 'He is a good man – the best fucker I know.'

'He is,' Pepper agreed, unable not to laugh at Otto's casual drop of the F-bomb. She was wearing a star-print dress that had felt like a good choice when she put it on in Finn's apartment earlier, but now she wished they had gone back to shower and change. It would have been nice to meet Finn's friends when she was not quite so sticky-skinned – or wearing something that could easily have been fashioned from a pair of clown's underpants.

Otto, however, did not seem to have noticed her dress. He was far too busy ushering them over to one of the tables and commanding that they sit down, before assuring them that he would look after their every need. No sooner had Pepper deposited her bag on the floor and arranged herself on a chair than Otto was back, four bottles in one of his big bony hands and three large wine glasses in the other.

'This one,' he said, brandishing the first of the wines, 'is fucking beautiful. You have to try it.'

'Oh, I really shouldn't, I'm—' Pepper began, but Otto was having none of her excuses.

'Drink,' he instructed, thrusting a glass into her hand.

Pepper bowed her head obediently, sniffing the small measure of white wine before taking a sip.

'That is delicious,' she said. 'So light and sweet.'

'Like me, heh?' Otto's entire body seemed to rock with laughter as he reached for another bottle. His light-brown hair kept slipping over his forehead and covering his eyes, and every time it happened, he flicked his head to one side as if he had a tic. In fact, Pepper thought, as she swilled the next measure around in her glass, Otto never seemed to stop moving, whether he was pouring, fetching bottles, drinking, or telling a story that required him to make a huge number of exaggerated gestures. Pepper could not work out if he was drunk, high, or plugged into the nearest socket.

After he had given them tasters of six different wines from various regions, Otto was distracted by the arrival of a group of young women, and promptly swept off to greet them, kissing each of their cheeks and waving his arms around like a human windmill.

'Wow,' Pepper said to Finn, raising her glass. 'He is . . . Wow.'

'*Ja*,' he agreed. 'Wow is exactly the right word. He has always been like this – the wave machine of a party, the one who will supply the midnight oil and keep it burning until morning. Sometimes, he can seem too much, too exhausting – but,' he added, his eyes following his friend as Otto retreated behind the bar at speed, 'everyone loves him. He is very good for our business, even if he does drink his way through our stock.'

'He does?' Pepper stared at the empty glass Otto had abandoned on their table. 'And that's OK?'

'Of course.' Finn shrugged. 'It is not all that much really, and it helps him to stay energised. It is hard to be an entertainer every single night of the week, but Otto is an expert.'

Pepper was far too sozzled herself now to condemn anyone else's drinking habits.

'So,' she said, her hand seeking out Finn's muscular thigh, 'if Otto runs things in here and Clara is the head chef next door, that means you get to enjoy both?'

Finn tapped the side of his head. '*Ja!* That is because I am the brains.'

'Well, obviously – the brains and the beauty.'

She had meant it as a joke, but Finn didn't disagree with her.

'Do you ever muck in?' she asked him. 'Chop vegetables or collect empty glasses?'

Finn pulled a face. 'Only if I have to, when somebody is ill or something. But I prefer to be behind the scenes.'

Otto skidded to a halt beside them.

'Everything all right here, fuckers?'

Finn put his exasperated head in his hands.

The restaurant next door was full to capacity, so it wasn't until much later that Clara joined them. Pepper's first thought was that she was tall – almost as tall as Finn – with long chestnut curls that she quickly untied and shook out over her shoulders. Despite wearing striped chef's trousers and a stained white apron, she looked as if she'd strolled in right off the end of a catwalk. As soon as she realised who Pepper was, she dragged her stool closer to the table and began chatting away to her as if they'd known each other for years.

'It is great to have someone to practise my English on,' she confided, even though she was clearly as fluent as Finn. 'Sometimes, I think, I choose the wrong word, and the true meaning can turn out to be something crazy.'

'You have nothing to worry about,' Pepper assured her. 'You are pretty much perfect, as far as I can tell.'

'Finn is supposed to teach me,' she said, nudging him with an elbow. 'But he is always away, off doing this or that, travelling around the world while the rest of us are sweating like dogs in this place.'

Otto, who was passing, let out a long howl.

'*Dummkopf!*' Clara shouted at his departing back. Then, leaning in closer to Pepper, 'He is even crazier than a dog.'

'I think he's brilliant,' she said. 'People must love him – look how busy it is.'

The bar was full of people now, as was the street outside. Everyone seemed to know not only each other, but Otto, Clara, and Finn, too. He wasn't exaggerating earlier when he told her how popular Freunde was – it was after two in the morning and the night was showing no sign of winding down. Pepper, who was starting to feel the effects of an early morning flight, followed by sex and multiple hours of exploring, drinking and singing, gave in to a yawn that she had been trying to suppress for ages, and rested her head against Finn's shoulder.

'Your girl needs sleep,' Clara ordered, tossing her curls around like the star of a shampoo commercial. At some point during the course of the past hour, she had swapped her chef's uniform for cropped jeans and a plain white shirt, and had painted her lips fire-engine red. She also chewed gum incessantly, explaining to Pepper that she was trying to quit smoking.

'Every day, I wake up and I feel sick from it,' she said, wrinkling her pretty nose. 'I stand out on the street there every night, talking, drinking, smoking – it is not good for me.'

'Shut up and have a fucking shot, heh?' put in Otto, who had overheard as he scooted past from one of his many trips to the bar. Clara swatted him away like she would a fly, then smiled helplessly at Pepper.

'Now you see what I am up against?'

Finn, who'd had his back turned talking to a couple at the next table, looked round and kissed Pepper lightly on the lips.

'Shall we go home?' he asked, and she nodded, elated at the prospect of more time alone with him. It had been such an enjoyable evening, but she guessed that Clara was probably only chatting to her to be polite – she almost certainly had other people to catch up with.

As they stood to leave, Clara put a hand on her arm.

'Finn told me just now that you went singing?'

Pepper grinned. 'We did.'

'Not once in twenty years have I seen that man sing,' Clara exclaimed. 'And he is very, what is the word? *Entspannt* – relaxed. You are bringing out a side to him that I have never seen.'

Impossibly touched, Pepper gripped Finn's hand a fraction tighter.

'You are good for him,' Clara added with a brisk nod. 'I hope that it is the same for you?'

'Oh, yes, of course,' Pepper assured her, wondering if she had ever been so happy.

Because it was true, wasn't it? It didn't matter if she found herself lacking, because Finn liked her exactly the way she was.

25

The bed was empty when she awoke, but there were traces of Finn everywhere. In the tangled sheets and dented pillow, in the ripe, musky scent of the air and the half-empty bottle of red wine on the wooden floor.

Pepper sat up and rubbed her eyes, tried to run a hand through her hair and found she couldn't. It was a jungle knotted by sex, by exploratory hands that had tugged and stroked. As she recalled the events of the previous night, she felt a shiver go through her and let the covers drop, biting her bottom lip as they brushed against breasts that were sensitive to the touch. She recalled the sensation of Finn's mouth at her throat, on her chest, down across her stomach and lower, his tongue seeking her out, driving her onwards until her eyes were closed, and her head was thrown back.

She jumped as a door opened and shut on the floor below, then pulled up the sheet and clamped it under her arms when she heard feet on the stairs. Finn's tousled blond hair appeared first, followed closely by his smile and two glasses of what sounded a lot like Alka-Seltzer.

'*Hallo, Hübsche*,' he said, flopping down onto the bed.

'Hey.'

Pepper felt coy all of a sudden, embarrassed by the torn condom wrappers littering the floor and the discarded knickers she knew he must have passed on his way across the bedroom.

'You look nice,' he said. 'I like this new hairstyle.'

'Whatever happened to, "Beer then wine, you'll feel fine"?' she groaned, clutching her head with both hands.

'This is the Otto effect,' Finn explained, handing her a glass. 'He has a reputation in Hamburg for breaking people.'

'Well, consider me broken,' she said, forcing herself to down the fizzing liquid, then almost gagging as her stomach lurched in protest.

'First, we should have a reviving shower,' Finn instructed, taking each of her elbows in his hands. 'Then food.'

He took her to a small café called – rather wonderfully, Pepper thought – Pauline, which was tucked away amidst a warren of narrow residential streets. On the opposite side of the road, there was a small grassy area framed by trees, and Pepper watched bleary-eyed as an old man threw a tatty tennis ball for his even-older dog.

Finn, who had gone inside to order, returned to their table with water, apple juice and coffee.

'You need to stay hydrated,' he said.

'How are you not hungover?' she asked, starting on her juice. 'Are you secretly a robot?'

Finn squared his shoulders and stiffened his arms. 'I am a Dalek,' he said, through clenched jaws, and Pepper laughed.

'It's no good,' she told him. 'You still look better than most people, even as a machine.'

'Perhaps, I am a love machine?' he joked, and Pepper groaned.

Their breakfast arrived on three tiers, like an afternoon tea, and Pepper's mouth watered as she took in the plates piled high with an assortment of hams, cheeses, scrambled eggs, salad, pastries and a whole basket of bread.

'To soak up the wine,' Finn said, and beamed at her over the rim of his coffee cup.

Pepper let him do most of the talking while she made her slow way through as much of the food as she could. The morning had begun overcast as before, but the sun leached through as they ate, warming their upturned faces and Pepper's bare toes. Anticipating a day of exploring, she had opted for trainers, but had kicked them off as soon as she sat down. Removing her shoes was a childhood habit that had stuck, and Pepper could remember being endlessly told off by her irritated mother, who was forever tripping over them.

Pepper speared a slice of tomato and turned to Finn.

'Has Otto always been . . .'

'A madman?' Finn guessed.

'I was going to say energetic.'

Finn thought for a moment as he chewed his way through a particularly dense slice of rye bread.

'Mostly, yes,' he said. 'We all used to be that way, to be partying all the time, but then Clara and me, we both grew up – grew tired of it. Otto still likes to play.'

'Is he seeing anyone?' she asked, but Finn shook his head.

'No – he drives them all crazy. His last girlfriend got fed up of waiting for him to come home every night. He is at the bar until five or six every morning, then back at four the next day. He sleeps between, so that does not leave much time for anything else – or anyone else.'

'What about Clara?' Pepper asked. 'She is so beautiful.'

'*Ja*,' Finn agreed. 'But again, she is too busy with the restaurant. We used to joke that we were all married to each other, the three of us and that Freunde is our child.'

'A very popular child,' Pepper pointed out, and he smiled.

'She keeps us busy – too busy for any real children.'

Pepper paused with a rolled slice of ham halfway to her mouth. Lowering her fork, she considered what she could say to that. She and Finn had not discussed babies – it was way too soon and too serious a topic. But by making this statement, was he inviting her to begin a conversation about it? Pepper had made peace with the fact that she would probably not meet anyone soon enough to have children, but that was before Finn had come along.

'Children take up a lot of time,' Finn went on, nodding as if in agreement with himself. 'And with Otto,' he added, 'it is like I already have a child to look after. Clara and I are his mama and papa.'

'Well,' Pepper said, still unsure of quite how to respond. 'He is very lucky to have you both, in that case.'

Finn extracted the last chunk of cheese and offered it to her.

'I am the lucky one,' he said, popping it into her open mouth. 'Because now I have you.'

Leaving the Pauline waitress with clean plates and a huge tip, she and Finn crossed the main road and made their way through an urban market area. Stalls had been set up all along the streets, buskers played music, carts offered everything from ice cream to beer to henna tattoos and everywhere Pepper looked there were happy faces. When Finn pointed out a funfair across the street and suggested a ride on the big wheel, Pepper bulged out her cheeks as if she was going to be sick.

'The hangover is still lurking,' she told him. 'Don't encourage it.'

They meandered along pavements cluttered with people, Pepper stopping every so often to take photos on her phone of the street art while Finn stood to one side, his hands in his pockets and a gratified expression on his face as he watched her.

'I like this,' he said, looping an arm around her shoulder and knitting his fingers together with hers. 'Seeing you falling in love with the city that I love. It makes me happy.'

Pepper felt, as she always did when he touched her, an enormous flood of warmth. She had never met anyone who lived their life so completely in the moment. Finn did not seem to let anything grind him down – not work, not the past, not his tricky relationship with his father. He could toss all those concerns aside and focus on the here and now, which she had never, *ever*, been able to do. The more time she spent with Finn, however, the more she was becoming attuned to his way of thinking, and of seeing the world and his place within it. If she could only learn to compartmentalise as he did, Pepper knew she would be happier.

She carried on taking photos, snapping cartoon cats, pink-and-white polka-dot walls and a spray-painted waterfall scene that dominated one side of a building. As Finn led the way north into the buzzing Karolinenviertel neighbourhood, she spotted her first mosaic of the day on a wall outside a boutique clothing store.

'Hair of the Otto?' Finn suggested when they drew level with a bar that was blasting reggae music into the street, but Pepper shook her head.

'I can't.' She grimaced. 'I daren't risk it.'

'Poor Pepper pot.' He kissed the top of her head. 'Coffee instead?'

She agreed to a peppermint tea, but even that was a struggle to drink. Whatever fizzing nectar Finn had given her in the bedroom that morning was fast wearing off, and as the heat of the day intensified, so did Pepper's nausea. Loath to be boring, however, she battled on, exclaiming with pleasure when Finn suggested they visit the flea market, or *Flohschanze*, as it was known in Hamburg, even though the thought of browsing was making her feel weak.

'I just need to—' she said, crumpling down to sit on the kerb.

'Sorry,' she added, apologising a further three times as Finn crouched beside her.

'I'm being pathetic, I know.'

He watched her suppress a yawn.

'Here,' he said, moving behind her until she could lean back against his chest. 'What are you thinking about?' he asked a moment later, his mouth only inches from her ear.

Pepper shivered at the feel of his breath against her neck.

'That I'm going to miss you when I have to leave tomorrow,' she said.

Finn rubbed the tip of his nose against her bare shoulder.

'Perhaps,' he said, 'you will not have time to miss me.'

'What do you mean?' Pepper half turned so she could see his face.

'I was supposed to have a meeting next week, about the restaurant,' he explained. 'There is talk of opening a second site, but we need some more investment.'

'That sounds . . . exciting?'

'I spoke to Clara last night, asked her if she would go alone, because I want to spend more time with you.'

'I can't stay here until next week, though.' Pepper's face fell. 'I have to work.'

'*Ja*, I know that,' he said, only now giving in to a wicked grin. 'But that does not stop me coming to visit you.'

26

It felt to Pepper as if she had barely arrived in Hamburg before it was time to leave again, but at least she did so knowing exactly when she would next see Finn. There was obviously a very large geographical issue standing in the way of their relationship – if she could yet call it that – but neither Pepper nor Finn had brought it up in conversation yet. The small matter of a five-hundred-mile distance between them seemed like nothing compared to their growing feelings, and Pepper was reluctant to throw obstacles in their path when they were progressing along it so seamlessly.

Moving work commitments around in order to have free time for him had unfortunately not been easy, and she felt guilty for letting people down at the last minute. When she called a local mum to explain that her weekly life drawing class would not be taking place, Pepper received a rather sanctimonious telling-off and, in a fit of desperation to make it up, had agreed to help out at the woman's youngest child's birthday party.

It was always with a certain amount of trepidation that she accepted a booking of this type – not because the kids themselves caused much trouble, even when they were full of enough sugary treats to climb up the walls, run across the ceilings and back down the other side – it was more due to the behaviour of their parents. Over the past three hours, Pepper had experienced a range of complaints, from the hysterical: 'No, no – Sebastian simply mustn't do *anything* involving paint, it's full of harmful toxins', to the ridiculous: 'Jemima must be told that her drawing is the best one, other-wise there'll be a tantrum, and nobody wants to see one of those today, do they?', and the well-meaning yet impractical: 'If Daisy could only use bamboo brushes and vegan glue, that would be great? We're raising her as animal-product-free and eco-aware.'

The gang of six- and seven-year-olds at the party – including Sebastian, Jemima and Daisy – had all been having a lovely time sticking fake flowers, dried pasta and sprigs of tinsel on their paper plates until their mums and dads butted in, and by four p.m., when the cake was being cut and party bags were being dished out, Pepper was about ready to dig herself a big hole in the beach and climb into it.

She took the longer route home, idling on the high street and browsing through the rails at her favourite charity shop, where she found a pretty lemon-yellow dress that could have been brand new, save for a small tear along the zip. It never failed to baffle Pepper how easily people would discard things, rather than going to the trouble of fixing them. It would only take her ten minutes with a needle and thread to close the hole, and she'd have something nice to wear when Finn arrived.

It had been a hectic few days, but she had somehow managed to fit an entire spring, summer, autumn and winter clean of her house around a mosaic course, two evening candle-making classes and today's party. Pepper had been grateful for all the distractions – especially as her mother had been in a listless and disinterested mood when Pepper paid her a visit as usual on Tuesday. Despite knowing that her daughter had been in Hamburg, she did not ask how the trip had gone, or anything at all about Finn. The incident with the brooch felt like it had happened to someone else.

Pepper had been dragging her feet as she made her slow way home but quickened her pace as she saw Josephine leaning against her front gate, hurrying out an apology for having kept her waiting.

'Nonsense, darling.' Josephine followed her to the door. 'It couldn't matter less. I should have rung first to check if you were at home.'

'Tea?'

'Lovely,' Josephine said, following her inside and settling into a squashy armchair in the front room while Pepper headed into the kitchen.

'Earl Grey if you have it, please.'

'I haven't got any biscuits,' Pepper said a few minutes later, elbowing open the door and gingerly putting two full mugs down on the coffee table. 'I'm a terrible host.'

'And I'm a terrible guest,' countered Josephine. 'Not only do I show up unannounced, I also forget to bring any cake. Or any gin, for that matter.'

'Our waistlines will thank us,' Pepper said, then instantly regretted it. Over the past few weeks, her friend seemed to have shrunk before her eyes.

Josephine laughed merrily when Pepper told her about that morning's party, rolling her eyes at the mention of demanding parents.

'I was never like that, of course,' she mused. 'My four practically ran wild growing up – they were like the feral cats that used to come into the garden and do their business in my herb patch.'

'I don't think my mum would have noticed what I was eating, doing or painting with,' Pepper said blithely. 'Even when she was there in the room with me, she felt absent.'

Josephine looked for a moment as though she might pry further, then thought better of it.

'Anyway.' Pepper brightened. 'How are you? How are you feeling?'

'Fine, all fine.' Josephine fiddled with the buttons on her blouse. 'Are you looking forward to our second little jaunt?'

'Of course!' Pepper sat forwards in her seat. 'Barcelona. I still can't believe it. But are you sure that you want me to come? I mean, I don't want to impose and—'

'Oh, do pipe down, darling,' Josephine said. 'You are part of this little adventure of mine now, so I'm afraid there's no wriggling your way out of it.'

Josephine went to cross her legs, only to wince and place her foot back down on the carpet. 'What's the matter? Are you hurt?' Pepper had leapt instinctively to her feet.

'Just a bit of cramp, that's all – perfectly normal for an old crone like me.'

'If that's the case, then why can't you look me in the eye?' Pepper pressed gently. 'There's something you're not telling me.'

Josephine took a deep breath, her hands knotting together in her lap as she stared around at Pepper's living-room walls, at the photos, paintings and large vase of cabbage roses in the window – a gift from a happy customer.

'I went to London this morning,' she began. 'On the train.'

'Right . . .' Pepper had returned to her seat, her mug clasped in both hands.

'I was there to meet with a doctor.'

Josephine fixed Pepper with a look that stilled her.

'A specialist in Parkinson's disease.'

Pepper wanted to stick her fingers in her ears and scream. She tried to speak, but nothing but suffocated air came out. Josephine's mouth was downturned, and her eyes had lost their trademark foxy glint.

'You're not trying to tell me that you—?' Pepper asked, her voice catching in her throat. Josephine struggled for a few moments to remain composed, then she smiled a sad sort of smile.

'I'm afraid so. The little horror has progressed to stage three now, which is dire enough that I will soon have to take up my daughter Georgina's offer and join her over in Australia,' she said. 'Terribly frustrating to be losing my independence, of course, but Georgie is adamant.'

Pepper had lost the ability to speak and mouthed at her friend in horror.

'So, you see why I needed to go on these trips now – and also why I could not risk going alone,' Josephine went on calmly, as if she was discussing a shopping list, not a debilitating illness.

'I manage quite well, most of the time,' she went on. 'But lately it's been . . . Well, I have found it rather more difficult.'

'I . . . I'm so sorry.' Pepper put down her tea, her hands flailing uselessly in the air. 'I don't know what to say. I can't believe it. It's awful.'

And it was. It was all too much to take in – first the story of Josephine's big love affair, and now this devastating diagnosis and the fact that she was going to move away to the other side of the world. So soon after Pepper had found her, too. She felt the weight of everything sitting heavily across her, the panic rising like lava inside her chest.

Illness frightened her, but death terrified her – the thought of losing anyone else she cared about made it feel as if the world had been whipped away from underneath her, as if she was about to plummet to earth without a parachute, with nothing and nobody to stop it. Knowing that her friend was in pain made Pepper want to weep, but she knew she must be stronger than that; she must be as brave as her dear friend was being.

'Do you know,' she said shakily, when Josephine fell silent, 'I have just this moment remembered that I hid a packet of Hobnobs in the microwave for emergencies. Can I interest you in one?'

Josephine managed a smile. 'Attagirl!'

Pepper made it as far as the hallway before the tears came. Running through into the kitchen, she scrubbed them furiously from her cheeks with a tea towel, but she could not stem the incoming tide of dread. She already knew enough to know that there was no cure for Parkinson's disease. Josephine was going to become increasingly frail and there was nothing either of them could do about it.

Josephine would not be drawn on the subject further, except to say her symptoms were being managed by her medical team, so over the next few hours, they chatted about anything and everything else, dipping biscuits into their tea while each did their best to sidestep around the conversation crater Josephine's bombshell had created. They discussed Barcelona, and Josephine

asked after Finn, braying with delight when she heard that he
would be flying in the day after tomorrow.

Pepper made them a simple dinner of vegetarian sausage
stew, served with soft, crusty white rolls that Josephine happily
slathered in butter, declaring the feast 'delectable'. She seemed
more relaxed now that she'd shared her secret, but Pepper was
still reeling. By the time she had walked her friend home and
traipsed slowly back through the muggy Aldeburgh streets, she
felt exhausted, yet wired at the same time, and headed straight
out to the studio.

The idea had come to her in Hamburg, as Finn, his hand in
hers, took her around the city, showing her one impressive landmark after another. He knew so much, and was so passionate in
the way that he spoke, that Pepper had found herself enthralled.
She wanted so much to recreate that feeling now and have
something to show for her time spent there, her time spent with
him. She loved the idea of a mosaic, not made of broken pieces
but of painted tiles, each slotting perfectly into place to make a
whole.

She began by sketching out the striking medieval bell tower
of the Rathaus across five blank tiles, then lay a further eight
down on the table and drew the outline of the Elbphilharmonie
concert hall, complete with its cresting-wave rooftop. In the
courtyard of the Mahnmal St Nikolai church, Finn had shown
her a haunting bronze sculpture that he loved called 'Angel on
Earth', which was of a woman stretching away from hundreds
of grasping hands. Pepper decided that she would recreate it
now, and unthinkingly gave the figure her own features.

As Pepper worked, she thought about Finn, of the way he had
looked at her as they lay tangled together between the sheets, of
how much they had laughed as they strutted around like Tina
Turner, and how proudly he had introduced her to his closest
friends.

For once, she didn't obsess over the little details, choosing
instead to trust her instincts. She stayed there for a long time;
until the light drained from the day and was replaced by a thick

and heavy blackness. Her hands reached for her paints, for more blank tiles, for the volume dial on the stereo.

The only time she paused was when she thought she heard a noise outside in the garden, felt the unmistakable weight of another person's gaze. But when she turned abruptly to look, there was nothing there.

Nothing but the shadows.

27

Pepper broke the surface of the swimming pool with a gasp, her eyes and throat stinging from the chlorine. She was out of breath, panting with effort, but it felt good to move her limbs and get her heart pumping.

She had stayed up until the early hours in her studio the previous night, crouching over the table until her shoulders and back ached, wholly focused on her work. The tiles she had painted were now laid out on the workbench drying, and for the first time in years, Pepper had not destroyed a single one.

When she woke up that morning, she had thought immediately of Josephine, the news of her dear friend's devastating diagnosis and the fact that she would soon be moving away to the other side of the world smashing into her afresh. Those thoughts had followed her here to the pool, chasing her under the surface as she kicked and pulled her way up, and down, and back, and forth. And it was not just Josephine who was with her, but Bethan, too. Her sister had so loved to swim, had so often run fearlessly into the sea, leapt off the diving board from its highest tier.

The fact that the water had been the thing to take her had always felt immeasurably cruel, but Pepper knew it was madness to blame it. Now, when she swam, it was as much for her sister as herself.

Heaving herself up the rickety metal steps five minutes later and wrapping her towel around herself, Pepper stood shivering for a moment on the coarse wet tiles, the sounds of the pool echoing around her. She could see that the smaller children's bathing area was being cleared for a private group, and as she reached the ladies' changing room entrance beside it, she recognised some of the residents and staff members from The Maltings.

Thankfully, however, Samuel did not seem to be among them. She had no real desire to bump into him when she was red-eyed, wet-haired and wearing a swimming costume that had seen better decades.

'Pepper, is that you?'

She froze, hardly daring to turn around.

Samuel had just emerged from the men's changing room clad in nothing but blue shorts, a pair of goggles dangling from a rubber strap around his neck.

'Are you all right?' he asked as he approached.

'Yeah.' Pepper sniffed. 'It's just the chlorine in here – makes my eyes water.'

Samuel folded his arms across his bare chest.

'You sure?'

What was it about people asking if you were OK that always made you want to cry?

Pepper stared down at her bare toes, willing herself not to crack.

'I'm fine,' she mumbled.

'You can tell me if something's troubling you,' he said. 'I know we don't know each other all that well, but I'm a good listener.'

As he said it, he angled his head so that one of his ears ended up about an inch from her face.

'You're a weirdo,' Pepper said loudly, right into it, laughing as he bobbed his head up and down like a nodding dog.

'See – you feel better already, don't you?'

'Much,' Pepper agreed. 'But I still maintain that you're a total weirdo.'

'Takes one to know one.'

'Touché.'

They grinned at each other.

'Bethan would have really loved you,' she said then, surprising herself. The only conversation she and Samuel had ever had about her sister was a brief one the first or second time they'd met. He didn't know the full story of how she'd died, just that she had.

'I wish I'd met her, in that case,' he replied. 'Do you think she might even have gone out with me?'

'Probably.' Pepper tried subtly to rearrange her towel, only for it to slip from her grasp and drop to the floor. Hastily scooping it up, her cheeks burning, she added, 'I seem to remember that Bethan had three boyfriends when she died, and she hadn't even turned eight yet. A serious maneater, that one.'

'My sister's the same,' Samuel said regretfully. 'Me and my two brothers are all useless – Esi puts us to shame.'

'There are four of you?'

He nodded. 'Yep. My poor mum, right? Imagine two more of me.'

'I bet she's very proud of you,' Pepper said, wriggling down into her towel. Her skin was beginning to crinkle up like a crisp packet that had been baked in an oven.

'Do you have any other brothers or sisters?' he asked, and Pepper felt her face fall.

'No. Just me. My parents didn't stay together for very long after Bethan died. It was as if a part of us all went with her – my family was shattered into pieces, and I guess we've never fitted together again since. Not properly.'

'That is sad.' Samuel looked crestfallen. 'And you said your sister was only seven when she died? Do you mind me asking how it happened – was she ill?'

Pepper took a very deep and steadying breath.

'Yes and no,' she said. 'She was born with epilepsy but hadn't shown any signs of it for years – no fits or anything. My parents never used to let her out of their sight, but as the years passed and there were no incidents, they – well, I say they, but I mean we, all of us – started to relax. Then, one evening, she was having a bath before she went to bed and—'

Pepper stopped abruptly as a lump caught in her throat. She could not bring herself to look at Samuel, but she could feel concern radiating off him.

'I was downstairs,' she went on. 'Drawing or something. I had my Walkman on. My dad was at work, and someone came to the door, one of the neighbours. I didn't hear them knocking, and so my mum came down to answer it and got chatting. But in the meantime . . .'

She trailed off with a shudder.

'By the time my mum went back upstairs, Bethan had been under the water too long and—There was nothing anyone could do.'

'Jesus.' Samuel sounded wretched. 'That's horrible. I'm so sorry.'

'I often think what would have happened if I hadn't been drawing,' she whispered. 'If I had answered the door instead of my mum. Would my sister still be alive if I had?'

'Maybe,' he allowed. 'But maybe you simply would have called to your mum and she would have come downstairs anyway. You can't allow yourself to think like that, you know – that's a sure-fire way to drive yourself downhill.'

'I know,' Pepper said dully. 'It hasn't stopped my mother, though. I know she blames herself. Probably blames me, too,' she added, knowing there was no 'probably' about it.

When she finally glanced up at Samuel, she saw that he was frowning, his head on one side.

'You know,' he said, 'I've been around death a fair bit in my life, what with being an almost-famous surgeon and all.' He gave her a flicker of a smile. 'And I found that a lot of the time, beautiful things can happen in the wake of it. Death doesn't have to be a full stop to life.'

'It was for Bethan,' Pepper said shortly, feeling suddenly defensive. 'She doesn't get to carry on with her story.'

'Of course she does,' Samuel said gently. 'She's here with us right now, isn't she? Being part of our story.'

Tears pricked at Pepper's eyes with such insistence that she had to screw up her face.

'Listen, I shouldn't have brought it up,' she hastened. 'Forget I said anything. I should go. I— I'll see you around.'

The look of pity in his eyes as she turned and fled haunted Pepper for the rest of the day.

28

Finn arrived in Suffolk on a scorching day.

It felt to Pepper as if a dripping curtain of humidity had been pulled right across the east coast of England, and despite opening all the windows of her ancient Volvo en route to Stansted Airport, Pepper still felt clammy in her mended yellow dress and hoped the beads of nervous sweat she could feel would not show up on the flimsy fabric.

She needn't have worried. As soon as Finn spotted her through the throng of people milling around in the arrivals lounge, he strode across and swept her right up into his arms, just as he had done in Hamburg, pulling loose her ponytail before kissing her until she laughingly demanded to be put down.

Back in Aldeburgh, he took his time exploring her cottage, picking up ornaments and examining photographs as he went.

'You were very cute as a little girl,' he told her, pointing to the image of a five-year-old Pepper on the beach, a grin on her face almost as large as the lump of seaweed she was proudly holding up for the camera. 'And you are very sexy as a grown-up one.'

A blushing Pepper clanked around making real lemonade in the kitchen, while Finn ventured out into the back garden, crouching down to smell her flowers and peering through the windows of her studio. When Pepper tossed the keys towards him along the path, he let himself in and opened every drawer and cupboard that wasn't locked, extracting coloured beads, splintered shards of mosaic tile and brushes of every size, shape and function.

'This place is an artist's treasure trove,' he said with enthusiasm. 'I feel like the hobbit Bilbo Baggins when he finds the cave of Smaug.'

'I hope you're not comparing me to a dragon,' she exclaimed, and Finn shook his head.

'No. But you are just as hot.'

He was even more delighted when he spotted the red pepper mosaic he had made her in Lisbon framed and hung on the studio wall, but when he asked ultra-casually if she had done any more of her own work recently, Pepper shook her head. She did not feel ready to show him the tiles she had painted yet.

It was such glorious weather that she suggested they set up a table and chairs outside.

'I haven't actually got a barbecue,' she told him regretfully. 'But I do have veggie burgers in the freezer?'

'Will they go with champagne?' he asked, brandishing a bottle as Pepper slid a tray under the grill. 'I brought some – it is a gift to you from Freunde.'

Pepper did a little shimmy and adopted a sultry French accent as she said, '*Ah oui, monsieur*, with these fizzy bubbles you are really spoiling us.'

'Ooh la la,' he replied, with rather less poetic flair, making Pepper laugh as he attempted to ease the cork out with his teeth.

'Careful you don't take your eye out!' she said in mild alarm, then squeaked as Finn put down the bottle and pulled her into his arms.

'What about the champagne?' she asked, wriggling half-heartedly. 'Don't you want any?'

Finn buried his head in her neck.

'There is only one thing in here that I want.'

Pepper's clothes were halfway over her head when they were interrupted by a knocking at the front door.

Yanking down her frock and giggling like a giddy hyena, she hurried along the hallway to answer it.

'He-llo-oo— Oh! Hello, Samuel.'

Pepper faltered as she took in the slightly apologetic expression on his face, and the limp bunch of tulips in his hand.

'For you,' he said, offering her the flowers. 'I felt like I said the wrong thing at the pool yesterday, offended you or something, and I just wanted to say sorry.'

He grimaced.

'It's not the first time this massive gob of mine has got me into trouble.'

'You didn't. I mean, I wasn't.' Pepper took the tulips and brought them up to her nose for a sniff.

'Thank you. They're lovely. But really, there was no need. I was just feeling morose. It catches up with me occasionally.'

She pulled up the strap of her yellow dress. It had been slipping down over her bare shoulder all day, and now she wished she'd worn a bra underneath.

Samuel put his hands into his pockets and rocked backwards on his trainers. 'My pleasure. Oh, and sorry for just turning up here out of the blue, too. Jilly Howarth had your address on file, and I was going to do the whole Interflora thing, but then I thought the personal touch would be better, but what I should have done was call first – or message. I hope you don't think I'm weird.'

'You know I absolutely do . . .' she replied. 'Not.'

Samuel smiled properly for the first time since she had opened the door. Then, inclining his head to the side, 'Are those burgers I can smell?'

'Oh bugger!' Pepper took a step backwards. 'They're probably burning – hang on. Come in, come in, I'll just be a sec.'

She left him in the hallway and ran back to the kitchen, where she was greeted by a large black cloud and the scream of her smoke alarm.

'Oops!' she cried, donning her oven gloves and trying not to choke as she retrieved the tray of very burnt veggie patties.

'Everything all right in here?'

Samuel had followed her in and was using his arm to windmill a path to her through the smoke. She noticed that the back door was propped open – Finn must have gone back out to the studio. He would have heard the shrill beeping if not.

'Can you pass me that broom?' she asked Samuel. 'It should be in the corner over there – that's right, behind that saucepan stand.'

He located it and passed it over, and Pepper paused to rub the moisture from her eyes. She knew the smoke alarm was on the ceiling just inside the door, but she couldn't make out exactly where. She had just jabbed the broom handle up to where she thought the button might be, when something small, dark and furry flew out of the corner and hit her square in the face.

'Aaaaargh!' she screamed, dropping the broom and running blindly towards the back door.

'Pepper!'

Finn had run along the garden path and caught her in his arms.

'What is it?' he asked aghast. 'What is going on?'

As he glanced over her shoulder towards the kitchen, Pepper felt him stiffen.

'There is a fire?'

Pepper didn't answer him, she was still too busy bashing away at her own face and hair.

'Something flew out at me!' she cried, shuddering as she remembered the cold scratch of claws against her cheek.

Samuel had now emerged like a magician through the smoke, and Pepper saw him and Finn give each other a curious once-over.

'Did you see where it went?' Pepper asked him, stepping away from Finn and going back towards the house. 'Is it still in there?'

'I dunno what you're on about,' Samuel said with a shrug. He looked amused by the strange turn of events, but for once, Finn was not smiling.

Back in the kitchen, the smoke was beginning to clear, but the alarm had reached a deafening pitch.

'Oh, shut up!' yelled Pepper, picking up the broom from the floor and hurling it towards the ceiling. She had aimed right, but instead of connecting with the off switch, the wooden handle smashed through the casing. Plastic pieces rained down, but the ringing continued its shrill screech. If anything, thought Pepper in mounting exasperation, all she'd actually done was anger it.

Retrieving the broom for another try, she noticed something attached to one end of it.

Screaming for the second time, Pepper lobbed the offending brush across the room, where it connected with Samuel's head.

'Ow!' he cried, then, 'WHOA!' as the bat abandoned the broom and flapped past an inch from his nose.

'We must all stay calm,' ordered Finn, who was rolling up his sleeves. Grabbing a tea towel from beside the sink, he swung it through the air, only to swear when the bat fluttered away out of reach.

'Mate, we got this,' said Samuel, pulling Pepper's apron off the hook on the back of the pantry door and leaping about a foot in the air.

Pepper stood with her back against the wall and watched them. With every missed swipe and wasted jump, Finn was growing more frustrated. It was clear both men wanted to be the one who rescued the little intruder, but so far the bat was doing a sterling job of evading capture. Finn was definitely the more agile of the two, but Samuel had the edge when it came to height and, by choosing the apron, he also had a far bigger net at his disposal.

'Shouldn't we just open the windows and leave it alone?' suggested Pepper. She was beginning to feel sorry for the Houdini bat, and it was also becoming increasingly difficult not to laugh.

Finn was bright red in the face now, while Samuel had somehow managed to rip two of the buttons off his shirt. What had begun as the two competing against each other had soon merged into them against the bat – and there was a very clear winner emerging.

'Stop moving, you asshole!' Finn growled through gritted teeth.

'Bollocks!' Samuel fell sideways against Pepper's kitchen table. 'I almost had him then.'

'We must corner him,' Finn instructed. 'I will go long, you stay midfield.'

Oh God, thought Pepper, giving in to helpless laughter, they had moved on to football lingo now.

There was an almighty crash as Finn whipped his tea towel through the air and took out a jam jar of coloured sand on the windowsill.

'Hey.' Pepper took a step forward. 'Be careful!'

Finn barely turned.

'Sorry,' he said. 'I will buy you a new one.'

'That is hardly the point,' she protested, then ducked as Samuel came flying across the room towards her, both arms raised and the apron billowing out behind him like a cape.

'Watch out!' he yelled, but the warning came too late for Finn. There was a crunch, followed by a grunt, and both men went tumbling to the floor.

'Oopsy,' giggled Pepper.

'*Scheisse!*' moaned Finn.

'My nuts,' muttered Samuel.

The bat, meanwhile, snuck out from its hiding place inside the lampshade and fluttered serenely away into the night.

29

'I can't remember the last time I did this.'

Finn paused in his application of sun lotion, one outstretched leg smeared white.

'Did what – ate ice cream?'

Pepper looked down at the scoops of salted caramel and Belgian chocolate that were beginning to melt and run down the sides of her cone.

'Yes – but also just sat on the beach, on a blanket, with a man,' she said. 'It's nice – I should really try to do it more often.'

Finn smiled at her, his hands returning to their task.

'You are lucky,' he said. 'To have this beach so close to your home. In Hamburg we have the river, as you know, but it is not the same as this. There is something very special about the sea; the feeling you get when you stand – or sit – and look out at it.'

Pepper bit into her wafer and a shoal of crumbs cascaded down the front of her swimsuit.

'Leave them,' said Finn slyly, as she attempted to fish them out. 'Something for me to nibble on later.'

Samuel had stayed long enough for the three of them to finish the bottle of champagne the previous evening, after which she and Finn had called for takeaway and sat together under a blanket on her sofa, feeding each other duck pancakes and prawn crackers dipped in sweet chilli sauce. Eventually, it got so late that Finn had fallen asleep, his long limbs dangling off her settee at all angles and his blond hair tossed artfully against the cushion. Loath to wake him, Pepper had crept around clearing up, stacking empty bottles in the recycling bag and using a dustpan and brush to sweep all the remnants of her broken jar into the bin. The tea towel that Finn had commandeered to catch the bat had ended up filled with ice for the lump on his head – a souvenir from his mid-air slam dunk with Samuel.

Once everything was washed, dried and put away, she had gone back into the front room and lowered herself down onto the carpet until she was sitting cross-legged beside him, allowing herself a few precious moments to take in the light stubble that was just starting to re-emerge across his jaw, the shadows his lashes cast across his cheeks and the soft fullness of his lower lip. The need to kiss him had burnt through her, the compulsion to touch him too strong to ignore. Leaning forwards, Pepper had pressed her own lips hesitantly against his own.

Finn didn't open his eyes; he simply gave in to a sleepy half-smile and pulled her against him, hoisting her up onto the sofa until she was lying across him. Wrapping his arms tightly around her, he had drawn her close until her body slotted in around his.

'Hallo,' he murmured, and when he kissed her, Pepper had felt all her recent anxiety drain away. Finn was her spoonful of medicine, her remedy to the trials she faced – being with him made her feel protected from the world, and from herself, too.

'You're right,' she agreed now, stroking her big toe along the underside of his foot. 'I don't know how people cope living in big cities. It must feel so claustrophobic. At least with the sea stretched out in front of you, it feels as if there's a way out.'

'That is very important to me,' he replied, his expression more serious now. 'I think that moving around so much when I was growing up has made me a nomad – the thing that scares me the most is being trapped somewhere, unable to come and go as I please.'

'You can come and go here as much as you please,' she assured him.

'*Danke.*' He put a hand over hers. 'I am happy to hear that.'

Pepper had spent most of the morning and early afternoon showing Finn around her home town, starting with a walk along the shingle beach to Thorpeness, where he had stared up in awe at the House in the Clouds, followed by a wander past the 16th-century moot hall and lunch at Aldeburgh's famous fish and chip shop. He'd had something appreciative to say about it all, from the rusted edges of the famous Britten Shell sculpture on the beach to the cluttered storefronts along the high street, and had made Pepper stop endlessly so he could take photos of the pastel-coloured houses, charmed as visitors so often were by the names displayed on decorative plaques beside front doors. Was Sun Trap Cottage the best place to catch a tan, he wanted to know? And did a family of anglers reside at the Bait Station?

Finn was also enchanted by Aldeburgh's many gift shops and art galleries and helped himself to a number of business cards belonging to local artists whose work he was keen to sell through his website. It was coming along very well, he told Pepper. All he needed now was the right collection to launch it – a showstopper of a piece. Something that would blow people's minds and put his website firmly on the map. When she asked him what kind of thing he was looking for, however, Finn had simply shrugged helplessly.

'When I see it, I will know.'

'I'm glad you like my hometown,' Pepper told him now, selecting a sun-warmed pebble from between Finn's feet and balancing it on her knee. 'I was worried you might find it too twee.'

'Twee?' He looked confused, and Pepper grinned.

'You're so fluent, I forget that English is not your first language,' she said. 'Twee means too quaint and cute – excessively pretty.'

'That is why it is the perfect home for you,' he said, not missing a beat.

'Oh, stop!' She laughed, but Finn didn't join in. He was looking at her thoughtfully.

'Remind me again,' he prompted. 'How do you and Sam know each other?'

'Samuel? Oh, he works at one of the residential homes where I volunteer, looking after kids and young adults with severe brain damage.'

'Because of your sister?' he asked. 'Was she sick like that before she died?'

Pepper did not want to talk about Bethan today. Finn was supposed to be the happy part of her life, the person who enabled her to put thoughts of her late sister to one side for a few hours.

'She had epilepsy, and it was a fit that caused her accident,' Pepper muttered, her words tumbling out one on top of the other.

'This is difficult for you to talk about.'

Finn shifted closer to her on the blanket. The beach was busy with families, groups of friends and waddling toddlers with buckets full of shells in their pudgy hands – Pepper felt as if every single pair of eyes was on her, pitying her.

There's that weird loner who teaches art. The one with the dead sister.

Finn didn't say anything for a few minutes, just pressed his bare leg against her own – a gesture of solidarity that almost broke through Pepper's resolve not to cry.

'You miss her still?' he asked. 'You feel like it is unfair that she died, and you survived?'

'Yes.' Pepper nodded. 'I do.'

Finn ducked as a football appeared from nowhere, narrowing missing his head.

'First a bat and now a ball – everything is out to get me in this place!' he exclaimed.

Pepper saw that his smile was back in place and felt her whole body sag with relief.

'Come on,' she said, clambering to her feet and reaching for his hand. 'It's high time you found out just how cold the North Sea can be.'

Wincing as the sharp edges of pebbles dug into their bare feet, they wobbled down to the shoreline, both gasping as a freezing wave splashed up over their legs.

'*Scheisse!*' swore Finn. Letting go of Pepper's hand, he dived forwards under the water.

'Nooo!' Pepper shook her head when he re-emerged and beckoned for her to join him.

'It is not all that cold once you get in,' he promised, through teeth that were definitely chattering.

'I'm perfectly fine where I am, thank you,' she said, but before she could retreat to dry ground, Finn stood and started pulling at her arm until she half staggered, half fell into the sea.

Pepper laughed as she swam after him, her flailing arms bashing water into his face until he gripped her wrists, lifting her up with ease until her legs were wrapped around his waist. Conscious of the children paddling only a few feet away, she wriggled clear, swimming further out until there was a decent distance between themselves and prying eyes.

'It's bloody freezing!' she wailed, squeezing icy water out of her hair.

Finn slid his hands across her bottom.

'Are you getting warmer now?' he asked, and Pepper felt herself stir. She and Finn had made love on her sofa the previous night, and then again in her bed that morning, each of them driven by the same uncomplicated longing that was coursing its way through her now.

'I want to tell you something,' he said.

'Um, I think I can guess what . . .'

'Oh.' Finn glanced down at his shorts. 'No, not that.'

'It's actually very impressive,' she observed. 'In water this cold.'

Finn smiled but didn't laugh.

'I have been thinking about perhaps taking a break soon,' he told her. 'From Freunde.'

'You have?'

Pepper pushed Finn's wet hair off his forehead. Her own she had bundled up into an untidy knot, but strands of it had escaped and were stuck like seaweed to her cheeks and throat.

'I want to focus on my website for a while,' he went on. 'Get it ready to launch in the springtime.'

'Good idea,' she said, wondering where he was going with this.

'So, I also thought,' he added, his hands closing around her waist. 'That perhaps I could work here?'

'In England?' Pepper was startled. 'What – you mean here? In Aldeburgh?'

'At the moment, I think it makes more sense to call it Cold-Brrrr,' he replied, lifting his arm out of the water to show her his goose bumps. 'But yes – here.'

Pepper opened her mouth, then closed it again.

'I know it is still the very beginning for us,' he went on. 'But I feel—' He stopped, taking a breath. 'No, *I know*. I know that I want to be with you – to try and make things work between us. I do not like being away from you, and today I realised that perhaps I do not have to be. Clara and Otto will be fine for a few months without me. I can move here while I finish the website, then after that we can see.'

'And you would want to stay with me, in my little house?' Pepper asked, even though she knew that must be exactly what he was planning. She felt all at once equal parts terrified and exhilarated at the prospect, at his confidence in their connection and his desire to be a permanent fixture in her life. It was happening so fast, maybe even too fast. But then again, hadn't meeting Finn been the best thing that had happened to her for years? Wasn't it true that she had wanted to be swept off her feet by a man who was both capable and romantic her entire life?

'Of course, this can only happen if it is what you want,' he added. 'If you get fed up of the sight of me, I promise to go.'

'No, no!' Pepper hushed him with a kiss. 'I could never get fed up of you.'

'*Danke*,' he said, his smile now every bit as wide as it had been that first day in Lisbon.

'I mean it, what I said before,' he told her, gathering her against him until Pepper could knit her feet together in the small of his back. 'About wanting to be with you.'

'You are a smitten kitten,' she teased, blinking as small waves splashed up and over them.

'The fact is,' he murmured, cupping her face in his hands. 'I am falling in love with you.'

30

Finn's declaration of love lifted Pepper up so high that for days after he flew home to Hamburg, she still felt as if she were floating.

Love. Finn was falling *in love* with her.

She had faltered when he said it, her words falling out in a tumble as she tried to make sense of what was happening. She felt as if she'd been yanked up into a jet stream of feeling and had no choice but to let herself be swept away by the moment. She knew that it was all happening fast, just as she knew that it was all utterly bananas, but she also knew that she had never felt this way about anyone before, and never been made to feel this full by someone else. Pepper was fit to bursting with unbridled joy, with possibility, with generosity – she wanted everyone in the world to feel as she did, to be loved and to love.

Because she did love Finn. She knew she did. This was exactly what love was supposed to feel like. It was what she had been holding out for her whole life.

Any fears that she may have had about Finn living too far away for their relationship to stand a chance had been allayed. He liked her enough to move countries. He was so confident that what they shared was the real thing, that he was willing to uproot his entire life to be with her, to make a go of it, to not give up but give it everything he could.

The more Pepper thought about it, the more astounded she felt. But she also felt bigger and bolder somehow, as if his unwavering belief in her, and in them, had been exactly the boost she needed to toss aside her lingering self-doubt. Not only did she stand taller and walk prouder, she also painted feverishly. With the Hamburg landmarks complete, she began on Lisbon, recreating a dripping wet orange tree with figures side by side under its branches, a molten sunset set off by darkened rooftops, trailing petals, tiny azulejos, jaunty trams and winding cobbled streets draped in tiny lights.

Every image she created reminded her of a moment – a lingering look or a tentative touch, a kiss stolen beneath the stars or a breath caught up in a web of emotion – and as she conjured up each one, barely pausing to lower one brush before picking up the next, Pepper finally understood the lesson she had failed to learn all those years ago: that art, real art, made you feel.

With only a matter of days left until she and Josephine would fly to Barcelona, Pepper packed her teaching schedule full, even venturing into London one afternoon to host a team-building session at a corporate office in Canary Wharf. Rediscovering her own passion for art helped to energise her, and she knew she was doing her job better as a result. More people than ever were asking for details of her classes, calling to see if she could squeeze them into candle-making, collaging or life drawing. Her little studio had never seemed so busy, and Pepper felt proud – prouder than she had ever allowed herself in the past.

Each evening, she and Finn would FaceTime each other from under the covers of their respective beds, sharing stories of their day and making plans for what they would do once he came to live in Aldeburgh. Pepper had already made space for his clothes, cleared a shelf in her bathroom cabinet and created an area in her front room where he would be able to set up his laptop. The house was ready, she was ready – now all she needed was him.

It was now the evening before her flight to Barcelona, and Pepper was on her way to meet her father and his wife-to-be at a local pub for dinner. When her dad had called earlier that day to invite her, Pepper had been surprised. Although she spoke to her dad fairly regularly, she didn't go to Kent to see him very often and had never met the woman who would soon be her stepmother. He had promised that it would be 'low-key', then threw her slightly by adding that he was keen for the two of them to 'bond' before the wedding.

Now that Finn was moving to Suffolk almost as soon as she and Josephine returned from their trip, Pepper felt more able to face the upcoming nuptials – not least because she would now have a proper boyfriend to take along as her plus-one. There was also a small part of her that still longed to spend time with her dad, whom she had been so close to as a child. That man, the one who'd let her ride up on his shoulders, who'd take her and Bethan rock-pooling, played football with them and read them bedtime stories at night, felt at times like an apparition – one that Pepper had dreamt up in her head.

Arriving at the bistro pub a few minutes early, Pepper was shocked to find her mother already seated at the table.

'Mum, you're here.'

'So I am.' Her mother was giving nothing away. Like Pepper, she had made an effort with her appearance, and was wearing a pale gold shift dress, her hair neatly blow-dried.

'You look nice,' she said, hanging her denim jacket on the back of a chair before sitting down.

Her mother blinked absently as if she hadn't heard.

'Is that a dress?' she asked.

'A jumpsuit.' Pepper tried a smile. 'Flattering on the bum, but a real pain when it comes to having a wee with any sort of ease.'

'I see.'

In an effort to keep the conversation flowing, Pepper asked what she had been up to since she last saw her a few days ago, being careful to make sympathetic noises when her mother bemoaned the builders that had been putting in a new kitchen next-door, and exclaiming in delight when she admitted that she'd won ten pounds at the Bingo.

'I didn't know you even went!'

'And you?' her mother eventually enquired. 'Anything I should know?'

She had always phrased it that way, as opposed to asking Pepper if there was anything she actually wanted to tell her. Just as it had when she was a teenager, the question rankled.

'Oh, you know me – all work, work, work.'

She had tried to tell her mum about Finn twice now, but each time she seemed to get nowhere. She couldn't tell if her mother simply didn't care, or if her words had not penetrated. There would be no choice soon, though – she would have to acknowledge his existence once he was living down the road.

Her mother looked tired as she reached for her sparkling water.

'Is it tomorrow you go away on holiday? Benidorm, was it?'

'Barcelona,' Pepper corrected. 'Should be fun – lots of art to see.'

'Right.' Her mother unrolled her napkin and lay it across her lap.

'Did Dad tell you this dinner was a chance for you and Keira to bond, too?' Pepper asked, grasping onto the one thing she hoped would, in fact, unite the two of them. But her mother had stopped listening. Her attention had been diverted by a waitress dropping a tray of empty glasses, and after a moment, she lowered her head and rested it on her hands.

'And you're still happy to go to the wedding?' Pepper went on.

Her mother nodded faintly.

'I, er. I have someone I want to bring – a guest.'

'Oh?' Her mother looked up at that, her gaze suddenly so focused that Pepper was taken aback. For a moment or two, she said nothing, merely fiddled with her fork.

'Well?' her mother went on, and Pepper couldn't tell whether she was angry or simply interested. 'Are you going to tell me who?'

Pepper went to reply but was interrupted by the arrival of her dad. Martin Taylor was slim and pale with the dishevelled grey hair and crinkled blue suit of someone who had been blown in sideways by a gale. In contrast, his fiancée, Keira, looked immaculate in a dove-grey clinging dress, ivy-coloured pashmina and a pair of scarily high black patent stilettos. Having never met her before, Pepper was gratified when Keira offered her a shy smile of greeting. The two of them must be about the same age, she thought numbly, accepting a brittle hug from her father.

'Sorry we're late,' Keira said, as Martin sat down beside his former wife. 'The sat nav went absolutely doolally and kept shouting at us that we were going the wrong way. It was all, "perform a U-turn" here and "you are going the wrong way down the street" there. I'm amazed we made it at all, to be honest with you.'

'That's OK.' Pepper passed her a menu. 'It's nice to finally meet you.'

'Ditto.' Keira glanced across at Martin. 'I thought it would be nice to get together before the big day. I mean, it won't be long now before we're all family.'

Pepper's mother cleared her throat, her expression thunderous.

'Wine?' blurted her dad, reaching for the list and hiding behind it. 'There's a nice Riesling here, if anyone fancies that?'

'Riesling is German, right?' Pepper checked, and he nodded. 'In that case, yes please.'

'We had a lovely bottle of that at that fish restaurant in Berlin, didn't we, Mart?' Keira was twiddling a dark-brown curl around her finger.

'Your dad took me there for our first mini break,' she confided to Pepper. 'I'd never thought much about Germany before then, if I'm honest, but it was great. So much to see and all that history.'

'I just got back from Hamburg,' Pepper said. 'I loved it.'

'What were you doing there?' demanded her mother, who seemed to have been switched off sleep mode for once. 'I thought it was Lisbon that you went to, Philippa?'

'It was,' said Pepper patiently. 'I went to both, remember?'

Her mother took a sip of water and coughed.

'City breaks are all the rage these days, aren't they?' Keira continued. She seemed blissfully unaware of any tension, but Pepper could almost feel the sharp tips of her mother's eye-daggers as she pointed them across the table. 'It's so easy to pop off for a sneaky little weekend away.'

'Is that what the two of you did when you started your affair?' her mother asked politely.

'Mum!'

Pepper looked across at her father, who had turned a violent shade of crimson.

'It's all right,' Keira reassured her. 'This can't be easy for you,' she said kindly. 'Either of you,' she went on, turning towards Pepper.

'It's fine.' Pepper glared at her parents. 'I'm sure she didn't mean to be rude, did you, Mum?'

Her mother said nothing, she merely fixed Pepper with a withering stare.

There was an awkward pause.

'I think I'll just find out where that waitress has got to,' muttered Keira, dropping her napkin on the table as she tottered away.

'You promised to be civil,' Martin hissed at his ex-wife. 'Keira is trying her best. You could at least meet her in the middle.'

'I shouldn't like to meet her anywhere,' Pepper's mother said rudely. 'I'm only here to support Philippa.'

'Come on, Mum.' Pepper was almost pleading. 'There's no need to start a row. We're all grown-ups here.'

She distinctly heard her mother tut in reply.

'Just spit it out,' she said wearily. 'Whatever it is you want to say, get it out now before Keira gets back.'

'I wish you wouldn't do that,' her mother replied.

'Do what?'

Pepper's father picked up his wine glass only to realise it had yet to be filled.

'Talk to me as if you're the parent and I'm the child.'

Feeling wounded, Pepper recoiled in her seat. There were so many words fighting to get out, so much injustice in what her mother was saying.

'Maybe I am guilty of that,' she said coldly. 'But only because I've had no choice. Someone had to look after you, didn't they? Someone had to step up after Bethan died.'

'Don't you dare say her name,' her mother said, in a hissing sort of whisper.

'Why not?' Pepper retorted. 'She was my sister.'

'And *my* daughter.'

'Please,' said Pepper's father, sounding drained. 'Let's not do this. Not tonight. This is supposed to be a happy evening. I had hoped we could focus on the future for once.'

'Tch!' her mother spat. 'That is typical of you, Martin – running away from anything remotely difficult, trying to pretend that the past never happened.'

'How could I pretend?' he exclaimed. 'When you would never let me forget, even for one sodding moment? Bethie was my daughter, too – you have never made allowances for that. I'm sorry for what happened, we all are, but it was an accident. We should be able to carry on with our lives and be happy. It doesn't mean we love her any less.'

'An accident,' her mother echoed bitterly, shaking her head.

Pepper looked at her father. He looked as if he had aged five years in the past five minutes, and her heart went out to him, out to all of them, for all their sorrow, for all they had been through and were still going through. She knew her mother was in pain, but she wished that she would just try – it was time she forgave herself for still being here, for being alive.

'I'm sorry, Trin,' said her dad. 'It was a silly, stupid accident – a tragedy. But it was nobody's fault.'

'That's the thing, though, Dad.' Pepper got slowly to her feet. 'Mum thinks it is someone's fault – my fault.'

'No, darling.' Her father was shaking his head now, as if trying to rid his mind of her words. Pepper braved a look at her mother and found her ashen, her face pinched with misery.

'I'm going to go,' she said. 'I'm sorry. I need to go. I can't, I just can't.'

Fumbling for her jacket and bag, Pepper stumbled blindly towards the door and pushed it open, hurrying towards her car. She felt numb, as if her blood had ceased to move, her heart squeezed to a standstill by the same tight fist that seemed to have wrapped itself around her throat.

'Wait!'

It was Keira, breathless having run across the pub car park in her high heels.

'Don't go, please.'

Pepper hung her head.

'I think I have to,' she said. 'It's not you – it's my mum. I find it— It's too difficult. If I stay, I'll only upset her more. I never seem to know the right thing to say, you know?'

Keira took a timid step closer.

'Marty told me,' she said. 'About your sister. That must have been so hard.'

Pepper sighed.

'You can't change the past, unfortunately,' Keira went on. 'You probably think of me as some young bimbo, but I have seen a lot, and been through a lot. My family have their own fair share of skeletons, and there's plenty in the past that could wreck us, if we let it. But we don't, because we're a family – and families pull together.'

'Mine doesn't seem able to,' Pepper said helplessly. 'We scatter and hide.'

'It might seem that way,' she said. 'But you all came here tonight, didn't you? That must mean something. Even if you're bickering, at least you're all doing it in the same room.'

Pepper was too overwrought to take in what she was saying, too tired of being stuck on a wheel that never seemed to stop circling, churning up the same dirt over and over.

'I guess I'm just tired of nothing ever changing,' she said, fighting back the tears. 'I'm so tired of it.'

Keira deliberated for a second, then opened her arms and enveloped Pepper in a hug.

'What's this for?' she muttered, her arms dangling down by her sides.

Keira sighed, her arms tight around Pepper.

'Because you look like you need it,' she said.

31

Less than sixteen hours after she had walked out on dinner with her parents, Pepper arrived in Barcelona.

She had barely managed to sleep, and when she picked Josephine up in a taxi with the swollen eyes of someone who has clearly been crying, her friend had known at once that something was wrong and did her best to coax the truth out of Pepper over watery cups of coffee in the departure lounge of Stansted Airport.

But it wasn't fair to burden Josephine with her problems – especially not when the older woman had so much to contend with already. Now that Pepper was aware of the Parkinson's, she could see that it was progressing with a steadfast determination – one that made Josephine's dauntlessness in the face of it all the more remarkable. Pepper had noticed her friend's facial expressions beginning to change, as if the effort of holding up a smile was becoming too great. It was a cruel affliction for anyone to bear, but it felt doubly cruel to see it strip away the vitality from someone who was so full of joy and mischief. Josephine was refusing to discuss the fact that she was now walking with the aid of a stick, telling Pepper in no uncertain terms that 'ignorance is bliss, so please let's just pretend that the horrible thing isn't there'.

Despite a markedly dour start to the day, Pepper's mood quickly improved as they drove through the wonderfully chaotic Spanish city. Barcelona was a place that overflowed with life. From the bonnet-to-bumper stream of traffic on the roads to the endlessly bobbing sea of tourists spilling along the pavements, it felt to Pepper as if there was movement and mayhem at every turn. Turning to help Josephine step down from the bus at the main square of Plaça de Catalunya, Pepper almost got the pair of them flattened by a passing Segway tour.

'Golly,' Josephine said, as they retreated hastily to a nearby wall.

'This place is an absolute riot!'

Pepper blew air into her cheeks as she stared around.

'I don't even know where to look first,' she exclaimed. 'Has it changed a lot from when you and Jorge came here?'

'Rather!' Josephine grinned. 'There were trams rather than trucks back in 'sixty-six,' she remarked, curling up her nose as one of the latter heaved past belching petrol fumes. 'And market stalls rather than all these glamorous-looking shops. In fact, I remember it being a quiet and dusty little place.'

'Well, it's the opposite now.'

'I know.' Josephine grasped her hand. 'What a thrill! I suspect that you and I are going to have a marvellous time here.'

Lisbon had been muted by drizzle when Pepper had bid it farewell, Finn's rainbow-striped umbrella the only bloom of colour as he pulled her against him for a goodbye kiss in the narrow lane beside her hotel. Barcelona was a carnival by comparison, and every surface, statue and upturned face was basking in brilliant sunshine. It was hot, but not uncomfortably so, and the longer she and Josephine sat watching the friendly pandemonium unfolding, the more at ease Pepper felt. The heat was working its way into her sleep-deprived limbs, relaxing her knotted muscles and lulling her into a strangely serene state.

'Righto, that's enough rest. Where would you like to begin?' Josephine asked, turning to Pepper. 'Jorge and I practically lived in Park Güell when we were here . . . Although, you simply must see La Rambla – it's iconic. And I have been so longing to set foot on a proper sandy beach.'

'Whoa, there!' Pepper said with a laugh, pointing to the bags at their feet. 'We should probably check in first, no? And don't bite my head off for saying this, but it would probably be a good idea if you rested for a bit.'

'Nonsense!' Josephine lifted her chin defiantly. 'I assure you, darling. I am absolutely fine. Fighting fit! Eager to beaver! Gung-ho for hotfooting!'

'I don't want you to overd—' Pepper started to say, but Josephine was adamant. Planting her stick firmly on the ground, she got shakily to her feet.

'Come, come.' She beckoned Pepper with a hand. 'Lots to see – no time to dilly-dally.'

Pepper gave in to a sigh that became a smile.

'You're the boss,' she said.

They began by walking the length of Barcelona's most famous street, La Rambla, each of them wide-eyed in a mixture of glee and bafflement as they tried to take in the madness around them. Groups of travellers streamed along like cut-out paper dollies, chummy stall owners yelled and corralled, music blasted out from speakers and dark-haired local children bashed against adult legs as they nipped and weaved their way through the crowds.

'It reminds me of Piccadilly Circus in London,' Pepper said, staring around. 'Only with fewer neon signs.'

'You should get a job here,' suggested Josephine, gesturing towards where a man had set himself up sketching caricatures for people. 'You would make an absolute killing.'

'He is way better than me,' Pepper retorted, to which Josephine rolled her eyes heavenward.

'It was busy along here even in 'sixty-six,' she told her. 'Jorge and I used to sit and idle over coffee for hours, he watching the world go by, and me watching him. I remember falling in love with this beautiful silver anklet, and Jorge haggled with the vendor, eventually getting him down to 750 pesetas, which would be around three-fifty nowadays.'

'How lovely!' Pepper exclaimed. 'Do you still have it?'

'Alas.' Josephine looked wistfully down at her bare ankles. 'It was in a box of my things that went missing during the move, but I never used to wear it anyway. It would have felt disloyal to Ian, I suppose.'

'Maybe we should get you another one?' Pepper said. 'There's bound to be a place along here that sells jewellery.'

Josephine shook her head. 'You are very sweet,' she said. 'But there really is no need.'

To escape the hordes, they veered right off the main strip and found themselves in a vast indoor market packed with food stalls. There were mountains of fruit, blocks of cheese almost as big as the Britten Shell and enough slices of cured meat to paper the walls of Pepper's house. Fresh fish stared out at them from trays of crushed ice, their unseeing eyes reminding Pepper of the marbles she kept in jars on her studio shelves.

Tucked away at the back they found a tiny refreshment stand and ordered a glass of fresh coconut juice each, followed swiftly by a second. But while Pepper deemed it the creamiest, most delicately delicious drink she had ever tasted, Josephine pulled a face and said, 'If you ask me, darling, it would be much improved by a healthy dose of gin.'

'You're incorrigible,' Pepper stated, linking her arm through Josephine's as they left the market and skirted along the very edge of La Rambla.

Even when you were being bulldozed from every angle by fellow visitors, it was impossible not to appreciate the beauty of the architecture. Pepper almost got a crick in her neck gazing up at the tall houses on either side of the street, with their ornate balconies and grand, shuttered windows. Tiny birds flitted among the branches of the plane trees, dipping and diving for dropped morsels of food, and from somewhere in the distance, she heard the distinctive chime of church bells.

'I want to bottle it all and take it home with me,' she gabbled to Josephine. 'Everywhere I look, there's something I want to draw or paint.'

Pepper had brought her proper camera with her, and now she began taking endless photos, zooming in to capture a flurry of bubbles being blown by one of the strange living statues, and the young woman leaning out from a high window, her cigarette trailing smoke as she surveyed the scene below. Every face in the crowd was a potential story, every frame of her lens a work of art.

'I can see why Jorge wanted to come here,' she said. 'This is Arcadia for an artist.'

'Indeed.' Josephine was smiling. 'And, my dear, this is only the very beginning.'

Eventually, they reached the end of the road and stepped out under the watchful shadow of the towering Columbus Monument. Pepper admired the noble profile of the illustrious and intrepid explorer, who glared out across the glistening sweep of the Mediterranean.

'Jorge and I used this fellow as a marker when we went out on our many forages around the city,' Josephine told her, tilting her chin to get a better look. 'Good old Chris here prevented us from becoming lost many a time, as I remember it.'

'Far more romantic than Google Maps,' reflected Pepper, but Josephine was lost in a memory, her pale blue eyes watery and her fingers laced tightly together on the handle of her walking stick.

'Hey.' Pepper touched a hand to her shoulder. 'We can go back to the hotel if you want to – just say the word.'

'Hush.' Josephine blinked and pointed across the road with her cane. 'Gung-ho, remember? The beach is just over the road. I am afraid that a paddle before dinner is non-negotiable.'

Pepper did not need Josephine to point out that the seafront area had changed beyond recognition since the mid-sixties, because an ultra-modern promenade dominated the shoreline. Boats of every size, shape and level of luxury were packed into the harbour, an enormous drawbridge linked a wooden walkway to a floating shopping centre, and kiosks selling everything from ice cream to beer to buckets and spades had been set up at intervals all the way along the water's edge.

For Pepper, who was used to the genteel layout of Aldeburgh, the beach came as a bit of a shock. They could barely see the sand for sunbathers, many of whom, to the obvious pleasure of Josephine, appeared to be in the midst of a party. Teenagers kicked balls to one another, shirtless waiters ferried trays of beer, while gulls the size of albatrosses picked at discarded food wrappers, squawking in outrage whenever somebody attempted to shoo them away.

'Bloody hell!' cried Pepper, as a football whizzed past only inches from her head.

'Isn't it marvellous, darling?' Josephine exclaimed, shrugging out of her voluminous kaftan and dumping it, along with her capacious tote bag, onto the sand. Laying down her stick and rearranging the front of her blue-and-white striped swimsuit, she gave Pepper an exaggerated wink and declared, 'I'm going in!'

Pepper was just unrolling her towel when a man with a thick rug of chest hair and a white sailor's hat lurched into view bearing a tray of bright-green drinks.

'Mojito, mojito – only three euros!'

'No, *gracias*,' Pepper put up her hand.

'Yes please, lady. Very good mojito. Very good price.'

Recalling what Josephine had said about the absent gin in the coconut juice, Pepper relented.

'Oh, go on then,' she said, handing over a ten euro note and ignoring the voice in her head that was berating her because the cups and straws were plastic. She must save them for future collages. Digging two holes in the sand with her heel, she propped the cocktails inside and, extracting her phone, took a photo.

Attaching the picture to a WhatsApp message, she wrote: 'I think I just met the Barcelona version of Otto. Miss you!' and added five kisses for good measure.

Finn replied less than a minute later.

'In that case – run!' she read, laughing when she saw that he'd added a dancing man emoji.

'Oh whoopee – is that for me?'

Josephine was back from her swim and dripping water like a washing-up sponge.

Pepper helped her to sit down on the towel, then passed across one of the mojitos.

'To you!' they cried in unison.

'To us,' corrected Pepper.

Josephine removed her straw and took a large gulp, only to splutter in disgust.

'What's the matter?' Pepper had yet to taste hers. 'Is it gross?'

'Worse.' Josephine shuddered. 'They haven't put any damn rum in it.'

32

Pepper woke to a text message from her mother.

Rubbing her eyes, she swiped her finger across the screen, then sat bolt upright in bed, staring at the little grey box of text. It contained just two words: I'm sorry.

Her mother had never apologised to her before – not ever.

Pepper wondered what she was referring to. Was her mother sorry that they'd had a row in the pub? Or was she merely sorry that she'd got pregnant with Pepper in the first place?

She typed back a reply, deleted it, then tried another.

What should she say? That she was sorry, too? She did feel slightly guilty for abandoning the dinner, but not for what she had said, because it had all been true. If anything, she should have said it a long time ago. She ought to call her mother, ask her to explain exactly what she meant by 'I'm sorry' and have it out properly. But Pepper was reluctant to risk another argument. Being here in Barcelona had brightened her up, like Brasso on a copper kettle – she didn't want yet more strife to take away that shine.

In the end, she settled for: 'Thanks. We can talk when I'm back', feeling the air tighten in her chest as she pressed send. It was ridiculous that a civil exchange of messages with her own mother made her feel so jittery, but then again, their relationship was strained and fragile – had been for so long now that Pepper should have become accustomed to it. But she never had. There was always the hope that things would change, that she would be forgiven.

And it was the hope that hurt most of all.

Determined to put thoughts of her mother aside, Pepper sent another message, this time to Finn, then busied herself getting ready for a second day's exploring. She and Josephine had stayed down at the beach until sundown the previous evening, before finding a nearby taverna and sharing a feast of fresh grilled sardines, tangy tomato and onion salad and a basket of warm bread, all washed down with a jug of sangria. Much later, with full stomachs and heavy eyelids, the two of them had wandered back towards the hotel through a city that showed no sign of winding down for the night. Pepper was asleep almost before her head touched the pillow.

Closing the door to her room behind her, Pepper spotted Josephine coming along the corridor in a flowing purple skirt and matching blouse, her stick and UFO hat in hand.

'Darling!' she proclaimed. 'I was just coming to knock for you. Thought we could forego the buffet breakfast downstairs and get to the park nice and early?'

Pepper had spent countless hours poring over photos of Park Güell, and when she and Josephine walked in through the ornate gates of Gaudí's hillside utopia half an hour later, it felt utterly surreal, as if she had wandered right into a dream.

'I can't believe we're actually here,' she said, her hand on the strap of her camera. 'I feel like I have déjà-vu, which I realise makes me sound completely bonkers.'

'Well, goodie,' Josephine replied. 'Because all the best, most interesting people are.'

They had only got as far the courtyard just inside the park entrance, but already Pepper had spied Gaudí's iconic and resplendent mosaic dragon perched above them in the centre of a wide, stone staircase.

'I have always been a fan of art that one is permitted to touch,' Josephine said, moving away from Pepper to run her fingers across a swathe of broken tiles set into the back wall of an alcove.

'Wonderful!' she breathed. 'And would you look at that stonework.'

Pepper peered up at the little stone houses that contained the ticket office and café, smiling when she saw twisted turrets atop each one.

'They look as if they're made from gingerbread.'

'Certainly a feast for the eyes,' observed Josephine. 'Jorge knew so much about Gaudí – did I tell you that mosaics were his favourite art form?'

'He and I have that in common.'

'What is it that draws you to those in particular?'

Pepper thought for a moment. 'I remember being told the story about finding a pot of gold at the end of a rainbow when I was little,' she said. 'But it always made more sense to me that it would be a mosaic – because of all the colours, you know?'

'That is a lovely notion.' Josephine's expression softened. 'And it would make a fabulous subject for a painting.'

'I find it satisfying, putting all the pieces together and creating something whole,' she went on. 'It started with jigsaws when I was tiny and progressed from there. I suppose I like things to be in the right place, to have a purpose.'

The two of them had begun to make their way up the steps, and in spite of the early hour, there was already a jumble of visitors huddled around the striped dragon. Unlike them, Pepper had no interest in posing for a selfie with it, but she did want to examine the sculpture in more detail, trace a finger over its blue, orange and yellow scales and the rippled arches of its back. The creation was over a century old, but it had none of the tells of age she had expected to find. Each polished piece seemed to glow, as if the dragon really did have fire in its belly.

Josephine had fallen silent, a faraway look on her face.

'Apologies,' she said absently. 'I was just thinking about what Jorge said to me the first time we came here. We stopped right here,' she put a hand on the dragon's head. 'Here on these steps, exactly where you and I are standing now, and he told me that in his mind, we are all mosaics. All of us a sum of our parts. I have thought about that a lot throughout my life.'

'And do you agree with him?' Pepper asked.

'Oh, absolutely.' Josephine looked down at the dragon rather wistfully. 'This little fellow here has lasted all these years because of his cracks, not in spite of them. Being imperfect has made him stronger. And isn't that what mosaics really are – something beautiful from something broken?'

There was a lump in Pepper's throat that she was forced to swallow before she could reply.

'Do you think he ever came looking for you?' she asked. 'Jorge?'

Josephine's hand tremored as she clasped it over Pepper's.

'If he did, my darling, then I was not aware of it.'

'He broke your heart,' she stated. 'Didn't he?'

'Oh, almost certainly,' agreed Josephine, her voice neutral. 'But perhaps the cracks he left behind made me stronger in the end.'

A queue had formed behind them as they talked, so she and Josephine continued up the central steps until they reached the Hypostyle Hall. Impressive stone columns stretched up like attention-seeking arms towards a honeycomb ceiling, pockets of which were decorated by large, circular mosaic collages. Pepper made her way to each one in turn, recognising the pattern of the sun and of the sea. It was intricate and inventive work, executed so beautifully, and as she looked, Pepper found herself struck by a deep sense of shame. Pepper had wanted to make a name for herself as an artist since childhood, but until recently, she'd let her insecurities and yearning for so-called perfection stop her from really trying. If she continued to do so, was she letting down those who had lit such a burning trail throughout history for her to follow? Standing here now, it felt as if she would be.

There was a curved pathway behind the hall, and they followed it up and around, Josephine using her stick and Pepper for support as the incline steepened. At the top they discovered a wide veranda that overlooked the park entrance. Undulating bench seats had been carved out neatly along each side like cresting waves, and every surface bar the dusty ground was festooned with shattered pieces of glazed and painted tiles. It all appeared haphazard and spontaneous – just like the sea itself, thought Pepper – but she knew how much painstaking planning and placing it must have taken to achieve such a mesmerising result.

What kind of pattern would her own life make, Pepper wondered, if she were to lay out all the pieces.

'Jorge used to joke that you could see the Eiffel Tower from here,' Josephine told her.

They had made their way to the front of the veranda, to where an exquisite view of the city awaited. A cheerful morning sun was beating down on them now, the glorious Spanish heat as relentless as the marching feet of a soldier. Pepper was thankful for the floaty folds of her thin cotton dress, and the copious coatings of sun cream she kept reapplying.

'We must find him,' Pepper said beseechingly. 'I bet he would be so thrilled to see you.'

'Hmm.' Josephine continued to stare out over the rooftops.

'I cherish my memories of Jorge,' she said. 'And of myself during that summer I spent with him. We were both so young and insouciant; the world was simply our playground. Jorge was and likely still is the most incredible man, but I am beginning to wonder if seeing him again is the right thing. Going back to Lisbon and coming here with you has been everything I hoped it would be – and more.'

She turned to face Pepper, a telling smile on her lips.

'But there is always a risk when you dig up the past that you will unearth something you don't want to find. Jorge and I, our story ended then – to hanker after it is pure sentimentality.'

Pepper looked away, unable not to think of Bethan. In those first, awful weeks following her little sister's accident, when the world felt as if it had been tipped over like a fishbowl, she wished that it had been she who drowned. She had lost so much of who she was, and the future seemed so impossible. But Pepper had known even as the thought came to her that it was foolish. Life was something – it was precious.

'It's not making you feel too melancholy, is it?' she asked. 'Being here?'

Josephine patted her arm. 'Only in a good way. Now, food time soon, I think. I don't know about you, darling, but I am absolutely ravenous.'

Pepper was halfway through agreeing when her phone vibrated inside her bag. Expecting it to be a reply from Finn, she was dismayed to find a message from the DVLA instead, reminding her that they would be taking out her car tax payment via direct debit. She must have made a small noise of disgruntlement, because Josephine gave her an enquiring look.

'Everything all right?'

'Yeah.' Pepper opened her message inbox, then did the same with WhatsApp, but there was nothing there, nothing from Finn. It wasn't like him to ignore her – he was usually super-punctual at getting back to her.

'I was just hoping it would be Finn,' she said, feeling as lame as she sounded.

'I see.' Josephine frowned down at the screen. 'Well, I'm sure he's just busy. He has that air about him, doesn't he? One of those men with people to see and places to be.'

'I guess so,' Pepper said, trying her best not to be despondent. It was still early, after all. Finn didn't exactly keep office hours – as far as she could tell, he got up whatever time suited him. And knowing him, he'd most likely had a late night at Freunde. Perhaps Otto kept him drinking out in the street until six in the morning and he was sleeping it off.

Just in case, she texted him again. A quick: 'Call me when you wake up. Miss you' and added a heap of kisses at the end.

There, she thought, feeling slightly cheered by the sight of the two grey ticks telling her the message had been delivered. She was bound to hear from him soon. There was nothing at all to worry about.

But as she and Josephine made their way out of Park Güell and headed back down the hill, Pepper could not shake the feeling that she had somehow missed something important.

33

The day that had started out pleasantly tepid was now hot, and Pepper gazed appreciatively up at the sun as they walked, marvelling at its power. The park they had just left behind was in the La Salut neighbourhood in the north of the city, which was a sprawling mix of residential high-rise buildings, shops, cafés and several large hotels.

They traversed streets lined by neatly sculpted trees and stopped to admire acid-pink bursts of bougainvillea tossed artfully against walls. Palm fronds cast skeletal shadows across pavements, car horns blared, and a gentle breeze chased lilac petals into dusty corners. Just as she had been in Lisbon and Hamburg, Pepper found herself easily captivated, her senses reeling as she took in the new sights, sounds and smells – so many of which were different from the ones she encountered at home. Barcelona was everything that Aldeburgh was not, in terms of its colour wheel, its loud-and-proud cacophony of noise, and the sheer size of the buildings. Where Lisbon had been all nooks and crannies, Barcelona was wide open.

Josephine chatted away almost non-stop, pointing out flowers that had broken through cracks, dogs straining at leads and the curled slug-like moustache of a man selling newspapers outside the Metro station. With every step, she seemed to remember more about the city, and she kept clapping her hands in unbridled delight every time a memory struck. This would have been fine if she did not keep forgetting about her stick – Pepper had to retrieve it from the ground so many times that she lost count.

After a quick breakfast of coffee and the lightest, fluffiest omelette Pepper had ever tasted, Josephine announced that she wanted to visit Casa Batlló, a grand six-storey residence in the heart of the city, which Gaudí had been commissioned to renovate in the early nineteen-hundreds.

'Welcome to Jorge's dream house,' she said, sweeping up her arm and leaning back on her stick in order to see right to the top. 'The two of us only came here together once, but we stayed for hours and hours. Jorge was reluctant to leave at all – he said that as far as he was concerned, there could be no better place.'

Pepper consulted the leaflet they had been given at the ticket office.

'It says here that it's also known as "the house of bones" or "house of yawns",' she said, squinting upwards. 'That must be because of the balconies.'

'Curious, aren't they?' Josephine agreed. 'And look at those thin stone columns – don't they remind you of fish bones?'

Pepper nodded, utterly enthralled by what she was seeing, by the creativity and imagination.

The change in temperature as they crossed the threshold only served to reinforce just how hot it was, and although the sunshine had been lifting Pepper's spirits ever since they arrived, it was still a relief to get some respite.

'Isn't it simply marvellous?' Josephine declared, coming to a stop in the centre of what was once a formal dining room. A wide front-facing window was made up of intricate panels of coloured glass, while Gaudí's fascination with water was evident everywhere, from the strange droplet design on the ceiling to the wave-like curves on the walls. Not a single detail had been overlooked, and Pepper experienced a rush of satisfaction as she slid her fingers over one of the moulded brass door handles.

'Gaudí really did think of everything,' Pepper remarked, stopping to admire the spiral folds around the central light fitting. 'It's like being at the bottom of the ocean.'

Yet more magic awaited them in the central stairwell, which was bathed in light and tiled in a myriad wash of blues. The closer they climbed to the top of the house, the paler the ceramic tiles became, as if they were rising up from the depths of the sea to its surface.

'This part of the house was Jorge's favourite,' said Josephine, tapping her stick against the thick glass panels separating them from the inner chamber. 'Have a look through and tell me what you see.'

Pepper crouched down on her haunches and rocked from side to side.

'Oh, wow,' she breathed. The glass panels were rippled, making it seem as if the blue tiles behind them were moving like shifting water. Back and forth she bounced on her heels, eyes wide and heart open. It was miraculous – the further she ventured along the roller-coaster tracks of Gaudí's imagination, the more inspired she felt. He had been by no means an orderly and tidy artist, but it was exactly his penchant for the chaos of nature that made his work so appealing, and so real. Gaudí, she was sure, would have scoffed at the very idea of artistic perfection – he simply looked at the world, thought about how it made him feel, then did his very best to recreate that feeling for others. It was what Pepper had been trying to do with her painted tiles – express all that wonderful love she felt for Finn.

Although, of course, to really achieve the level of greatness that someone like Gaudí had, she would eventually need to share her work, not keep it locked away in a cupboard.

'I knew it,' Josephine said happily as Pepper stood up with a smile of wonderment on her face. 'I knew you would love this place just as much as my dear Jorge did. I would wager it's an even better tonic for the soul than gin, although don't tell anybody else I said that.'

'I have never seen anything quite like it,' Pepper said. 'I keep expecting fish to swim past.'

'That is exactly what Jorge said.' Josephine beamed. 'He told me that when he became as rich and famous an artist as Gaudí, he would build us our own home, even better and more fantastical than this one. It was his dream.'

'Do you think he ever managed it?' Pepper asked. She had been wanting to ask this question for a while – ever since they had tried and failed to find a trace of Jorge online. 'When I was young, I used to dream about becoming all sorts of things.'

'You are still young,' Josephine said gravely. 'I know you may not always feel that way, but you'll have to trust me on that. As for Jorge, I cannot say for sure. I always encouraged him to pursue his art, but he was also an incredible chef. I imagine he could easily have made a career for himself by sticking to that vocation. I used to tell him that there was as much artistic merit in fine cuisine as there is in fine art, which he found rather amusing, as I am sure you can imagine?'

'I can barely manage beans on toast,' confessed Pepper. 'Some wife I'll make.'

Josephine stared for a moment out into the open shaft of the stairwell. There was a strange echo in here, Pepper realised, much like the one you find at swimming pools or empty concert halls. It lent an almost ethereal quality to what was already a dreamlike setting.

'Is that what you want then, darling? Josephine said, turning back to face Pepper. 'To get married?'

Pepper reddened. 'I guess so. I mean, I used to think I didn't really care all that much, but that was before.' She hesitated, feeling suddenly embarrassed.

'Before you met Finn?'

Pepper squirmed. 'Does that make me sound like an idiot? It's such early days with me and Finn, but now that he's coming to live with me, I don't know, it just feels different – more grown-up than any other relationship I've had, even if we are both behaving like a pair of lovestruck teenagers.'

'You are not an idiot,' Josephine said, tutting at Pepper as they pressed the button for the lift that would take them up to Gaudí's dragon-esque roof terrace. 'You are just in love, my darling, and love makes fools of us all, does it not?'

'I really hope it does not,' Pepper said, slipping her phone out of her pocket and finding the screen still blank.

'Unfortunately, as with anything as momentous as love, it carries with it a certain amount of risk. There is always the risk you will be rejected, or hurt, or deceived – but the rewards are too great to pass up. I would wager that most people who have had their hearts broken would still keep the chapters of their story that contained love, rather than tear them out. Because what are we without love, really?'

Pepper was not thinking about Finn now, but about Bethan. About how she would still rather have had those seven years with her sister, than never known her at all, even taking into consideration the pain of her own grief, and how much havoc Bethan's death would wreak. Pepper knew that she was who she was because of her sister, not in spite of her.

'How did you know?' she asked Josephine. 'That you were in love with Jorge, I mean?'

The lift had arrived, and the doors slid open to reveal a gaggle of schoolchildren, each one clutching a clipboard and chattering away excitedly in Spanish.

One of Josephine's eyebrows twitched.

'That is a very good question,' she said, stepping forwards as Pepper followed. 'But I fear now may not the best time to answer.'

And with that, for the time being at least, Pepper had no choice but to be satisfied.

34

Finn finally replied to Pepper's message as she was dressing for dinner later that evening, telling her that he also missed her very much and asking lots of questions about what she had been up to and how she was finding her first experience of Spain. It had not surprised her to learn that he had visited Barcelona many times before, and when she asked him to recommend somewhere nice for food, he promptly responded with a list.

Now she and Josephine were sitting opposite one another at a small restaurant called Bodega Joan, which had a dark-wood interior, strings of garlic bulbs hanging in clusters from the ceiling, and wicker baskets of various sizes decorating the walls. It was also, according to Finn, one of the best establishments in the city to sample paella.

'I thought we would have trouble getting in,' Pepper said now, picking up the earthenware jug of sangria and topping up each of their glasses. Aside from herself and Josephine, there were only four other tables occupied.

'That is because we're rather early for dinner, darling,' said Josephine.

'Half past eight? Early?'

'The locals won't venture out until ten to eat – perhaps even later, given that it's a Saturday.'

'If I waited that long to eat, my stomach would eat itself,' Pepper said seriously, pulling off a chunk of the bread that their waiter had not long ago brought over, and Josephine smiled.

'It's funny,' she mused, watching as Pepper dug her knife into the butter. 'But since my diagnosis, my appetite has been boringly lacklustre. I am supposed to be keeping my strength up and all that gubbins, but I have been struggling to feel very enthusiastic about English food. The same is certainly not true here – that was part of the reason I wanted to revisit this city, to find a morsel or two to reignite my taste buds.'

'I knew I should have made sure you took a siesta,' Pepper implored. After she and Josephine had left Casa Batlló, the older woman had promptly crossed the road towards yet another of Gaudí's architectural wonderlands, La Pedrera, and insisted they go inside.

It was the rooftop of this particular building that was its standout feature, and instead of boring chimneys and ventilation towers, the innovative artist had created an army of stone guardians to watch over his city. Pepper had felt like a pawn on a giant chess board as she gazed up at each one in turn. Many of the sculptures had been decorated in pieces of broken tile, and she and Josephine had traced the patterns with their fingers as they meandered up and down steps and along pathways, all the while playing a game of hide and seek with the sun.

By the time they emerged, pink and dehydrated three hours later, the afternoon was drawing to an end and, having skipped lunch in favour of worship at the esteemed altar of Gaudí, both were hungrier for dinner than a nap. Pepper continued to be astounded by her friend's determination to remain upbeat and relatively energetic, but she still worried that Josephine was perhaps pushing herself too far.

'I think tomorrow, we should have a more relaxing day,' Pepper suggested now, picking a slice of orange out of her glass and sucking it. 'A boat tour, maybe? Or back to the beach?'

Josephine gave a little grimace.

'Both those ideas sound delightful, but I am afraid we already have plans.'

'We do?'

Josephine tapped the side of her nose with a finger.

'All shall be revealed tomorrow, darling.'

The paella arrived, vast and golden and overflowing with enormous pink prawns and gigantic mussels. It was fresh from the stove and steaming hot, the smell so enticing that both Pepper and Josephine leant forwards in their seats, their mouths open and their eyes alight.

'Golly, this looks divine,' Josephine said, helping herself to a huge portion. 'Make sure you scrape that spoon across the bottom of the pan,' she told Pepper. 'The *socarrat*, that's the singed stuff, has the very best flavour.'

'Is that another of Jorge's pearls of culinary wisdom?'

'Indeed it is. He was full of them, you know. And he enjoyed teaching.' She eyed Pepper over the table. 'The two of you have a lot in common, when I come to think about it – the art, the teaching, the misfortune to end up with me by your side.'

She had obviously been joking as she said the last, but Pepper felt the need to argue back regardless.

'How could being around you ever be viewed as a misfortune?' she exclaimed. 'My life has become so much richer since I met you. I have learnt so much and experienced things I never thought I would, seen things I never have. Hell, I would never have met Finn if it wasn't for you!'

Josephine took a delicate mouthful of paella and dabbed at the corner of her mouth with a napkin. The restaurant was getting steadily busier, and they could hear the sound of pots being banged down and staff shouting to one another.

'I am by no means perfect,' she said. Then, when Pepper pulled a face. 'Honestly, darling – I have made some very iffy decisions over the course of my life. I have not always been honest with the people I was supposed to love and trust the most.'

'Do you mean about Jorge?' Pepper asked. 'The fact that your husband never knew about him?'

'Yes.' Josephine speared a prawn but didn't eat it. 'But there is more to the story, more that I have not yet relayed to you.'

Pepper reached for her sangria to wash down her most recent forkful of paella. Josephine was right, the *socarrat* was the best bit.

'The thing is,' the older woman began, waiting until Pepper had lowered her glass before continuing, 'when I told you that I never heard from Jorge again, and that I gave up when he did not reply to any of my letters, that wasn't strictly the truth.'

'Oh.' Pepper went very still.

'Two summers after I had first met Jorge, my life felt as if it had fallen completely apart. I had been married to Ian for less than a year, pregnant for most of it, and scared absolutely witless about becoming a mother for the first time. In those days, it wasn't in the slightest bit unusual for a girl of nineteen, as I was then, to be starting a family – but that didn't make it any easier. I kept thinking that once the baby arrived, once I was holding them in my arms, all the fear would fall away. I trusted that my body and those so-promised motherly instincts would take over, but then Georgina arrived, and I felt . . . Well, I felt indifferent, if I'm completely honest with you. There was just this big, dark hole where I thought all the love would be, and it seemed to suck me down into it. For the first few months after she was born, I was floating, rudderless, utterly lost and so very terrified.'

'Oh, you poor thing.' Pepper lifted an instinctive hand to touch her, then changed her mind and lowered it again. 'Was it post-natal depression?'

Josephine fussed absentmindedly with her mass of frizzy grey hair.

'I deduced later that it must have been,' she said. 'But nobody talked about such things then. It was all "pull your socks up" and "less fussing, more getting on with it". There was no real support on offer, or certainly none that I experienced, and Ian was at a loss as to how to help me. The poor man sought refuge at work, while back at our home in London, I slowly but surely went into decline. I knew that Georgina needed me, and at first it was enough to go through the motions of feeding and cleaning and comforting, but after a while I became fixated on the idea of escaping – from her and from Ian. I honestly believed that they would both be better off without me.'

She paused briefly to gather her thoughts, and Pepper wondered if she should interject. But then, what could she say? She had never been a mother, so she could only begin to guess at what her friend had gone through.

'I had a little bit of money saved,' Josephine went on. 'My father had passed away not long before Ian and I got married and he had left me some. It had been our plan to save it, create a trust for Georgina, so she had something there as a safeguard, or for when she needed it for her studies, or to buy a home of her own one day. It was so important to me that she have it, that option for independence that I had so craved – but all of a sudden, my escape felt more important. I knew that if I didn't get away I would go mad, it was as simple as that. I waited for a Bank Holiday weekend and managed to persuade Ian to take Georgina to visit his parents alone. He could see that I was struggling, even if he pretended not to, and so he agreed, even though Georgina was still so young. I should have been sad to see the two of them drive away, but I'm ashamed to admit now that I wasn't – I was relieved.'

Pepper, who had never met Ian Hurley, tried her best to imagine the scene. It was difficult to pull together a picture from the limited photographs she had seen, of Josephine and her much-taller, jolly-looking husband. She had always presumed that they must have had a happy marriage, but all she really knew was that it had been a long union, and that the couple had welcomed three further children. Georgina had emigrated to Australia, of course, where she worked as a midwife, Toby and Patrick lived next-door to each other in suburban Surrey and ran a very successful property development business, while Bunty, the 'surprise' youngest, was an architect and had recently moved up to Scotland.

Pepper wondered if any of them had ever been told this story.

'I thought that if I could just get myself back to Lisbon and see Jorge again, I would feel better. I would be able to sleep again, feel like a human being again – like myself again. I was convinced that it was the only way.'

Pepper's eyes widened.

'You went back again?'

'I know,' Josephine shook her head. 'I know what you're thinking – why would I go off and leave my baby behind to look for a man who had, to all intents and purposes, rejected me? Why would I do such a thing?'

'You weren't well,' Pepper reminded her gently. 'You have to make allowances for that.'

'I was a coward,' Josephine replied firmly. 'What I should have done is ask for help. Instead, I ran away from the two people I was supposed to love most in the world – who loved me the most.'

'But did it help?' Pepper asked, seized by a sudden urgency. 'Oh my God – did you find him? Did you find Jorge?'

Josephine lifted her shoulders. 'Getting away did help,' she said, sounding abashed. 'I felt immediately happier as soon as I got there, but what I should have felt was guilt – ashamed to have abandoned my husband and young daughter and run off in search of another man. I kept waiting for the reality of what I was doing to hit me, but it didn't – not for the two weeks I spent hunting – unsuccessfully, I might add – for Jorge. That was how long it took for the guilt to catch up with me. I remember it so clearly, waking up one morning and knowing, just knowing, that I had to go home. In that moment, I missed Ian and Georgina so much that I almost stopped breathing. I started running around the room I had rented, throwing my belongings into a bag and wailing my head off like a demented banshee. I was so glad, then, to not have found Jorge after all. I could not believe how close I had come to losing everything.'

'Wow.' Pepper breathed. The paella was still sitting half-eaten on her plate, forgotten.

'What happened after you got back?' she asked.

'Poor Ian,' Josephine said, extracting a tissue from her cavernous handbag and dabbing at her eyes. 'He was so relieved to see me. I had left a note saying I needed some time alone, but he had no idea where I had gone, and the dear man had searched all over England for me. My family were beside themselves, and my daughter—'

She took a long, steadying breath.

'Georgina had been so fretful without me. Ian told me that she never stopped crying out for me, that she had barely slept and was refusing food. I cannot bear to think about what I put her through, what she endured because of me, the one person who was supposed to love and protect her over everyone.'

Her tears were falling steadily now, but Pepper felt at a loss as to what to say. Instead, she reached across the table and put a hand on her friend's arm. She was so slim, so fragile.

'Gosh, I'm such a silly old bat,' Josephine muttered, blowing her nose. 'I didn't know that talking about all this stuff would still have such an impact on me. I'm so sorry.'

'Please don't apologise,' Pepper soothed. 'I think you're amazing. You swam when you very easily could have sunk – and you did go back. Don't forget that. You left, but not forever. Not like—' She pulled herself to an abrupt halt.

This was not about her.

Josephine didn't seem to register. She was staring down at the golden rice in the dish between them. Sensing that her comforting hand was no longer required, Pepper removed it.

'Ian forgave you for disappearing?'

A nod.

'Did you tell him where you had been?'

Josephine closed her eyes briefly, as if in a wince. 'No, never. I know I should have told him. I tried to, many times. But in the end, it would only have hurt him more and he deserved better than that – better than me, in truth. I have been trying very hard to forgive myself for my whole life, and clearly' – she gestured towards her face – 'I haven't been able to do so. And if I am unable to forgive myself, then what chance would dear Ian have had?'

Pepper opened her mouth to attempt a rebuttal, then shut it again. She understood about forgiveness, and how the passing of time sometimes offered little comfort. People go on about forgiving and forgetting, but do they ever really do so? When something is profound enough to change a life, can it ever be forgotten? And should it be? Josephine was entitled to feel all this pain, a fact that Pepper appreciated more than most, thanks to her mother.

'You didn't let what happened define you, though, did you?' she said at last. 'My mother has allowed my sister's death to define her whole existence.'

'Losing a child . . .' Josephine visibly shuddered. 'I don't think anything could be harder than that. Pain of that kind changes a person permanently, I'm afraid. She will never be the woman she was before it happened.'

'I know that.' Pepper's voice was small. 'But she could be happier than she is, if she would only try a bit harder. Everything is black to her, there is no light at all. No matter what I do, I can't make her see that there are still plenty of reasons to be happy, and things to enjoy.'

'Is that why you stay?' Josephine asked. She had taken a few sips of her sangria now, and the colour was returning to her cheeks. 'In Aldeburgh? Even though most of your friends have gone?'

Pepper did not want to think about the fact that Josephine would soon be gone, too. Instead of replying, she merely shrugged.

'I hope your mother is not the sole reason you are still there,' Josephine went on, her tone low now and laced with caution. 'Because this is your life – you must live it for yourself.'

'I might have agreed with you a few weeks ago,' Pepper said, picking up her fork once more. 'But now that Finn is coming to live with me, I have everything I need to be happy, right where I am. I honestly believe that he is the missing piece I have been waiting for, and as soon as he's there, everything else will fall into place.'

For a moment or two, Josephine said nothing, then she raised her glass.

'Shall we drink to that, then?' she asked, as Pepper followed suit.

'To what, exactly?'

'Oh darling, isn't that obvious? To love, of course!'

35

Having left Bodega Joan even more full of affection for Finn than she was of paella, Pepper attempted to FaceTime him as soon as she was back in her hotel room, but her call went unanswered.

She stayed up for as long as she could, flicking through TV channels she could not understand and sketching absentmindedly in the pad she had brought along in her hand luggage, drawing on a day spent in the company of Gaudí for inspiration. She may not be here in Barcelona with Finn, but she had decided that she still wanted to include the city in her painted tile project. It made her excited to think about how she would recreate the stunning mosaics in Park Güell and capture that trapped sense of movement she had felt in Casa Batlló. The work distracted her, but she still felt deflated switching off the bedside light hours later, her phone resolutely empty of new messages or calls.

The next morning there was still no word, but Pepper could see from the soul-crushing blue ticks that Finn had both received and read her messages, which meant he was choosing not to get in touch. What could have happened in the past twelve hours to make him suddenly ignore her? Pepper trawled fruitlessly through her brain, trying to come up with a solution and failing, her frustration at not knowing what was going on causing her to stub her toe painfully on the bathroom door and stab herself in the eye with her mascara wand.

When she found Josephine downstairs having breakfast, in very high spirits having slept well and late, her friend knew at once that something was amiss.

'I hope you're all set for a morning's fun. I have that lovely surprise booked for us first, then I thought we could take an afternoon mosey around the old neighbourhood where Jorge and I stayed?'

Pepper sat down more heavily than she had intended.

'Sounds great.'

'Darling.' Josephine's tone was determinedly breezy 'Why don't you simply call him and get it over with?'

'Call who?' Pepper attempted to sound surprised.

'There is no fooling an old fool,' Josephine snipped. 'I know a lover's tiff when I see it etched across someone's face. Trust me, if the two of you have it out sooner rather than later, it won't have time to fester.'

Pepper pulled a face.

'Come on now,' Josephine crowed. 'Off you toddle.'

'But I—'

'SHOO!'

With a drawn-out sigh that would have won gold at the Grumpy Teenager Olympics, Pepper heaved herself up and took her phone outside into the hotel courtyard, her shoulders drooping as the heat settled across them.

Taking a deep breath, she called Finn.

One ring. Two rings. Five rings.

He wasn't answering.

Instead of going to voicemail, the call ended abruptly, as if someone at the other end had cancelled it. Pepper now felt even worse than she had five minutes ago. She couldn't understand what was happening, and whether or not she should be concerned for his safety. A life with no Finn in it was impossible to comprehend – Pepper felt sick at the mere thought. But it was unfair of him, ignoring her like this. If she had not heard anything by the evening, she decided she would have no choice but to call Freunde and ask Otto or Clara for help.

Feeling slightly less despairing now that she had a plan of sorts, Pepper returned to the table.

'Better?' Josephine arched an enquiring brow.

'Yes and no.' Pepper put her phone into her bag. 'Let's not talk about it any more. Now, tell me more about this cunning plan of yours.'

Josephine grinned. Her expression was even more mischievous than it usually was.

'Go and fill up at the buffet,' she urged. 'Then we can get going.'

'Oh my God – you didn't?'

Pepper stared at the shiny red Vespas that were parked at a jaunty angle by the kerb, her mouth falling open as Josephine tittered with amusement.

'I am afraid I did. This was how Jorge and I used to get around the city, except in those days the scooters were very different from these beautiful beasts, of course.'

Pepper could not be sure if she was referring to their vehicles of choice for the hour-long tour, or the two young men that would be driving them.

'We will start along the beach,' her guide, Tomas, told her, handing Pepper a helmet and helping her to adjust the chin strap. 'Then go around to the north, stop for some photos, and back along all the best roads for seeing our sites.'

'Er, *gracias*,' she said. Glancing across to check on Josephine, she found that her friend was already in the pillion position, both legs and arms wrapped snugly around Ignacio, who was a few years older and a good foot taller than his colleague.

'Are we ready, ladies?' he called, as Pepper hopped onto the smooth leather seat. Unsure of where to put her hands, she felt around behind her, only for Tomas to indicate his waist.

'Hold me here, please,' he instructed. 'It is easier for me to balance – and safer for you.'

'OK.' Pepper turned even redder than the paintwork. She barely had time to register the fact that her hands were now full of young Spanish man before they were off, zooming along the narrow side street in a burst of such unexpected power that Pepper found herself gripping Tomas even tighter.

Ignacio and Josephine led the way, and Pepper shut her eyes in fright as the two men weaved them out into the traffic at speed, dodging cars and tooting their horns at any tourist who dared get in their way. When she heard Tomas cough as if he was trying to catch his breath, she relaxed her arms a fraction and tried her best to remain as still as possible.

Once she got over the fear factor, Pepper started to realise that it was actually quite a fun way to travel, and what made her even happier was the sight of her friend up ahead, her arms brazenly outstretched and her head thrown back, clearly loving every second. When they pulled up beside one another at a set of traffic lights not far from all the beach bars, Josephine reached across and squeezed Pepper's hand.

'Isn't this blooming marvellous?' she yelled, as both Ignacio and Tomas revved their engines in anticipation of a green light. 'This is really living!'

Pepper laughed – it was impossible not to – but as soon she did they hurtled off once again and the warm wind flooded into her open mouth, along with one or two insects. As Pepper coughed and spluttered, she heard a great whoop coming from her friend up ahead, and her chokes dissolved into laughter.

The sky today was an uncompromising shade of the clearest blue, the sun within it bright and ringed with gold. The deeper they ventured into the city, the more there was to see, and when Ignacio and Tomas pulled over so they could take photos from up behind Park Güell, the view made Pepper fall into a silent state of awe. From all the way up here, Barcelona could almost be quiet. The traffic was muted, the canopies of the trees turning the streets from grey to green and the people were merely dots – stitches on a tapestry.

'Do you want to swap?' Josephine asked slyly, throwing a look in her driver's direction. 'Ignacio is very funny – keeps telling me jokes about the English that I can't for the life of me seem to work out. I have been laughing along with him, of course.'

Pepper chuckled. 'I'm very happy with Tomas,' she assured her. 'He is a strong and silent type, which suits me just fine.'

'Shall we get a photograph with them?' Josephine asked, beckoning the two men over with an enthusiastic hand. Ignacio, who was the tallest, kindly offered to take the selfie, and Pepper rested her head against her friend's, knowing this would be yet another moment she would never forget. As she clambered back behind Tomas, however, she could not help but think what Finn would say if he could see her, and how happy he would be to hear she had spent the morning with her legs wrapped around another man. A really childish part of her wanted to send him the selfie, but she knew that was the disgruntled side of her worry talking. This was Finn. He was different. She had to believe that if he wasn't getting back to her, then he must have a very good reason.

Pepper told herself to put the subject away and concentrated instead on how glorious it felt to have the wind rushing through the ends of her hair, and the sun beating down on her bare legs. Thank heavens she had worn shorts today instead of a dress – flashing the people of Barcelona her pants was definitely not something she wanted to tick off the bucket list.

The next time they stopped at a set of lights, Tomas reached down and moved Pepper's hand from his waist to the moped throttle, putting his own over the top.

'When I say,' he said loudly, 'you pull – yes?'

What was this, Carry On Vespas?

'Yes – er, OK.'

The light turned green, Tomas said 'now', and Pepper eased her hand backwards on the handle, feeling the roar of the engine vibrating through her fingers.

'Bravo!' yelled Tomas. 'Now you are driving.'

Although it was not quite Michelle Pfeiffer in *Grease 2*, Pepper felt very pleased with herself.

For a few exhilarating minutes, she had been the one in control, and it had felt so damn great.

36

It was with slightly bandy legs that she and Josephine ambled through the Barri Gòtic quarter that afternoon. While Gaudí's various haunts had felt like other worlds, the cobblestone streets and Gothic churches down here transported them to another time.

As a city, Barcelona was grander than Lisbon, but it was no less fascinating to behold, and as they strolled under stone arches, past ruined cathedrals, lively water fountains and café tables buried under a sea of tanned, sprawling limbs, Pepper felt more and more overwhelmed by a need to capture what she was seeing. Her camera was not enough; it would only tell half the story. She needed a pencil and paper, some paints and an easel.

Seemingly immune to the steadily rising heat of the day, Josephine powered through the lanes as fast as her stick would allow, exclaiming in delight every time she saw a landmark that she recognised.

'Jorge and I kissed on this wall!' she would cry, sinking down and pressing a hand to the stone. 'Do you know, we never let go of each other's hands – barely ever. It was as if the two of us were conjoined, for heaven's sake, so helplessly infatuated that we could not bear to let go, even for a moment.'

'That's what love should feel like,' Pepper told her, picturing herself and Finn, wrapped up in each other's arms as he led her through Hamburg. Josephine, however, had not replied, merely peered closely at Pepper, as if trying to work her out.

'This is one of the prettiest squares in the city,' she announced a little while later. 'Plaça Reial. Of course, it was far less popu-lated with all these fancy restaurants when Jorge and I used to while away the hours here – the only other creatures we ever saw were other artists. Oh, and the pigeons of course.'

'I like these streetlamps,' Pepper said of the two posts flanking a grand, central fountain.

'I guessed you might,' Josephine said appreciatively. 'Gaudí again. Jorge sketched them, if I remember rightly. The two of you would so have got along.'

'We still could,' Pepper tempered lightly.

Josephine's face had been thrown into shadow by one of the square's many palm trees, and her expression gave nothing away.

'Maybe.' She looked away towards the edge of the square. 'Now, shall we walk beneath the porticoes? The stonework is simply divine.'

It was many hours later that Pepper was finally able to persuade her to sit and rest for a while, and even when they had located a free table tucked away along a narrow lane, Josephine refused to get a pot of tea, opting instead for a jug of sangria and insisting that Pepper share.

'I am pulling the Parkinson's card on this one,' she said, waving away Pepper's refusal. 'You have to do as I say, because I am old and dying.'

'Oi! Less of that, please.'

'We have earned it,' she proclaimed. 'And how often are you in a beautiful Spanish city, with nowhere to be and nothing to do except feel the sunshine on your bare toes and enjoy a little late-afternoon tipple?'

'Fair point.' Pepper accepted a glass. Then, after two more, she felt brave enough to try calling Finn, screwing up her face when it went straight to voicemail. His recorded message was in English rather than German, and Pepper wondered if that was for her benefit, or something to do with his work. Perhaps now, she thought numbly, she might never get an opportunity to ask.

'Do you want to talk about it, darling?' Josephine raised a braceleted arm and shooed away a hovering mosquito.

Pepper shook her head.

'Maybe later,' she said. 'I want to hear more about you and Jorge.'

The sun continued to drift lazily across the sky as they sat, sharing stories and a second jug of sangria as the city edged its way from daytime to dusk. Pepper was torn between a desire to bask in the moment and a need to give in to the rising tide of unease that was beginning to course through her at the thought of something being wrong with Finn. Was that simply the hand that life had dealt her? Was she destined to lose everyone she held dear – first Bethan, then Finn, and soon Josephine? It felt horribly as if the happiness that had been dangled tantalisingly close to her was now about to be ripped away.

When Josephine giddily suggested a third jug, Pepper scraped back her chair.

'First, we must find some food,' she said, even though her stomach felt as shrunken and gnarled as a walnut. 'Then we can talk about more alcohol.'

Eight on a Sunday evening was apparently a far more popular time to eat than on Saturdays, and it took a further hour of wandering before the two of them found a place to eat. On first glance, the little restaurant Cal Pep did not look like much, with its long counter, low ceiling and laminated menus, but everyone inside was Spanish, which according to Josephine was a very positive sign.

The two of them sat up on tall stools and sipped cava served in small tumblers. Their server – a thickset man in a sauce-splattered white apron – shook his head when they began asking questions about the food, telling them briskly that he would bring them a selection of his own choosing.

'I like him,' Josephine said approvingly. 'A man that takes charge of a situation – not many of those left.'

Pepper thought of Finn, and how content she had been to let him take the lead when she was in Hamburg. He was a 'take charge' type of man. Well, perhaps except where errant bats were concerned. Remembering the incident now, she relayed the story to Josephine, who laughed so much that cava came out of her nose.

'This Samuel chap sounds fabulous!' she enthused. 'Why haven't you introduced us yet?'

'I will when we get back to Suffolk,' Pepper promised. 'I'll do a meal for you both or something.'

'Speaking of which . . .'

Their tapas arrived, the plates piling up until every free space on the countertop was filled. There were still-sizzling Padron peppers zebra-striped from the grill, melt-in-the-mouth frittata oozing butter, a rich and creamy Russian salad, thinly sliced chips crunchy with salt, warm bread painted with fresh tomatoes and dripping with olive oil, delicately flavoured seabass fillets and a thick, meaty sausage served over hot, spicy beans.

'Get gobbling,' ordered Josephine, when Pepper made no move to begin.

'It's not every day you get to eat food like this, you know.'

She was right. Pepper scooped up a forkful of frittata, her eyes widening as her taste buds came instantly to life. She hadn't been able to face eating much at breakfast that morning, and now found she was starving. As the delicious dishes rapidly disappeared, Pepper began to feel more human again, less wrung out than she had for the past few hours.

'Thank you,' she said to Josephine, as their satisfied server removed the final empty plate and topped up their glasses with more cava. 'I needed that.'

'A full stomach equals a full mind.' Josephine tapped the side of her head. 'You've put some fuel in the tank, and now you can think more coherently.'

Pepper picked up her paper napkin and began shredding it methodically into pieces.

'I'm worried about Finn,' she said. And then, because she had run out of excuses of why not to, she told Josephine what had been going on.

'I understand why you're so concerned,' was the first thing she said, then she pondered for a moment. 'The way I see it,' she said, 'Finn is a straight-talking sort. I can't see him simply ignoring you, apropos of nothing.'

'That's what I thought,' Pepper said dully. 'Just a day or so ago, he was all set to come and live with me, but now that feels like it won't happen. I know, I know!' Pepper held up both her hands as she saw the look on Josephine's face. 'I'm catastrophising – but I can't help it.'

She groaned loudly, her head rocking back until she was staring at the fluorescent strip lighting on the ceiling.

'Everything was so perfect, and now this. It feels so bloody unfair!'

'Welcome to life, darling.' Josephine sighed. 'A series of complicated conundrums, one after the other. I am almost twice your age, and they still appear to be coming thick and fast.'

'I hate that you have to leave Aldeburgh,' Pepper said then. It was the first time she had admitted it out loud, and for a horrible second, she thought Josephine might cry.

'Oh, darling,' she said eventually, drawing in a long, shuddering breath. 'I hate that I have to leave you, too.'

'I'll be OK.' Pepper sniffed. 'I'll muddle through – we both will.'

'Just don't forget that you have choices.' Josephine was looking at her earnestly now. 'If things with Finn are not destined to be, then you can still take charge of your future. You don't need a man to dictate the pace, or the progress.'

'What if he's changed his mind?' More bits of desiccated napkin fluttered to the floor. 'What if he doesn't want to move to Aldeburgh after all?'

Josephine sipped her cava, her eyes not leaving Pepper's.

'All you really need to ask yourself is: do I want to be with Finn for the long haul?' she said. 'If the answer is yes, then you must do everything you can to make it work, even if that means making some big changes to your life.'

'But I can't.' Pepper rubbed at her eyes in agitation. 'I can't leave Suffolk.'

'Can't?' Josephine raised a single eyebrow. 'Or won't?'

It was dark by the time they left Cal Pep, but the streetlights cast a marmalade glow across the cobbles. The air carried the rich scent of a hundred kitchen windows propped open, and notes of music danced past them from bars that were only now beginning to usher in the night.

'Do you know, I think I may have overdone it a tad,' remarked Josephine, wobbling unsteadily on her walking stick. With her frizzy grey hair brushed out and her long green trousers dusting the cobbles, she reminded Pepper of a dandelion.

'No, we are not walking back,' Pepper said firmly, stepping in front of Josephine as her friend attempted to scuttle past the waiting line of taxis.

'Bossy boots!' Josephine blew a friendly raspberry at Pepper as they slid across the backseat.

It didn't take them long to reach the hotel, but instead of waiting for Pepper to pay the driver, Josephine opened her door on the traffic side of the car and clambered out.

The next few seconds seemed to happen in slow motion. There was a loud honking of horns, a screech of alarm and a male voice shouting. Before Pepper could even untangle herself from the seatbelt, Josephine had been hoisted up in the air by a tall man in a hooded top, and the motorbike that had almost hit her was speeding away, its driver yelling obscenities over his shoulder.

Rushing around the bonnet of the taxi, Pepper practically fell across Josephine, who had just been lowered gently to the ground by her rescuer.

'Are you OK?' she exclaimed, then, when Josephine nodded, 'You gave me the scare of my life. What were you thinking? Jesus Christ, woman!'

Glancing up, she was just about to start thanking the man when he pulled down his hood and smiled at her.

'Wh—?'

Josephine beamed up at them both from the pavement.

'Finn, darling!' she giggled. 'Aren't you a sight for sore eyes?'

37

In spite of the fact she had come less than an inch from death by angry motorcyclist, Josephine batted away Pepper's suggestion that she see a doctor.

'Not a scratch on me, thanks to this one,' she said, linking an arm through Finn's. 'But I will let you come up and make me a hot toddy, if you insist.'

'No more alcohol!' Pepper implored, signalling to Finn with her eyes to back her up.

'You heard what the lady said,' he told her obediently. 'I think it is best that we get you into bed.'

'But it's my final night.' Josephine tried to wheel around as they reached the hotel entrance. 'I was rather hoping to go out dancing. Jorge and I would go down to the beach at sunrise and dance across the sand. Did I ever tell you that?'

'You did.' Pepper smiled. 'And if you want me to wake you up before sunrise so we can go and do the same thing together, then I will.'

This seemed to satisfy her, and between them, they managed to get Josephine into the lift and up to her room without too much trouble. Finn boiled the kettle for tea while Pepper helped Josephine remove her make-up and wash her face. There was a black scuff mark on the hem of her beautiful trousers where they had been run over by the motorbike.

'Are you sure nothing hurts?' Pepper checked.

'Only my pride,' Josephine said, extracting a packet of ibuprofen from her washbag and swallowing two dry. 'And I'm too old to worry about that now, thank heavens.'

Pepper's heart still raced. Her friend could so easily have hit her head, or had her arm broken.

When they emerged from the bathroom, Finn was nowhere to be seen. Pepper held Josephine's tea up to her lips so she could sip it, then tucked the sheets in around her and switched on the bedside lamp.

'I'm only a few doors down, so just call my phone if you need me. It doesn't matter what time it is.'

'Thank you, darling.' Josephine was already closing her eyes. 'And thank Finn for me too.'

Finn. Their knight in efficient German armour. Where to even begin?

Letting herself out of Josephine's room, however, Pepper almost tripped right over him. Finn was sitting on the carpeted corridor, his back against the wall.

'Hallo,' he said.

Pepper slid down until she was sitting beside him.

'Hey.'

'I'm sorry,' they both said at once, and Finn jerked his head backwards in surprise.

'What have you got to be sorry for?' he asked. 'You have not done anything wrong.'

Pepper chose to ignore the implication behind his words – that he *had* done something wrong – and said instead, 'All those calls and messages. You must have thought I was a right old nag.'

'No.' Finn was adamant. 'I should have called. I did not want you to worry, but I knew that if I spoke to you, then I would have to tell you. And I wanted to—' He stopped, clearly struggling. Pepper pressed her knee against his.

'Tell me what?'

Finn's hands found the drawstring of his hoodie and he pulled each one until his face disappeared from view.

'*Scheisse*,' he muttered, banging the back of his head against the wall. '*Scheisse, scheisse, scheisse.*'

'Listen, Finn.' Pepper's voice sounded steadier than she felt.

'Whatever it is, you can tell me. I'm not a monster, you know. I won't bite.'

He was still hidden in the depths of his hoodie, so Pepper hooked a finger in the gap and eased it open.

'Why don't you start,' she said, 'by telling me why you flew all the way out here. I mean, not that I'm not thrilled to see you – I am – but I would probably have been fine to wait until you came to Suffolk in a few weeks' time.'

At this, Finn emitted a grunt.

Pepper prised the material apart until she could see his eyes, then knelt in front of him, her hands resting on her knees.

'It was Clara's idea that I come,' he said.

Pepper had not been expecting that.

'And it is not so far,' he added, finally pushing back his hood. His hair was sticking out at all angles, but for once, Pepper did not feel able to reach across and smooth it down.

'And I am glad that I came,' he said. 'I had been sitting outside the hotel for two hours, waiting for you. Every car that pulled up, I was staring at it, hoping it would be you. So, when I saw Josephine, I got up and ran.'

'Thank God you did,' she said. 'You're her hero.'

'But not yours?' he probed gently.

Pepper sighed and rubbed at the beginnings of a headache. There had been too much sun and alcohol today, and nowhere near enough water. Finn sat forwards, his dark-blue eyes hopeful. He wanted to kiss her, but Pepper could not let herself melt into his arms – not yet.

'I think we must talk,' he said.

'We must,' she agreed. 'But not here.'

There was no sofa in Pepper's hotel room, just a single hard-backed chair, so she and Finn had little choice but to perch on the edge of her double bed. Pepper could feel the tension simmering between them – tension that had, up until this point, been driven by their mutual desire. Today, however, that feeling had shifted. There was no trace of the energetic and affable man who had dragged her through the rain in Lisbon now – this Finn was tormented and edgy.

For something to do, Pepper fetched two glasses from the bathroom and filled them with bottled water, handing one to Finn as she sat back down.

'*Danke.*' He drained it and turned to face her.

'I am afraid I have some bad news.'

She knew from his stricken expression that it must be bad. Someone close to him had passed away, perhaps? Or something had happened with the business?

'Whatever it is,' she told him, 'we can get through it. I'm here for you.'

'It is Clara,' he said, so forlornly that it could only be the very worst of news. Pepper was muted by dread as she pictured the tall, strikingly beautiful German woman who had been so kind to her.

'She . . . she's not?' Pepper began.

'Sick?' He almost laughed. '*Nein* – of course. She is fine. In fact, she is happy, considering.'

'I don't understa—'

'Clara is pregnant,' he said, again in the same flat tone.

'Oh.' Pepper was so relieved that her whole body seemed to deflate. 'Well, that's good news, isn't it? I mean, I assume she will need to take some time off work, and I guess that also means you will have to stay in Hamburg for a while longer than we planned – but that's OK. I can fly over and see you more often in the meantime. We'll find a way. You're not cross with Clara, are you? It's wonderful news.'

Finn merely grunted.

'It is!' she persisted, increasingly puzzled by his reaction. 'You should be excited that one of your best friends is having a baby.'

'Having my baby.'

Pepper went to reply, but the words fused together in her throat and she coughed, hard and loud and painfully.

Finn sighed, his gaze now fixed on the carpet.

'I am sorry,' he said. 'The baby, it is mine.'

This could not be happening.

'What do mean, the baby is yours?'

This had to be a prank. His weird Anglo-German sense of humour was failing to translate, and in a minute he would explode with that big-hearted laugh of his and tell her that it was all a joke.

'I mean exactly that.' Finn sounded frustrated now. 'Me and Clara had sex – one time. It happened at a festival two months ago. We all went – me, Clara, Otto – there was a lot of beer, a lot of drinking. It was a stupid thing – we laughed about it the next day.'

Pepper hated to ask, hated herself for even entertaining the thought, but she had to be sure.

'And it's definitely yours? There isn't any chance that it could be someone else's?'

'Pepper,' Finn tempered wearily. 'Clara is one of my oldest friends. She would not lie to me about this – it is not what she planned either. But, you know, she is thirty-eight, she wants to keep it.'

'Of course,' Pepper said numbly. 'Of course she does.'

'You are angry?' he stated, as Pepper stood up and began pacing around the room.

'No,' she said, managing to keep her voice level despite her gathering tears. 'I'm not angry. I just need a bloody moment to take this in.'

'It is a shock, I know,' he said wretchedly. 'But me and Clara, we are not going to get married or something. It is not the nine-teen-fifties. My life is not going to change all that much.'

'Oh, for heaven's sake, Finn!'

He stared at her, his eyes the wide of the wounded.

'Of course your bloody life is going to change,' she said, gritting her teeth. 'A baby changes everything – you must see that?'

Finn shook his head in bewilderment, his thick butter-gold hair flopping across his forehead. Pepper wanted to run scream-ing from the room, but she could not make herself move. What a fool she had been to believe what they had was real – what a fool to think that she could meet and fall in love with the romantic hero she had been holding out for her whole life. She had known right from the start that what they had was too good to be true, and now fate had turned over the cards and played her happiness off the table.

'Please don't give up on me, Pepper,' he said then, attempting to placate her by remaining calm. 'I thought that you wanted to give things with us a proper go?'

'I did,' Pepper snapped. 'I do! But this is . . . It's too much . . .'

The air-conditioning unit clanked in the corner, and upon noticing it, she shivered.

'Here!' Finn started to pull off his dark-blue hoodie to offer it to her, but Pepper was already reaching for her own cardigan. They stood for a few seconds, both unsure what to do next. Finn spoke first.

'Shall we raid the minibar?' he suggested hopefully.

Pepper sighed.

'I'm not sure getting drunk is going to solve anything.'

'I only meant one,' he tempered. 'To remove this . . . this edge.'

'You go ahead,' she told him. 'I've had more than enough tonight.'

Overcome by another need to move, Pepper began pacing around the room again. The butterflies she always had around Finn had been replaced by angry bees – she could imagine them swarming out of her mouth like something out of a horror film.

'*Salud.*' Finn raised his glass of whiskey half-heartedly.

'What are you drinking to?' Pepper asked. 'Impending fatherhood?'

He frowned at that, his forehead creasing.

'I am sorry,' he said.

Pepper crossed the room to sit beside him. 'I know,' she said. 'I don't know why I'm being such a bitch. You've come all this way. I'm just . . .' She gestured helplessly. 'I don't know. In shock, I guess?'

'You are not the only one.' Finn stared down into his glass. 'I cannot believe it.'

'If I was a nice person, I would be saying congratulations,' she said sourly. 'Having a baby, becoming a parent – it's an incredible thing.'

'But?' Finn looked at her. His eyes looked almost black in the lamplight.

'But as happy as I am for you both, I'm also sad. I don't know whether to laugh or cry.'

'I did both things,' he admitted. 'At first, I did not believe that it could be true. I accused Clara of lying, of being jealous.'

Pepper's eyes widened.

'But that was stupid,' he continued. 'She loves me as a friend – nothing more.'

'For now,' Pepper murmured. 'But in time, maybe the two of you w—'

'No!' Finn shook his head. 'Never.'

'A baby changes everything – will change *everything*,' she countered. 'You have to do whatever it takes to look after it and,' she added, thinking of her father, 'support Clara, too.'

Finn looked askance and took a gulp of whiskey before replying.

'Clara understands,' he said. 'I told her that I am not going to change my plans. I want to be with you.'

Relief flooded through Pepper.

'I want that too,' she said, but when Finn then put his arm around her, she felt her whole body tense up.

'Clara has her parents in Hamburg and a lot of friends,' he went on. 'We will get someone in the restaurant to cover for her, all will be well.'

Pepper was confused.

'Where will you be?' she asked, and Finn smiled for the first time.

'With you,' he said simply.

'But you can't!' Pepper moved away from him. 'You can't leave Hamburg now.'

'Of course I can.' Finn was nonplussed. 'That is what I want to do.'

Could he really be saying this? Pepper chewed on her bottom
lip in agitation.

'You know me, Pepper,' he said, as if that explained things.
'The reason that I am happy in my life is because I do not
compromise. I know what I want, and I go after it.'

And he had, hadn't he? He had chased after her in the street,
had pursued her until she gave in. What had seemed so romantic then now felt tainted by his singlemindedness. And while
Pepper could allow that he might be in shock, she was dismayed
by his determination to distance himself from his own child. It
felt too close to home.

'I think the time for putting yourself first may have ended,'
she told him. 'Soon, there will be another person to prioritise,
one that will mean more to you than any ambition – or any other
person.'

Finn had been taking sullen swigs of whiskey while she was
talking, and now he was staring moodily down into the bottom
of his glass.

'I thought that we wanted the same thing,' he said, his shoulders slumped. 'I thought you were happy that I was coming to
live with you. You tell me one day that you are falling in love with
me? Well, this is love – it endures beyond mishaps and
problems.'

'Finn.' She sighed. 'Don't you see?'

He shook his head, seeming irritated now.

'I don't want to be someone that you end up resenting,' she
whispered, barely trusting herself to speak in case she started to
cry. 'I have enough of that in my life already.'

Finn put his glass down on the bedside table and pushed a
hand through his hair, gripping it as if he wanted to pull it out.

'I know!' he exclaimed, gripped by a sudden burst of energy.
'You can come to Hamburg – live with me.'

Pepper was already shaking her head.

'*Ja!* Why not? I will teach you to speak German. And you
don't have to work; I have plenty of money from Freunde. You
can help me with the website – we can travel the world together,

or you can stay at home and paint all day, whatever you want. I will look after you and Clara. It would work, I know it. Things will be great.'

Pepper allowed herself a minute to imagine it. Finn was offering her adventure, companionship, security, love – all the things she had wanted for so long; the things she told herself would make her life complete. And now, here they were, being handed to her freely and genuinely, without question.

'I— I don't know.' She faltered as his expression fell.

'I'm not giving up on us, I'm just trying to do the right thing by everyone.'

'Maybe, it is time that you stopped thinking for everybody else?' he replied bitterly. 'Perhaps, for this little while, try to think only about yourself?'

He made it sound so easy.

'I don't know, Finn.' It was barely a murmur. 'I don't know what to do.'

He shifted his position until he was facing her again.

'You are in shock,' he said steadily. 'Of course you are, so take some time. Think about what you want, because I know already what it is that I want.'

'But how long do I—' She stopped again, words had abandoned her. It was so hard to look at him and see the man she had known, the one so right and so ready to be with her.

Finn took her hand. 'I will wait,' he said. 'Take as much time as you need. I will be waiting.'

Pepper thought he was about to stand up and walk away and braced herself for the sorrow of seeing him go. But instead, Finn leant forwards, taking her face in both his hands and pressing his forehead against hers.

'The only way that this will change our future,' he said, 'is if you let it.'

38

The trip to Barcelona had only lasted four days, but it was a different Pepper that arrived back in Aldeburgh.

Never before had she felt so conflicted, so unsure whether to laugh at the absurdity of life or shout obscenities at how unfair it was. It was no longer clear to Pepper what she wanted, or where she was heading. The ground had opened up below her and all the lights had gone out, and now she was falling without end, in limbo and with no idea which direction to turn. All the while, the same thought rebounded through her mind over and over: Finn was having a baby with someone else.

She knew she had changed, because the old Pepper would have taken her frustration out on the work she had created, but when she laid out her tiles on her studio workbench, thinking she would destroy them, she found that the urge to do so was no longer there. Just as her feelings for Finn had not dimmed in intensity, nor had the love and hope and happiness that seemed to flow from each image – they were still every bit as powerful.

And so, Pepper set to work creating more, and the work became her salvation. Tiles were soon piling up in the bottom of her studio cupboard, each one a tribute to something she had seen or a feeling she had experienced in Barcelona. She painted Vespas with laughing faces and trailing hair, a simmering pan of paella so large she needed six squares to finish it, and she sat up late into the night trying to recapture even a sniff of Gaudí's unmistakable magic. While she worked, she wrestled with her problems, determined to face them rather than grouting over the gaps. Thoughts of Finn were her constant companions, there in morning when she woke and always with her in the dark. He had spent the night in her hotel room in Barcelona, but she had woken before dawn to find him gone, a note left on the pillow reminding her that he would wait.

That had been a week ago, yet Pepper was still no closer to a decision.

Today, however, she had lifted the needle from her spinning mind in order to host a candle-making class in her studio. She had five enthusiasts seated at her table, each one clad in an apron that was becoming steadily doused with soft wax. Jars of essential oils, sprigs of dried herbs, cinnamon sticks and matches littered the table, while coils of wick snaked along the floor.

Making candles was both messy and smelly, but the sessions always proved to be popular – especially around Christmas time, when people wanted to craft a gift. Today's bunch – who varied in age from nine to ninety-two – were very nice, but also very slow. The day was supposed to have finished over an hour ago, but a few were still deciding on a fragrance.

'Try not to overthink it,' she said to Sally, who ran one of the gift shops on the high street. 'You can't go wrong with citrussy notes or vanilla.'

'I want an aroma that will relax me,' Sally mused, squinting at the small print on a bottle of eucalyptus oil.

'In that case,' Pepper said, making for the door, 'you need lavender. I'll just pop into the garden and get you some.'

Swerving to avoid a chair that another of her pupils chose that exact moment to push back, Pepper skittered sideways and knocked a large bottle of white spirit onto the floor.

'Oopsy,' she trilled, swallowing the seven or so much ruder words that had sprung to mind.

She had just deposited the lavender on the table and was heading inside to get a cloth when her phone started ringing. It was then that Pepper remembered her vow to call her mother when she got back from Spain – a vow she had failed to keep.

'Mum? Hi. I know, I said I'd call – I'm sorry. It's just been busy. Work's been busy.'

'It's fine,' her mother replied, for once with enough buoyancy to sound convincing. 'I'm just on my way round to you, actually.'

'But it's Monday.' Pepper stopped halfway along her garden path.

'Yes, I know,' said her mother. 'I— Well, I thought we could go for a walk?'

Her mother wanted to spend extra one-on-one time with her – was choosing to do so?

'Er, OK.' Pepper said, unable to mask her surprise. 'But don't bother coming all the way here. Shall I meet you by the coastal path, in say ten minutes?'

'Sorry, everyone,' Pepper said, addressing the room two minutes later. 'Something's come up and I have to pop out. Feel free to stay and finish. You all know what you're doing, right?'

There was a chorus of nods.

'Right, when you go, can the last person make sure they shut and lock the studio door behind them? Just leave the keys on the kitchen worktop. And don't worry about clearing up,' she added, pausing with one arm through the sleeve of her denim jacket. 'I'll clear everything up in no time when I get back.'

She found her mum waiting at the foot of the beach path, sparse grass behind her and the wide, salt-and-pepper spread of stony beach ahead. It felt unusual to be meeting her like this, on a non-designated day and not in a pre-scheduled place, and to make matters even more astonishing, her mother was actually smiling.

'Have you won the lottery or something?' Pepper asked as she drew closer. She and her mother rarely hugged and never kissed each other hello, but today her mother extended a hand of greeting.

'Are we shaking hands now?' Pepper said bemusedly. 'Very formal.'

'Sorry.' Her mother went to snatch it away, but Pepper caught hold of her and gave the hand a brisk shake.

'There we go,' she said lightly. 'Not weird at all.'

Her mother's mouth had gone rather lopsided, as if she was trying hard to suppress a grin.

'I thought that we . . . Oh, never mind. Anyway, shall we?' She gestured to the path. 'I thought it might be nice to walk along to Thorpeness, get an ice cream or something?'

Any moment now, Pepper thought. Any moment now I will wake up.

They began by talking about Barcelona, her mother gazing mostly towards the far horizon as Pepper told her about Park Güell, Casa Batlló and La Pedrera, trying her best to explain how it had felt to be surrounded by the work of such an imaginative genius.

'I'm only vaguely aware of Gaudí,' her mother confessed. 'But I always did like mosaics.'

She did?

Pepper was about to reply when they were both distracted by a dog bounding along the path, all long floppy ears and lolling pink tongue. Bethan had begged incessantly for a puppy, had scrawled the word at the top of every birthday and Christmas list she made. Her mother had not been keen on the idea, but Pepper's dad was more easily persuaded. Bethan would creep onto his lap while he watched the news and curl her fingers around his, promising that she would be a good girl, that she would do all the walking herself, that if he said yes to a puppy, she would never ask for anything else ever again.

If the accident had never happened, her sister would have got her way in the end. Pepper was sure of it.

She began to collect things as they walked – pebbles, feathers, twine, plastic bottles and sweet wrappers – slipping it all into a canvas tote bag she'd slung over one shoulder. It was the kind of thing her fastidiously clean mother would usually screw her nose up at, but today she didn't comment. She did not say much, in fact, seemingly content to listen as Pepper brought up one safe subject after another – what she planned to wear to Martin and Keira's wedding, the drama series about corrupt police officers that she'd just discovered and was watching every night, the outdoor watercolour class she hoped to launch soon. When Pepper filled her in on the Vespa tour she and Josephine had taken, and what her friend had said about 'beautiful beasts', her mother laughed. *Actually laughed.* Pepper almost fell off the path in shock.

She ran out of topics just as they reached Thorpeness, but by then, it was clear her mother had a plan of where she wanted to go next.

'Look,' she said, as the village green came into view on their left, covered as it always was by waddling ducks and geese. 'The House in the Clouds is just up ahead – do you remember it from when you were little?'

'Of course I do.'

She and Bethan had spent so many happy days down on the beach as children, lying on their tummies side by side on the warm stones, gazing up at the distant house and making up stories about the people who lived in it. Pepper could remember teasing Bethan that you could see right across to Belgium from the top floor, and that once upon a time, fairies had been found living at the bottom of the garden.

'There's a secret in every room of that house,' she would tell her. 'If you stand on the path outside and whisper your secret into the wind, the house will keep it for you.'

'It reminds me of Bethan,' Pepper said quietly, testing the subject that so often caused her mother to spiral downwards into abject misery. She saw her take a deep breath.

'Yes,' she said. 'Bethie always loved it. But I've always found it more reminiscent of you.'

'Me?'

'You're the one who's most like it,' her mother said. 'Ever since I can remember, you've been walking around with your head in the clouds.'

Where was the sullen tone? Where was the weary, withering look?

'I try not to do that any more,' Pepper said, as they turned down the lane that would lead them right to the house. 'I learnt my lesson.'

Her mother stopped walking and Pepper glanced back.

'What?'

Her mother said nothing at first, she simply stood and picked listlessly at the bobbles on her over-washed cardigan. She looked less prim and put-together today and had swapped her sensible heels for a pair of plimsolls and put on a floral blouse instead of her standard navy or cream. It made her seem softer somehow, more vulnerable, but with her sharp elbows and hunched shoulders, she reminded Pepper painfully of Josephine.

Sliding her phone out of her pocket, she realised that she'd been alone with her mother for almost an hour now, but for the first time since Pepper had reached adulthood, she had not been starkly aware of every awkward passing minute. She had always thought it was her mum who had driven the wedge between them, but perhaps they had been equally evasive.

'This is weird,' she blurted.

Her mother's expression gave nothing away.

'Weird how?'

'Us, here, spending time together doing something other than sitting in your house or shopping.'

'We used to do it all the time,' she said. 'Before Bethan was born, it was always just the two of us.'

Pepper swallowed. Her lungs felt flat and unyielding.

'You always wanted to be outdoors as a child,' she went on. 'I used to joke with your father that we'd brought the wrong baby home from the hospital, because Martin and I were such homebodies. With you, it was always the beach – you wanted to play chase with the waves and collect shells for all your collages.'

'I still do both those things,' Pepper told her, and was surprised when her mother smiled.

'I don't think I'm all that different from my childhood self, not really.'

'In some ways, you are very much the same,' her mother allowed, finally moving forwards again. When she drew level with Pepper, she lifted a hand, as if she wanted to touch her, but then dropped it again.

They walked on in silence, less companionable now, and Pepper rummaged through her mind in search of something to say. She wondered where Finn was, and what he was thinking about right at this moment. Were the two of them connected enough that their individual thoughts would throw a rope around the other's and draw them in? Or was it more realistic that Finn was simply concentrating on work, or his pregnant best friend? It was horrible not speaking to him every day, but she couldn't see how they could slip back into their FaceTime habit until she had made a decision.

'Philippa.'

Her mother had come to a halt again. They were so close to the House in the Clouds now that Pepper could make out the pattern of the curtains at its windows and hear the faint sound of a family perhaps sharing a picnic lunch in its front garden. Just beyond them lay a windmill, its sails frozen forever in the shape of a kiss.

'I wanted to say,' her mother began, falling silent as Pepper's phone began to ring.

'Aargh! Sorry, Mum. I'll just . . . Oh, it's my neighbour, Mrs Hill. That's strange – she never calls. Hang on.'

'Pepper! Dear oh dear – where are you, love?'

'In Thorpeness,' Pepper said, feeling mystified. 'Whatever's the matter?'

'Do you have your— No, I can see it. No matter. I will come and get you – can you go to the green and wait for me there?'

'Why?' Pepper became more insistent. 'What's the big hurry?'

'I saw smoke.' Mrs Hill faltered. 'Don't worry, love – I called 999 and they're on their way.'

'Hang on – there's a fire?' Pepper felt fear plummet like a potted snooker ball into her stomach. 'Where?'

Mrs Hill took a breath.

'Go to the green now and wait there,' she repeated. 'I'll be with you in five minutes.'

39

'No, no, no!'

Pepper slammed the door of Mrs Hill's pink Fiat behind her and hurtled towards her cottage. Smoke was billowing out above the roof and she coughed as the acrid smell filled her throat.

'Philippa!' she heard her mother shout, but she didn't stop. Shovelling her way through the crowd that had assembled like ghouls on the pavement outside, Pepper flung herself into the house, hurtling along the hallway and across the kitchen.

She had known as soon as Mrs Hill had said the word 'smoke' that it would be her studio. The candle-making class left unattended; the spilt bottle of white spirit never mopped up – Pepper had done this to herself.

There was a loud crack as the glass in the studio door shattered and fell, and Pepper watched on in muted horror as flames began to lick their way out through the gap. All her materials, her paints and mosaic tiles in their little tins, her charcoal and paper and feathers and glue, the red pepper Finn had made for her, the stack of tiles she had so lovingly been painting since she met him. It was the best work she had ever done – the most real and honest thing she had ever created. And now it was burning. It was all turning to ash.

Without stopping to think what she was doing, Pepper lifted her T-shirt until it was covering her nose and mouth and stepped further along the path. She could feel the heat of the flames on her skin, and hear the roar as they gathered pace, not caring what they stole, or who they hurt.

There was a chance.

She had locked her Barcelona-themed tiles in the cupboard with the others just a few days ago. She could get in there and kick it open somehow, snatch them all before the fire caught up with her, save something of her love story.

Pepper took a few more steps forward, looking for a way in. The heat was almost unbearable now, the smoke growing ever thicker. She should wait until she heard sirens, but logic was fast losing the battle.

'Philippa!'

She heard her mother's scream just as she reached the blackening studio wall, but ignored her, instead aiming a kick at what was left of the window and watching it shatter. She felt something rising up inside her chest – not fear or misery, but rage.

Red hot rage.

The cupboard was right there – she could see it, she could reach it, she could save something, she could kick down the door, this door and the other door – the bathroom door. She could pull her sister out of the water and bring her back.

Roaring with frustration and anger, Pepper set off at a run, determined to leap over the flames. She heard a shout and felt someone's hands on her shoulders, yanking her backwards and down to the ground.

'Let me go!' she screamed, twisting and writhing away.

'Philippa,' she heard her mother cry. 'Please!'

'I need to save her!' she wailed, incoherent now. 'I can still save her.'

The smoke was absolute now. It blinded and choked as the flames crackled and crashed. Pepper was still struggling, but she could no longer see which way was forward or back, she could only see the same blackness that she had on that day, and on every other day that followed. A horrible gaping wound where her baby sister should have been.

'We need to get out of here.'

Her mother was on the ground beside her, her voice a low croak.

'It's not safe, sweetheart. My girl, my precious girl.'

'Mum?'

Pepper turned and groped for her mother. Trinity had fallen silent, her eyes huge in a face blackened now by smoke. She would never leave her, Pepper realised then, and with a sob she pulled herself up, dragging her mother to her feet and back towards the house.

Neither of them had been able to save Bethan. But as they stood out in the road, the blue lights from the fire engine rotating a pattern across cheeks that were pressed one against the other, Pepper wondered if perhaps the time had come to salvage something from the mess that her sister's death had left behind. On her final morning in Barcelona, she had kept her promise to Josephine and walked with her down to the beach. They had searched through the music on her phone for a suitable song as the whispers of a pastel dawn began to appear at the far boundaries of the sea, and then they had stood up, and they had danced to welcome in the new day.

Josephine had danced for Jorge, and for her memories of a love that she would never forget.

Pepper had danced for Bethan.

40

Finn's invitation arrived three days after the fire.

He had spared no expense, and Pepper had to smile when she saw the embossed gold lettering that spelled out the name of his website.

He had called it 'The Pelican'.

Beside a quirky sketch of the bird in question – also in gold – were the details of a launch party-cum-exhibition, which was being held at Freunde, in Hamburg, in just over three weeks' time. There was also a handwritten note from Finn, which simply said:

'I found the perfect artist, so I thought, why wait? See you at the party.'

That was so like him, she thought, pressing the note to her chest. Assuming that she would be there and not even entertaining the idea that she would not. The two of them had messaged back and forth a handful of times over the past few days, and upon hearing about the fire, Finn had immediately rung her to express his sympathy – and to check that she was all right.

He missed her, he had said. And Pepper agreed that she missed him, too. But at no time during their conversation did she mention moving to Hamburg, and good as his word, neither did Finn. They stuck to safe topics, and Pepper did not mention the baby except to ask how Clara was doing. When she had filled Josephine in on the pregnancy news on the flight back from Barcelona, her friend's initial reaction was: 'I thought safe sex was all the rage these days?'

Then, when Pepper had merely sighed, she'd added, 'So foolish, taking a risk like that. I thought Finn was a sensible sort of fellow?'

'So did I,' Pepper had agreed in a desultory tone, although she could not find it in herself to berate him too harshly. Nobody was immune from the occasional slip-up, and there was no point playing the blame game. Clara and Finn had been friends for a long time; they had drunk too much and had a fumble that went too far. It was as simple as that. No great crime – just very unfortunate timing.

To be speaking to him again had settled her conflicted heart somewhat, and now that Pepper knew she would see him in just a few weeks, she felt as if some of the pressure had been lifted. She would definitely know by then what she was going to do, she was sure of it.

Propping the invitation upon the living-room mantelpiece, Pepper collected her things and for once remembered to lock the front door behind her. It was a non-negotiable must, as far as her temporary landlady was concerned, along with removing all hair from the shower plughole and not leaving teabags in the sink.

Her mother had not changed all that much.

Pepper missed her studio horribly, but the sting of losing it had been tempered by the people of Aldeburgh, many of whom had rallied around to help. As soon as word of the fire got out – which had not taken very long at all, given Mrs Hill's fondness for a good old gossip – offers started coming in from all over the town. Sally from the gift shop – who blamed herself for the fire even though, as she told Pepper, 'I never even tried out my candle, so it can't have been me' – had lent her the empty flat above her high-street store to host her sessions, while the landlord of the Turbot had donated a table large enough to accommodate groups and unearthed a set of six chairs from the pub store room. Mrs Hill herself had stepped in to help call and reschedule appointments while the new room was still being set up, and the ladies from the RSPCA charity shop organised a coffee morning that raised enough donations to buy Arts For All a second-hand camera and laptop.

For so many years, Pepper had imagined herself to be isolated and lacking in friends, but over the past week, she had been proven wrong countless times over.

She was loved here in her hometown – she could feel it.

Everything had been sorted out so efficiently that Pepper had only needed to cancel a handful of sessions in the end, and she had enjoyed ordering boxes of new craft materials on the company credit card she had taken out years ago, yet never used.

It was as if the fire had wiped the slate clean; given her the chance to start afresh with the things that mattered most. Stuff could always be replaced, and walls put back up – the only thing she still felt sad about was her collection of painted tiles. If the fire had happened even a few weeks earlier than it had, Pepper would not have lost anything she had created herself – a fact that baffled her now when she thought about it.

Those tiles had represented the time she had spent with Finn, and with Josephine, too – time that she cherished almost more than any other in her life. She knew the fact that they were gone did not mean those memories would vanish along with them – those moments that had taught her so much, about herself and what she wanted – but she couldn't help but feel sad that nobody else would ever get to see them. Not since she was a teenager had Pepper been proud enough of a piece to show to anyone, but that was exactly how she'd been starting to feel about her tiles. She had planned to show Josephine first, then perhaps even Finn. Now, neither would ever get the chance. Of course, logic told her that she could start again – paint the same scenes and generate the same emotion – but that did not feel right somehow.

Something else would happen to reawaken that artistic spirit that Pepper now knew had never really gone away – and this time when it did, she would not hesitate to listen.

She was in the flat above the shop unpacking a box of brand-new tile clippers when there was a knock on the door.

'It's open!' Pepper called.

'Hello, darling – I'm not interrupting anything, am I?'

It was Josephine, looking resplendent in flowing blue silk.

'I just wanted to bring you this,' she said, swinging a carrier bag at Pepper with the hand that wasn't clutching her stick.

'It's gin, of course – but there's another little something in there that I thought you might like.'

'You really shouldn't have,' Pepper said, drawing out a hard-edged rectangular parcel wrapped in brown paper. Inside, she found a framed black-and-white photograph of a young couple sitting atop a low wall patterned with tiles. From the spread of rooftops behind them and the glint in the smiling eyes of the woman, there could be no mistaking who it was or where it had been taken.

'Is this . . . ?' Pepper gasped.

'Not the best quality, I'm afraid, but then it is almost as old as I am,' Josephine said, bustling over to the kitchen area and opening the freezer.

'Please say there's some ice in here.'

'Third drawer down.'

Pepper was still gazing at the photo. The man was dark and handsome, with a broad, intelligent-looking face and thick fore-arms – one of which was resting casually on the young woman's bare thigh.

'Josephine, is this you and Jorge?'

'Yes, yes,' Josephine was now struggling to open the lid of the gin. 'Damn these hands,' she muttered.

'Here.' Pepper hurried over and helped her out. 'But we really shouldn't be drinking pink gin in the middle of the afternoon.'

'Poppycock!'

Josephine dashed a healthy measure into each glass, sighing with pleasure at the sound of the ice cracking.

'Once I get to Australia, I'll be under the stern watch of Georgina, and I'm telling you now, my darling, gin o'clock will very quickly become a fond but distant memory.'

'I love this photo,' Pepper told her, taking a sip of her gin and spluttering as the neat spirit hit the back of her throat. 'You both look so young, so carefree.'

'And so we were.' Josephine smiled. Today was a good day – Pepper could tell. There was a colour in her friend's cheeks, and she'd taken the time to apply a dash of lipstick.

'Why did you choose this one to give me?'

'Well, because it's the only one I have . . .'

'Then I mustn't take it!' Pepper was aghast. 'I mean, I'm really flattered and everything, but you should keep it.'

'Whatever for?' Josephine fixed Pepper with one of her stares. 'Darling girl, once I leave here, it is probable that I will not return. No, no – let me finish. I wanted to go back and relive that summer I spent with Jorge, and so I did, thanks to you. It has been so wonderful, seeing it all again and remembering how blissfully happy we were. But now I have done all that, and it's time to move on to what's next.'

Pepper couldn't bear it. She closed her eyes, as if somehow the words would become less true if she didn't watch them being said.

'I am going to organise all my affairs before I leave,' Josephine went on. 'And the first of those is this photo. You are a part of my story now, so it's only right that you get to keep the only physical piece of it that I have. Georgina won't even know who it is in the photo – if I take it with me, it will only end up forgotten, plonked in a shoebox underneath a bed and left to gather dust. At least if you take it now, I know it will be seen in the way it was intended to be. It is the way I want you to remember me. As that young, adventurous girl with an open heart and nothing holding her back from what she wanted. Promise me that you will keep it?'

'Of course I will,' Pepper was crying now, she couldn't help it. 'Sorry,' she blurted, wiping her face with the back of her hand. 'I'm a wreck lately – a watering can with extra holes.'

'Darling girl.' Josephine took a step closer and put an unsteady hand on her arm. 'You have been through a lot – and I don't

mean just Finn and the fire,' she added. 'I know how much you
miss your sister – I can see it. Grief is an absolute beast. When
Ian died I felt as if all the threads holding my patchwork pieces
together had unravelled at once; I was this great big useless heap
on the floor.'

'How did you get from there to here?' Pepper asked, looking
down again at the photo. 'I feel like the broken bits of me have
never mended.'

Josephine sipped her gin, a smile playing around her lips as
she considered this.

'You know, if you thought about it,' she said. 'If you put your
artist hat on, then really thought about it, you would realise that
you already know the answer to that question.'

Pepper opened her mouth, but Josephine talked over her.

'Now,' she said, pulling out one of the rickety pub chairs and
eyeing it with mild alarm. 'You promised me in Barcelona that I
could have an introduction to that wonderful-sounding Samuel
chap.'

'You want to meet him now?' Pepper asked. 'As in, tonight?'

'No time like the present,' Josephine trilled, lowering herself
down and wincing with the effort. 'I'm in both the silk and the
red lippy, and I would rather that neither went to waste – no
offence, darling.'

Pepper, who was already reaching for her phone to make the
call, rolled her eyes.

'What did your last slave die of?' she joked.

Josephine cackled.

'Why, exhaustion, of course.'

When Pepper sent Samuel a message asking if he was free for dinner, he rang rather than texted back.

'Had to check it wasn't a prank call,' he had said. 'This is *the* Pepper, right?'

'That depends . . .' Pepper had rolled her eyes at Josephine's enquiring glance. 'Which one do you consider to be *the* one?'

'Oh, y'know? Blonde, tells bad jokes, always covered in splodges of paint . . .'

When Pepper then explained that she had someone who wanted to meet him, and asked if he would like to come to hers for a meal in order to do so, an excited Samuel had fired about twelve consecutive questions asking if this person was single, and why she needed Pepper there as a third wheel.

'She is single,' Pepper had told him carefully, 'but she's also leaving town soon, so I am afraid marriage is probably out of the question. Oh, and it won't just be me third-wheeling,' she'd added, suddenly struck by an idea. 'My mum will be there as well.'

'This is going to be some blind date,' he had replied. 'But OK. Why don't you come to mine? I'm a dab hand in the kitchen, especially when I have a mysterious lady to impress.'

'Make that two mysterious ladies,' Pepper had reminded him. 'Unless you've secretly been dating my mum this whole time.'

'Chance,' he had retorted cheerfully, 'would be a fine thing.'

Samuel lived in a maisonette not far from The Maltings, and as Pepper eased her vast Volvo up onto the kerb outside, he opened the front door, spilling light and music out to greet them. He was wearing a grey and white striped apron and had a wooden spoon covered in what looked like tomato sauce in one hand.

'Golly,' muttered Josephine, who had been busy becoming fast friends with Pepper's mother during the drive over. 'You look just like that actor, you know, the one in the alien film.'

'Sigourney Weaver?' said Samuel, catching Pepper's eye as he bent to kiss Josephine's cheek.

'I think you mean Will Smith, right?' she corrected. Her mum was still hovering uncertainly by the car, so Samuel strode out to offer her his hand.

'You must be Pepper's mother?'

'Trinity.' She looked for a moment as if she was going to curtsey, but thankfully settled on a handshake instead.

'Samuel,' he said. 'Feel free to call me that, or the Chief, which is one of my many monikers. Or, of course, you could also call me the Fresh Prince of Aldeburgh, which is one-hundred percent going to be another one after tonight.'

'I hope we're not imposing,' Pepper heard her mum say as they filed into the house.

'We brought wine.' Pepper put a bottle of red down on the table, which Samuel had set with proper placemats and candles. 'This is such a nice place.'

And it was. The décor in the living-cum-dining room was understated yet thoughtful, with little touches here and there making it feel homely rather than bachelor pad-ish. Pepper's eye was immediately drawn to a large photo collage hanging above the sofa, which showed what could only be Samuel's two brothers, sister and parents indulging in various acts of foolhardiness. Like him, they all had warm and open expressions, and she could almost hear the laughter coming from some of the more animated pictures. Many of the photos had been taken in what looked like holiday locations, and almost all of them featured food of some kind.

'I hope you're all hungry,' Samuel shouted through from the kitchen. There was the sound of a cupboard door opening and closing, followed by a drawer, then he re-emerged carrying four wine glasses.

'Not for me, thanks,' said Pepper, then for some reason lifted her hands and began miming a steering wheel. 'I'm driving.'

'What are we having?' asked Josephine, who had settled herself into an armchair and was flicking through the *Big Issue*.

'Spag Bol.' Samuel glanced at each of them in turn. 'I hope that's all right? Please say there are no veggies in the house.'

'I never refuse meat from a man,' Josephine said blithely, and Samuel bellowed with laughter just as Pepper said firmly, 'Josephine!'

'Shall I help you in the kitchen?' her mother said, but Pepper interrupted.

'No, please let me. You stay here and keep this one on a tight leash.'

Samuel was still chuckling as he scooped a strand of spaghetti out from a pan boiling on the stove top.

'Mind out,' he said, and lobbed it against the wall where it bounced off and landed with a slithery splat on the floor.

'Not quite done yet.'

'I thought that was an urban myth,' said Pepper. Then, seeing a lump of Parmesan on the worktop. 'Shall I grate?'

'That'd actually be, er, great,' he said cheerfully, pulling open a large drawer which clanked slightly, and passing over a four-sided cheese grater. The kitchen was small but well thought-out, with ample preparation space and a classic Belfast sink. Samuel had a range of fresh herbs living in pots along his windowsill, and a Tottenham Football Club calendar hung on the wall above the light switch.

'It's really good of you to have us all over,' said Pepper, pull-ing out one of the two stools that were tucked under a narrow breakfast bar and settling herself into it. 'I would have happily hosted at mine.'

'I like being the host with the most,' he told her, turning from where he was stirring fresh basil into the Bolognese sauce. 'And I wasn't sure you'd want the extra stress, not after what happened recently.'

She had told Samuel about the fire over the phone earlier.

'It has been a bit of a nightmare,' she allowed. 'The fire never got anywhere near the main house, thank God, but the smell was horrendous. I haven't checked the pond yet, but I bet Mr and Mrs Ribbit have moved out in protest.'

'And Mr and Mrs Ribbit are . . . ?'

'My frogs.'

The corners of Samuel's mouth twitched.

'Of course,' he said. 'Silly me.'

'The worst thing is,' Pepper went on, her eyes not on him but on the lump of Parmesan she was shredding, 'I had started painting again – for myself, I mean. I hadn't done anything I liked for years, but I thought that this time—' She sighed as the familiar regret washed over her. 'I thought maybe, just maybe, I'd created something worth seeing – worth showing other people.'

She glanced up to find Samuel staring at her, the wooden spoon in his hand immobile.

'You mean you don't normally show people your art?' he asked slowly, and she shook her head.

'Not for years – not since I quit my degree before it even began.'

'I just assumed you had a great big stash of work somewhere,' Samuel admitted. 'I thought it would be all over your house, but I could tell none of those paintings were yours when I came over that one time.'

'You could?' Pepper was surprised. 'How come?'

Samuel thought for a moment.

'None of them felt like you,' he said simply.

'Well, you were right about that,' Pepper told him. She had

grated far too much cheese now, so she started absentmindedly eating it. 'Nothing I made had felt like me for a long time; then this summer, after I got back from Lisbon, I was inspired. I started a collection of tiles, and do you know what – they were pretty good.'

'I'm sure they were,' he agreed, turning down the heat under the sauce. There were orange droplets all down the front of his apron where a bubbled-over splatter had got him.

'Well,' she went on gloomily, 'nobody will ever see them now. I stupidly locked the whole lot in my studio cupboard, which is now nothing more than a pile of ash.'

'That is annoying,' Samuel concurred. 'But you shouldn't let it beat you down too much. I mean, you still painted them, right? You still did it. That can only be a good thing. Now you know you can do it – create something you're proud of that feels like you.'

'I guess so.' Pepper tucked her hair behind her ears and chewed at her bottom lip. 'But what if I can't? What if that was a fluke – a one-time thing?'

'Incoming!' called Samuel, and Pepper had to duck to avoid being hit with wet spaghetti. This time the pasta stuck fast to the wall, and she laughed as Samuel gave a cheer.

'I get what you're saying,' he told her, crossing to the sink. Steam enveloped him a moment later and turned the windows white. 'I felt the exact same way the first time I assisted on an appendectomy. There was no reason for me to think I had done anything but an excellent job, but I still doubted myself.'

'How did you overcome it?' Pepper asked eagerly.

Samuel put the pan of drained spaghetti back on the stove top.

'Easy,' he said. 'I just did it again. And again. And on the tenth or eleventh time, it became easier. I trusted my skills more and my anxieties less. You didn't really need me to tell you that, though, did you? You already know what you have to do.'

Pepper watched on in silence as he heaped spaghetti onto four plates and plonked large mounds of Bolognese on top. She knew he was right; she did know what to do. She understood why she hadn't for so long, why she now could, and what she needed to keep her creative momentum going.

She had to believe in herself.

42

Pepper didn't know if Samuel had chosen spaghetti Bolognese on purpose as an icebreaker, but it certainly made the experience of eating an amusing one.

There was no way of consuming it without dribbling sauce over your chin or scooping a heap onto your spoon only to have it slither off back onto the plate. Even Pepper's mother raised a smile when Samuel sucked in an extra-long strand of pasta with such gusto that the end whipped him across the nose.

Pepper had tucked her napkin into the neck of her shirt without preamble, and Josephine followed suit, although she managed not to get a single drop of sauce on herself.

'You look as if you've taken a stroll through an abattoir,' she remarked to Samuel when they had finished. He was still wearing his apron, and it was covered with splatters of sauce.

'Maybe this is why I'm single,' he told them, topping up Pepper's water glass then checking that everyone else had wine. 'Because you can't take a messy toad like me anywhere.'

'Toad?' Pepper chuckled. 'You're welcome to move into my pond, if you like? You're bound to attract a mate that way.'

'Gee.' Samuel deadpanned. 'Thanks.'

'I would absolutely allow you to court me if I didn't have to leave,' Josephine told him. 'What is that word? The one that describes an older lady with a younger lover?'

'Cougar,' replied Pepper and Samuel at the same time.

'That's it! Marvellous!'

'Is that what you're looking for, then?' Pepper asked Samuel. 'Someone older and wiser?'

'Someone non-amphibian would do,' he drawled. 'I don't really have a type. As long as she finds my jokes funny, then I'm hers.'

'Oh dear,' Pepper said gravely. 'Looks like you'll be alone forever, in that case.'

'For that,' Samuel said, pushing back his chair, 'you can help me with pudding.'

Half an hour and four bowls of very good treacle tart and ice cream later, they retired to the sofa area, Josephine sinking down into an armchair that looked older than all four of them combined and Pepper's mother perching awkwardly on a swivel chair. She had not said much throughout the meal, but she seemed to Pepper to be more relaxed than usual and had laughed along with the rest of them rather than going off into one of her vague trances. It was clear her mother liked Samuel, and Pepper wondered if she would take as quickly to Finn. That's if she ever got the chance to meet him. She could not imagine her mum boarding a flight to Germany to visit him, even if she did seem stronger in herself. She was still too tied to home, too anchored to the past – Pepper understood, because at the start of this strange, eventful summer, she had felt the same way. Now, however, she found herself torn – she wanted to be in two places at the same time.

Samuel had put on some music, and Pepper sat listening for a moment, enjoying the gentle flickering of the candles and the soft banter being traded from sofa to squashy armchair. She felt at ease here, more so than she had in a long time, and wondered if it was to do with the setting or the company. Certainly, it had been ages since she'd been around her mother and not felt twitchy, but things had changed between them since the fire. Her mum seemed more engaged, more interested in what she was saying or doing, more willing to offer support. It was a nice feeling, but Pepper didn't know if she quite trusted it yet. When it came to her mother, the ground was always fragile, and there was no way Pepper would embark upon a tramp across a frozen lake unless she had a very strong rope to hold onto.

Somehow they had got around to the subject of her dad's wedding, and Pepper turned her head away from the candles, ready to re-engage.

'What was that?'

'I was just telling Samuel here that your date has fallen through,' Josephine said.

'It has?' Pepper's mother piped up. 'That's a shame.'

She couldn't be sure if the comment was genuine or sarcastic. No Finn meant her mum would have her all to herself. She was just about to reply, when her mother went on, 'Why don't you come instead, Samuel?'

'MUM!'

Josephine looked between them. 'I agree,' she said, and Pepper rolled her eyes. 'I think that is an excellent idea. Weddings are utterly tiresome most of the time,' she went on. 'If Samuel goes along with you, it's bound to be a hoot.'

'I love you too,' Samuel said, blowing Josephine a kiss.

'But there's no time,' Pepper protested. 'It's in Guernsey,' she added to Samuel. 'So, you'd have to get a flight, and the hotel is probably booked up by now.'

'Samuel can have your room,' said her mother. 'I booked a double, so we can share.'

'But—'

'But nothing.' Josephine was clapping her hands now. Her stick had slipped down from where she'd balanced it against the arm of her chair and Pepper bent to retrieve it. 'It makes perfect sense – your mother and I agree, so I am afraid you're overruled.'

'But what about Samuel?' Pepper said, feeling exasperated. 'I'm pretty sure he gets a say, too.'

They all turned to find him smiling broadly.

'I'm game,' he said. 'As long as it's all right with you? I've never been to the Channel Islands before – kinda fancy it.'

How had this somehow become her decision?

Pepper could not help but think of Finn, and how put out he would be when he learnt that Samuel was attending the wedding in his place. She had been so looking forward to having him on her arm, proving to her parents that she was not the sad habitual single after all, that she had found a wonderful man who loved her just as much as she loved him. But everything with Finn felt sullied now and difficult. He probably would still have come to the wedding had she asked him, but until now, the thought hadn't even crossed her mind.

She looked towards her mother, who was smiling expectantly, and to Josephine, whose mischievous twinkle was waiting. Samuel was harder to read, but if Pepper had to guess, she would have said he was hopeful of a yes.

'Of course you should come,' she said, groaning good-naturedly when Josephine whooped. 'But don't blame me if none of the bridesmaids agree to give you their number.'

Samuel laughed.

'How did you know that was what I was thinking?'

Pepper tapped her temple.

'Telepathic, obviously. Now, if you point me in the direction of your loo?'

'Upstairs, door on the— Actually,' he grinned. 'If you're tele-pathic, you'll probably work it out for yourself.'

Pepper could still hear the three of them laughing as she scampered up the carpeted stairs and smiled to herself as she tried the first door. It was an airing cupboard.

The second door she opened was clearly a bedroom, so she shut it quickly, glimpsing only a white duvet cover and dark-blue pillows. The third door led into a tiny boxroom that housed a desk, shelves and a complicated array of exercise equipment and weights. Pepper was about to go into reverse when she spotted something vaguely familiar tucked in beside the computer. Checking over her shoulder, she stepped quietly into the room, sure she must be mistaken. But no, it was what she'd thought it was.

'Hello, again,' she said.

It was the ugly toy cat from the fête. She could not believe he'd kept it.

43

Pepper had gone from feeling anxious about her father's wedding to genuinely looking forward to it.

She was sad not to have Finn with her, but relieved that Samuel was now going to be there in his place. He was so relaxed and cheerful – and the effect he had on her mother felt near-revolutionary to Pepper. As the three of them drove towards Gatwick Airport, her mother, who was on the backseat, could not seem to stop giggling at everything Samuel said, and Pepper, who was driving, kept swivelling her eyes to the rear-view mirror, increasingly bemused by what she was witnessing.

Her mother *never* giggled.

If Samuel was feeling in any way awkward about being Pepper's plus-one for the weekend, he was keeping it well hidden. But then, she could not imagine him ever feeling ill at ease in any given situation – that was a trait he shared with Finn. Just as Pepper had been drawn to the magnetism of one man's unabashed confidence, so she was allured by the other. Finn had encouraged her to go after what she wanted, while Samuel made all the big stuff seem smaller. That must be the remnants of the doctor in him, she guessed – if he told her that everything was going to be all right, she would believe him.

It was lunchtime when they reached the departure lounge, and Samuel insisted on treating them all to a bite at the posh oyster bar – a bizarre outlet to have in an airport, Pepper pointed out – but when the tray arrived, he quailed.

'Confession: I've actually never tried one,' he said, lifting a gnarly shell up to his nose for a cursory sniff, then lowering it again warily as if it were a scorpion.

Pepper and her mother, who had both grown up on the coast and therefore eaten oysters pretty much since birth, had a lot of fun showing him how to get the little wrigglers down in a single gulp, laughing when he finally got one in only to clamp his lips together, blow out his cheeks, and clutch at his throat in horror.

'Why are these things a delicacy?' he half-choked, and promptly downed half a jug of water.

After a very short flight on a very small plane, the three of them touched down in Guernsey to bright sunshine and a brisk wind. Pepper, who knew even less about the Channel Islands than she had about Lisbon, found herself instantly captivated. It was only a short taxi ride from the airport to the Dove Hotel in St Peter Port, where the wedding was taking place, and everything she saw through the window, from the rows of thatched stone cottages to the bursts of wildflowers and the far-reaching blue skies, was beautiful.

There was a short queue of arrivals at reception, so it took a while to get checked in and settled. Pepper had managed to book herself the last available single room; she had drawn the line at actually sharing a double bed with her mother, using the excuse that she planned to see the wedding reception through until the end, and didn't want to crash in late. The truth was, it felt too soon to be cuddling up beside her. Their relationship may have improved slightly over the past few weeks, but she wasn't sure if she wholly trusted it yet. Feeling slightly guilty as they headed towards the stairs with their bags, Pepper suggested that they all meet in the bar for a pre-dinner drink once they'd freshened up.

'You two go ahead,' her mother said. 'I might take a bath, read my book.'

'Just don't light any candles, whatever you do,' joked Pepper, who had gone right off the things.

Trinity smiled weakly. 'See you at dinner,' she said, and as Pepper watched her drift away, she caught Samuel's enquiring eye.

'Everything OK?' he asked.

Pepper frowned.

'Hope so.'

Once in her room, she hung up her outfit for the following day, then took a quick shower to wash off the journey and pulled on the white sundress she'd bought in Portugal. She had been wearing it the first time Finn kissed her. That night in the bar with the spilt beer and the cabinet covered in goggly eyes felt like an eternity ago. So much had happened since then. Meeting him had yanked a stopper out of her life, and everything since then seemed to have rushed at her like flood water – falling in love, travelling, dealing with first Josephine's bombshell, then Finn's, followed by a devastating fire and now this, a weekend away with the few pieces of her family that were left. It made Pepper's head spin just thinking about it.

Samuel was already sitting at the bar when she went back downstairs, a half-full pint of beer in front of him and a book open in his lap, which he closed with a smile as she approached.

'What are you reading?'

He held it up.

'A poetry anthology?'

'Don't make that face! Poetry is all the rage.'

'You continually surprise me,' she mused, ordering herself a red wine. The wooden bar top was so polished, Pepper half expected to see her reflection in it.

'Shall we sit outside?' Samuel asked, as she tried and failed to get comfortable on the equally polished stool next to him.

The terrace was bathed in soft apricot light and a gentle breeze teased the ends of Pepper's newly washed hair. From here they could see straight down to the marina and the English Channel beyond, its surface sparkling like cut glass as the sun made its way down in the west. The Dove Hotel gardens stretched out below them, a carpet of green scattered with droplets of water from an earlier sprinkling. Pepper strained her ears, but the birds were quiet now, nestled down for the night in their leafy dens in order to wake with the dawn.

For a while, they simply sat in companionable silence, sipping their drinks and absorbing the ambience.

Then Pepper's phone buzzed.

It was Finn, telling her how excited he was to be seeing her soon. She was flying over to Hamburg for the launch party only a few days after arriving back from Guernsey, and every time she thought about it, her insides twisted into knots. After not having travelled abroad once in her entire life, Pepper calculated that she would soon have taken ten flights over the space of one summer – an appalling tally for the planet. But then, the circumstances had been extraordinary.

'All good?'

Pepper glanced up at Samuel, then back down at her phone.

'Yeah,' she said, tapping out a quick reply. 'It's just Finn, checking in.'

'Right. And how is my bat-rescuing rival?' he asked. 'Still impossibly handsome and ridiculously charming?'

Pepper swallowed.

'Actually,' she began, then hesitated, unsure of how much to tell him.

'Trouble in the proverbial paradise?' he guessed, and Pepper cringed.

'You could say that.'

By the time she had got him up to date, they had finished their first drink and ordered themselves a second round.

'Mate . . .' Samuel said, his mouth pulled into a line.

'I know.' She grimaced. 'Things with me and Finn, they've become so complicated so quickly. And now he wants me to go and live with him in Germany . . .'

Samuel didn't say anything to that. He merely swilled his beer around in his glass, a thoughtful expression on his face.

'In the beginning, it was all so perfect,' she went on. 'But now, suddenly, there are all these barriers between us – endless hurdles that we have to clamber over, just to be together.'

'Which famous poet was it that compared falling in love to conquering a mountain?' Samuel asked.

Pepper took a forlorn swig of her wine.

'Probably all of them.'

'The tougher the climb the better the view from the top, and all that,' he said.

'But what if I get to the top and find that I can't see? What if the view is shrouded in clouds?'

'Speaking in metaphors is a sure sign of a decent red,' he joked.

Pepper pulled a face at him over the rim of her glass.

'I just wish I knew what to do,' she moaned. 'Why does it have to be so hard?'

'Do you want to know what I think?'

'Yes, please.'

'I think you already know exactly what you want but admitting it – even to yourself – is proving too scary. I think people always know what they want, deep down. Instinct is a powerful thing, but you'd be amazed how often people ignore it. Doing the thing that makes you happy first and foremost doesn't make you selfish, you know? It makes sense. To do anything else would be dishonest, both to yourself and the people whose best interests you are trying to keep at heart.'

'Are all failed doctors as smart as you?' she asked, still feeling glum.

'Hey! Not failed, just fed up, remember? And yes.'

He smiled slyly.

'Listen, I know the two of us haven't known each other all that long, but I can tell you've been a lot happier these past few months. If being with golden boy Finn makes you happy, then perhaps that is a good thing – maybe it's exactly what you need. But against that, it has to feel real. You have to feel like you. I've always been a big believer in a partner helping you be your best self, not your worst.'

'My worst self is worse than most,' she muttered.

'How so?' Samuel folded his arms when she didn't reply.

'Come on,' he urged. 'There's a good hour before dinner yet, and a whole lot more beer waiting to be drunk. I have nowhere else to be but right here – so you may as well use me as your sounding board. And anyway,' he added. 'I'm a right nosy Norbert, me – why do you think I became a doctor?'

'Remember what I told you about my sister?' she began, hearing the tremble in her voice.

'Yes.' He frowned. 'You mean about the accident?'

'Well, on the day it happened,' she went on, careful to keep her voice low in case anyone at the other tables was listening, 'my mum kept saying over and over that she'd left Bethan alone – that she should have been watching her. But she wasn't, and that was down to me, really. It was an accident, but it could have been avoided.'

Pepper was not looking at Samuel now, she was picturing her sister. The enormity of what had happened assaulted her afresh, as it always did, like a fist buried hard and deep into her stomach. She felt winded by pain.

'My mum didn't speak to me again for weeks after that night – she could barely bring herself to look at me.'

She trailed off, not wanting to cry in front of him.

'Pepper, I'm so sorry.'

The lightest touch on her shoulder.

She shrugged, still unable to speak.

'But you know it's not your fault, right?'

Pepper sighed.

'Sometimes I believe that, but then other times I can't help but blame myself.'

Samuel shook his head. Pepper could read sympathy in his expression.

'You were what – ten?'

'Thirteen. So?'

'So, you were only a kid.'

'But I let her down,' she said. 'I let them both down – Bethan and my mum.'

'Pepper,' he said, waiting until she looked at him. 'It was an accident. What happened to Bethan was nobody's fault – not really. It was a stupid, horrible accident.'

Her father had said the same thing, and so had Keira. But it was easier for them – they hadn't been there.

Pepper shook her head and fought the urge to put her hands over her ears. She wanted to drown out his kind words. This was her guilt – the mound upon which she had somehow ended up building her entire life.

'Your mum doesn't blame you, does she?' Samuel asked. 'That's not the reason the two of you are so uncomfortable around each other?'

'You noticed then?' Pepper's head was in her hands.

'If that really is the case, then it's wrong of her,' he said gently. 'I don't mean to intrude or anything, but there is so much wrong with that. You can't carry on as if this whole thing is your fault, and she can't carry on letting you.'

Pepper thought longingly of Finn, of how safe she had always felt in his arms, away from the reality of all this – of her life. He had never asked her these questions or pushed her to confront her demons. Finn was accepting of who she was right now, and what the two of them could be in the future – he had never thought to delve into her past.

Samuel turned in his seat until he was facing her and put his large hands on each of the elbows that she had clamped so rigidly to her sides.

'This is why you can't decide what to do about the Finn situation,' he said kindly. 'Because your life is on hold, stuck in a weird limbo – and I'm afraid it will be until you have this thing out with your mum properly.'

Pepper looked at him; she felt wrung out from the effort of not crying.

'You really think so?'

'Trust me,' he said, offering her a smile that didn't quite reach his eyes. 'I know so.'

44

Pepper managed to push aside any lingering emotions long before they sat down for dinner. She could have kissed Samuel, who not only kept the conversation going at their table but invited others to join it too, thus ensuring that by the end of their first evening in Guernsey, the three of them had become acquainted with at least half the wedding party.

Her mother, however, seemed to retreat into herself more with every passing hour. She kept staring vaguely off into space, losing the thread of a conversation and forgetting to reply when someone asked her a question. Pepper knew the circumstances were likely getting to her – she was about to attend the wedding of her ex-husband, after all – but she wished her mother would at least try to battle through. She had always accepted her misery so passively; it seeped into her like water would a sponge. Not for the first time, Pepper found herself feeling helpless, wanting to help but not knowing how, then ending up frustrated with both herself and her mother.

In the end, she was glad to wave her off when she went up to bed. And even though she knew the mood had changed, Pepper still went to sleep later that night with hope in her heart – hope that they could at least make it through the following day without any drama.

'Is that what you're planning to wear?' was her mother's opening comment, as Pepper met her in the hotel reception area the following morning.

Pepper prickled.

She had been delighted to unearth the shocking pink dress amongst a sea of boring black ensembles on the rail at Oxfam. It was a couple of sizes too large for her, but Pepper thought she had done a decent enough job of taking it in around the bust area. She loved the way the sweeping chiffon skirt tickled her ankles, the hem hanging just high enough to show off her trusty gold sandals. Her hair had dried all crinkly the previous night, so she hadn't needed to do much more than pin a few bits up, and she'd even painted her nails a deep, rich blue. The overall effect had worked quite well – or so she had thought.

'I was going for a "Molly Ringwald at the end of *Pretty in Pink*" vibe,' Pepper replied, putting her clutch bag down on the arm of a sofa.

'And look,' she added, pointing to her chest. 'I'm wearing the brooch you got me.'

The clock on the wall confirmed that it was past eleven, which must be why her mum felt it was acceptable to be drinking prosecco.

'But no hat?' her mother went on. She was dressed in a predictably understated pastel-blue trouser suit, complete with matching bag, shoes and pillbox hat with a tiny veil attached.

'Please don't do this all day,' Pepper said wearily.

'I'm only making conversation.'

'No, you're not. You're picking.'

'I was just saying th—'

'Yes, Mum, this is what I am wearing, and what's more, I like it. I think it looks nice. And I'm sure the Guernsey sunshine is not harsh or dangerous enough for me to require a hat.'

'I suppose all of *her* family will be properly attired.' Her mother sniffed. 'You know she comes from money?'

'Good for her,' Pepper countered, in a snappier tone than she had meant to. Building a new and more honest relationship with her mother was never going to happen if Pepper allowed herself to be drawn into sniping matches. It was clear her mum was on edge – probably because she was about to meet the family of her ex-husband's new wife – and it was understandable that she would be keen to make a good impression.

Pepper decided to be the bigger person.

'Shall I get a glass, too, so we have a toast?' she suggested. 'To being here, on this beautiful island?'

Her mother almost smiled.

'If you insist, Philippa.'

They made it through the ceremony without incident, Pepper on one side of Samuel and her mum on the other. He had dressed for the occasion in a lightweight grey suit, and after catching sight of Pepper in her upcycled frock, had proclaimed her to be 'pretty as a pink-ture', to which she groaned and rolled her eyes in mock despair.

It was impossible not to get caught up in the romance of it all, and when Keira floated by in her flouncy white dress, the tears on Pepper's cheeks were of genuine happiness. No expense had been spared when it came to the decorations, and as they were ushered into the ballroom where the wedding breakfast was taking place, Pepper was amused to find monogrammed 'Mr and Mrs' balloons, goldfish in vases on the tables and photos of the happy couple strung up like bunting around the walls. She had only seen her father for long enough to say a brief congratulations but noted that he looked happy – if a little exhausted. That was to be expected, Pepper had thought, when you married someone twenty-two years your junior. For the first time, she wondered now if Keira would want any children of her own and was surprised to find that the idea wasn't all that horrifying. It might even be nice to have a new baby in the family.

There was champagne circulating and bottles of wine on every table, and Pepper continued to drink as the first two courses came out. She had been seated at a separate table from the others, and assumed that Keira was the one behind it, having witnessed the frostiness between Pepper and her mum at the pub all those weeks ago. She must have thought she was doing her new stepdaughter a favour by teaming her up with a group of people her own age.

'How do you know the bride?' she asked the girl next to her, who was tall and blonde with a place card that read 'Hayley' in swirly letters.

'Pony Club,' she said, smearing half a dish of butter onto her bread roll. 'Kezza used to ride when she was younger, but she gave it up to crunch numbers instead.'

'I thought she was a secretary,' Pepper said, contemplating her smoked salmon. The lemon wedge had been wrapped in muslin – she must slip it into her bag to use for a collage.

'Nope, global marketing manager,' Hayley told her. 'Whatever one of those is. You'll have to excuse me – I work as a riding school instructor, so I have very little idea about the corporate world.'

'Me neither,' Pepper agreed. Then, glancing across at the empty seat on the other side of her, 'Do you think whoever Evangeline is will mind us pinching her starter?'

'Oh, I shouldn't think so.' Hayley leant across and picked up the plate. 'She's not coming – couldn't drag herself away from her new sister.'

'A new sister?'

'Yeah.' Hayley topped up Pepper's wine. 'It's a long story with a very happy ending. Anyway, who are you here with?'

'My mum is over there,' Pepper told her, pointing across and catching Samuel's eye. He had tucked his napkin in around his shirt collar and gave her a thumbs-up.

'She's a beauty like you,' Hayley said. 'And that guy reminds me of a younger, hotter Will Smith.'

'You're not the first to say so.' Pepper laughed. 'But don't tell him that, whatever you do. We don't want him getting a big head.'

'I doubt he'd care much what I thought,' Hayley pointed out, as she looked from Samuel back to Pepper. 'From the way he keeps staring over in your direction, I would say there's only one person at this wedding whose opinion means anything to him.'

Pepper almost choked on her champagne.

'You've got it all wrong,' she said, scooping up a slice of the missing Evangeline's salmon. 'We're just friends.'

'That's what I used to say about Billy,' Hayley said, resting both her elbows on the table and knotting her fingers together. 'And we just celebrated our first anniversary.'

Pepper's second 'congratulations' of the day was interrupted by someone tapping their knife against a glass, and she turned in her seat just as her father stood to make his speech.

'I want to start by thanking you all for coming,' he began, and Pepper swilled from her glass, only half listening as he rattled on about what a fantastic job the bridesmaids had done, and how lucky he was to have found such a wonderful woman to marry.

So far, so standard.

'I also wanted to mention my beautiful daughter, Philippa,' he went on, to which Pepper shifted uncomfortably in her seat. 'Who I am so happy to see here today.'

He paused for a moment as he searched through the faces, eventually finding Pepper's and crinkling his eyes with affection.

'I know that I haven't always been the best dad,' he blundered on, his voice cracking as Pepper felt the heat rising up across her cheeks. 'I probably could have done more, been around more, been on your side more,' he added, this time looking towards his ex-wife. 'Keira has made me realise that I need to do better, and that I have some making up to do. I hope this can be the first of many apologies, and perhaps the first brick towards all of us building a better future – one where we can better support one another.'

There was a crash as Trinity's chair hit the polished wooden floor, and Pepper knew she could not have been the only person who heard her mother's audible sob as she fled from the room.

45

'Mum?'

Pepper gave the toilet cubicle door a tentative knock.

'Are you OK?'

Nothing. She put her ear against the wood, heard a faint sniff.

'Come on, Mum,' she tried again. 'Don't take what Dad said to heart – you know he didn't mean it as a dig at you.'

Pepper recoiled as the toilet lid was slammed down, only just stepping back just in time to avoid falling into the stall when her mother yanked open the door. Her face was flushed with tell-tale anger and she looked blotchy beneath her carefully applied make-up.

'There was no need to follow me, Philippa,' she said, so coldly that Pepper shrank away. 'Your father won't have taken too kindly to you disappearing in the midst of his big moment.'

'His speech was ill-judged,' Pepper said, not simply to comfort her mother but because it was true. If her father had something to say to her, he should have done it in private. Now the entire wedding party knew about their tempestuous family history.

'Yes, well.' Trinity shook the excess water off her hands. 'We can agree on that, I suppose.'

'I think we agree on lots of things,' Pepper said, folding her arms. 'We both think drinking copious amounts of champagne is the best way to get through today, when it clearly isn't, we both agree that I probably should have worn a hat, and we both agree that Dad has become a soppy idiot.'

'He always has been,' her mother said. 'Even when I needed him to be strong, he couldn't quite manage it. He was worse than useless when Bethan—' She faltered.

'Had a fit in the bath and drowned?' Pepper said, astonished at her own courage. Her hands were trembling, and she could feel the heat rising into her cheeks, but she was still relieved to have said it, because she was so damn tired of it all – the resentment, the guilt, the grief that had stolen away her mother and left her with this bitter and detached shell of a woman. Samuel was right – it was time they discussed what had happened.

'Yes, I remember what happened,' she continued, when her mother simply gaped at her. 'I was there, remember? I have been here every bloody day since.'

Her mother emitted a small scoffing sound. She was attempting to reapply her lipstick in the mirror now, but Pepper could see her hand beginning to shake. Unlike poor Josephine, however, it wasn't because of a horrible, incurable disease – it was fear and rage, pure and unequivocal.

'You moved out the first chance you had,' she argued. 'Just like your father did.'

Pepper felt her resolve to be reasonable slipping away.

'I never wanted to go, Mum, I felt like I had to. All that misery was draining the life out of me. I needed a break from this compulsion you have to dwell on what happened all the time, as if I could ever forget, as if I could ever forgive myself. Don't you think I go over and over it in my head every single day? Don't you think I would swap places with Bethan in a second, if I could? What would you have me do, Mum? Be miserable forever – is that what you really want? Would my being sad make up for not answering the door that day?'

For a moment, her mother's grey eyes seemed to soften, but it was only because they had filled with tears. Almost as soon as the glimmer of something close to regret was visible, it was gone again, and her mother was moving towards the door.

'Please don't walk away.' Pepper went to grab her arm and missed. 'You have to stop, Mum,' she said, not caring how loud she was being. 'You can't keep punishing us.'

'Leave me alone, Philippa. I am warning you.'

Pepper ran after her along the carpeted hallway.

'Or what?' she yelled. 'What will you do? Tell everyone it's my fault that my sister died? Because everyone already knows that, Mum – you've made sure of it, for fuck's sake!'

Her mother hated swearing, she always had, and now she turned back to face Pepper, her neck and face red, her eyes darting around as if she were a cornered animal.

'I had to,' she croaked.

Pepper went still.

'What do you mean?'

'I don't know how to stop,' her mother stuttered, staring down at hands that were still shaking. 'I don't know how to stop being angry.'

Pepper thought of all the beautiful things she had created, only to destroy. The painstaking time she had taken to get her creations as close to perfect as they could be, only to find them always lacking. When she brought down her hammer each time, the blow had hit her as deeply as she thought she deserved.

'I know,' she said, moving towards her mother. 'I know.'

'I just . . .' Trinity looked at her imploringly, her bloodshot eyes wet. 'I didn't mean to blame you, I was scared, I still am scared to face up to it. I was trying to hold us together, hold myself together. But your father knew – he's always known it was my fault.'

She was crying so hard now that Pepper tried to hug her, only to be pushed away.

'Don't.' Her mother shuddered. 'I don't deserve sympathy – what kind of mother allows this to happen to her family? What kind of person?'

'Hey.' Pepper tried to soothe her. 'It's OK. Things happen, stuff gets broken, friends get ill, marriages end, studios get burnt down, your boyfriend gets another woman pregnant – there is nothing so bad that it can't be fixed. And Dad doesn't blame you,' she added.

Her mother was trembling now from head to toe, but when Pepper tried again to put an arm around her, she shrank away.

'I can't!' she cried, her voice high and shrill. 'I just can't.'

'Pepper?'

Samuel had just emerged from the ballroom, his eyes wide.

'You might want to,' he began, raising a hand. 'We can hear you,' he explained, his voice low. 'Through the doors.'

Pepper looked at her mother, at the self-loathing that was seeping out of her like pus out of a wound, and found herself overwhelmed with pity. She was no longer angry, or even resentful at the way she had been treated – she was simply sad.

'Mum,' she began, but Trinity was already hurrying away from them, away from the guests, away from a conversation that hurt far too much.

Pepper let her go.

46

'Are you all right?'

Pepper had forgotten that Samuel was standing there, that he had been a witness.

'Sorry,' she said, but he was shaking his head.

'I feel like this is my fault,' he said. 'Going on at you last night to have things out with your mum – I should have kept my snout well out.'

'You didn't go on at me,' Pepper insisted. 'And I appreciated your advice – you were right. I perhaps should have waited for a time when the two of us hadn't been drinking, though.'

By rights, Pepper knew she should be feeling the effects of the alcohol she had consumed, but the altercation with her mother had sobered her up. All she felt now was numb.

'Don't beat yourself up about it,' he told her. 'You know as well as I do that it doesn't count as a proper wedding until something kicks off. Force any family to spend time together and there will always be a ruckus of some kind or another – especially if you add booze to the mix.'

'I should have waited until we were back home,' Pepper groaned. Now that her surge of courage had subsided, she felt ashamed. 'My choosing right now to have it out with my mum is not very fair on her, or on Keira – or my dad,' she added, with less conviction.

'It's done now,' Samuel said simply. 'What your mum needs now is time, and the best thing you can do is give her some space. I know your instinct is to look after her,' he went on, as Pepper made as if to move, 'but sometimes you have to put yourself first. This is one of those times.'

Samuel pushed the ballroom doors open with his foot, but Pepper backed away.

'I think I'll just go to my room.'

'What, and miss the chance to dance to "Agadoo" with me?'

Pepper folded her arms across her shocking-pink bodice.

'"Agadoo"?'

'Hell yeah!' he said. 'I want to push pineapple, shake a tree and sing with a Goddamn hula melody.'

'Oh my God, you know the lyrics?'

'And all the moves! Come on, you can't deny a man his "Agadoo" moment.'

The disco was just beginning as Pepper followed him across the room, and she swerved to the side as a little boy slid past her on his knees. The DJ had opted to start the night with a movie soundtrack mega mix, and there were currently at least thirty arms windmilling around to 'Greased Lightning'.

They found Keira smiling up at her new husband, and as soon as she turned and saw Pepper, she hurried over and pulled her into a hug.

'What was that one for?' Pepper asked, taken aback yet again by the unexpected show of affection.

Keira smiled. 'This time, you looked as if you needed it.'

'Well, thank you.' Pepper smiled, then laughingly filled Keira in on Samuel's 'Agadoo' plans.

'I had better go and make sure they play it, in that case,' she said.

'So, the newest member of my family is an angel,' Pepper stated, watching her glide away in her poufy dress.

'I'm very glad you think so.'

It was her dad, red-faced and wonky-bow-tied.

'Is everything OK?' he asked hesitantly. 'With Trin— Your mum?'

Pepper caught the lie just before she let it out.

'Honestly?' she said. 'No, not really. I know you meant well with that speech, Dad, but it really upset her. I'm trying,' she began, glancing up at Samuel, who smiled encouragingly. 'I'm trying to mend things between us, but it's not easy. Everything with Bethan, it just ...' She fell silent and stared hard at the wooden floor.

'I know.' He put a hand in the crook of her elbow, stroking her arm with his thumb. 'I blame myself. Neither of us handled your sister's death in the way we should have. God! It's taken me the best part of twenty years to be able to say that out loud,' he added, letting out a huge breath. 'I never wanted to deal with the grief, but Keira made me realise that I had to.'

'She's a wise lady.' Pepper smiled, raising her eyes. 'You did good.'

'Yes.' He nodded, looking around. 'Yes.'

'Martin, they're about to play our song!'

Keira was swishing her way back through the throng of dancers, both her arms outstretched towards him.

'Go,' Pepper urged, as he dropped his hand.

'OK,' he agreed. 'But we'll talk more when I'm back from the honeymoon, yes?'

She watched him go, her heart lifting as he wrapped his arms around his new wife's waist. He had managed to find love again, despite all the odds; forgiven but never forgotten.

The opening bars of 'Fix You' by Coldplay had begun, and a crowd of guests were forming a circle around Keira and her dad.

'What about my "Agadoo"?' Samuel pouted.

'I think we can safely say the universe has spoken,' Pepper told him gravely. 'And decided that on this occasion, it is very much Aga-don't.'

'Boom!'

'I hope you're having fun?' she added. 'I know it's nigh-on impossible to say no to the combined persuasive power of Josephine and my mum, but if you'd wanted to bail out on this weekend, I wouldn't have judged you.'

'Are you kidding?' Samuel said easily. 'Beautiful place, free bar, great company . . .'

'Now I know you're taking the mickey. Great? Us? With all the drama?'

'I know,' he gave her a sidelong look. 'Hanging out with you is even better than watching a season finale of *Grey's Anatomy*.'

'You're a *Grey's* fan?' Pepper looked at him with new respect.

'I like shouting at the TV when they get things wrong,' he told her. 'I'm all like, "Mate, don't cut that, she'll bleed to bloody death!"'

'It's more about the love stories than the medicine really, though,' she said slyly. 'And I seem to remember you mocking me once for daring to believe in all that mushy love stuff?'

'Even I'm not immune to the charms of McDreamy,' he joked. 'I mean, I am only human.'

'I'm surprised you didn't give yourself that nickname during your own doctoring days,' she threw back.

'I should have,' he agreed. 'Might have helped me have better luck with the ladies.'

'So, you haven't been on any more dates recently, then?'

'Nah.' Samuel turned to face her.

'There are plenty of women here that would happily scoop you up,' she said quickly. 'You should get out and, you know, get your flirt on. Hanging out with me is seriously cramping your style.'

'Not true,' he countered. 'You're the groom's daughter – that makes you the third most important guest. I'm punching if anything.'

Coldplay was drawing to an end now, everyone singing along and swaying together from side to side. It was a great choice for a first song – Keira really had fixed her father.

'Do you think it will ever get easier for me and my mum?' she asked Samuel, her head on one side as she continued to watch the dancing.

'I think you both want it to,' he allowed. 'Which means you're probably halfway there.'

'Some days, it feels possible,' she told him. 'But then on others, I can't even imagine it. I worry that our roles in the story are too deeply ingrained now to change.'

'So, leave that story behind,' he said. 'And start a new one.'

47

Pepper half expected her mother to slam the door in her face when she went to knock for her just after breakfast the following morning, but she didn't look remotely angry. What she did look was tired. Her usually impeccable appearance had been marred by dark circles under her eyes, hair that was scraped back and unwashed, and nails bitten down to the quick.

'Am I late?' she asked vaguely. 'Do we need to check out?'

'Nope.' Pepper strode into the room, taking in the empty bottle of white wine lying sideways on the carpet, the remains of a room service scrambled eggs congealing on a tray. 'Our flight isn't until five, and I've arranged with the hotel to store our luggage until later. We can drop off the keys and our bags on our way out.'

'Our way out where?'

'Samuel and I thought we could walk along the coastal path,' she said evenly. 'There's a place I want to see that I think you'll really like.'

'So, it will be just us?' she clarified. 'Not Martin?'

'Just us.'

'Fine.' Trinity pulled the sleeves of her hotel robe down over her wrists. 'Give me ten minutes or so to get dressed, I'll meet you both in the lobby.'

In the end, it was closer to half an hour before her mother emerged, but Pepper didn't mind. The sun was out, they were on a beautiful island, and she'd ended up having a really fun time last night – there were plenty of reasons to be happy today.

Her mother still looked rather frayed around the edges, but she had managed to spirit a picnic lunch from somewhere, which a grateful Samuel stowed in his bag.

The three of them set off, weaving their way down towards the water without saying much.

It was not an uncomfortable silence, however, more of a measured calm, and when Pepper stole a glance across at her mother, she looked utterly lost in thought. That was to be expected, though. Yesterday had been a big day – and not just for Keira and her father.

They meandered through narrow streets past tall, square buildings, shops, pubs and a grand, mottled church. Hanging baskets overflowed with flowers, colourful strips of bunting fluttered along the High Street, and pigeons peered inquisitively from window ledges and the tops of walls.

There were far more boats in the harbour here than there had been in Barcelona, and the yellow marble of the sun above the hundreds of masts resembled a vast game of KerPlunk. Pepper was enchanted by the quaint beauty of the place, by the bright yellow phone boxes and deep blue post boxes, and by the smiles on the faces of the locals.

'According to the leaflet I discovered on the hotel reception desk, if we follow this path here,' Pepper said, pointing off to the right, 'it will take us around the coast. Then we need to head inland at a place called Petit Bot Bay.'

'Sounds good to me,' approved Samuel. He was in shorts and a bright yellow polo shirt today and kept stopping every few yards to brush midges off his front.

It wasn't long before the paving slabs gave way to a gritty shingle, and the crunch of their shoes as they walked across it added a steady percussion to the swish and fold of the sea.

'You OK back there, Mum?'

Her mother raised her eyes. They still looked a little bloodshot, Pepper noted. Perhaps she should have left her mother to rest. When she and Samuel had concocted their plan in the early hours of the morning, it had felt important to Pepper that she follow through with it. The place she wanted to show her mother only existed on Guernsey.

'I may have drunk a bit too much wine,' her mother allowed, pausing as they came to a fork in the path. They could continue along the edge of the coast or take a detour through a wooded area. Pepper and her mother agreed they were happy either way.

'Come on.' Samuel headed towards the treeline. 'If there was ever a place for spotting pixies . . .'

Pepper could smell the earthy tang of wild garlic and hear the gentle chatter of birds. The trees were tall and slim like Samuel, each one leaning inland as though buffeted by wind.

There was a fallen log just off the path, and Pepper bent to touch it. She never had been able to resist running her fingers over the springy fur of moss.

'This is a bluebell wood,' her mother said. She had moved off ahead and was examining a sign. 'What a shame it's too late in the year for them.'

'If you like bluebells, I'll happily paint you some,' Pepper found herself saying, thinking wistfully of the lilac tile she had so painstakingly created all those weeks ago only to smash it. Despite not having done any new work since the fire, she had been trying hard to keep hold of the inner confidence that had bloomed inside her when she was painting her city scenes. Far from being anxious about the prospect of giving her mum something she had made herself, Pepper found that she loved the idea.

They walked on, Pepper doing her best to commit as much of the scenery as she could to memory. She appreciated how much things had been left to grow wild here, and how the signs they passed were inscribed stones rather than ugly structures made from metal or plastic. Not that they needed much help with direction – it was impossible to get lost when the sea was calling out to them, its gentle roar preventing them from straying too far.

When they emerged back out into the sunshine, it was to a steep hilly path that wound up and across the cliffs, the trodden line of the path nipping and twisting like a dropped ribbon through the grass. Samuel was halfway up the first slope when he stopped abruptly and beckoned for her and her mother to catch up.

'Look,' he breathed, smiling as a mother duck waddled into view with her two downy ducklings following carefully behind.

'Makes up for missing bluebells,' Pepper said, stepping cautiously out of the way so the birds could pass. 'I don't think I've ever seen a duck so far from water before – unless they go in the sea? Do they, Mum?'

Her mother didn't answer, so Pepper turned, shocked to see her face wet with tears.

'Sorry,' she stuttered, as Pepper fished in her bag for a tissue and, finding none, pulled out the spare pair of socks she'd chucked in there just in case. She expected her mother to at least smile when she saw them, but she didn't even seem to notice.

'This is why I never drink white wine,' she said, dabbing her eyes. 'Turns me into an emotional wreck.'

'I think white wine does that to all of us,' Samuel said comfortingly.

Pepper knew she should put an arm around her mother, or touch a hand to her shoulder – something, *anything*, even the smallest form of contact – but she didn't want to risk upsetting her more, as she had last night. She understood now that when it came to her mother, small steps forward were the only option.

'I don't think it's too much further to the beach now,' she said, as they crested the clifftop and peered down at waves that were slamming up against the rocks. Pepper was reminded anew that they were on a small island – a floating collection of stones and minerals, plants and trees, houses and people. A tiny dot on the landscape of an entire world.

She glanced across at Samuel. He was so different from Finn but had somehow become an equally vital cog in her life. The closed bud of their friendship had blossomed this summer into something she truly cherished. She had never thought to introduce Finn to her mother – had been too wrapped up in her own time with him to invite any complication the single occasion he had flown over to see her – but Samuel now not only knew her mum, he also understood how tricky things were between them and tried his best to help.

'This must be it,' she said, as a spoon-shaped cove of caster sugar sand came into view below them. Rough stone steps led away down the hillside, and Samuel used his foot to push aside the sticky tendrils of goose grass that were growing across them. The landscape in Guernsey was charmingly unkempt – a scruffy-haired poet as opposed to a slick film star – and Pepper liked it all the more because of it. It was impossible to know what her mother thought – she had fallen silent in the aftermath of her tears and did not answer when first Pepper, and then Samuel, pointed out the heather, or the sprigs of white straggly flowers, or the grand-looking houses perched high above them.

It felt good to step off the trail and onto the damp sand of Petit Bot Bay beach. Waves scurried importantly up to greet them, bowing in a wet salute before returning back out to sea. Large, flat stones littered the shoreline, their speckled surfaces reminding Pepper of the boiled egg she'd had for breakfast and making her stomach rumble.

'Anyone hungry?'

Her mother was squinting out at the horizon, her eyes searching for what, it was impossible to tell.

'Pardon?' she murmured. 'Oh, I . . . No, not at the moment. But you two go ahead.'

Pepper looked at Samuel, who lifted his shoulders.

'It's OK.' Pepper touched her mother's arm. 'We can wait.'

'Do you mind if I sit here for a while?' asked her mother, her gaze fixed on the water.

'Sure.' Samuel had begun to move away, and Pepper went to follow, to give her mother some space, then she hesitated.

'Mum?'

Her mother opened her eyes a fraction wider.

'I'll be just over here, if you need me.'

She had been saying the same phrase ever since she was a teenager but wondered now how sincere she had been. For years, Pepper had prodded at her mum's grief, looking for chinks into which she might slide a little comfort, but the less success she had, the more it became an exercise in simply going through the motions. Today, however, the words sounded different, and Pepper did not have to search long to work out the reason why.

It was because for the first time ever, she finally felt able to help.

48

Pepper could still remember the first mosaic she had ever made.

Her mother had collected her from school, her bright red coat straining over the swell of her baby sister Bethan, and taken her down to the beach.

'Pick up as many pretty shells and pebbles as you can find,' she had told Pepper, pushing a little bucket into her hands. 'Mummy will wait here for you.'

Pepper had done as instructed, picking her way along the shoreline where the stones were their shiniest. Every few paces, she had turned, looking back over her shoulder to make sure her mother was still there, that she could still make out the scarlet blur of her in the distance.

When her bucket was full, they had taken it home where her mother had washed all the pieces, laying them out on a tea towel to dry while she mixed up a bowl of plaster. This she spread inside the cardboard lid of a shoebox – 'right to the edges, see?' – explaining to Pepper how she could create a picture from half-burying all her treasures in its grainy surface. Seeing her picture come to life had felt magical, and it was a sensation she had carried with her always – that feeling of rightness, and of coming alive. It had ignited the artist in her, and that flame had not gone out. Not even in the darkest of times.

It had always been her light.

'This is it, Mum. This is what I wanted to show you.'

Trinity stared up at the small building in front of them, taking in the oval stained-glass windows, ornate crosses and miniature turrets.

'It looks like a church,' she said, and Pepper smiled.

'It is. Well, it's a chapel – the Little Chapel, to be exact.'

Her mother still looked mystified.

'I have never heard of it,' she said.

'Neither had I, until I started looking up Guernsey earlier this week,' she confessed. 'But isn't it amazing?'

'It's certainly . . .' Samuel paused, raising a hand to shield his eyes from the sun. 'Something.'

'The whole thing is decorated in shells, glass, pebbles and broken china,' Pepper told them, unable to keep the excitement from her voice. 'It's essentially a giant mosaic.'

As they moved forwards to take a closer look, Pepper realised that it wasn't simply the chapel that had been adorned with broken fragments, but the walls, archways and steps around it, too. She was aware of the familiar tickle of inspiration as she took in all the colours, shapes and patterns, a new delight revealing itself with every step she took. There were diamond-shaped panels of white and green, stars of yellow shards and crowns of amber, sapphire and terracotta. There were daisies and willow trees, roses and birds, geometric patterns and painted faces split in two. It was chaos, but there was harmony, just as Pepper had known there would be.

'What do you think?' she asked Samuel, as the two of them emerged from the far exit of the chapel and made their way back around to admire it from the front.

'I think it looks like a place that elves would live in,' he replied. 'But I like it.'

'Park Güell in Barcelona is a lot like this,' Pepper told him. 'But on a much larger scale.'

Her mother had been examining the little grotto-cum-garden to the left of the chapel, but now she joined them, a real smile on her face for the first time that day. The walk had clearly done her some good. The hangover she'd had when Pepper knocked for her that morning seemed to have gone, and her quiet poise was well on the way to returning.

'You know,' Pepper said. 'I have always loved mosaics, because I saw them as a sort of jigsaw puzzle – only one where I got to decide what picture to make. Putting everything back together, as I saw it, made me happy. I wanted things to be as perfect as possible – and anything I found lacking, I simply tossed away.'

Samuel was smiling at her as well now, the sun behind him making the tips of his ears glow.

'But all that time, and actually until very recently, I was missing the whole point,' she went on. 'It wasn't until Josephine said something to me a few weeks ago that I realised I'd been looking at things all wrong.'

'What do you mean?' her mother asked, tucking her hair behind her ears as a light breeze scurried past them.

'Well, what do you see when you look at this chapel?' Pepper asked.

Trinity shook her head in confusion.

'Go on,' Pepper urged. 'Just look at it right now and tell me what you see.'

'I see lots of colours,' she said. 'And patterns.'

'And?' encouraged Pepper. 'Do you like it?'

'Yes. I mean, it's certainly very striking – very beautiful.'

Samuel coughed. 'It's a masterpiece if you ask me – must have taken ages.'

Pepper laughingly agreed.

'What do you think makes it so beautiful, Mum?' Pepper pressed, watching her closely.

'All the pieces,' she said. 'All the broken pieces.'

'Yes!' Pepper exclaimed. 'When we look at this chapel, or at any mosaic we ever see, we look at the pieces, not at the cracks around them.'

'I would argue that we do,' Samuel put in. 'I guess, we just don't see them – we don't take them in.'

'Exactly!' Pepper took a few steps forwards and placed her hand on the chapel wall.

'The thing is,' she said, her eyes now solely on her mother, 'I think you and I have been guilty of looking at the wrong thing for years.'

Her mother frowned, still not quite understanding.

'The cracks,' Pepper went on, tracing a finger along one as she spoke. 'We have focused so intently on the fault lines of our lives that we forgot to appreciate all the beauty – the good things we still had left after Bethan died.'

'I couldn't see any of them,' her mum said then, her voice choked with pain. 'Everything was tarnished by what happened, by the accident.'

Pepper froze. It was the first time she had ever heard her mother refer to it as such.

'First Bethan died, then your father left. I had you, but it felt as if I didn't. I was so scared of the pain that I pushed you as far away from me as I could. I was scared to even love you – my own daughter.'

She crumpled over then, her hands finding her knees, and Samuel hurried towards her, his arms open.

'It's OK,' he said, as she fell into them and began weeping against his chest. 'I've got you. Let it all out. That's right.'

His eyes found Pepper's and she stepped forwards, letting him envelop her in the same embrace. For a moment her mother stiffened, and then she threw her own arms around her daughter, pulling Pepper tightly against her and saying over and over again that she was sorry, and that she loved her. Samuel didn't say a word, he stood stock still and strong as they leant against him, both overwrought but for once not despairing, just holding tight and close and feeling like they never wanted to let go. Pepper knew that if they tried, they could make something beautiful from all the broken pieces. It might not be perfect, but it would be theirs.

Samuel lowered his arms, and Pepper stepped back and looked past him for a moment, to where the Little Chapel sang with a thousand colours, each lit up by a brilliant sun. The pieces of a rainbow splintered not into a pot of gold, but into a promise: of a future untethered by hope.

And by love.

49

This time when Pepper walked through the arrivals lounge of Hamburg Airport, there was no Finn waiting to lift her up in his arms.

It felt like only days ago that she had last been here, at the start of something so fresh and so thrilling, to see a man she had fallen for on the beat of that first hello. Her heart then had been fit to burst with possibility, but now it felt leaden. Nothing that had happened was predictable – or even fathomable. Pepper had jumped into the slipstream and clung on for the ride, and now here she was, arrived at what could well be her final destination.

She had messaged Finn to tell him what time she landed, but gently refused his offer to come and collect her himself and wondered now if he would be fed up with her as a result. That was silly, though – the Finn she knew was not capable of such pettiness. His enormous heart and unflinching determination to remain upbeat were two of the reasons she loved him so much.

After checking into her Airbnb apartment and changing from her jeans into a plum-coloured crushed velvet dress, Pepper began refamiliarising herself with Finn's enigmatic neighbourhood. She avoided the neon lights and stumbling drunks along the Reeperbahn and made sure not to stroll past Freunde either. With only a few hours to go until the launch party began, Finn was bound to be there, and Pepper did not want to catch him unawares. She was also gut-churningly nervous, her stomach tied in more knots than she'd seen on ropes along the marina in Guernsey.

The valiant sun that had become such a loyal companion throughout her stay in the Channel Islands hadn't made it as far as Hamburg, but it was no real loss. Pepper thought the charcoal-smeared sky made the city's Gothic architecture seem all the grander, providing the perfect backdrop to all the tall red-brick buildings and moody dark trees.

As she ventured further, passing the metal palm trees in Park Fiction and the mirrored waves atop the roof of the Elbphilharmonie, Pepper was reminded yet again of her lost tiles, and how much she had been looking forward to showing them to Finn. It would have been nice to give him a token that proved how much her first visit to this city had meant to her, and how much the time she spent with him meant, too.

Taking out her phone to check the time, Pepper found a message waiting.

'Good luck tonight, darling. Don't do anything I wouldn't do (or would!).'

Josephine had signed off with a flurry of kisses and a winking face made from a semi-colon, dash and closed bracket, which for some reason made Pepper want to weep. She wished her wonderful mischievous friend were here with her, but despite receiving an invite directly from Finn, Josephine had chosen not to make the trip.

'Three's a crowd,' she had said, adamant even when Pepper had begged her to reconsider. 'You will want some time alone with him – trust me, darling.'

Pepper had no idea how she would feel when she saw Finn, but it was about time she found out.

She had only just rounded the corner of the street when she felt an arm slide around her shoulders from behind. Startled, she yelped, leaping about a foot in the air as she did so.

'Sorry, love!'

Otto was addressing her in a very strange cockney accent.

'That's all right, guv,' she threw back, and his mouth cracked open in a smile.

'How are you, Cool Peppers?'

'Oh, you know,' she said, patting his back as he pulled her into an extremely tight hug. Her neck was so constricted against his bicep that she could barely get the words out.

'*Ah, scheisse,*' he cried, swinging backwards like an orangutan. 'The baby, yeah? Can you believe it, man? Those fuckers.'

'Literally,' Pepper drawled, and Otto slapped both his hands against his knees in amusement.

'You will be a very good stepmother,' he said cheerfully, and Pepper dropped her eyes. She could smell alcohol on Otto's breath, and see a faint trail of capillaries across his nose and cheeks.

'Are you OK?' she asked, consumed suddenly by the idea that he might not be. Of course, Finn and Clara having a baby together would affect him, too – they were his best friends.

Otto made a show of shrugging.

'Shit happens,' he said, although with perhaps less gusto than he had intended. Pepper did not know him well enough to delve any deeper, so instead she told him the one thing that she knew would be true, whatever happened.

'The baby will be amazing – and you will love it. We all will.'

'*Ja.*' He nodded. '*Ja.*'

'Come on, then,' she chivvied, linking an arm through his. 'You can escort me to the party.'

Both the restaurant and the bar sides of Freunde had been done up for Finn's launch, with plinths replacing tables so that works of art and sculptures could be displayed. Waiting staff circulated with trays of wine and champagne, others with iPads and tablets, and there was a vast TV screen arranged at the far end of the room, a digital clock underneath it counting down. The website was scheduled to go live at exactly midnight, and it was then, Otto explained, that Finn would reveal the identity of his mystery artist – the person who had brought his concept to life. The room hummed with anticipation, and Pepper soaked it all in as Otto dragged her around to meet various groups of people, introducing her every time as 'Cool Pepper', punctuated by a bellow of mirth.

She had been feeling pretty good about her clinging plum dress until she saw Clara. Despite being in the early stages of pregnancy, which Pepper understood to be sickly, bloated and uncomfortable, she was wearing impossibly tight cigarette pants and a very expensive-looking periwinkle silk shirt. With her endless legs and her thick chestnut hair pulled back into a high ponytail, she looked like a racehorse being paraded around a winner's enclosure. Everyone at the party seemed to gravitate towards her, and there was an awful lot of air-kissing going on. When Clara spotted Pepper, however, she appeared to falter.

To put her at ease, and because Pepper never had been able to bear any sort of uncomfortable atmosphere, she lifted a hand and waved, smiling across with as much warmth as she could muster.

Visibly relieved, Clara mouthed '*danke*', lifted her champagne flute of orange juice in Pepper's direction, and the two women offered each other a silent toast. Pepper took a sip of her drink and found that her only thought was of the baby, and how lucky he or she was to have parents as glamorous and capable as Clara and Finn.

There was no sign of the man himself, although Pepper was surprised to discover the sketch she had done of him in Lisbon hanging on one of the walls. Finn must have moved it here from his flat.

Bending over to peer at the label underneath, she saw a circular red sticker next to some German words that she could not decipher.

'It says, "not for sale".'

Pepper wheeled around, her heart a tight fist.

It was Finn.

50

For a moment, neither of them said anything.

They simply stood and stared at each other, a smile playing around Finn's lips but an intensity in his eyes. Pepper had forgotten how it felt to be held within his gaze, to feel as though she was stuck fast to a web of mutual desire.

'Hey, you,' she managed at last. 'It's really good to see you.'

Finn beamed at her.

'*Ja*, very good,' he agreed. 'Thank you for coming, I know it is a very long way, a very big deal. But can you believe it? I did it.'

'You most certainly did.' Pepper looked around in admiration. 'It's incredible,' she told him. 'You are incredible.'

Finn nodded in agreement, and Pepper had to fight an absurd desire to laugh. He looked as good as she had ever seen him look this evening, in a sharp navy suit and emerald-green tie embroidered with – Pepper squinted – pelicans.

'Love the tie!' she said. 'Very apt.'

'It was you who gave me the idea. I am sad not to see the pelicans on you tonight, although this dress is very nice,' he said, raising a hand as if to touch her, then lowering it again.

'They were toucans,' she reminded him, and Finn laughed.

'Toucan, pelican – potato, *kartoffel*.'

Pepper could feel herself being drawn into his bubble, could sense the room around them being smudged away as she focused on him, and only him. Now that she was so close to Finn again, her body ached for him, her cheeks flushed with telltale longing. All she wanted to do was lie back and let the pleasure wash over her – over both of them.

'Come.' Finn put a warm hand in the small of her back. 'There are some people that I want you to meet.'

Pepper let herself be led across the room to where a rather stern-looking man with the heavy brows of an owl was helping himself to a glass of red wine. Beside him, a slight woman with deep-set celestial-blue eyes and piles of ash-blonde hair was contemplating a mini bruschetta.

'*Mein Junge*,' she cried, pulling Finn against her. '*Das ist wunderbar!*'

'*Danke, Mama*,' Finn said, ushering Pepper in closer.

'This is Philippa,' he explained.

'Aha!' The woman found a napkin for her bruschetta and put it down on the table, before clasping both Pepper's hands in her own.

'*Der Künstler – sehr gut.*'

Pepper fumbled out a hello and a thank you, glancing from the woman – who must surely be Finn's mother – to the flinty man at her side, who she deduced could only be his father.

'Malcolm,' he barked, extending a ramrod straight arm. 'Pleasure.'

As they exchanged small talk, Pepper marvelled at how different Finn was from his dad. He may well have inherited Malcolm's height, broad shoulders and direct stare, but his features and softness all came from his mother, who she had just learnt was called Hanna.

As Finn stepped away to greet some more new arrivals, she leant towards Pepper.

'You must be excited, *ja*?'

'Yes. Very excited for Finn – he's worked so hard, and I know how much this website means to him.'

Hanna looked slightly puzzled by this but made no further comment except to smile at her with warmth. Pepper noticed her exchanging a look with her husband.

'I should' – she began, motioning towards the bar area – 'go and get a top-up. It was nice to meet you both – enjoy your evening.'

'Pleasure.' Malcolm nodded. He was so stiff – like an uptight colonel from an old war film. No wonder Finn found it difficult to connect with him properly – he was intimidating.

She met Finn again on the way back from the bar, and, emboldened by a second glass of champagne, put a hand on his arm. He looked down at her, but only for a second, distracted as he was by the chattering groups of people on every side.

'I am sorry,' he said, grimacing with frustration. 'Now that you are here, I just want to steal you away, back to my home, but I have to be the host for a while. We will have time together later – is that OK?'

Pepper made herself let go of him, her hand dropping to her side only for Finn to gather it up again and press her fingers against his lips.

'I love you,' he said, and then he was gone again.

She spent the next few hours orbiting the party, watching Finn from a distance while his friends, colleagues and family flocked around him. Otto made several heroic attempts to pull her into conversation, but each time she made polite excuses and slipped away back into the corners.

As midnight grew steadily closer, the level of anticipation in the room swelled. Pepper stared around at all the faces she did not recognise, wondering which of them was the mystery artist. Whoever it was had made a tidy sum this evening, as every single piece from their collection had apparently been sold to a private buyer, someone who – according to Otto – had been given an early preview ahead of the website's official launch.

'Five thousand euros,' he had whispered in Pepper's ear. 'Five fucking thousand.'

Now it was only ten minutes to go until the big reveal, and Pepper made sure that she was positioned close to where the artwork – whatever it was – had been hung on the back wall of the restaurant, a black sheet concealing it from view.

Finn had disappeared a while ago – presumably to go over his speech – but as she squinted through the assembled crowd of heads, seeking out his thick sweep of golden hair, she caught the eye of an approaching Clara instead and stiffened.

'Hallo, Pepper,' she said, the timid beginnings of a smile on her face as she made her way over. 'I hope you are having a good time?'

'Sort of.' Pepper decided to be honest. 'I met Finn's parents.'

At this, Clara glanced across the room towards where Malcolm and Hanna were still standing, their backs against one of the long tables.

'It is a big deal for them to be here,' she explained. 'They are nice people, but . . .' She shrugged, and Pepper nodded to show she understood.

'Finn told me about his father when we first met – how difficult he is to impress.'

'*Ja.*' Clara tossed her ponytail over her shoulder. 'When he told him about the baby, all he said was "oh".'

'Just "oh"?'

Clara rolled her eyes.

'His mother is different – she cannot say enough nice things. I think that she is very happy, you know. But his father . . . He needs more time. He is very conservative, and of course, Finn and I, we are not married.'

'Well, baby news is always quite a lot to take in, whatever the circumstances,' Pepper said, sounding more defensive than she really felt. 'What I mean is, it must have come as quite a shock to you, let alone Finn's parents. It wasn't as if the two of you were even seeing each other when it happened . . . Were you?' she added, when Clara did not immediately agree.

'*Nein,*' she said firmly, her tone unequivocal. 'It was stupid, just one night. I hope you don't think that we—'

'It's OK, I don't,' Pepper said hurriedly. 'Finn explained it all. I don't, you know, blame you or anything.'

'*Danke.*' Clara regarded her for a moment through flawlessly made-up eyes. 'You are very understanding, very kind. I am glad that Finn has you in his life now – you are good for him. A good influence,' she said.

Pepper felt her cheeks heating up from the compliment.

'Is Otto looking forward to becoming an uncle?' she asked, guessing that he would soon be referring to himself as one.

Clara nodded.

'Otto is like my little brother,' she said, her smile widening as they heard the man in question bellowing something about it being 'two fucking minutes to go, bitches'.

'He is such a mad baby – being around him is good practice for when I become a mother. We are a family,' she added. 'We all care about each other. Finn and I – we will make it work, and he will make it work with you. I don't want you to worry about anything.'

Pepper did not know how to answer. Instead, she said teasingly, 'So, you and Otto never . . . ?'

Clara clapped her hands as if Pepper had just revealed the punchline to a hilarious joke.

'*Mein Gott!* Is that what you think? Otto is not in love with me,' she exclaimed. 'He loves the bottle, and his friends, and different girls every night of the week.'

'And you?' Pepper probed. 'Who do you love?'

Clara's hand dropped to her stomach, and she fixed Pepper with a no-nonsense stare.

'This one,' she said. 'There is nothing more important now – or ever again for me.'

There it was. So simple and undeniable.

The baby was more important than anything or anyone else, than any friendship fractured by complicated feelings. Finn and Clara must have thought they were in control of their situation, that they were good enough friends for one no-strings hook-up to affect them, but it had. They had created a new piece for the puzzle of their lives, one around which all the others must be built, and there was nothing else to do but feel thankful. Happy and grateful that such a beautiful picture would soon begin to take shape for them both.

'I don't think I have said this yet.' Pepper offered a smile. 'But congratulations.'

'*Danke.*' Clara's big brown eyes softened. 'Ah,' she said, glancing over Pepper's shoulder, 'Ah, look-look – here is Finn for the big *Enthüllung.*'

Everyone in the room shuffled forwards and made a semicircle around their host, their phones poised ready to make videos and take photos. Otto made everyone laugh with a flamboyant shushing, and a photographer who had been hired for the night crouched down on his haunches in front of Finn.

Pepper felt suddenly apprehensive for him – and for whoever it was whose work was about to be shown. The pressure they must be feeling, what with all the expectation in the room, must be palpable. Even knowing that her portrait of Finn was on one of the walls here made her feel peculiar enough – a severe case of imposter syndrome that had been gurgling away in her stomach all night.

Someone had passed Finn a microphone, which he held up to his lips now, waiting until the room had fallen silent before beginning to speak.

'Hallo, *Freunde,*' he began, his eyes searching until they found Pepper's.

'I am going to speak in English tonight, because there is something I need someone to hear, and to understand.'

He smiled then, and Pepper was transported back to those steps in Lisbon, back to that square where they had sheltered from the rain, to the moment she had known that this time, it was different. That he was special.

'The story begins at the start of this summer,' he said.

'And with a girl I have been waiting my whole life to meet.'

51

Pepper could not believe he was doing this.

She wanted to flee, but her legs were fence posts buried deep in concrete. All she could do was stand, rooted to the spot, the air constricting inside her chest as it became clear what Finn was talking about.

Her.

'I think when it concerns art,' he said, 'curation comes not from knowledge, but from instinct. We, all of us, choose based not on what we know, but what we feel.'

He tapped a hand against his chest.

'All the pieces I have selected for my website' – Finn smiled as a cheer went up in the room – 'are there because they made me feel something when I saw them, and because I want to share that feeling.'

Another cheer.

'So, when I saw this person, this woman . . .'

His eyes flickered once again to Pepper.

'I felt something right away, in the first moment. We all laugh when someone says they have fallen in love at first sight, but why? We do it with cars, with clothes, with art,' he went on, gesturing around. 'So, why not with people?'

There was a murmur in the audience as people either nodded or shook their heads, and Finn watched on, smiling as he always seemed to, amused at life and its many beguiling twists and turns. He saw so much, Pepper thought – more than she could claim to see. It was why he was so easy to love, because he was so interested.

'I have always been a person who goes after the things that

they want,' he said, this time looking across at his parents. Pepper read nothing but affection on his mother's face, but his father's expression was unreadable.

'And I am proud of the things I have achieved – my business here, this website.'

Yet another cheer went up.

'And now, it would seem, I have something very special coming to me that I did not plan.'

Finn looked towards Clara, who shifted from one spiky stiletto to the other.

'But that I know I will fall in love with as soon as I see him or her.'

There was a smattering of laughter as Finn held up two crossed fingers.

'I thought that I had learnt all the lessons I needed,' he went on. 'I was arrogant in that way, and I was a fool – a *dummkopf*. This girl that I met, she has taught me that there is still much to learn, about what is important, about who matters the most, and why sometimes it is better to do what you must instead of what you want. I am a better man because of her,' he said seriously. 'And tonight, I can launch my website because of her.'

Now he really had gone too far, Pepper thought, trying to catch Finn's eye to illustrate how confused she felt. He wasn't looking at her, though, he had turned and was reaching for the edge of the sheet behind him. There was a small intake of breath as he gathered up the material in one hand, and then a gasp followed by rapturous applause as the cover fell to the floor.

Pepper did not clap, or move – she simply stared, her mouth falling open and her heart thudding like a trapped bird against her chest.

This must be some sort of trick, or sorcery, or she must be seeing things. Perhaps this was all a dream and she was still asleep in her cottage back in Aldeburgh? Because what she was looking at couldn't be true – those could not be her tiles up on the wall. Her collage of Hamburg, of her love story with Finn, all the moments they had shared and the places they had been, of her feelings captured as swirls of colour – a picture not only of time spent, but of wounds healed and lessons learnt.

Pepper had thought them lost; scorched, cracked and blackened by fire – yet here they were, pristine and perfect, right in front of her eyes.

'Philippa.' Clara nudged her gently. 'Go up – Finn is waiting.'

They were all waiting. Every face in the room turned towards her, each one intrigued and admiring. She had gone from being the awkward girl in the corner to the artist whose work had so captivated them all.

Pepper took a blundering few steps forwards, her cheeks burning with the red-hot heat of a hundred pairs of eyes. She brought her hands up to cover her face, but a laughing Finn pulled them down again, leading her on reluctant legs towards the pattern of tiles, and throwing his arm around her with pride.

She blinked as a camera started flashing, trying to shield her eyes only for Finn to lace his fingers through hers, lowering her hand and telling her she must smile.

'This is crazy!' she said at last, relieved to find herself laughing rather than sobbing. She was so overwhelmed that she could hardly remember any words at all, let alone utter them.

'How did you? How did this happen?'

Finn chuckled, lifting her chin with a finger and turning her face towards his.

'You really cannot guess?' he exclaimed, as the photographer moved in for another shot.

Pepper frowned, still not understanding, then the truth hit her like a great wave, almost knocking her right off her feet.

There was only one person who could have been behind this – the same person she had to thank for being here in the first place, for meeting Finn, for the fact that those tiles on the wall behind them existed at all.

'Josephine,' she said. 'It was Josephine, wasn't it?'

'Maybe . . .'

Finn still had his arm around her, and now he moved so he was facing her, so he could look at her properly.

'But how?' Pepper exclaimed. 'I didn't tell anyone about this project. I locked all the tiles in my cabinet, inside my studio – and my studio burnt to the ground.'

'I am sorry.' For a moment he looked downcast. 'But now you can build an even better one. I sold all these,' he added proudly. 'Five thousand euros is waiting to be transferred to you.' Pepper shook her head in disbelief.

'They weren't for sale,' she said helplessly, and Finn replied with one of his great bellows of mirth. 'Someone bloody stole them!'

'Not me!' He held up both hands.

'What if I'd wanted to keep them?' she went on. 'I've spent the past few weeks mourning the loss of them, and now suddenly, here they are again. Am I supposed to just accept it all?'

'You are not cross?' For a moment, his face fell. 'I can return them to you, if that is what you want?'

Was it what she wanted? Pepper was conflicted, trapped between the opposing towers of shock and pride.

'I can't believe they sold,' she said. 'All that money for something I created.'

'Of course they did.' Emboldened by the astonishment in her voice, Finn bent down and planted a kiss on the end of her nose. 'They are beautiful, Pepper – a masterpiece. But you are right,' he went on. 'They were not mine to sell. I should not have just assumed.'

'Josephine must have broken in somehow,' said Pepper, more to herself than him. 'That wily old fox.'

'I am sure she will explain everything to you herself,' Finn said. 'She will be happy that the secret is finally out.'

'What about you?' she asked. 'Do you have any more secrets you need to tell me?'

'This was my best one,' he replied. Then, when Pepper found she could not find any words, he pulled her back into his arms.

'Will you come home with me tonight?' he asked, his voice muffled by her hair.

Pepper sighed, unable not to think of Clara, and of the baby.

'Just to talk,' he said, as if he could see right through into her mind and was reading her thoughts as they unfurled. '*Bitte.*'

She had made it back into the bubble, thought Pepper. Back where it was safe. And so, she wrapped her arms around his waist, squeezing herself against him until there were no spaces left between them.

'OK,' she said. 'On one condition.'

'Name it.' Finn stepped out of their embrace and reached for her hands, toying her back into the room.

'You tell me who my mystery buyer is.'

'That,' Finn said, letting go of her hand, 'is something that you can definitely work out for yourself.'

52

She knew what would happen if she followed Finn into his bedroom, waiting in the open doorway while he lit candles and closed the blinds. She knew that once she let him pull her down onto the duvet, there would be no going back. The two of them as drawn to the other as they had been right from that first moment.

He had told her that he loved her at the party, but the tiles she had painted must have told him the same thing weeks ago – he would have known as he unwrapped each one and slotted them together. Now, as they lay together under the covers, Pepper could feel the weight of that sentiment pressing down on them and felt crushed by expectation.

'I have missed you very much,' he said, his finger tracing a circle on her stomach, across her hips, lower. 'I thought that you might not come – that you had decided it was all too much. The baby, the distance that we are from each other.'

He paused to kiss her, first her cheek, then the hollow of her throat.

'I missed you, too,' she assured him. 'There was just so much happening at home, the fire – and after Barcelona, I wasn't sure how I felt, or what was the best thing to do.'

'And now?'

'It feels nice to be here,' she said decidedly. 'What you did for me tonight. Nobody has ever done anything like that before – I still can't quite believe it.'

'That is not quite true,' he tempered. 'It was more than one person who did it, remember?'

'Well, you both had faith in me.'

Pepper itched with a need to follow up her words with something self-effacing, about how she wasn't worthy of such esteem, that her work was average at best – but she stopped herself. She was the only person telling herself this story, over and over, which meant that she was the only person who could bring an end to it all, to that inner insistence that the things she created were not good enough. She had to write herself some new rules and start living by them.

'You are very talented,' he told her, his nose resting against hers. 'I have a list as long as Otto's bar tab of people who want one of your pieces, and who are very willing to pay for them.'

'But I—' she started to protest, then stopped herself again.

'That is amazing,' she managed. 'Thank you – thank you so much, for everything.'

'Do not thank me.' He smoothed the hair back from her face. 'It is just good business sense. You are a commodity now – my meal ticket.'

'Well then, feel free to feast away!' she joked, yelping as Finn promptly took her at her word and disappeared beneath the covers.

'Oi!' she cried, pulling him back up. 'You promised me talking only.'

Finn frowned as he peered down at their naked, entwined bodies.

'It is a bit late for that now.'

'I feel bad.' Pepper sighed.

'Why? Because of Clara?'

She nodded.

'There is nothing like that going on between us,' he said, and she could tell he was having to work hard to keep the exasperation from creeping into his voice. 'That is why it still feels a little bit unfair, you know? Like the right things happening to the wrong people.'

'At the wrong time,' she finished.

'Maybe there is never a good time for a baby, because nobody is ever really ready to be a parent.' Finn screwed up his features. 'This is what everyone tells me – even Mama.'

'I think what they mean to say is that there's never a bad time,' she chided, kissing his downturned mouth. 'You are going to love this baby and be an incredible father.'

He stared at her for a moment, searching her eyes, checking that what she was telling him was true, and that there was no cause to worry.

'If you say it, then I will believe it.'

'I can't tell you that it will be easy,' she said. 'There will be some very difficult days and lots of complicated feelings, but you will be OK. You are the most capable and confident man I have ever met, and I know you said in your speech earlier that I had taught you things, but the truth is, I have learnt so much more from you. You have shown me that it's important to be brave, and to fight your own corner. That there is little point holding on to anything that makes you unhappy, when it is often such a small part of who you are, and what your life is all about.'

'I see you,' he said. 'There is a sparkle there.' He touched her cheek. 'That was not there before – or maybe it was, but you kept it hidden, buried underneath all those layers of . . . what? Sadness? Guilt?'

'Both.' Pepper swallowed so as not to cry, and Finn pulled her closer. 'But you're right – I have changed for the better. I think that falling in love with you has made me stronger, made me see myself in the way you see me. I feel like a lot of my confusion about the past has settled, and I can move forwards and help my mum to do the same.'

She sighed, her head buried against the soft downy hair on his chest. There was a part of Pepper that wanted to stay right where she was, here with a man who loved her, who would support her, who meant so much to her. But then, there was the other side of the pebble, the one that didn't catch the sunlight and shine like a dropped penny on the shoreline. The half of Pepper's life that ran a business she loved, had a great network of people around her who had shown that they were friends in the truest sense, and a mother who was only now beginning to come back to her.

She could not have both.

'Don't cry.' Finn wiped away her tears with his thumb.

'I can't help it.' Pepper sniffed, taking a long shuddering breath before raising her eyes to his.

Finn searched her eyes, looking for a way to soothe, and then he saw it. The truth.

'You came here to tell me it is over.'

It wasn't a question.

'No.' She shook her head. 'I didn't know what I was going to do until I got here. I saw you in the centre of your world tonight, so loved and so happy. I watched you, and I could see that you were in the right place, where you are meant to be. You belong in this world, with these people and with your child.'

She smiled, hoping that he would follow her lead, but Finn's expression had darkened.

'You say that you love me,' he said, his voice low, 'but you refuse to try. Don't you believe that we are worth fighting for? Look at the way we met, how we were put together – that must mean something to you?'

'It does!' Pepper shuffled up on her elbows. 'Of course it does. Loving you is the best feeling I have ever had, next to painting. This summer has been the best of my life. Finn, before this summer, I had never even been abroad; I was existing, not really living, but now I feel the opposite way – I feel as if I could do anything. Such a big part of that is because of you, but it's so fragile. If I left now and moved here, it would all fall apart – I would fall apart.'

Finn did not look angry now so much as defeated, and Pepper shut her eyes against the anguish she felt.

'This is not my world, Finn. I don't belong here. Things with my mother, they're finally starting to hurt less, and I think we have a real chance of rebuilding our relationship – our whole family do. I want to be there; I don't want to run away. I'm not being selfless by saying that, it's what I want.'

'Why can't you have both?' he asked. 'Be here, but sometimes be there? You will not even try?'

'You deserve better than someone who would need to try,' she said. 'You deserve someone who knows for sure, straight away. Just like you did with me, that day on the steps in Lisbon. You always knew better than me, believed with more determination than me, gave away more of your heart than me.'

'I can believe enough for both of us,' he said desperately. 'If you would only let me.'

'I know you would, and you're so incredible to even offer. You know, I used to feel like a fool for being such a fan of love, but meeting you and loving you,' she said determinedly, 'has taught me a lesson about love that I could never have learnt from a film or a book.'

She gave herself a moment's composure, thinking of Josephine and Jorge, of the love that had been captured so beautifully in the photo that now hung, pride of place, on her bedroom wall.

Their love story had never dimmed; it had carried on throughout her friend's entire life, had comforted her, and led her to adventure. It didn't matter that their lives went in different directions, what mattered was the moments they had shared. The love remained because Josephine had not forgotten it, just as Pepper would not forget Finn.

'I didn't know it was possible for one person to experience so much love. I thought that there wasn't much of any in my life, but there is so much. I think I had to fall in love with you to realise it. And I want you to know that I will always, always, always love you, Finn.'

Pepper smiled at him through her tears and took his face in her hands.

They kissed for all they had shared, and for every future moment they would spend apart; they kissed for custard tarts and wet shoes slapping across rain-soaked cobbles; they kissed for his thigh against hers on the seat of a bus, an airport embrace that earned them a cheer; they kissed for eggs in cups and errant bats, for paddling in the sea and drinking beer in the sunshine. They kissed for all the pieces of their love story.

But most of all, they kissed each other goodbye.

53

Pepper found Josephine in the same place she had found her back in the spring, sitting with an easel on Aldeburgh's wide stony beach.

This time, however, there was no painting coming to life on her canvas – it was as blank as the sky above the water, her brushes as dry as the driftwood that was scattered like leaves amongst the pebbles. Despite the warmth of the afternoon, Josephine had wrapped herself up in a pale blue pashmina that matched her eyes.

'I thought I would find you here,' Pepper said, putting her bag down on the ground and unfolding the canvas camping chair she had brought from the flat.

Josephine's smile was faint.

'I wanted one last look at the view,' she said.

'I can't believe you fly tomorrow,' Pepper said forlornly, and Josephine sighed.

'Yes, it has come around far too speedily, hasn't it? It's a funny thing, you know. When I was in my twenties, it felt as if life was one endless gallivant, but I also thought that by the time I reached this ripe old age, I would be ready to stop. Fact is, I am nowhere near ready – I want nothing more than to keep going, but my body' – she held up a tremoring hand as proof – 'clearly had other ideas.'

'Not your body,' corrected Pepper. 'A horrible, unforgivable and cruel disease.'

'The doctors keep reminding me that Parkinson's is not fatal.' Josephine scoffed. 'But it is a death sentence to spontaneity, and independence.'

'Don't let it be!' Pepper insisted. 'Don't allow it to crush your spirit.'

'My darling girl.' Josephine shifted on her deckchair and winced as if in pain. 'You know as well as I do that it would take more than a spot of Parkinson's to knock this old bird down. But let's not talk about things that are guaranteed to put a dampener on the day. Tell me about Hamburg – was the party a big success?'

'In a moment.' Pepper reached down for her bag and extracted two cans of pre-mixed gin and tonic. 'First, I thought we should have a toast.'

'Oh, goody!'

Pepper cracked open both drinks and handed one across.

'To Josephine Hurley,' she said solemnly. 'The funniest, most fabulous and sneakiest woman I have ever met.'

Josephine tittered with amusement as she took a sip.

'Sneakiest? I must say, I have no idea what you're getting at.'

Pepper lowered her can.

'The tiles!' she exclaimed. 'My collection of work that you stole and gave to Finn!'

'Ah.' Josephine chuckled. 'That.'

'I still don't understand how you did it – or when?'

Josephine looked out towards the water for a moment, her gaze drawn by the gentle swish of the waves. Pepper wondered if like her, Josephine found the repetitive nature of the sea a comfort – a force of nature that you could always rely upon to follow the same pattern.

'It all started one evening, when I received a rather interesting phone call from your mother.'

Pepper almost choked on her gin.

'As it turns out,' Josephine went on, clearly enjoying herself, 'she spied on you.'

'What? Spied on me how? Why? When?'

'She told me that she'd headed over to your house one night, because she wanted to talk to you about something. She arrived at the front door and knocked, but you never came, and so she tried the handle, and it was open. Then she made it as far as the garden path before she saw you, so intent on what you were doing that you didn't even see her standing there. She explained that it was the first time she had seen you painting in years, and that you looked so enraptured. She was mesmerised, I suppose. And she didn't want to break the wonderful spell you were under, so she waited. But then you did the most extraordinary thing.'

Pepper looked down at her shoes, shame casting flames across her cheeks.

'You smashed the tile you had just painted – and your mother told me that it was so beautiful. She could not understand why you would do such a thing, and neither could I, at first, but then, as I got to know you better, I guessed what it was that drove you. It was guilt, seeping in and infecting your self-confidence. God knows, I can recognise that. I spent years crippled by it myself, of course.'

'Why didn't she say anything at the time?' Pepper asked. 'Why didn't you?'

'I can't speak for Trinity, but I remained quiet because I didn't want to embarrass you, darling. Besides, telling a person never has as much impact as showing them. Your mother thought, and I agreed, that if we could find a way to show you how good you were, then you might just believe it. After you and I went away together that first time and you met Finn, I could see that he had effected a change in you, and I hoped – correctly, as it transpired – that his positive influence would lead you to create something beautiful. I tipped off your mother when we returned, told her to keep an eye out, and soon she was pinching a few pieces every few days.'

'How did she?' Pepper began, but then she realised. Of course, her mother would have a spare set of keys – it had been Trinity's parents' cottage once upon a time. As for the studio, Pepper was forever tossing her set of keys for that down on the kitchen worktop whenever she went out – that's if she even remembered to lock it.

'We both agreed that you were selling yourself far too short, young lady. And I was only too eager to be of service. In fact, it was often I who tipped her off when you were out of the house. After the fire, I know she wanted to tell you, but by that time I had already been in touch with Finn and he was adamant that it remain a secret. He assumed, rightly I imagine, that you would not have allowed him to buy them if you had known.'

'Finn didn't buy them,' she said. 'He sold them to some mystery person.'

Josephine looked as if she was going to laugh.

'What?' Pepper persisted. 'Do you know who it is?'

'Naturally.' She smiled. 'As do you.'

Pepper was confused, but then it dawned on her. There was only one person it could be.

'Finn. Finn is my mystery buyer? But that makes no sense.'

'He loves you, darling,' Josephine reminded her. 'So it makes perfect sense.'

For a second, Pepper was stilled by an image of him. Saying goodbye to Finn was one of the hardest things she had ever had to do – and now she had to bid farewell to Josephine, too.

'I half hoped that he would be here today,' Josephine confided, but Pepper shook her head.

'Oh – so not the romantic reunion I was wishing for, then?'

'Finn is exactly where he belongs,' Pepper said firmly. 'As am I.'

Disappointment flashed briefly across Josephine's face, but then she shrugged.

'Sometimes people come into our lives right at the time when we need them the most, to help us transition or to realise what it is we need. Perhaps Finn was that person for you?'

'Just like Jorge was for you,' said Pepper, and the older woman's eyes became watery.

'Yes,' she said. 'But there is something I must tell you about Jorge.'

There was a wistfulness to her now that made Pepper lean forwards in her chair. She took another sip of her drink, trying to read her friend's expression.

'That evening in Lisbon, when I went off for a wander by myself,' she began, and Pepper nodded. 'Well, I found the restaurant that his family used to own.'

'You told me,' Pepper interrupted. 'You said there was nobody there who knew him?'

'Yes, well.' Josephine gave her a shifty look. 'I may have . . . Well, let's just say, there might have been a bit of fibbing on my part. His family were still there. I met his daughter, in fact – she was so beautiful, had his eyes. She told me that Jorge, bless his heart, had passed away a few years previously.'

'Oh no!' Pepper cried. 'Why didn't you tell me?'

Josephine dabbed at her eyes with her pashmina. A breeze was rolling in from the sea now, blowing her frizzy grey halo of hair in all directions.

'Grief is a very private affair, as you know,' she said quietly. 'And honestly, I didn't want to end the story so soon, for myself or for you. I loved seeing how inspired you were by our little quest. If you had known the truth, you might not have come with me to Barcelona – and I so wanted us to go. Going back to those places reminded me of what was important. Namely, spending as much time as I have left with those who love me the most. My children have wanted to look after me for so many years, and I have pushed them away time and time again. Now it's time to stop all that.'

Pepper nodded as she thought of her own mother, of all the years they had wasted. She was going to miss Josephine almost as much if not more than Finn, but her leaving was the right thing.

'What am I going to do without you?' Pepper pulled down the sleeve of her cardigan to wipe her eyes as Josephine raised her gin and tonic in another toast.

'Drink!' she said. 'And laugh as hard as you can, as often as you can – the same goes for love. That one is an important one. And you must keep creating – nurture your talent and share it far and wide, my darling.'

'I thought I might start by painting all the places in the world that my sister and I wanted to see,' Pepper told her. 'Something to keep me occupied while my studio is rebuilt.'

They were still toasting one another and laughing when they heard the crunch of feet on shingle. Turning in their chairs, Pepper and Josephine waved across at the two people coming to join them.

'She looks radiant today, your mother,' Josephine said. 'The first time I met her, she was like this little dormouse, all curled up and shut off from the world. Now she's positively glowing.'

'I gave her a present this morning,' Pepper confided. 'A drawing that my sister did, which somehow found its way to me this summer. She loves it – she's put it up on the fridge.'

'How wonderful!'

'I hope you don't mind them being here?' Pepper went on. 'They both wanted the chance to see you before you go. Now I understand why my mum was so insistent!'

'Of course I don't mind.' Josephine gripped her stick, preparing to stand. 'It makes me very happy to know that I'm leaving you in such good hands. Because they are not only here for a silly old crone like me. They're here because they love you, Philippa.'

Her mother had reached them now, but Samuel was still a little way behind. He had stopped to pick something up, a stone or a shell, perhaps, and when he glanced up and saw Pepper staring across at him, he smiled.

It was if a light had been switched on.

EPILOGUE

Ten years later . . .

The door of the gallery was propped open when they arrived, and a shaft of sunlight lay like a fallen sail across the wooden floor.

The woman took her husband's hand as they crossed the threshold, her fingers tightening around his involuntarily as she saw the tiled mural on the far wall.

'There it is,' she whispered, hushed into reverence by her own enchantment. They had come so far, the two of them, had waited so long to be here.

'Hallo.'

The woman smiled at the little boy walking towards them. He was wearing an apron dotted with paint stains, and from the looks of things, had also got some in his blond hair.

'Can I help you?' he asked, his English flavoured with the German he had grown up speaking.

'I hope we came to the right place,' she began, stopping when the boy beamed at her.

'Are you from Australia?' The idea seemed to thrill him. 'They have pelicans there as big as cars!'

'Cars, you reckon?' The woman chuckled. 'That sounds about right.'

'Hamburg does not have many pelicans,' he added, rather sadly. 'Only in the zoo.'

'Oh, but you do have the headquarters of the Pelican website – that's a huge deal.'

'*Mein Papa*,' he said, flashing them an apologetic grin when he realised he had lapsed back into German. 'My father. He is the boss.'

'Then he is the one who owns the first work by Philippa Selassie over there,' the woman's husband put in. 'We came all the way from Australia to see it.'

The little boy's eyes widened at this information, and he wiped both his hands on the front of his apron.

'My father is the one who discovered her,' he said proudly, stumbling slightly over the longer English word.

'I know,' the woman confided. 'And it was my mother who helped to make sure he knew just how talented she is. That's why we came to see her work for ourselves, because Philippa meant a lot to my mum.'

There were tears in the woman's eyes now, and she blinked them hurriedly away.

'May we?' she asked, and the boy nodded with enthusiasm.

The couple followed him to the back of the room, to where the spread of tiles was mounted inside a simple gold frame. It was a few minutes before any of them spoke again, each drawn in by the fable playing out in front of them, by the dashes of colour, intricate patterns, exquisite details and the pure life force that seemed to flow between each one.

'Does it have a name, this work?' the man asked eventually, turning to the little boy.

'No.' He shrugged, scratching at a spot behind his ear.

'But my father, he sometimes calls it "*Die ersten Stücke der Liebe*" – but only to me.'

'Do you know what that means in English?' the woman asked, smiling as the boy's face lit up with another smile.

'*Ja*, of course,' he said. 'It means "The First Pieces of Love".'

ACKNOWLEDGEMENTS

It is to you, dear reader – and indeed to all readers of romantic fiction – that I must say my first thank you. Your support and passion for this genre is what keeps us authors plugging away day after day, and I feel enormously privileged that you chose my book from the many hundreds out there in the world.

To my wonderful agent, Hannah Ferguson, thank you for always being unfailingly wise, kind, strong and brilliant. And that goes for the whole team at Hardman & Swainson – you all work so hard, while all I do is sit around in my pants making up stories. I am very lucky.

Kimberley Atkins, you were with me right at the start of this journey and for some reason wanted me back again. For this and a million other reasons, I am extremely grateful. Editing is your super power and I hope that together we can make this book fly even further than Superman, or Iron Man, or even, er, Dumbo. (Well, I had to get a Disney mention in somewhere!)

To the incredible team at Hodder & Stoughton, you are all shiny pennies in my wishing well of publishing dreams. Thank you for making me feel so very welcome from the first moment I signed on the dotted line. Eve Hall, you nailed it yet again with this title. Amy Batley, you are so organised it puts Kondo to shame. Myrto Kalavrezou, you've made me love publicity more than pubs (which is quite a feat). Jo Myler, this cover is a fresh and feel-good slice of beauty. Libby Earland, you and Imogen succeeded in making me look far less like a foot than I ever have before, and Helen Parham, your copyedit has definitely made me look cleverer. Massive thanks to you all – and the rest of the team at large.

To the early readers, bloggers, reviewers, tweeters, hashtag-gers, Instagrammers and book champions far and wide, if I could kiss all of you, I would, even if it gave me a cold sore. Thank you for doing what you do and sharing my books with friends, family and followers. You are the big beating heart of this industry; I love you all very much.

I could easily sit here and thank each of my author friends one by one, but happily there are just too many of you now to make that feasible. From the Book Camp crew to my Nearest & Dearest chums and those who are always there at the end of the phone (or at the bar) when I have needed you, thank you for propping me up and reminding me that we have the best job in the world. Every time I think about all the new people I have met and can now call friends, my heart swells fit to burst. I have found my people.

To my friends and family. Most of you are mystified as to what exactly it is I do when I shut myself away for weeks – often months – on end, but you're always there when I re-emerge (somewhat more frazzled) on the other side. It is you who keep me laughing, keep me inspired, keep the bar staff busy at my launches and keep me wanting to be the best writer that I can. And for that, you get the biggest slice of my thankful pie.

And lastly (not leastly) to Mum. I wish you could love your-self even a fraction of the amount you love me, but it doesn't matter if you can't. I have enough in my heart for both of us.